New Library of French Classics
HENRI PEYRE, SERIES EDITOR

◇◇◇◇◇◇◇◇◇◇◇◇◇◇◇◇◇◇◇◇◇◇◇◇◇◇◇◇◇◇◇◇◇◇◇

Our judgment on literature, like those on the music, the painting, the thought of past ages, stands constantly in need of revision. With some laziness, many of us have accepted an arbitrary choice made by teachers or critics of an earlier generation, which declared only certain novels by Stendhal, Balzac, Flaubert, Zola, or by German, Russian, Spanish novelists, to be "masterpieces" and passed off other works as "minor."

The present series is intended to reconsider such archaic choices. Our age has reassessed the fiction of the eighteenth century, once placidly ignored, and that of seventeenth-century France, and rediscovered many a tale of the Renaissance.

A number of less well-known novels of the nineteenth century touch us more than many of the more celebrated volumes by Balzac or Flaubert, by Dickens or Turgenev, conventionally accepted as most fit for schoolboys. After all, Balzac wrote many other novels than EUGÉNIE BRANDET and LE PÈRE GORIOT, and in the eyes of good judges, maybe better ones. Stendhal is not all enclosed in LE ROUGE ET LE NOIR. Zola is at least as original in LA FAUTE DE L'ABBÉ MOURET as he is in NANA, and a much greater poet and portrayer of love in the first of those two novels. Even in our own century, novelists who have been neglected by translators and publishers may well appear to a later generation equal to others who have been temporarily acclaimed outside of France.

The purpose of this series is to bring some of those half-neglected yet highly significant novels from French literature to American readers. The translators are persons of established competence both as masters of the French language and as talented writers. The novels should afford psychological insight, social criticism and enjoyment to those who may discover them in their American version, and, in the poet's words, "give grace and truth to life's unquiet dream."

HENRI PEYRE

Other translations in preparation:

AXEL
by Villiers de l'Isle-Adam

BEATRIX
by Honoré de Balzac

L'INSURGE
by Jules Vallès

LE PAYSAN DE PARIS
by Louis Aragon

LE VESUVE
by Emmanuel Robles

L'AGE INGRAT
by José Cabanis

THE
SIN OF
FATHER
MOURET

by
Emile Zola

Translated by Sandy Petrey

PRENTICE - HALL, INC.
Englewood Cliffs, New Jersey

THE SIN OF FATHER MOURET
by Emile Zola, translated by Sandy Petrey
© 1969 by Prentice-Hall, Inc., for this translation
Copyright under International and Pan American Copyright Conventions
All rights reserved. No part of this book may be
reproduced in any form or by any means, except for
the inclusion of brief quotations in a review, without
permission in writing from the publisher.
13-810523-5
Library of Congress Catalog Card Number: 69-19595
Printed in the United States of America *T*
Prentice-Hall International, Inc., London
Prentice-Hall of Australia, Pty. Ltd., Sydney
Prentice-Hall of Canada, Ltd., Toronto
Prentice-Hall of India Private Ltd., New Delhi
Prentice-Hall of Japan, Inc., Tokyo

CONTENTS

THE SIN OF FATHER MOURET

BOOK ONE

❖❖❖❖❖❖❖❖❖❖❖❖❖❖❖❖❖❖❖❖❖❖❖❖❖❖❖❖❖❖

I La teuse came in and put her broom and feather duster against the altar. She was a little late because she had just started to make soap, a task she performed every six months. She crossed the church to ring the Angelus; in her haste she bumped into benches and limped even more than usual. The bell cord hung from the ceiling near the confessional. It was a plain, frayed rope ending in a large knot which showed the dirt of many hands. She tolled regular strokes, pulling on the cord with all her bulk, then she lost control and rolled back and forth in her petticoats, her bonnet askew, her broad face flushed with blood.

After giving her bonnet a light tap to straighten it, la Teuse came panting back to sweep the altar. Dust held on tenaciously; every day it seemed to be glued to the platform's poorly fitted planks. The broom grumbled angrily as it reached into the corners. When she took off the altar cloth, she was furious to see a new hole worn through the very center of the large upper cover, already patched in twenty places. The under cover was visible; it was folded double and was itself so thin and transparent that she could see the consecrated stone framed in the painted wood of the altar. She beat the dust from this linen browned by great age, vigorously ran her duster along the gradine, and replaced the liturgical cards she had dislodged. Then she climbed a chair and removed the yellow cotton covers from the cross and two of the candlesticks. The brass was tarnished and dull. "Merciful heavens," la Teuse muttered to herself, "do they ever need a good cleaning! I'll use the tripoli stone on them."

Then, running on one leg, swaying and shaking so much that the floor was in danger of splitting, she went to the sacristy for the missal. Without opening it, she laid it on the lectern, next to the Gospel, so that it faced the altar. And she lit the two candles. As she was leaving with her broom, she glanced around to make sure the Lord's housekeeping had been satisfactorily done. The church was asleep except for the bell cord near the confessional, which was still swinging in a long graceful motion, stretching from the vault to the floor.

Father Mouret had just come down to the sacristy, a small cold room off the dining-room hall.

"Hello, Father," said la Teuse as she put down her cleaning implements. "My, but you were lazy this morning! Do you realize it's six fifteen?" And she went on without giving the smiling young priest time to answer: "I've got a bone to pick with you. The altar cloth has another hole in it. It doesn't make sense. We've just got one spare, and I've been putting my eyes out for three days trying to get it in shape. If you keep on like this, you'll have poor Jesus naked."

Father Mouret was still smiling. He said happily, "Jesus doesn't need so much linen, my good Teuse. When you love him, he's warm enough, he's treated royally."

Then he turned toward a small cistern and asked, "Is my sister up? I haven't seen her."

"Miss Désirée came down ages ago," replied the servant. She was kneeling before an old sideboard where they stored the folded vestments. "She's already with her chickens and rabbits. She was expecting some chicks yesterday, but they didn't hatch. You know what that does to her!" She broke off to ask, "You want the gold chasuble, don't you?"

The preoccupied priest had washed his hands and was mouthing a prayer. He simply nodded his head. The parish had only three chasubles—a purple one, a black one, and one made of golden cloth. The last was used on days when white, red, or green was necessary, and it had acquired extraordinary importance; la Teuse lifted it religiously from the shelf lined with blue paper where she laid it after each ceremony. She put it on the sideboard, carefully lifting the cambric which protected its embroidery, a depiction of a golden lamb sleeping on a golden cross surrounded by broad golden rays. The fabric was especially worn around the folds, and tiny specks flaked off continuously. The raised ornamentation was rubbing itself away. This chasuble gave rise to great worry in the house. Everyone anxiously watched it disappear bit by bit. The priest had to wear it almost every day; how could they replace it, how could they buy the three chasubles it substituted for when the last golden threads were gone?

La Teuse laid the stole, maniple, cordon, alb, and amice on top of the chasuble. But she kept talking even while giving her full attention to adjusting the maniple on the stole to form a cross and to arranging the cordon so as to outline the revered initial of Mary's holy name. "This cordon's not much good," she muttered. "You're going to have to break down and buy another one, Father . . . You can afford it. I'd twist you one myself if I just had the hemp."

Father Mouret did not answer. He was preparing the chalice on a small table, a large old chalice made of silver gilt standing on a bronze foot, which he had just taken from a cupboard made of white wood used to store holy vessels and linen, holy oils, missals, candlesticks, and crosses. He laid a clean Communion cloth across the cup, put the silver-gilt paten containing the Host on it, and covered everything with a small linen pall. As he was hiding the chalice by pinching the two folds in the golden veil matching his chasuble, la Teuse cried out, "Wait, there's no corporal in the burse. Last night I got all the dirty Communion cloths, palls, and corporals to get them clean—by themselves, of course, not with the other dirty things . . . I didn't tell you, Father, I just started to make the soap. It's really thick! It'll be a lot better than last time."

And as the priest was slipping a corporal into the burse, decorated with a golden cross on a gold background, preparatory to putting the burse on the golden veil, she went on animatedly, "By the way, I forgot to tell you. That rascal Vincent isn't here yet. Do you want me to serve Mass, Father?"

The young priest looked at her sternly. "Oh, it's not a sin," she continued with her good smile. "I did it once, served Mass, when Father Caffin was here. I do it better than little brats who laugh like heathens when a fly buzzes into the church. I may wear a bonnet and be sixty years old and big as a house, but I respect the good Lord more than any pesky kids . . . I caught them playing leapfrog behind the altar again the other day."

The priest stared at her and shook his head. "A hole, that's

3

what this village is," she grumbled. "There aren't a hundred and fifty people here. There're days, like today, when you can't find a living soul in Artauds. Even kids in diapers head for the vineyards. And you can bet I know what goes on there—vines growing out of rocks, dry as thistles, the wildest country anybody ever saw for miles around. If an angel doesn't come down to serve Mass, Father, you don't have anybody but me. Or maybe one of Miss Désirée's rabbits, begging your pardon."

But at that moment Vincent, the younger Brichet child, softly opened the sacristy door. His unruly red hair and his small, shining gray eyes infuriated la Teuse. "Oh, here's the little sinner," she cried. "I bet he's been up to some mischief! Come on up, you little brat; the Father's afraid I might make the good Lord dirty."

When he saw the child, Father Mouret picked up the amice. He kissed the cross embroidered in the middle of the cloth, put it on his head for an instant, then brought it down to the collar of his cassock and crossed and tied the cordons, right over left. Next, beginning with the right arm, he put on the alb, symbol of purity. Vincent had crouched on his haunches and was turning around him, adjusting the alb, making sure that it hung evenly on all sides, two fingers from the floor. Then he gave the cordon to the priest, who pulled it tight to remind himself of the bonds of the Saviour during His Passion.

La Teuse, jealous and hurt, remained standing. She was trying not to say anything, but her tongue itched so much that she soon started in again. "Brother Archangias came. There's not a single kid in school today. He ran off fast to go to the vines and pull the little wretches' ears for them. You'd better see him. I think he has something to tell you."

Father Mouret held up his hand for her to be silent. He had not said another word. He was reciting the sacred prayers as he picked up the maniple, kissed it, and draped it over his left forearm as a sign of the labor of good works; he kissed the stole as well, before crossing it over his chest as a symbol of his dignity and power. La Teuse had to help Vincent adjust the chasuble; she tied the thin cordon so the vestments did not droop in the back.

"Holy Mother! I forgot the cruets," she stammered as she rushed to the cupboard. "Come on, hurry up, you rascal!" Vincent filled the cruets, little phials made of coarse glass, while she hurriedly opened a drawer to get a clean towel. His left hand holding the chalice by the knop, the fingers of his right hand resting on the burse, Father Mouret, without removing his biretta, bowed deeply before a Christ of black wood hanging over the sideboard. The boy also bowed; then, holding the cruets under the towel, he left the sacristy, followed by the priest, who was walking with his eyes downcast, lost in profound devotion.

◇◇◇◇◇◇◇◇◇◇◇◇◇◇◇◇◇◇◇◇◇◇◇◇◇◇◇◇◇◇◇◇

II THE EMPTY CHURCH WAS ALL WHITE ON THIS MAY MORNing. The bell cord near the confessional was hanging motionless again. The colored lamp was burning like a red spot against the wall to the right of the tabernacle. After placing the cruets on the credence, Vincent came to kneel to the left of the altar steps. The priest genuflected before the Sacraments and went to lay the corporal on the altar. He placed the chalice in the middle of the corporal, opened the missal, and returned to genuflect once more. He crossed himself aloud, folded his hands before his chest, and began the great divine drama, his face completely pale in faith and love.

"Introibo ad altare Dei."

"Ad Deum qui laetificat juventutem meam," mumbled Vincent, his rump on his heels. He swallowed the responses of the litany and psalm and gave his full attention to watching la Teuse prowl around the church. The old servant was casting nervous glances at one of the candles. Her agitation seemed to increase when the priest, bowing low, his hands clasped, recited the *Confiteor.* She stopped, struck her chest, and continued to glance at the candle even though her head was bowed. The priest's calm voice and the altar boy's muttering alternated for a time.

"Dominus vobiscum."

"Et cum spiritu tuo."

And the priest, after opening his hands and reclasping them, said with emotional fervor, *"Oremus."*

La Teuse could keep still no longer. She went behind the altar to clean the candle with the end of her scissors. It was guttering, and two large wax tears had already been lost. When she came back to her place after arranging the benches and making sure that all the fonts contained holy water, the priest, his hands on the edge of the altar cloth, was praying in a low voice. He kissed the altar.

Behind him the little church was pallid in the morning light. The sun had not yet risen above the roof. The *Kyrie, eleisons* quivered through the little whitewashed barn topped by a bare-beamed, flat roof. On each side, three high, clear-glass windows, cracked and broken in many places, opened to admit crude, chalky light. Fresh air forced its way in to expose mercilessly all the poverty of this forsaken village's God. A wooden gallery ran across the rear wall above the main door, which was never opened and was overgrown with plants. A mill ladder led to the gallery, which groaned under the wooden shoes striking it on feast days. Near the latter stood the confessional, made of poorly joined panels and painted lemon yellow. The baptistry, an old holy-water font with a masonry stand, was next to the small door facing the confessional. Finally, two small altars surrounded by wooden railing stood on each side of the center of the wall. The one on the left, dedicated to the Blessed Virgin, displayed a large Mother of God made of gilded plaster, her light-brown hair regally topped by a golden crown. In her left arm she held a naked, smiling Jesus whose little hand contained the starry globe of the world. She was walking in clouds; winged heads of angels were under her feet. The right-hand altar, where Masses for the dead were said, was surmounted by a Christ of painted cardboard, a counterpoint to the Virgin. The Christ, about the size of a ten-year-old child, was suffering his death agony in a most disturbing way: his head was thrown back, his ribs jutted out, his stomach was ripped open, his limbs were twisted and splattered with blood. The church also contained a pulpit, a square box reached by five steps rising next to a grandfather clock in a walnut case whose dull ticks shook the church like the beats of an enormous heart hidden somewhere under the tile floor. All along the nave, the fourteen Stations of the Cross—fourteen crudely executed pictures in thin black frames —spotted the wall's whiteness with the yellow, blue, and red of the Passion.

"Deo gratias," Vincent muttered after the lesson had been read. The mystery of love, the immolation of the holy victim, was prepared. The altar boy took the missal and, being careful not to touch its pages, carried it to the left, toward the Gospel. Each time he passed the tabernacle he twisted in a desultory genuflection. Then he returned and stood to the right, crossing his arms as the Gospel was read. The priest, after making the sign of the cross over the missal, crossed himself on his forehead, to say that he would never blush at the holy word; on his mouth, to show that he was always ready to confess his faith; on his heart, to indicate that his heart belonged to God alone.

"Dominus vobiscum," he said as he turned around and blinked at the church's cold whiteness. *"Et cum spiritu tuo,"* responded Vincent, again on his knees. After reciting the offertory, the priest uncovered the chalice. For a moment he held the paten containing the Host level with his chest as he offered it to God for himself, for those present, and for all the faithful, living or dead. Now, without touching it with his fingers, he slid the chalice to the edge of the corporal and rubbed it carefully with the chalice cloth. Vincent had gone to the credence to get the cruets, which he then offered to the priest, the one containing the wine before that containing the water. The priest now offered for the whole world the half-filled chalice, put it back in the center of the corporal, and covered it with the pall. Next, after praying again, he returned to have thin streams of water poured over the tips of his thumbs and index fingers in order to purify himself of the

7

smallest trace of sin. When he had dried his hands with the towel, la Teuse, who had been waiting her turn, emptied the cruets into a zinc container on the corner of the altar.

"*Orate, fratres,*" the priest said aloud; he was facing the empty benches, his hands spread wide in an appeal to all men of goodwill. And, turning to the altar once more, he proceeded in a lower voice. Vincent was lost in the long Latin sentence he was garbling. At that very moment yellow flames came in through the windows: the sun, responding to the priest's appeal, was coming to Mass. It lit large gilded patches on the left wall, the confessional, the altar of the Virgin, and the big clock. A hollow crack shook the confessional. The Mother of God was given a nimbus by the dazzling light on her crown and golden cloak; her painted lips smiled tenderly at the Christ child. The clock, warmed by the light, struck the hour with greater vigor; the dust dancing in the sun's rays became a multitude of the faithful filling the benches. The little church, the whitewashed barn, was filled with warm legions. Small sounds of the countryside's happy awakening penetrated the church: the grasses breathing freely, the leaves rubbing themselves in the heat, the birds preening their feathers and making the first wing strokes of the morning. The countryside even joined the sunlight in the church; a large service tree was reaching up next to one of the windows, shooting branches through the broken panes and stretching its buds as if to look inside. The plants on the steps were visible through the main door and threatened to invade the nave. The large Christ, still shadowy in its corner, was the only dead thing in this throbbing onrush of life; the flesh daubed with ocher and splattered with lacquer still suffered its death agony. A sparrow came to perch on the edge of a hole in the window, looked around and flew away. But he reappeared almost immediately and silently swooped down between the benches next to the altar of the Virgin. A second sparrow followed. Soon they were coming from every branch in the service tree to hop tranquilly about on the tile floor.

"*Sanctus, Sanctus, Sanctus Dominus Deus Sabaoth,*" said the priest softly, his shoulders bent slightly forward. Vincent rang the bell three times. But the sparrows, frightened by this sudden song, flew away with such a beating of wings that la Teuse, who had just gone into the sacristy, ran back to scold them. "The beggars are going to get everything dirty. I bet Miss Désirée's been giving them crumbs again."

The awesome moment was drawing near. The body and blood of a God were about to descend to the altar. The priest kissed the altar cloth, folded his hands, and made multitudinous signs of the cross over the Host and chalice. He was ecstatic with humility and gratitude as the prayers of the canon fell from his lips. His posture, his gestures, the inflections of his voice, all said how small he was, how overwhelmed at being chosen for such a task. Vincent came to kneel behind him, took the chasuble in his left hand, lifted it slightly, and prepared to ring the bell. The priest, his elbows on the edge of the table, pronounced the words of consecration over the Host he was holding between the thumb and index finger of each hand: *"Hoc est enim corpus meum."* Then, after genuflecting, he slowly raised the Host as high as he could reach, following it with his eyes while the prostrate altar boy thrice rang the bell. Next he consecrated the wine: *"Hic est enim calix."* His elbows again on the altar, he bowed and elevated the chalice, following it with his eyes, his right hand grasping its knop, his left hand supporting it from underneath. The great mystery of Redemption had just been renewed; the adorable Blood was flowing once again.

"Just wait, just you wait," threatened la Teuse, shaking her fist in an attempt to frighten the sparrows away. But the sparrows were no longer afraid. They had returned while the bell was ringing and were now brazenly hopping on the benches. The constant tinkling delighted them now. They responded with small cries which broke into the Latin words like the pearly laughter of free urchins. The sun warmed their feathers; the church's soft poverty enchanted them. Cheeping, pecking, fighting over the crumbs on the floor, they made themselves at home as if they were in a barn whose window had been left open. One of them perched on the smiling Virgin's golden veil, another came nimbly up to examine la

Teuse's petticoats, and the sight of such daring infuriated her.

At the altar the swooning priest, his eyes fixed on the sacred Host, his thumb and index finger joined, did not hear this invasion of the nave by the warm May morning, by the rising tide of sun, greenery, and birds which flowed to the very base of the Calvary where damned nature was suffering its death agony.

"Per omnia saecula saeculorum," he said.

"Amen," responded Vincent.

After the Lord's Prayer, the priest raised the Host above the chalice, broke it into two equal parts, then removed a particle from one of the halves and dropped it into the Precious Blood to show the intimate bond Communion would create between him and God. He said the *Agnus Dei* aloud, recited very softly the three prescribed prayers, and performed his act of unworthiness. With his elbows on the altar and the paten under his chin, he partook of both parts of the Host at the same time. Then, after folding his hands before his face in ardent meditation, he used the paten to gather the holy particles of the Host fallen on the corporal and dropped them into the chalice. A small piece stuck to his thumb, and he rubbed it off with the tip of his index finger. And, crossing himself with the chalice, the paten again under his chin, he drank all the Precious Blood in three swallows, consuming the divine sacrifice to the last drop without removing the cup from his lips.

Vincent had gone to the credence to get the cruets. But the door of the corridor leading to the presbytery opened wide and banged against the wall to admit a pretty twenty-two-year-old childlike girl hiding something in her apron. "Thirteen! Thirteen of them!" she cried. "Every single egg was good." She half-opened her apron to reveal a brood of swarming chicks covered with new feathers and staring with the black points of their eyes. "Just look at them! Aren't they cute! The little darlings! Oh, look at the little white one climbing up on that other one's back. And that one there, the speckled one—he's already beating his wings! The eggs were really good! Not one was sterile."

La Teuse, who, despite everything, was helping at the Mass

by passing Vincent the cruets for ablution turned and said aloud, "Hush up, Miss Désirée! Can't you see we're not done yet?"

A strong barnyard odor came through the open door, blowing like a sudden burst of fermentation across the church, through the warm sunlight which had now reached the altar. Désirée remained standing for a time, completely absorbed in the little world she was carrying. She glanced at Vincent as he poured the wine for purification and at her brother as he drank this wine so that none of the holy substance of Christ's body would remain in his mouth. And she was still there when he came back, holding the chalice with both hands, to receive on his thumb and index finger the wine and water of ablution before drinking these as well. But the mother hen was looking for her chicks; she began clucking outside and threatened to enter the church. Cooing maternally to the chicks, Désirée left at the very moment when the priest, after putting the chalice cloth to his lips, was passing it around the edges and inner portion of the chalice.

It was the end. The actions of grace had been rendered up to God. The altar boy went to get the missal for the last time and brought it back to the right-hand side. The priest put cloth, paten, and pall back on the chalice; then he again pinched the veil's two large folds and laid down the burse in which he had enclosed the corporal. All his being was now burning with gratitude. He asked heaven for the remission of his sins, for the grace with which to live a holy life on this earth, and for life everlasting hereafter. He was engulfed by this miracle of love, by this continual immolation which nourished him every day with the blood and flesh of his Saviour.

After reading the prayers, he turned and said, *"Ite, missa est." "Deo gratias,"* Vincent responded. Then, turning to kiss the altar, he came back once more, his left hand under his chest and his right hand extended, to bless the church filled with the sunlight's pranks and the sparrows' uproar.

"Benedicat vos omnipotens Deus, Pater et Filius, et Spiritus Sanctus."

"Amen," said the altar boy as he crossed himself.

The patches of sunlight had grown larger, the sparrows were bolder. While the priest was on the left platform, reading the Gospel of St. John announcing the eternity of the Word, the sun was setting the altar ablaze, whitening the false marble panels, devouring the light of the two candles, whose short wicks were now nothing but two dark spots. The triumphant star surrounded crucifix, candlesticks, chasuble, and chalice veil with its own nimbus, and all this gold paled under its rays. After the priest, his head covered, had taken the chalice, genuflected, and left the altar to return to the sacristy, preceded by the altar boy carrying the cruets and towel, only the sun remained in the church. It was now sole master. It had reached the altar cloth and was brilliantly illuminating the door of the tabernacle to celebrate the fertility of May. Heat rose from the tile floor. The whitewashed walls, the large Virgin, even the large Christ quivered with the vitality of new sap, as if death had been conquered by earth's eternal youth.

◇◇◇◇◇◇◇◇◇◇◇◇◇◇◇◇◇◇◇◇◇◇◇◇◇◇◇◇◇◇◇◇◇

III La teuse hurried to put the candles out, but she did not leave immediately because she felt she simply had to chase away the sparrows. When she took the missal back to the sacristy, Father Mouret had washed his hands, put away the vestments, and left. He was already in the dining room, breakfasting on a cup of milk.

"You really have to make your sister stop throwing bread in the church," la Teuse said when she saw him. "She started that cute little trick last winter when she decided that the sparrows were cold and the good Lord could feed them if anybody could. You'll see, she'll end up making us sleep with her hens and rabbits."

"We'd be warmer," the young priest said happily. "You're always complaining, Teuse. Let's let poor Désirée love her animals the way she wants to. The innocent thing doesn't have any other pleasures."

The servant stood defiantly in the middle of the room. "Oh, you! You wouldn't mind if magpies built their nests right in the church. You don't ever get upset. You always think everything's fine and dandy. Your sister's awfully lucky you took her with you when you left the seminary. No father, no mother. I'd like to know who else would let her wallow around in a barnyard the way she does!" Then, relenting and changing her tone, "You're right, it'd be a real pity to bother her. There's not a mean bone in her body. She may be one of the strongest girls around, but she's really just a ten-year-old kid. You know, I still tuck her in bed every night. She's just like a baby—I have to tell her stories to put her to sleep."

Father Mouret had remained standing to finish his milk. His fingers were slightly reddened by the chill in the dining room, a large tiled room painted gray with no furniture except table and chairs. La Teuse picked up a napkin which she had laid in a corner of the table for breakfast. "You hardly use any linen," she muttered. "It looks like you can't ever sit down, you're always about to leave. Ah, if you had only known Father Caffin, the poor late priest you replaced. Now, *there* was a finicky man! He wouldn't have digested a blessed thing if he'd had to eat standing up. He was a Norman from Canteleu, like me. Oh, I don't think he did me any favor when he brought me to the wild country we're in. Good heavens, were we bored at first! The poor Father had had some rough going in our part of the country . . . Goodness, Father, didn't you put any sugar in your milk? Both cubes are still lying here."

The priest laid his cup down. "I must have forgotten," he said. Shrugging her shoulders, la Teuse looked straight at him. She folded the napkin around a slice of brown bread which had also been left on the table. Then, as the priest was leaving, she ran up to him, knelt, and said, "Wait, your shoes aren't even tied. I don't know how your feet stand these clodhoppers. You're so particular. You even look like you'd been spoiled! The bishop must have been a real buddy of yours to give you the poorest parish in the department."

"But," replied the priest, smiling again, "I'm the one who chose Artauds. You're in a foul mood this morning, Teuse. Aren't we happy here? We have all we need: we're living in heavenly peace."

She held herself back and even managed to laugh as she said, "You're a holy man, Father . . . Come see how thick my lye is. That's better than arguing." He had to follow her, for she might not let him leave if he did not compliment her on her lye. He was going out of the dining room when he tripped over a piece of plaster in the hall. "What's that?" he asked.

"Nothing," la Teuse answered in her most terrible voice. "Just the house falling down. But you like it, don't you? You've got all you need. Maybe you're right—Lord knows we've got plenty of holes. Just look at that ceiling. Is it cracked enough? If we aren't crushed to death one fine morning, we'll owe a monstrous candle to our guardian angel. But it's all right so long as you're happy . . . It's the same with the church. Those broken windows ought to have been fixed two years ago. The good Lord freezes in the winter. Besides, it'd stop the sparrows from coming in. I just warn you, I'll end up sticking paper in the holes."

"But that's a good idea," said the priest. "We could put up paper. And the walls are more solid than you think. The floor in my room doesn't sag anywhere except under the window. This house will see us all dead and buried."

They went into the small shed near the kitchen, and Father Mouret, anxious to please la Teuse, waxed ecstatic over the excellence of the soap. He had to smell it and let it flow through his fingers. Then the delighted old woman showed how motherly she could be. She no longer grumbled, she ran to get a brush. "You're not going to go out with yesterday's mud on your cassock! It'd be nice and clean if you'd just left it on the rail. It's still good, this old cassock is. Just be sure to pick it up when you cross the fields. Those thistles rip everything to shreds." And she made him turn around like a child as she shook him head to foot with the violent strokes of her brush.

"Fine, that's enough," he said as he tried to run away. "Look out for Désirée. I'll tell her I'm going out."

But just then a clear voice called out, "Serge! Serge!" Red with joy, bareheaded, her black hair pulled tightly into a bun, Désirée came running up to them. Her hands and arms were covered with filth, for she had been cleaning her hens. When she saw her brother, his breviary under his arm, about to leave, she laughed louder and kissed him squarely on his mouth, her hands thrown behind her so she would not touch him. "No! No!" she stammered. "I'd get you all dirty. Oh, what fun I'm having! You'll have to see the animals when you come back." And she ran away.

Father Mouret said he would be back for lunch around eleven. He was leaving when la Teuse, who had seen him to the door, called out her last bit of advice. "Don't forget Brother Archangias. Go by the Brichets' too. The wife came again yesterday about this wedding. Listen, Father, I saw Rosalie. She'd be happy to marry big Fortuné. Speak to old Bambousse again. Maybe he'll listen to you this time. And don't come back at noon like you did the other day. At eleven o'clock, right? Eleven o'clock."

But the priest did not turn around again. She went back in, muttering between her teeth. "He never listens to a word I say. He's not even twenty-six, and he's already having trouble with a swelled head. He could teach holiness to a sixty-year-old man, but he hasn't lived at all; he doesn't know a blessed thing about life. It's no trouble to the darling child to be as sweet as a cherub."

◇◇

IV FATHER MOURET STOPPED WHEN HE COULD NO LONGER hear la Teuse behind him, delighted to be alone at last. The church was built on a slight rise sloping gently down to the village. It stood like an abandoned sheepfold pierced by wide windows and brightened by red tiles. The priest turned around and glanced at the presbytery, a grayish hovel shoved against one side of the nave. Then, as if he were afraid of being caught once more by the endless chatter that had been buzzing in his ears all morning, he moved off to the right. He considered himself safe only when he was in front of the main door and out of sight of the house. Rain and sun had worn the church front bare; the red roof was topped by the dark profile of a bell in the center of a narrow stone square, from which a cord dangled through the tiles. Six broken, half-buried steps led to the high rounded door, cracked and devoured by dust, spider webs, and rust. It looked so pitiful on its wretched hinges that it seemed the first breath of wind would burst through and sweep the church. Father Mouret, who loved this ruin, went up the steps to lean against one of the double doors. The whole countryside lay before him as he shaded his eyes with his hands and scanned the horizon.

In May, a great surge of vegetation broke through this rocky soil. Colossal lavenders, junipers, and patches of tough grasses ran up the church wall to plant clumps of dark green all the way to the roof. At this time of morning the growth was at full strength, the primeval rush of sap threatening to carry away the church in a dense tangle of knotty plants. The heat hummed in a long silent effort to raise the shuddering stones. But the priest could not feel the heat of these laborious births. He simply thought the steps were unsteady and leaned against the other side of the door.

The countryside spreading out for six miles around was enclosed by a wall of yellow hills spotted by dark pine groves— a terrible country of dry wastes broken by rocky ridges. The few acres of arable land were laid out in bloody pools, red fields lined with rows of scrawny almond trees, gray tips of olive trees, and wild vines scoring the plain with their brown stems. It seemed that a great consuming fire had passed through this land to strew forest ashes on the heights and leave vicious light and heat in the low places. At rare intervals a little relief was afforded by pale green patches of wheat. No water was visible, the land was awful, it was dying of thirst and gave off great clouds of dust at the slightest breeze. In the far distance, the hills on the horizon revealed damp greenness, offering a glimpse of the neighboring valley made fertile by the Viorne, a river which sprang from the Seille gorges.

Blinded by the glare, the priest lowered his gaze to the village, whose few houses were scattered helter-skelter below the church. Miserable houses, made of dry stones and hewn boards, dropped along a narrow road without side streets. There were about thirty of them, some black from want and crouching in their own filth, others larger and brightened by pink tiles on their roofs. Thin, tiny gardens wrenched from the rock displayed vegetable plots separated by quickset hedges. Artauds was empty at this time of day. Not one woman at her window, not one child sprawling in the dust. Nothing moved except for flocks of hens walking back and forth along the road, scratching the straw, searching everywhere for food, walking right up to the doors yawning complacently in the sun. A large black dog sitting on his rump seemed to be guarding the entrance to the village.

Little by little a sense of laziness numbed Father Mouret. The rising sun bathed him in its warmth. He was being invaded by happiness and peace, and he relaxed against the church door. He began to reflect on this village of Artauds which had grown among the rocks like one of the valley's hardy plants. All the inhabitants were relatives; they all had the same name. They had to be christened in the cradle to be distinguished from each other. An ancestor, an Artaud, had come and established himself in this wasteland like a pariah. Here his family had grown with the fierce vitality of grass sucking life from the rocks to become a tribe, a commune where relationships went back for centuries and were lost. They married among themselves in shameless promiscuity. No one could think of an Artaud who had taken a wife from a neighboring village; only the girls went away. The villagers were born and died attached to this bit of earth, multiplying in their dung heap slowly, with the simplicity of trees growing from their own seed; no one had a very precise idea of the great world beyond the yellow rocks on which the Artauds vegetated. And nevertheless there were already rich and poor among them. Some hens had disappeared; heavy padlocks protected the chicken coops at night. One evening an Artaud had killed an Artaud behind the mill. It was a nation apart, lost behind this desolate belt of hills, a people born from the soil, a race of three hundred souls beginning time over again.

The priest himself retained the dead darkness of the seminary. For years he had not known the sun. He still did not know it; his eyes were closed to gaze at his soul, and he had only contempt for damned nature. For a long time, during the hours when he was prostrate in meditation, he had dreamed of a hermit's desert, of some hole in a mountain where nothing alive, no being, no plant, no water, could come distract him from contemplating the majesty of God. It was a surge of pure love, a horror of physical sensation. There, dying to himself, his back to the light, he could have waited to be no longer, to lose himself in the sovereign whiteness of souls. Heaven seemed to him completely white, with the whiteness of light, as if all purity, all innocence, all chastity, had caught fire. But his confessor scolded him when he spoke of his desire for solitude, of his need for divine simplicity; he was reminded of the Church's struggles, of the necessity of ministry. Later, after his ordination, the young priest came to Artauds at his own request, hoping to realize his dream of human annihilation. In the midst of this poverty, on this sterile soil, he could close his ears to the world's noise and live in the sleep of the saints. He had in part succeeded, he had been smiling for several months; hardly any movement from the village disturbed him, hardly any warm bite of the sun took him by the neck as he strode along the paths. He belonged completely to heaven; he did not hear the continuous births surrounding him as he walked.

The large black dog guarding Artauds decided to investigate Father Mouret, sniffed his feet, and sat on his rump once more. But the priest remained lost in the morning softness. The day before, he had begun the rituals of Mary's month. He attributed the great joy entering him to the Blessed Virgin's intercession with her divine Son. And how contemptible the things of earth seemed to him! How grateful he was for feeling poor! On taking orders, after losing his father and mother in a drama whose terrors he still did not fully know, he had left the family fortune to an older brother. Only his sister still bound him to the world. He had burdened himself with her out of a sort of religious affection for her simple mind. The dear innocent thing was so childish, so like a little girl, that she appeared to him as one of the poor in spirit to whom the Gospel gives the kingdom of Heaven. However, he had been worried about her for some time; she was becoming too strong, too healthy, too much life exuded from her. But even this barely disturbed his comfort. He spent his days in the inner world he had created for himself. He had abandoned everything to give his entire being. He closed the door of his senses, tried to liberate himself from bodily needs, was now only a soul delighting in contemplation. Nature offered him only snares and filth. He made it a point of honor to do violence to it, to scorn it, to release himself from his human mud. The just must appear insane to the world. Therefore he considered himself an exile on earth; he strived only for celestial things, for he could not understand how anyone could hesitate between an eternity of joy and a few hours of perishable pleasure. His reason deceived him, his desires lied. And if he moved forward in the way of virtue, it was especially because of his humility and obedience. He wished to be the lowest of all, subject to all, so that divine dew might fall on his heart as on dry sand. He said he was covered by disdain and confusion, unworthy of being rescued from sin. To be humble is to believe and love. Now he no longer relied at all on his deaf and blind self, on his dead flesh. He was nothing but God's plaything. Then, from this abasement in which he had thrust himself, a hosanna carried him above the contented and powerful into the brilliance of bliss without end.

Father Mouret had thus found in Artauds the delights of the cloister which each reading of the *Imitation of Christ* made him desire so strongly. As yet nothing in him had fought back. He was perfect at his first genuflection. There had been no battle, no trembling, as if he had been struck by grace and had completely forgotten his flesh. The ecstasy of God's approach which some young priests know, the blissful hour when everything is silent, when desires are only an immense need for purity. He had not put his hope in any creature. The belief that one thing is All makes a man impregnable, and he believed that God was All, that his own humility, obedience, and chastity were All. He remembered temptation being described as an awful torture which even the holiest must undergo. He had smiled. God had never abandoned him. He marched in his faith as in a suit of armor protecting him from the smallest blows. He remembered crouching in a corner and crying from love when he was eight years old. He did not know whom he loved; he cried because he loved someone very far away. He had always remained emotional. Later, he wanted to become a priest to satisfy that need for superhuman affection which was his only torment. He saw no way to love more abundantly; the priesthood satisfied the sources of his being, his adolescent dreams, his first manly desires. He awaited temptation, if it should come, with the calm of an inexperienced seminarian. The man in him had been killed—he felt it to be so. He was glad to know he stood apart, a castrated creature turned away from his natural self, branded as one of the Lord's sheep by his tonsure.

◇◇◇◇◇◇◇◇◇◇◇◇◇◇◇◇◇◇◇◇◇◇◇◇◇◇◇◇◇◇◇◇◇◇◇◇

V ALL THIS TIME THE SUN HAD BEEN WARMING THE BIG church door. Golden flies were buzzing around a large flower growing between two steps. Father Mouret felt a little dizzy, and he was about to leave when the big black dog barked furiously and rushed toward the gate of the cemetery to the left of the church. At the same time, a rough voice shouted, "Ah, you good-for-nothing brat, you can't come to school but you can come horse around in the cemetery. Don't try to deny it! I've been watching you for the past fifteen minutes."

The priest moved over to the cemetery and saw Vincent, his ear being pinched by the friar of the local parochial school. The child was almost suspended over the gully formed by the Mascle, a torrent whose white waters were hurled into the Viorne about six miles away.

"Brother Archangias." The priest spoke softly in an attempt to induce the frightening man to be merciful. But the friar did not let go of the ear.

"Ah, it's you, Father," he growled. "This little scoundrel's always hanging around here, and I don't even know what kind of mischief he gets into. I ought to drop him to the bottom and break his head. Heaven would be pleased."

The child was silent; he kept his eyes shut and tried to grab the underbrush.

"Be careful, Brother Archangias," said the priest, "he might slip." And he himself helped Vincent out. "Now, my young friend, what were you doing here? You ought not to play in cemeteries." The urchin had opened his eyes and now scampered away from the friar to claim sanctuary near Father Mouret.

"I'll tell *you*," he said, raising his intelligent eyes to the priest. "There's a warbler's nest in the briars under this rock. I've been watching it for more than ten days. The babies have hatched now, so I came to look at them this morning after serving Mass."

"A warbler's nest!" roared Brother Archangias. "Just wait." He ran off, picked up a clod on a grave, and hurried back to throw it into the briars. But he missed the nest. A second clod thrown more skillfully shook the frail cradle and dumped the little birds into the torrent. "That might keep you from prowling around here like a heathen," he said as he brushed his hands. "The dead people will come pull your toes at night if you keep walking on them."

Vincent, who had laughed to see the nest tumble down, looked around and shrugged his shoulders like the unsuperstitious young man he was. "Oh, I'm not afraid," he said. "Dead people don't move around much."

And, in fact, the cemetery was not in the least frightening. It was a stark piece of ground whose narrow walks were buried under the invading plants. The ground bulged in several places. Father Caffin's grave had the only stone; it was brand-new, its whiteness standing tall in the middle of the plot. Nothing else except broken wooden crosses made of dried boxwood and old cracked slabs covered with moss. There were no more than two burials a year. Death seemed far away in this hazy ground where la Teuse came every evening to fill her apron with plants for Désirée's rabbits. A gigantic cypress standing at the gate cast the only shadow on this forsaken field. The cypress, visible for nine miles around, was known throughout the region as the Hermit.

"It's full of lizards," added Vincent, who was looking at the church's crumbling wall. "It'd be great fun to . . ." But he leaped away when he saw the friar draw back his foot. The latter pointed out to the priest the disrepair of the iron gate, which had been corroded by rust and had one hinge hanging loose and a broken lock. "We ought to fix that," he said.

Father Mouret smiled without replying. And, turning to Vincent, who was playing with the dog, he asked, "Say, boy, do you know where old Bambousse is working this morning?" The child glanced at the horizon.

"He must be in his Olivettes field," he replied. "Besides, Father, Voriau can take you. He always knows where his master is." He clapped his hands and shouted, "Ha! Voriau, ha!" The big black dog stood wagging his tail for a moment, trying to read the urchin's eyes. Then, barking joyously, he ran toward the village. Father Mouret and Brother Archangias chatted as they followed him. A hundred yards down the path, Vincent sneaked away and returned to the church; he watched them carefully, ready to throw himself behind a bush if they turned their heads. He slid back into the cemetery like a snake, back into this paradise of nests, lizards, and flowers.

Meanwhile, as Voriau led the way down the dusty road, Brother Archangias was speaking irritably to the priest. "Give up the damned to hell, abandon these toads, Father. There's no way to make them pleasing to God short of hamstringing them. They're wallowing in irreligion just like their parents before them. I've been in this part of the country for fifteen years, and I've yet to make anybody a Christian. It's all over the day they leave me. They belong to the earth, to their vines and olive trees. Not one so much as sticks a foot in church. They're animals in a war with their rocky fields. Lead them by hitting them with a stick, Father, with a stick."

Then, catching his breath, he added with a horrible gesture, "Look. Artauds is like the brambles that eat the rocks around here. One was enough to poison the whole country. They clamp themselves on, they multiply, they thrive no matter what. The town's just like Gomorrah; nothing but a rain of fire from heaven could cleanse it."

"We must never despair of a sinner," said Father Mouret, who was calmly walking along in his inner peace.

"No, these people belong to the devil," said the friar, even more violently. "I've been a peasant like them. I dug the ground until I was eighteen. I know what I'm talking about. And later, at the institute, I swept floors, I peeled vegetables, I did every lousy job you can think of. I don't criticize the rough work they do. On the contrary, God prefers the lowly. But the Artauds are beasts, can't you see that? They act just like their pigs. They don't go to Mass; they make fun of the commandments of God and the Church. They love their miserable pieces of ground so much they'd fornicate with the earth if they could just figure out how."

Voriau, his tail in the wind, stopped and made sure that the two men were still following him before resuming his trot.

"There are indeed some deplorable abuses," said Father Mouret. "My predecessor, Father Caffin—"

"A useless waste," the friar interrupted. "He came to us from Normandy after some dirty scandal. When he got here, he didn't think about anything except his stomach. He let everything go to pot."

"No, Father Caffin did all he could, but I have to admit his efforts were almost useless. Even mine often seem to have no effect."

Brother Archangias shrugged his shoulders. He walked silently for a moment, swaying his large, slender body which seemed to have been rough-hewn by an ax. The sun beat down on his tanned leather neck and shaded his hard, razor-sharp peasant face. "Listen, Father," he said finally, "I'm too lowly to give you advice. It's just that I'm almost twice your age, I know this country, and that gives me the right to tell you you won't get anywhere by gentleness. Do you understand? Catechism is all that matters. God has no pity on impious people. He burns them. Keep that in mind." And when Father Mouret continued to look at the ground without opening his mouth, he went on: "Religion is losing ground in the country because people make it too sweet. Men respected it when it spoke like a master who didn't know what pity was. I don't know what they teach you in seminary now. These new priests cry like babies with their parishioners. God's not the same anymore ٬ . . You know what? I bet you don't even know your catechism by heart."

The priest, wounded by this will striving too roughly to impose itself on him, raised his eyes and said almost dryly, "That's fine, your zeal is praiseworthy. But don't you have something to tell me? You came to the church to see me this morning, didn't you?"

Brother Archangias answered brutally. "I wanted to tell you what I told you. The Artauds live like their pigs. I found out yesterday that Rosalie, old Bambousse's daughter, is pregnant. They all wait to get knocked up before they think about getting married. In fifteen years I haven't seen a single one who didn't head for the fields before going through the church. And they joke about it; they say it's a local custom!"

"Yes," muttered Father Mouret, "it's all very shocking. I'm looking for old Bambousse to talk about this very thing. We all want the marriage to take place as soon as possible. It seems the baby's father is Fortuné, the Brichets' son. Unfortunately the Brichets are poor."

"That Rosalie," the friar went on, "she's barely eighteen. She was damned on the school benches. It hasn't even been four years since I had her. I could tell she was a lost girl. Now I've got her sister Catherine, and she's just as bad. She's only eleven, but I can see she's going to be even more shameless. Every time you turn around she's hiding in some hole with that miserable punk Vincent. It doesn't do a damned bit of good to pull their ears until the blood flows, the woman in them is going to grow up no matter what. They've all got damnation in their skirts. They ought to be thrown out with the rest of the garbage so maybe we could get rid of their poisonous itch. It'd be great if every single girl were strangled at birth." Disgust and hatred for all women made him swear like a trooper. Father Mouret's face remained calm as he listened to this outburst, and he finally even smiled at such extravagant violence. He called Voriau, who had run into a neighboring field.

"Just look!" yelled Brother Archangias, pointing at a group

of children playing at the bottom of a gully. "There're the little bastards who miss school because they say they have to help their parents in the vineyards. You can bet that bitch Catherine's right in the middle of them. She likes to slide. We can see her skirts fly over her head. There, what did I tell you . . . See you tonight Father. Just wait, just wait, you little brats!"

And he ran away, his dirty bands flying behind him, his large, filthy cassock pulling up thistles. Father Mouret watched him swoop down among the children who were running away like a flock of frightened sparrows. But he had succeeded in catching Catherine and another child by the ears. He pulled them toward the village, holding them tight with his fat hairy fingers as he yelled insults at them.

The priest began walking again. Brother Archangias at times caused him strange misgivings. His very crudity made him appear to be the true man of God whom nothing attached to earth; he was completely given over to God's will, humble, uncouth, his mouth full of ordure to use against sin. And he himself despaired because he was unable to release himself even more from his body, because he was not ugly and vile, because he did not stink of saintly vermin. When he felt revolted by the friar's coarse language, by his overly eager brutality, he reproached himself immediately for his delicacy and pride as if these things were mortal sins. Should not he be dead to all worldly weakness? He smiled sadly when he remembered that he had almost lost his temper during the friar's burning sermon. This was pride, he thought, trying to destroy him by making him scorn simple people. But, despite himself, he was relieved at being alone, and he walked peacefully down the road, calmly reading his breviary, finally liberated from that bitter voice which so disturbed his dream of pure love.

◇◇◇◇◇◇◇◇◇◇◇◇◇◇◇◇◇◇◇◇◇◇◇◇◇◇◇◇◇◇◇◇◇◇◇◇

VI THE ROAD WOUND AMONG THE ROCKS FROM WHICH THE peasants had wrested tiny, scattered plots of chalky soil, and the dust in the deep ruts crackled like snow under the priest's feet. At times, when a particularly warm breeze hit his face, he raised his eyes from his book to see where this caress could have come from. But his eyes focused on nothing; they always remained vague and lost without really seeing the fiery horizon, the twisted lines of this passionate, dry country swooning like a sterile woman in heat sprawled under the sun. He pushed his hat down on his forehead to escape the warm puffs; he began peacefully reading once more, his cassock trailing behind him, raising a little cloud which rolled along the road.

"Hello, Father," said a passing peasant.

The noise of digging beside the road brought him out of his reverie. He turned his head and saw a few gnarled old men in the distance. In broad daylight, the Artauds were fornicating with the earth, as Brother Archangias had said. Sweaty brows appeared behind the bushes, puffing chests raised themselves slowly in an ardent attempt to impregnate, and his ignorance allowed him to walk calmly through all these couplings. His flesh could not be disturbed by the great act of love which was filling the beautiful morning.

"Stop it, Voriau! Don't eat me alive!" happily yelled a strong voice which silenced the dog's rabid barks. Father Mouret raised his head.

"It's you, Fortuné," he said, and he walked to the edge of the field where the young peasant was working. "I wanted to talk to you."

Fortuné was a big boy, strong-looking, his skin already hard, although he was about the same age as the priest. He was clearing a corner of the rocky field.

"About what, Father?" he asked.

"About what happened with Rosalie," the priest replied.

Fortuné began to laugh. He must have considered it funny for a priest to worry about that kind of thing.

"Bull!" he muttered. "She really wanted it. I didn't rape her. Too bad if old Bambousse won't give her to me. You saw how his blasted dog tried to bite me. He sics him on me all the time."

Father Mouret was going to say something further when old

Artaud, called Brichet, whom he had not seen at first, came out from the shade of a bush where he had been eating with his wife. He was tiny and humble-looking; age had dried him out.

"Somebody's been spreading stories, Father," he exclaimed. "The boy's as ready as can be to marry Rosalie. They grew up together . . . It's nobody's fault . . . There's lots of people who did what they did and don't live any the worse for it. It's not up to us to decide. You've got to talk to Bambousse. He thinks he's too good for the likes of us because of his money."

"Yeah, we're too poor for him," whined his wife, a big, sniveling woman who stood up after her husband. "All we've got in the world is this little field where the devil makes it rain pebbles all the time. It doesn't give us the bread . . . without you, Father, we'd have starved long ago."

Mother Brichet was the village's only religious woman. After taking Communion, she wandered around the presbytery, certain that la Teuse was keeping a couple of loaves for her from the last baking day. Sometimes she even took away a chicken or a rabbit that Désirée gave her.

"But there are simply too many scandals," said the priest. "We've got to have this marriage as soon as possible."

"But that's fine with us. We'll do it the minute the others will," said the old lady, very worried about her handouts. "Right, Brichet? We're not likely to be un-Christian and upset the Father, now are we?"

Fortuné was sniggering. "I'm more than ready," he declared, "and Rosalie is, too. I saw her behind the mill yesterday. It doesn't bother us a bit. We just laughed about it."

Father Mouret interrupted him: "All right, I'm going to talk to Bambousse. He's over in Olivettes, I think." The priest was walking away when Mother Brichet asked him what had become of her other son, Vincent, who had left that morning to serve Mass. Now, there was a brat who really needed the Father's advice. And she walked beside the priest for a while, complaining of her poverty, of the potatoes she could not have, of the cold spell that froze the olive trees, of the hot spell threatening to burn the meager harvest. She left assuring him that her son Fortuné said his prayers every morning and every night.

Voriau was leading Father Mouret when suddenly, at a bend in the road, he rushed into the fields. The priest had to take a narrow path up a hill. He was in Olivettes, the richest land in the area, where the commune's mayor, Artaud, called Bambousse, owned several fields of wheat, olive trees, and grapes. Meanwhile, the dog had run into the petticoats of a large brunette who laughed heartily when she saw the priest.

"Is your father here, Rosalie?" asked the priest.

"Over there," she replied, pointing, still smiling as she left the part of the field she was weeding to show him the way. Her early pregnancy was visible only in a slight swelling around her hips. She had the powerful, rolling gait of hard workers; she was bareheaded in the sun; her neck was red and covered by black hairs bristling like a mane; her green hands smelled of the plants she had been pulling up.

"Hey!" she cried. "Here's the priest wants to see you." And she did not leave—she remained to grin brazenly like a lewd animal. Bambousse, fat, sweaty, round-faced, left his work and walked nimbly over to meet the priest.

"I'll just bet you want to talk to me about repairing the church," he said as he brushed his hands, which were covered with soil. "No, no, no good, it's just not possible, Father. The commune doesn't have a cent. If the good Lord furnishes plaster and tiles, we'll furnish masons." This sacrilegious peasant joke made him burst into huge gales of laughter. He smacked his thighs, coughed, almost choked.

"I didn't come about the church," replied Father Mouret. "I wanted to talk about your daughter Rosalie."

"Rosalie? What did she do to you?" Bambousse asked with a wink.

The peasant girl was boldly staring at the young priest, examining him from his white hands to his feminine neck, amusing herself by trying to make him turn completely red. But he said bluntly, his face calm, as if he were talking of something which he did not feel, "You know what I mean, Bambousse. She's pregnant. She's got to get married."

"Aha, so that's it!" the old man muttered in his mocking way. "Thanks for running the errand, Father. The Brichets sent you, didn't they? His woman goes to Mass, and you give her a hand when she wants to set her son up for life, that's understandable. But I don't want to play. I don't like the rules. That's it!"

The surprised priest explained that the scandal had to be cut short, that he had to forgive Fortuné since he wanted to atone for his sin, and concluded by stating that his daughter's honor demanded a quick wedding.

"Ta-ta-ta!" said Bambousse as he waggled his head. "What nice words! I'm keeping my daughter, do you understand? All that doesn't have a thing to do with me. Fortuné's poor. He's not worth two cents. It'd be a fine state of affairs if all you had to do to marry a girl was do it with her. Good Lord! There'd be weddings day and night. Thank God I'm not worried about Rosalie. People know what happened to her; it doesn't make her bandy-legged or hunchbacked, and she'll marry anybody she damned well pleases."

"But her child?" interrupted the priest.

"The child? It's not here, is it? Maybe it'll never come. If she has the baby, then we'll have to see."

Rosalie observed the priest's lack of progress and felt she had to cover her eyes with her fists and moan. She even fell to the ground, displaying as she did so the blue stockings rising above her knees.

"Shut up, bitch!" yelled her furious father. And he savagely called her crude names, which made her laugh behind her clenched fists. "If I find you two together, I'm going to tie you both up the way you are and drag you naked and coupled through the streets for everybody to see. Shut up, I said . . . Just wait, you slut!" He picked up a clod and flung it at her from four paces away. It smashed against her hair bun, slid down her neck, and covered her with dust. Stunned, she jumped up and ran away, shielding her face with her hands. But Bambousse had time to hit her with two other clods; one only glanced off her left shoulder, but the other hit her so hard on the back that she fell to her knees.

"Bambousse!" shouted the priest, snatching away a fistful of pebbles he had just picked up.

"Let go, Father," commanded the peasant. "It was nothing but soft dirt. I should have used rocks. You don't know a thing about girls, do you? They're hard as nails. I could dunk that one to the bottom of the well, break her bones with a stick, and she'd still go do her filthy little tricks . . . Still, they're all the same way." He was gradually regaining his humor, and he drank some wine from a large flat bottle encased in a sparterie which was warming in the burning earth. And finding his hearty laughter again, "If I had a glass, Father, I'd be happy to offer you some."

"Now," the priest asked again, "about this marriage."

"Nope, sorry, it can't be done. Everybody would laugh at me. Rosalie's strong—she's as good as a man, you understand? I'll have to hire some boy the day she goes away. We'll talk about it again after the harvest. And besides, I don't like being robbed; it's always gimme, gimme, gimme, isn't it?"

The priest remained there a full half hour, preaching to Bambousse, talking to him of God, using all the arguments required by the situation. The old man had started to work again; he shrugged his shoulders, made jokes, became more stubborn. Finally, he shouted, "Look, if you asked me for a sack of wheat, you'd pay me for it, right? So why do you want me to let my daughter go for nothing?"

Father Mouret was discouraged as he walked away. A few paces down the path, he saw Rosalie sprawled under an olive tree with Voriau; the dog was licking her face and making her laugh. Her skirts flying and her arms beating the ground, she shouted to the dog, "You're tickling me, you dumb thing! Stop it!"

Then, when she saw the priest, she pretended to blush and gathered up her clothes, her fists again in her eyes. He tried to comfort her by promising to try another time with her father. And he added that she had to obey the old man, that she must not see Fortuné and make her sin worse.

"Oh, come on," she said, smiling in her brazen way, "there's no risk now, it's already there." He did not understand; he talked of hell where wicked women burn. Then, having done his duty, he left her, recaptured by that serenity which allowed him to walk unperturbed through flesh and its filth.

◇◇

VII THE MORNING WAS BECOMING TERRIBLY HOT. IN THE spring and summer, the sun transformed this vast amphitheater of rocks into a flaming furnace. The great star's elevation told Father Mouret that he had just enough time to get to the presbytery by eleven and avoid being scolded by la Teuse. His breviary read, his business with Bambousse completed, he hurried toward the distant gray spot of his church and the tall black rod which the big cypress, the Hermit, made on the blue horizon. The heat made him drowsy, and he began to dream of how lavishly he would decorate the chapel for the rites of Mary's month. The road rolled out a soft carpet of dust for his feet and displayed the purity of dazzling whiteness.

At the Croix-Verte, as he was about to cross the road leading from Plassans to la Palud, a carriage hurrying down the hill forced him to take cover behind a pile of stones. He was crossing the intersection when a voice called out, "Hey, Serge! Hello, my son."

The carriage had stopped; a man was leaning out. The young priest recognized one of his uncles, Dr. Pascal Rougon, called simply "M. Pascal" by the people of Plassans, where he cared for the poor without pay. Although he was barely fifty, his huge beard and bountiful hair were already white as snow and emphasized the kindly delicacy of his handsome features.

"What're you tromping through the dust at this time of day for?" he asked gaily, leaning farther out to clasp the priest's hands. "Aren't you afraid of sunstroke?"

"No more than you, Uncle," the priest replied with a laugh.

"Oh, as for me, I have the hood of my carriage. Besides, sick people don't wait. People die in all kinds of weather, my son." And he told him that he was rushing because of old Jeanbernat, the caretaker at Paradou, who had suffered a stroke during the night. One of his neighbors was taking his vegetables to sell in Plassans and had told the doctor about it. "He must be dead by now," he went on. "Still, I have to go see. These old devils are awfully tough." He was raising his whip when Father Mouret stopped him.

"Wait. What time do you have, Uncle?"

"Quarter to eleven."

The priest hesitated. He could hear la Teuse's frightening voice in his ears, telling him that lunch would be cold. But he was strong and said immediately, "I'm going with you, Uncle. The poor man might want to be reconciled to God in his last moments."

Dr. Pascal could not keep from laughing. "Him! Jeanbernat!" he cried. "You're out to convert *him*? Oh, well, it doesn't matter, come on. Just seeing you might cure him."

The priest got in. The doctor, who seemed remorseful about his joke, was especially attentive to him as he clicked his tongue to make the horse hurry. He was curiously studying his nephew out of the corner of his eye, as if he were making notes for a scientific observation. He curtly but jovially questioned him about his life, his habits, and the peaceful happiness he enjoyed at Artauds. And after each satisfactory answer, he muttered in a reassured tone, as if talking to himself, "Good, so much the better, that's perfect." He was especially inquisitive about the young priest's health. His astonished nephew assured him that he was marvelously well, that he never had vertigo, nausea, or headaches. "Perfect, perfect," repeated Uncle Pascal. "In the spring, you know, your blood churns. But you're strong, you really are . . . By the way, I saw your brother Octave at Marseille last month. He's leaving for Paris. He has a fine position in a big business there. Ah, the rogue's leading quite a life."

"What kind of life?" the priest asked naïvely.

To avoid answering, the doctor clicked his tongue. Then he said, "Yes, everybody's well, your Aunt Félicité, your Uncle Rougon, and the rest. That doesn't keep us from needing your prayers. You're the family saint, my boy; I'm counting on you for the salvation of the whole band." He was laughing, but in such a friendly way that Serge took no offense and even joked himself. "The only thing is," the doctor went on, "there're some in the barrel who won't be so easy to lead to Paradise. You'd hear some memorable confessions if they came to see you. They don't need to confess to me. I watch them all the time; I have their files at home with my plant collections and my notes. One day, it'll all make an interesting monograph. Then we'll see, then we'll see."

He was caught up in his childlike enthusiasm for science and almost forgot himself, but a glance at his nephew's cassock pulled him up short. "You're a priest," he murmured. "You've done well. Being a priest makes people happy. It involved you completely, didn't it, so you've turned out well. You'd never have been happy doing anything else. Your relatives went away like you, but their meanness didn't help them at all; they're still not satisfied . . . Everything's logical there, my boy. A priest rounds out the family. Besides, we had to have one. Our blood had to end up there. So much the better for you—you were the luckiest one of all." But he smiled strangely and stopped himself. "No, your sister Désirée was the luckiest."

He whistled, cracked his whip, changed the subject. The carriage had reached the top of a rather steep hill and was rolling through a desolate pass; it came to a plateau and moved onto a sunken road running along a high, endless wall. Artauds had disappeared; they were in the wilderness.

"We're getting close, aren't we?" the priest asked.

"This is Paradou," replied the doctor, pointing to the wall. "You've never been here? We're not even three miles from Artauds . . . It must have been truly magnificent, this Paradou. The park wall on this side is at least two kilometers long. But everything's been growing wild there for more than a hundred years."

"It has some lovely trees," the priest remarked as he looked up in astonishment at the masses of greenery spilling over the wall.

"Yes, that corner is very fertile. The park is a real forest right in the middle of all these bare rocks. Besides, that's where the

Mascle runs. I've heard about three or four springs, I think." And, in choppy sentences, digressing continually about wholly unrelated subjects, he told the story of Paradou, a kind of legend in the region. Under Louis XV, a lord had built a magnificent palace surrounded by immense gardens, pools, flowing water, and statues, a real little Versailles lost in the rocks under the great southern sun. But he spent only one season there; he arrived with a woman who never came out and who must have died there. The next year the palace burned, the park doors were nailed shut, even the holes in the walls were filled with earth; it was so well sealed that since that distant era, no one had looked into this vast enclosure filling an entire plateau in the Garrigues.

"I bet they don't lack nettles," Father Mouret laughed. "It smells wet all along the wall, don't you think, Uncle?" Then, after a silence, he asked, "Who owns Paradou now?"

"No one knows," replied the doctor. "The owner paid us a visit about twenty years ago. But he was so frightened by this snakes' nest that he never came back. The real owner is the caretaker, that old Jeanbernat. He lives in a summer house that's managed to hold together somehow. Look, it's that old gray hovel over there. See how the ivy covers its windows."

The carriage passed a once-lordly gate made bloody by rust, blackened by thorns, and boarded up on its inner side. A hundred yards away, the lodge where Jeanbernat lived was wedged into the park. But the caretaker seemed to have barricaded his house on the side facing the forest; he had made a narrow garden next to the road, where he lived with his back to Paradou, apparently not suspecting the immense ocean of greenery always rising behind him.

The young priest leaped to the ground and looked curiously around him, questioning the doctor as he hurried to tie the horse to a ring imbedded in the wall. "And that old man lives alone in this abandoned place?" he asked.

"Yes, completely alone," Uncle Pascal replied. But he checked himself. "He has a niece with him, a funny girl, a savage . . . Hurry up. Everything looks dead here."

VIII ASLEEP UNDER THE NOONTIME SUN, ITS SHUTTERS closed, the house was surrounded by the noise of huge flies buzzing in the ivy which climbed to its roof. A contented peace bathed this sunny ruin. The doctor pushed against the door of the narrow garden enclosed by a very high hedge. There, in the shadow of a section of the wall, stood Jeanbernat, stretching his tall frame, peacefully smoking his pipe, watching his vegetables grow in the great silence.

"What! You're up and about! Was this some kind of joke?" the astounded doctor cried.

"So you came to bury me, huh?" grumbled the old man roughly. "I don't need anyone. I bled myself—" He stopped short when he saw the priest and gestured in such a frightening way that Uncle Pascal hurried to intervene.

"This is my nephew," he said, "the new Artauds priest, a good boy . . . What the hell! We didn't run across the country at this time of day to hurt you, Jeanbernat."

The old man calmed down a little. "I don't want any inside-out collars on my property," he mumbled. "Just looking at one kills people before they know what hit them. You understand, Doctor, no drugs and no priests when I kick the bucket; otherwise, you'll have a fight on your hands. That one there can come in, though, if he's your nephew."

Father Mouret, bewildered, could think of nothing to say. He remained standing in the middle of a walk, examining this strange character, this hermit scored by wrinkles, his face made of baked clay, his limbs dried and twisted like bundles of rope, who seemed to bear his eighty years with an ironic disdain for life. When the doctor attempted to take his pulse, he became angry again.

"Leave me alone, dammit! I told you I bled myself with my knife! It's all done now. What stupid peasant had to go bother you? The doctor, the priest, why not the undertaker? But what do you expect, people are stupid. That doesn't mean we can't have a little drink."

He set a bottle and three glasses on an old table which he had put in the shade, filled the glasses to the brim, and proposed a toast. His anger was melting into mocking joy. "This won't poison you, Father," he said. "A good glass of wine is no sin. Why, this is the first time I've ever drunk with a cassock, no offense intended. Poor old Caffin, your predecessor, refused to argue with me—he was afraid." And he gave a hearty laugh as he went on: "Just imagine, he decided to prove to me that there is a God. So I worked on him every time I saw him. He finally had to put his tail between his legs and call it quits, the old goat!"

"What! There's no God?" Father Mouret shouted when he could speak.

"Oh, if you say so," Jeanbernat said mockingly, "we can start over . . . But I just warn you that I'm very good. In a room upstairs, there're thousands of books saved from the Paradou fire, all the eighteenth-century philosophers, a heap of books on religion. I've learned some fine things. I've been reading them for twenty years . . . Ah, right, I'm a dangerous opponent, Father."

He had stood up. He stretched out his hands in a sweeping gesture embracing the whole horizon, heaven and earth, and said solemnly, "There is nothing, nothing, nothing. When the sun is blown out it'll all be over."

Dr. Pascal had nudged Father Mouret. He was winking his eyes, studying the old man attentively and nodding his head to make him talk. "You're a materialist, then, M. Jeanbernat?" he asked.

"Me, I'm only a poor fellow," the old man replied as he lit his pipe. "When Count Corbière, my foster brother, fell off a horse and died, the children sent me to take care of this Sleeping Beauty park to get rid of me. I was nearly sixty years old. I thought I was done for. But death forgot me. And I had to make do as best I could . . . You see, when you live alone, you end up seeing things in a funny way. Trees aren't trees, the earth starts to look like a living person, rocks tell you stories. Stupid things. I know secrets that would flabbergast you. But what do you expect people to do in this wilderness? I read the books; it was more fun than hunting . . . The count, who swore like a heathen, always used to say, 'Jeanbernat, my boy, I'm counting on finding you in hell so you can take care of me down there like you did up here.'"

He made the same sweeping gesture and went on: "You see, nothing, there's nothing; all that's a big joke."

Dr. Pascal began to laugh. "It's a good joke, in any case," he said. "Jeanbernat, you're a puzzler. I suspect you of being a secret lover. I really think you were moved just now when you talked about trees and rocks."

"No, I promise," the old man muttered, "that's all gone now. Once, it's true, when we were friends and collected plants together, I was stupid enough to love all kinds of things in this great lying country. Fortunately the books killed all that . . . I'd like for my garden to be even smaller; I don't go outside but twice a year. You see that bench? I spend all my time there, watching my greens grow."

"And your walks in the park?" interrupted the doctor.

"In the park!" Jeanbernat repeated, apparently deeply surprised. "But I haven't set foot in there for twelve years. It's too big. It's dumb, all these trees that don't stop, moss everywhere, broken statues, holes where you almost break your neck every time you try to move. The last time I was there, it was so dark under the leaves, the wild flowers smelled so strong, such strange breezes blew down the paths, that I was almost afraid. And I barricaded myself in so the park wouldn't come here. A sunny spot, three feet of lettuce before me, a big hedge that blocks the horizon, that's already too much to make a man happy. Nothing, that's what I'd really like. Nothing at all, something so narrow that the outside could never come bother me. Six feet of dirt, if you like, to flop down on." He hit the table with his fist, suddenly raising his voice and yelling to Father Mouret, "Let's go, another drink, Father. You're not going to find the devil at the bottom of the bottle."

The priest was sad. He felt he lacked the strength to lead back to God this strange old man whose reason seemed to him peculiarly out of order. Now he remembered some of la Teuse's gossip about the Philosopher, the Artauds peasants' name for Jeanbernat, and bits of shocking stories ran vaguely through his mind. He stood up and made a sign to the doctor; he wanted to leave this house where he thought he smelled the odor of damnation. But, in his hollow fear, a strange curiosity held him back. He remained there, going to the end of the garden, looking searchingly at the vestibule as if attempting to see beyond, behind the walls. The open door revealed only the narrow stairwell. And he came back, looking for a hole, for some way to peek through this sea of leaves whose presence he felt as a heavy noise beating against the house with the sound of waves.

"Is the kid all right?" asked the doctor as he picked up his hat.

"Not too bad," Jeanbernat replied. "She's never around. She disappears for hours at a time . . . Still, maybe she's upstairs." He raised his head and called out, "Albine! Albine!" Then, shrugging his shoulders, "Yeah, right, she's a great hussy . . . I'll see you later, Father; at your service."

But Father Mouret did not have time to accept this challenge from the Philosopher. A door had just been thrown open at the end of the vestibule; a dazzling hole opened in the wall's blackness. It was a vision of virgin forest, a tunnel of vast woods under a shower of sunshine. In this lightning flash, the priest clearly perceived certain details in the distance: a large yellow flower in the center of the lawn, a sheet of water falling from a high rock, a colossal tree filled with a flock of birds; all of this drowned, lost, burning in such a torrent of green, such an orgy of plants, that the whole horizon was nothing but a vast blossom. The door slammed, everything vanished.

"Ah, the brat," Jeanbernat cried. "She was in Paradou again!"

Albine stood on the edge of the vestibule and laughed. She was wearing an orange skirt with a big red shawl tied behind her back, an outfit which made her look like a gypsy in her Sunday best. And she kept laughing, her head thrown back, her chest puffed with happiness; she was pleased with her flowers, with the wild flowers woven into her blond hair, tied to her neck, to her breast, to her thin arms, naked and bronzed. She was like a huge, strong-smelling bouquet.

"Oh, you're really cute," the old man scolded. "You smell so much like plants it makes you sick . . . Would you guess she's sixteen? She's just a little kid."

Albine brazenly laughed louder. Dr. Pascal, who was her good friend, let her kiss him. "So you at least aren't afraid in Paradou," he said.

"Afraid? What of?" she asked, her eyes opened wide in astonishment. "The walls are too high, no one can come in. There's nobody but me. It's my garden, all mine alone. It's awfully big. I still haven't found the end of it."

"But the animals?" the doctor interrupted.

"The animals? They aren't mean; they all know me."

"But isn't it dark under the trees?"

"Sure, it's shady; if it weren't for the trees, the sun would burn my face. It's nice in the shade, under the leaves." And she spun around, filling the narrow garden with the flight of her skirts, releasing the sharp odor of the vegetation she carried on her body. She had smiled at Father Mouret without self-consciousness, without worrying about the astonished way he stared at her. The priest had gone away. This blond child with her narrow face burning with life appeared to him as the mysterious and disturbing daughter of the forest he had glimpsed in a burst of sunlight.

"Say, I've got a blackbird's nest. Do you want it?" Albine asked the doctor.

"No, thanks," he replied with a laugh. "You'd better give it to the priest's sister. She likes animals. I'll see you later, Jeanbernat."

But Albine had tackled the priest. "You're the Artauds priest, aren't you? Do you have a sister? I'll go see her . . . But you can't talk about God; my uncle doesn't want you to."

"You're bothering us. Go away," Jeanbernat said with a shrug.

She leaped away like a goat, leaving a rain of flowers behind her. They heard a door slam and then heard laughter behind the house, clear laughter that died gradually, as if it came from the motion of an insane animal released in the grass.

"You'll see, she'll end up sleeping in Paradou," muttered the old man in his indifferent way. And, as he was seeing his visitors out, he went on: "Doctor, if you find me dead one fine morning, do me a favor and throw me in the dung heap there, behind my greens. Good night, gentlemen."

He let the wooden bar fall back into place across the gate. The house recovered its contented peace under the noontime sun, surrounded by the noise of huge flies buzzing around the ivy which climbed to its roof.

◇◇

IX THE CARRIAGE WAS AGAIN ON THE SUNKEN ROAD RUNNING along Paradou's endless wall. Father Mouret silently raised his eyes to look at the huge branches stretching over this wall like the arms of hidden giants. Noises came from the park: the rustling of wings, the trembling of leaves, branches cracked by secret leaps, great sighs bending young shoots, the very breath of life rolling through the tops of a nation of tree people. And at times, at the sound of a certain birdcall which resembled a human laugh, the priest worriedly turned his head to gaze all around him.

"What a girl!" Uncle Pascal said as he loosened the reins a little. "She was nine years old when she fell in that old heathen's lap. A brother of his was ruined, I don't know how. The child was boarding somewhere when the father killed himself. She was a real young lady too, already educated, reading, knitting, chatting, banging on pianos. And Lord, was she coquettish! I saw her when she came: she had holes in her stockings, her skirts were all sewed up, all kinds of little shirts and oversleeves, a pile of frills . . . Well, the frills lasted a long time!" He was laughing. A large stone almost made the carriage turn over. "If I don't leave a wheel on this devilish road!" he muttered. "Hold on, my boy."

The wall went on. The priest was listening.

"You understand," said the doctor, "that Paradou, with its

sun, its rocks, its thistles, could eat one outfit a day. The girl's pretty clothes were good for three or four bites. She came home naked—now she dresses like a savage. Today, she was still passable; but there're days when she's not wearing anything but her shoes and shirt . . . You heard her, Paradou is hers. She took it the day after she got here. She lives there, jumping out of the window when Jeanbernat closes the door, running off no matter what, going nobody knows where, into all sorts of lost places. She must have quite a time in that wilderness."

"Just listen, Uncle," Father Mouret interrupted. "It sounds like an animal running behind that wall." Uncle Pascal listened.

"No," he said after a time, "it's the noise of the carriage on the rocks . . . She doesn't bang on pianos now. I even believe she can't read anymore. Imagine a young lady brought back to the free state of nature, let go to have fun on a desert island. All she has kept is her dainty coquettish smile; that's still there when she wants it . . . Ah, right, if you ever hear about a girl to be brought up, I don't advise you to give her to Jeanbernat. He has a completely primitive way of letting nature take its course. When I risked discussing Albine with him, he told me it was bad to keep trees from growing the way they want. He says he's for the normal development of personality . . . That doesn't matter; they're both very interesting. I go see them whenever I'm in the area."

The carriage finally left the sunken road. There, Paradou's wall turned to stretch along the tops of the hills as far as the eye could see. At the very moment when Father Mouret was turning his head to take a final look at this gray barrier whose impenetrable sternness had begun to grate on his nerves, he heard the noise of branches being shaken and saw a cluster of young birches begin to wave good-bye from the top of the wall. "I told you some animal was running along there," the priest said.

But without a sign of anything human, with nothing visible except the birches bending more and more wildly, they heard a clear laughing voice call out, "I'll see you, Doctor. I'll see you, Father. I'm kissing the tree, the tree's sending you my kisses."

"Hey, it's Albine," said Dr. Pascal. "She must have run along beside our carriage. She can go through any kind of jungle she wants." And yelling in his turn, "We'll see you, darling. You're awfully big to wave to us like that."

The laughter increased; the birches bent lower and threw leaves all the way to the carriage. "I'm as big as the trees; all the falling leaves are kisses," said the voice. It was altered by distance, became musical, so much a part of the rolling breath of the park that the young priest could not stop trembling.

The road was improving. Artauds reappeared at the end of the scorched plain. When the carriage crossed the village road, Father Mouret would not let his uncle take him back to the presbytery. He jumped down and said, "No, thanks, I prefer to walk. It'll do me good."

"If you say so," the doctor said at last. Then, shaking his hand, "Oh, you'd be better off if you didn't have parishioners like that brute Jeanbernat. Still, you're the one who wanted to come . . . And stay healthy. Send for me for the least little thing, day or night. You know I take care of the whole family for nothing. Good-bye, my boy."

◇◇◇◇◇◇◇◇◇◇◇◇◇◇◇◇◇◇◇◇◇◇◇◇◇◇◇◇◇◇◇◇◇◇◇

X FATHER MOURET WAS RELIEVED TO FIND HIMSELF ONCE more alone on the dusty road. The rocky fields brought him back to his dream of severity, of inner life passed in the desert. The burning sun dried up the disturbing coolness which the trees along the sunken road had dropped on his neck. The skinny almond trees, the stunted wheat, the sick vineyards standing on both sides of the road, calmed him and drew him out of the troubled state into which he had been thrust by the overly lush breezes of Paradou. And Jeanbernat's blasphemies could not create even a shadow in the blinding light flowing from heaven to the scorched earth around him. He felt a strong sense of joy when he raised his head and saw on the horizon the immobile bar of the Hermit and the spot made by the church's red tiles.

But as he walked along, the priest was gradually overcome by another worry. La Teuse was going to be awful—his cold lunch must have been waiting for almost two hours. He saw her frightening face and heard the rush of words which would greet him, the angry noise of dishes which would continue for the entire afternoon. When he had crossed Artauds, his fear became so great that, gripped by cowardice, he wondered if it might not be better to walk around and come through the church. But as he was debating with himself, la Teuse appeared in person in the presbytery door, her bonnet askew, her fists on her hips. He bent his back; he had to go all the way up the hill under that stormy gaze weighing heavily on his shoulders.

"I really think I must be late, my good Teuse," he stammered at the last turn on the path. La Teuse waited until he was very close to her. Then she furiously looked right into his eyes without saying a word before turning to lead the way to the dining room, tapping her thick heels, so stiffened by anger that she almost lost her limp.

"I had so many things to do," the priest began, terrified by this silence. "I've been going as fast as I could." But she cut him off with another look, so rigid, so angry, that his legs seemed to collapse. He sat down and began to eat. She served him as dryly as a robot, slamming the plates down so hard that they nearly broke. The silence became overwhelming. He was so choked by emotion that he could not swallow his third bite.

"My sister has already eaten?" he asked. "That's good. You should always go ahead with lunch when business keeps me away."

No answer. La Teuse was standing and waiting for him to clean his plate before taking it away. Then, feeling that he could not eat if these implacable eyes were to continue to crush him, he pushed his plate away. This angry gesture resounded like the crack of a whip and jerked la Teuse out of her stubborn rigidity. She gave a leap. "So that's the way it is," she cried. "You're still the one who gets mad. Okay, I've had it. I'm leaving. You're going to pay for my trip home. I'm through with Artauds and with your church! And with everything!"

With trembling hands she removed her apron. "You must have seen I didn't want to talk. Is this any kind of life? Only idiots act like you, Father. Aren't you ashamed to be still eating when it's almost two? That's not the Christian thing to do, no, that's not the Christian thing to do." Then she stood squarely before him: "Okay, where have you been? Who did you see? What kind of business could have kept you out so long? If you were a child, you'd be whipped. A priest has no business being out on the roads under the sun like trash with no home . . . Ah, you're in great shape; your shoes're all white, your cassock's ruined. Who'll brush it for you, your cassock? Who'll buy you another one? Well, speak up, tell me what you did. My word, if people didn't know you, they'd think all kinds of funny things. And you want me to tell you what I think? I'm not dead sure they aren't right. People who eat lunch like this are capable of anything."

Relieved, Father Mouret let the storm pass. He felt something like nervous release in the old servant's thoughtless words. "Come now, my good Teuse," he said. "First you're going to put your apron back on."

"No, no," she cried, "it's over. I'm leaving."

He stood up and tied the apron around her waist with a laugh. But she fought back, stammering, "No, I tell you. No jokes this time. I see right through you. You just want to use your sweet words to calm me down. First tell me where you were, then we'll see."

He happily sat back down like a man who knows he has won. "First," he said, "you have to let me eat. I'm starving."

She was touched and said softly, "Of course you are! What a dumb thing to do . . . Do you want me to fix a couple of eggs? It won't take long. Still, if you have enough . . . And everything's cold. And I was so careful with your eggplant . . . It's in great shape now! It looks like an old shoe . . . It's a good thing you're not finicky about what goes into your stomach like poor Father Caffin . . . Oh, you have your good points, I don't deny it."

She was serving him as carefully as a mother as she talked. Then, when he had finished, she ran to the kitchen to see if the coffee was still hot. She was letting herself go; her joy at the reconciliation made her limp absurdly. Father Mouret ordinarily shied away from coffee, which gave him serious problems with his nerves; but under the circumstances, his desire to ratify the peace made him take the cup she brought him. And as he leaned back to relax at the table, she sat down across from him and repeated softly, like a woman tortured by curiosity, "Where did you go, Father?"

"But," he answered with a smile, "I saw the Brichets. I spoke to Bambousse . . ." And he had to tell her what the Brichets had said, what Bambousse had decided, how they looked, where they were working.

When she learned how Rosalie's father had reacted, she cried out, "Good heavens, as if the pregnancy wouldn't count if the child died!" Then she folded her hands and gave a look of mingled admiration and envy. "How you must have talked, Father! More than half a day to get to this fine result! And did you walk very slowly coming home? It must have been terribly hot on the road."

The priest, who had stood up, did not reply. He was about to speak of Paradou, to ask for information about it. But his fear of being questioned too closely, a vague kind of shame which he did not admit even to himself, made him refrain from mentioning his visit to Jeanbernat. He cut off more interrogation by asking, "And my sister, where is she? I don't hear her."

"This way, sir," said la Teuse. She put a finger to her lips and began to laugh. They went into the next room, a country drawing room papered with a pattern of large, faded gray flowers and furnished with four armchairs and a couch, all stuffed with horsehair. Désirée was stretched out asleep on the couch, her head on her two clenched fists. Her skirts hung down and revealed her knees, while her raised arms, bare to the elbow, accentuated the powerful lines of her breasts. She was breathing hard; her red, half-open lips showed her white teeth.

"Is she ever asleep!" la Teuse whispered. "She didn't even

hear you yell those things at me a while ago. Boy! She must be awfully tired. Just imagine, she was cleaning her animals until almost noon. After she ate she dropped there like a piece of lead. She hasn't budged since."

For some time the priest watched her with great feeling. "We have to let her rest as much as she wants," he said.

"Of course . . . Isn't it a pity she's so innocent? Just look at that big arm! When I dress her, I always think of what a beautiful woman she could have been. She would have given you some fine nephews, Father . . . Don't you think she looks like that big stone woman in the Plassans wheat market?"

She was referring to a Cybele recumbent on sheaves of wheat, the work of a pupil of Puget, which had been sculpted in the market's facade. Without commenting, Father Mouret pushed her gently out of the drawing room, telling her to make as little noise as possible.

And the presbytery retained its great silence until evening. La Teuse finished her soap in the shed. At the back of the narrow garden, the priest, his breviary fallen on his knees, lost himself in pious meditation as a continuous rain of pink petals fell from the flowering peach trees above him.

◇◇◇◇◇◇◇◇◇◇◇◇◇◇◇◇◇◇◇◇◇◇◇◇◇◇◇◇◇◇◇◇◇

XI THERE WAS A SUDDEN AWAKENING AROUND SIX O'CLOCK. Doors being opened and closed amid bursts of laughter created a din which shook the whole house, and Désirée appeared, her hair loose, her arms still bare to the elbows, shouting, "Serge! Serge!" Then, when she saw her brother in the garden, she ran up, sat on the ground for an instant, leaped back to her feet, and begged him, "Just come see the animals! You haven't seen the animals yet. If you only knew how beautiful they are now!"

She had to beg a long time. The barnyard frightened him a little. But he gave in when he saw tears in Désirée's eyes. She threw herself on his neck with the sudden joy of a puppy and laughed loudly without even drying her cheeks. "Oh, you're nice," she managed to say as she pulled him away. "You can see the hens, the rabbits, the pigeons, **my** ducks (they've got fresh water), my goat (his room is as clean as mine now). You know, I've got three ducks and two turkeys. Come on, hurry. I'll show you all of them."

Désirée was now twenty-two years old. Raised in the country by her nurse, a peasant from Saint-Eutrope, she had grown up in farm dung. With her head empty and free of any kind of serious thought, she thrived on the country's rich earth and open air; only her flesh matured, and she became a beautiful animal, fresh, white, red-blooded, firm-skinned, like a species of she-ass endowed with the gift of laughter. Although she wallowed in dirt from dawn to dusk, she still kept her delicate limbs, the supple lines of her hips, the bourgeois refinement of her virgin body; she had become a unique creature, neither lady nor peasant, a girl nourished by the earth, with the broad shoulders and narrow forehead of a young goddess.

It was undoubtedly her weak mind which made her like the animals. She was at ease only with them, she understood their language better than any human tongue, she cared for them with maternal tenderness. She lacked any kind of cogent train of reasoning, but she had an instinct which put her on their level and allowed her to know where they were hurt when they first cried out in pain. She created treats which they ravenously devoured, settled their quarrels with a gesture, seemed to know at a glance if their character was good or bad, told long stories with such abundance of precise detail on the habits of the smallest chick that she profoundly astonished those for whom one baby chicken is indistinguishable from another. Her barnyard had thus become a small nation where she reigned as absolute monarch, a nation with a very complicated organizational structure, disturbed by revolutions, inhabited by distinct beings, whose history she alone knew. The certainty of her instincts was so far-reaching that she could recognize the sterile eggs in a nest and tell in advance the number of babies to be in a litter of rabbits.

At the age of sixteen, when she entered puberty, Désirée experienced none of the dizziness and nausea felt by other girls. She simply acquired the stature of a grown woman, felt better, and filled out her dresses with the splendid bloom of her flesh. From that time on, she possessed this rounded, freely-moving figure, these sturdy limbs of an ancient statue, this verve of a healthy animal. She seemed to draw strength from the barnyard, to suck life up through her strong legs, as white and solid as saplings. And not one carnal desire arose in her lushness. She found continuous satisfaction in feeling animals swarming and multiplying around her. Manure heaps and coupling animals released a wave of fertility in which she tasted the joys of personal fecundity. Something in her rejoiced when the hens brooded; she laughed like a beautiful girl receiving a compliment as she carried her female rabbits to the males; she experienced the happiness of pregnancy in milking her goat. Nothing could be healthier. She was innocently filled with the odor and heat of life. No depraved curiosity drove her to worry about reproduction when she saw cocks beat their wings, when she heard females in labor, or when she smelled the billy goat poisoning the narrow stable. The peace of a beautiful beast always shone in her clear gaze empty of all thought; she was happy to see her little world multiply; she felt her own body grow as if she herself had been impregnated. She was so identified with all these mothers that it seemed she was the common mother, the natural mother dropping generative liquid from her fingers without any unhealthy tremor.

Désirée had been completely happy since she came to Artauds. She was accomplishing her life's dream, the only desire that would have tortured the childhood of her feeble mind. She owned a barnyard, controlled a place where she could raise animals as she chose. She buried herself there, built hutches for the rabbits, dug a duck pond, drove nails, hauled straw, allowed no one to help her. La Teuse had only to wash her face. The barnyard was located behind the cemetery; indeed, Désirée often had to go among the graves to retrieve a curious hen who had leaped over the wall. In the rear was a shed containing the rabbit hutch and chicken coop; the goat lived in a small stable on the right. In other respects the animals all lived together: the rabbits ran with the chickens; the goat cooled his feet among the ducks; the geese, turkeys, guinea hens, and pigeons socialized with three cats.

When Désirée appeared at the wooden barrier that prevented all these creatures from going into the church, a deafening uproar greeted her. "Do you hear them?" she said to her brother at the dining-room door. But after she had brought him in and was closing the barrier behind them, she was attacked so vigorously that she almost disappeared. Banging their bills, the ducks and geese pulled her skirts; the gluttonous hens jumped on her hands and pecked at them; the rabbits huddled on her feet and leaped up to her knees; the three cats perched on her shoulder; and the goat began to bleat at the back of the stable because he could not join her. "Leave me alone, you beasts," she cried; all those feathers, paws, and beaks rubbing against her tickled her so much that she laughed deeply. But she did nothing to get rid of them, rejoicing so much in feeling this life rush up and give her its downy heat that she would have let herself be eaten alive as she talked. Finally, only one cat was stubborn enough to want to remain on her back. "This is Moumou," she said. "His paws are like velvet." Then she proudly pointed to the barnyard and added, "You see how clean it is."

The barnyard had in fact been swept, washed, and raked. But the dirty water she had stirred up, the stable litter she had turned with a pitchfork, still exuded an odor so strong and uncompromising that Father Mouret felt himself gag. The dung heap rose against the cemetery wall in a great smoking pile.

"That's quite a heap, right?" Désirée said as she led her brother into the bitter vapor. "I piled up all of it, nobody helped me . . . Come on, it's not dirty. It cleans you. Look at my arms." She stretched out the arms she had simply plunged into a bucket of water, regal arms, proudly rounded, which had grown like sleek white roses in this pile of manure.

"Yes, yes," murmured the priest. "You've been doing a fine job. It's really pretty now." He was trying to reach the barrier, but she stopped him.

"Wait. You're going to see everything. You just don't

know." She pulled him into the shed and over to the rabbit hutch. "There're babies in every box," she said, enthusiastically clapping her hands. Then she discoursed at length about each litter. He had to squat and put his nose against the screen while she furnished minute details. The mothers, breathing hard and rigid with fear, shook their big, worried ears and looked askance at the two humans. There in a box was a hollow of fur where a living pile was pullulating, a vague blackish mass whose heavy breath seemed to come from a single body. Some babies ventured to the edge of the hollow and lifted their enormous heads. Farther on, they were already stronger; they resembled young rats, ferreting, leaping, their raised rumps spotted with the white button of a tail. These had the joyous grace of human children as they ran around the boxes, the whites of their eyes a pale pink, their pupils shining like jet buttons. And they suddenly panicked; they began to leap about, their thin paws browned with urine showing with each bound. They quickly huddled so closely together that their heads were no longer visible.

"You're what's frightening them," Désirée said. "They know me." She called to them as she took a crust of bread from her pocket. Reassured, the little rabbits came wandering up one by one; their noses curled up as they stood against the netting. And she let them stand to show her brother the down on their bellies before giving a crust to the boldest one. This made the whole gang run up and nudge one another without fighting; at times, three babies would take bites from the same crust; others escaped and turned to the wall to eat in peace; in the rear, the mothers were still panting defiantly, refusing the crusts. "Oh, the pigs!" cried Désirée. "They'd eat like that all day . . . You can hear them nibbling the greens they missed after we go to bed."

The priest had stood up, but she was not yet ready to stop smiling at her beloved children. "You see the big one there, all white with black ears. Well, he's crazy about poppies, he picks them out from the other plants. The other day he had a stomachache. It hurt under his rear paws. Well, I took him and kept him warm in my pocket. Since then he's been all well again." She pushed her fingers through the netting to rub their backs. "It feels like satin," she said. "They're dressed like princes. And they're just as prissy, too. Here, this one is always washing his face. He uses his front paws . . . If you just knew how funny they are! I don't say anything, but I'm always watching when they get into mischief. For instance, that gray one looking at us hated a little female that I had to take out of the box. They had awful fights. It'd take too long to tell you about. Well, the last time he beat her up, I was furious, and what do you think he did? That little rat crouched in the back and looked like he was dying. He wanted to make me think that he was the one with complaints to make . . ." She stopped, then, addressing the rabbit: "It doesn't do you a bit of good to listen to me. You're nothing but a little scamp." And, turning to her brother, she whispered with a wink, "He understands everything I say."

Father Mouret could no longer remain in the heat rising from the litters. The life swarming under this fur torn from the mothers' bellies had a strong breath whose power he felt in his temples. Désirée was slowly becoming intoxicated; she was happier, ruddier, stronger in her flesh.

"But you don't have to leave," she cried. "You always look like you're trying to run away . . . And what about my little chicks, they were born just last night." She took some rice and threw down a handful. The hen moved forward, clucking seriously to call her brood. The whole band of chicks followed, tweeting and roving about like wild birds who have lost their way. When they were in the middle of the grains of rice, the mother pecked frenetically, scattering the grains as she broke them. The babies pecked hurriedly at her side, adorable in their childhood, half-naked, round-headed, their eyes bright as steel points, their beaks so awkwardly placed, their down ruffled in such a strange way, that they looked like cheap toys. Désirée laughed happily to see them.

"They're darlings," she blurted as she picked up one of them in each hand and covered them with a storm of kisses. And the priest had to examine them as she said peacefully, "It's not easy to tell the roosters. But I'm never wrong. That one's a hen . . .

that one too." She put them back down. But the other hens came up to eat the rice. A big red rooster with flaming feathers followed them, raising his wide feet with considered majesty.

"Alexander's getting proud," the priest said to please his sister. Alexander was the rooster's name. He looked at the girl with his burning eye, turned his head, and spread his tail. Then he came to stand next to her skirts.

"He likes me," she said. "I'm the only one he lets touch him. He's a good cock. He has fourteen hens, and I never find a sterile egg—right, Alexander?"

She had bent down. The rooster did not run from her caress. It seemed that a rush of blood lit his comb. His wings beating and his neck stretched, he gave a prolonged cry which sounded as if it had been blown through a brass tube. He crowed four times, and every cock in Artauds answered, far away. Désirée was thrilled and happy to see fear on her brother's face.

"It splits your eardrums, doesn't it?" she said. "He's got a great voice. But I promise he's not mean. It's the hens who are mean. You remember the big speckled one, the one who laid yellow eggs? Day before yesterday, she hurt her foot. When the others saw the blood, they went crazy. They all ran after her, pecked her, drank her blood, and they had eaten every bit of her foot by dusk . . . I found her with her head behind a rock, not making a sound, letting herself be eaten up like an idiot."

The memory of the hens' cannibalism made her laugh. She calmly told of more cruelty, of young chickens with their rumps slashed to shreds, their insides pulled out, so that only their neck and wings were left, of a litter of little cats eaten in a few hours in the stable. "You could give them a Christian," she went on, "and they'd finish him off, too . . . And can they take pain! They get along very well with a broken limb. They can have wounds, holes in their body big enough to stick your fist in, and they still gobble up their meals. That's why I love them. Their flesh grows back in two days; their bodies are always as warm as if they had sunshine stored under their feathers. When I want to give them a party, I cut up some raw meat for them. And worms! I'll show you how they go for them."

She ran to the manure heap, found a worm, and picked it up with no disgust. The hens threw themselves on her hands. But she held the worm very high and amused herself with their gluttony before finally opening her fingers. The hens pushed, knocked each other down; then one ran away, chased by the others, with the worm in her beak. It was thus taken, lost, retaken, until one hen swallowed it with a great gulp. Then they all stopped dead, their necks twisted, their eyes round, waiting for another worm. Pleased, Désirée called them by name and spoke to them like a friend, while Father Mouret recoiled a few steps before this intensity of voracious life.

"No, I'm not feeling well," he told his sister when she wanted him to hold a hen she was fattening. "It upsets me to touch living animals." He tried to smile, but Désirée called him a coward.

"All right, and my ducks, and my geese, and my turkeys. What would you do if you had to take care of them all? Ducks are what's dirty. You hear them dipping their beaks in the water? And when they dive you don't see anything except their tails, straight as an arrow. The geese and turkeys aren't easy to manage either. It's great when they walk around, some all white, others all black, with their big necks. They look like ladies and gentlemen . . . But I wouldn't advise you to give your finger to some of them. They'd swallow it for you in one gulp. But they kiss mine for me, my fingers, see?"

She was cut off by the joyous bleating of the goat, who had finally broken through the poorly latched stable door. In two bounds the animal was next to Désirée and bending its front legs to caress the girl with its horns. The priest thought it looked like the devil with its pointed goatee and deep-set, crossed eyes. But Désirée took its neck, kissed its head, pretended to run, and talked of nursing at it. That happened often, she said. Whenever she got thirsty in the stable, she lay down and nursed at the goat. "Look, they're full of milk," she added as she hefted the animal's enormous teats.

The priest blinked his eyes as if he had been shown something obscene. He remembered seeing, among the gargoyles in the cloister of Saint-Saturnin at Plassans, a stone goat fornicating with a monk. Goats, stinking of lust, possessed by feminine whims and fixations, offering their hanging teats to all comers, had remained for him creatures of hell, sweating from lewdness. His sister had received permission to keep one only after weeks of begging. And when he came, he avoided being rubbed by the animal's long silky hair, defending his cassock from the approach of those horns.

"All right, I'm going to let you go," said Désirée, when she noticed his growing discomfort. "But first I have to show you something else . . . Promise not to scold me? I didn't ask you about it because you wouldn't have—if you just knew how happy I am!" She made herself a suppliant by folding her hands and putting her head on her brother's shoulder.

"Another bit of madness," muttered the priest, who could not keep from smiling.

"You want to, don't you?" she said, her eyes shining with joy. "You won't get mad . . . It's so pretty." And she ran to open a low door under the shed. A little pig leaped out into the yard. "Oh! the cherub!" she said. She sounded completely delighted as she watched him scamper out.

The piglet was all pink and charming; his snout had been washed in the stagnant water; he had a dirty ring near his eyes from his continuous splashing in the trough. He was trotting about, scattering the hens, hurrying to eat what had been thrown to them, turning sharply throughout the small yard. His ears flopped over his eyes, his snout sniffed the ground; his thin paws made him look like a toy on rollers. And, from behind, his tail looked like the string used to pull him.

"I don't want that beast here! Get it out!" yelled the angry priest.

"Serge, my good Serge," Désirée begged again. "Don't be mean. Look how innocent the dear little thing is. I'll wash his face, I'll really keep him clean. La Teuse got it for me. We can't give it back now . . . See, he's looking at you, he's smelling you. Don't be afraid. He won't eat you."

But she broke off in a fit of laughter. The bewildered pig had

54

just run between the goat's legs and knocked it over. It ran around again, squealing, waddling, terrifying the entire barnyard. Désirée had to give him a bowl of dirty water to calm him down. He dived into it up to his ears, gurgled, and spluttered as shudders passed over his pink body. His tail lost its curl and hung down behind him.

Father Mouret felt a final revulsion when he saw this filthy water being splashed about. Ever since he came to the barnyard, he had been having more and more difficulty breathing; flushes now burned his hands, chest, face. Little by little he had lost control of himself. He smelled in one diseased breath the fetid warmth of the rabbits and poultry, the lewd odor of the goat, the jejune fat of the pig. It was as if the air were filled with fecundity, and it weighed too heavily on his virgin shoulders. It seemed to him that Désirée had grown, that her hips had expanded, that she was waving enormous arms, that her skirts were sweeping the ground to raise this powerful odor making him lose consciousness. He barely had time to open the wooden fence, his feet were glued to the ground still moist from dung, he felt that he was held in an embrace by the earth. And suddenly, without his being able to stop it, the memory of Paradou and its huge trees, black shadows, and powerful odors came back to him.

"You're all red now," said Désirée when she joined him on the other side of the barrier. "Aren't you glad you saw it all? . . . Do you hear them crying!" When the animals saw her leave, they had pushed against the barrier and were emitting heartrending cries. The little pig gave an especially prolonged whine which sounded like a bent saw being struck by a steel bar. She curtsied and blew kisses at them, laughing to see them all there in a heap, as if they were in love with her. Then, holding her brother as they went to the garden, she blushed and whispered in his ear, "I'd like a cow."

He stared at her, already making a gesture of refusal. "No, no, not now," she added quickly. "Later we'll talk about it some more . . . There'll be room in the stable. A pretty white cow with red spots. You'd be happy to have good milk all the time . . . A goat, after all, is too little. And when the cow has a calf!"

She was dancing and clapping her hands, and the priest felt in her the barnyard she had carried away in her skirts. He left her in the garden, sitting on the ground in the bright sun, next to a hive whose bees, without stinging her, came buzzing up to hover like golden balls on her neck, along her bare arms, and in her hair.

◇◇

XII Brother archangias dined at the sacristy every Thursday night. He usually came early to chat about parish affairs, and for three months he had kept the priest informed about the entire valley. This Thursday, they were walking slowly around the church, waiting for la Teuse to call them. When the priest described his meeting with Bambousse, he was astonished to hear that the friar found the peasant's answer quite natural.

"He's right, that old man's right," the Ignorantine said. "You don't give away what's yours . . . Rosalie's not worth much; but it's always hard to see your daughter throw herself away on some poor good-for-nothing."

"Still," said Father Mouret, "marriage is the only thing that can stop the scandal before it goes further." The friar shrugged his shoulders and gave a disturbing laugh. He was almost shouting.

"If you think you're going to cure this part of the world with that marriage, you've got another think coming! Catherine'll be pregnant inside of two years. The others will all have their turn; they'll all end up the same way. The minute they're married, they don't care about anybody. These Artauds grow up in bastardy as if it were a kind of manure brewed especially for them. There's only one cure—I already told you about it— break the females' necks if you don't want the country poisoned. No husband, just hit them with a stick, Father, with a stick!" He calmed down and added, "Just let everybody handle his stuff the way he wants to."

And he spoke of arranging the catechism hours. But Father Mouret was distracted and paid no attention. He was looking below him at the village in the setting sun. The peasants were going home, silent men, walking slowly, moving like harried cows returning to their barn. The women standing by the hovels were calling out, gossiping vehemently with each other, while groups of children filled the road with the noise of their heavy shoes, pushing, fighting, tripping each other. A human smell rose from this heap of quivering houses. And the priest thought he was back in Désirée's barnyard, face to face with that endless swarm of multiplying animals. He felt the same heat of generation, the same continuous labor whose smell had made him sick. All day he had lived with this pregnancy of Rosalie's, and he finally thought of it as part of life's filth, of the flesh's drives, of the preordained reproduction of the species which sowed men like grains of wheat. The Artauds were a flock penned in by the four hills on the horizon, begetting, spreading out with each new litter from the females.

"Look!" yelled Brother Archangias, who had stopped talking to point to a big girl being kissed by her lover behind a bush. "There's another slut!" He waved his long black arms until the couple ran away. In the distance, on the red earth, on the bare rocks, the sun was dying in a last burning flame. Little by little, night fell. The fresh, warm scent of lavender was borne to them on the rising breezes. At times there was a great sigh, as if this vast earth, all scorched by passion, had finally cooled under the gray rain of dusk. Pleased with the lower temperature, Father Mouret, his hat in his hand, felt shadowy peace enter him once more.

"Father! Brother Archangias!" called la Teuse. "Hurry! Soup's ready." It was a cabbage soup whose strong vapor filled the presbytery dining room. The friar sat down and began slowly emptying the enormous plate la Teuse had just set before him. He ate a great deal; his throat gurgled so he could hear the food falling into his stomach. He kept his eyes on his spoon and said not a word.

"So my soup's no good, Father," said the old servant. "You're just pecking around in your plate."

"I'm not hungry at all, my good Teuse," answered the priest with a smile.

"Heavens! It's no wonder, when you eat the way you do. You'd be hungry if you hadn't had lunch at two o'clock."

Brother Archangias, after pouring into his spoon the last drops of soup from the bottom of the bowl, said tendentiously, "You must eat regular meals, Father."

Désirée, who had also eaten her soup without opening her mouth to speak, had followed la Teuse into the kitchen. The friar, left alone with Father Mouret, was cutting large bites of bread to eat while he waited for the main course. "Did you walk a long way?" he asked.

The priest did not have time to reply. A noise of steps, exclamations, and deep laughter arose at the end of the hall next to the barnyard. There seemed to be a brief dispute. A reedlike voice which disturbed the priest grew angry and began to speak rapidly before dissolving in a gust of joy.

"What is it now?" he said, leaving his chair. Désirée came bouncing back in. She was hiding something under her folded shirt and said animatedly, "She's funny. She didn't want to come. I held her by her dress, but she's awfully strong. She got away."

"Who's she talking about," la Teuse asked after running in from the kitchen with a dish of potatoes and a little bacon.

The young girl had sat down. With infinite care, she took a blackbird's nest containing three sleeping baby birds from under her shirt and put it on her plate. As soon as the babies saw the light, they stretched out their frail necks and opened their red beaks to ask for food. Charmed, Désirée clapped her hands. The sight of these animals she did not know plunged her into an extraordinary fervor.

The priest suddenly remembered the afternoon and shouted, "It's that Paradou girl!"

La Teuse had gone to the window. "That's right," she said. "I should have recognized her voice. She sounds like a cricket . . . Ah, the gypsy! Look, she stayed to spy on us." Father Mouret came to the window and thought he saw Albine's orange skirt behind a juniper tree. But Brother Archangias rushed violently up behind him, brandishing his fist, shaking his rough head, and thundering, "The devil take you, you little thief! I'll pull you around the church by your hair if I catch you casting spells around here."

A sudden burst of laughter, fresh and cool as an evening breeze, rose from the path, followed by a slight movement, the noise of a skirt flowing across the grass like a slithering serpent. Father Mouret, standing by the window, watched a pale spot sliding among the pines in the distance. The breaths reaching him from the country had the same powerful perfume of greenery, the same odor of wild flowers, which Albine had shaken from her bare arms, free body, and flowing hair.

"She's damned. She's a daughter of perdition," Brother Archangias grumbled deeply as he sat back down. He ate his bacon ravenously, swallowing whole potatoes served in place of bread. La Teuse could not make Désirée finish her meal. The big child stared ecstatically at the blackbird nest as she asked one question after another; she wanted to know what they ate, if they lay eggs, how you could tell the roosters.

But the old servant was suspicious. She stood on her good leg and stared at the young priest. "So you know the Paradou people," she said.

Then, simply, he told the truth and described his visit to old Jeanbernat. La Teuse exchanged scandalized glances with Brother Archangias. At first she said nothing. She simply limped furiously around the table and threatened to smash the floor with her stomping heel.

"In three months it seems you could at least have told me about these people," the priest said at last. "It would have been nice to know whose home I was visiting."

La Teuse stopped short, as if her legs were broken. "Don't lie, Father," she stammered. "Don't lie. You'll just make your sin worse. How dare you say that I haven't told you about the Philosopher, that heathen who's the scandal of the whole country. The truth is that you never listen when I talk to you. Everything goes in one ear and out the other . . . Ah! If you just listened to me, you could save yourself a lot of trouble."

"I told you a thing or two about those abominations, too," confirmed the friar.

Father Mouret shrugged his shoulders. "Well, I didn't remember," he said. "It wasn't until I was in Paradou that I thought I remembered certain things . . . Besides, I'd still have gone to the poor man, I thought he was about to die."

Brother Archangias, his mouth full, smashed his knife down and shouted, "Jeanbernat is a dog. He ought to die like a dog." Then, seeing the priest shake his head, he cut him off by saying, "No, no, there's no God for him, no repentance, no mercy. It would be better to throw the Host to the pigs than to take it to that infidel."

He took more potatoes and chewed them like a madman, his elbows on the table, his chin in his plate. La Teuse, her lips pinched, white from anger, was content to say dryly, "Stop. The good Father doesn't need anyone else; he has secrets from us now."

There was a heavy silence. For a while, the noise of the friar's jaws and the strange gurgling in his throat was all that could be heard. Désirée, her bare arms enclosing the blackbird nest still on her plate, leaned forward to smile at the babies; she spoke at length to them in a private babble which they seemed to understand.

"You tell people what you've done when you don't have anything to hide!" La Teuse cried suddenly.

And the silence began again. The old servant was especially exasperated by the mystery with which the priest seemed to have surrounded his visit to Paradou. She considered herself a woman unworthily deceived; her curiosity was injured and bleeding. Withdrawn into herself, she marched around the table, not looking at the priest, not talking to anyone. "Heavens! That's why we eat so late! . . . We gad about the country without saying anything until two in the afternoon. We go in houses with such bad reputations that we don't even dare say where we've been. Then we lie, we betray everybody . . ."

"But," gently interrupted Father Mouret, who was forcing himself to eat so as not to make la Teuse even angrier, "nobody asked me if I went to Paradou. I didn't have to lie."

La Teuse seemed not to hear. "We rub our cassock in the dirt, we come home looking like a thief. And if a good woman interested in us asks us things for our own good, we push her back, we treat her like a woman of no importance, a woman we can't trust. We hide like a spy, we'd rather die than say a single word. We don't even care enough to cheer up our home by telling what we saw." She turned to the priest and looked him squarely in the face. "Yes, all that's for you. You have secrets. You're mean."

And she began to cry. The priest had to comfort her. "Father Caffin used to tell me everything," she said. But she was calming down.

Brother Archangias, apparently completely undisturbed by this scene, was finishing a large piece of cheese. It was his opinion that Father Mouret had to be kept in the right track; it was good for la Teuse to let him feel the bit. He emptied a final glass of wine and leaned back in his chair to digest.

"Anyway," the old servant asked, "what did you see at Paradou? At least you can tell us about it."

Father Mouret smiled and described in a few words Jean-bernat's singular way of receiving him. La Teuse assaulted him with questions and interrupted him with indignant exclamations. Brother Archangias clenched his fists and shook them. "May heaven destroy him," he said. "May it burn them—both him and his witch."

Then, in his turn, the priest tried to get more details about the Paradou couple. He listened most attentively as the friar told of monstrous deeds. "Yes, that devil came and sat in school one morning. A long time ago. She must have been about ten. I let her. I thought her uncle sent her for first Communion. For two months she revolutionized the class. She had made them love her, the brat. She knew games, she invented things with leaves and rags. And smart too, like all the daughters of hell. She was best on catechism . . . Then, one fine morning, the old man busted in right in the middle of the lesson. He was raving about breaking everything, shouting that the priests had taken his child away. The police had to come throw him out. The girl had run away. I saw her through the window, laughing at her uncle. She had been in school on her own for two months, and he didn't know about it. An earthshaking story."

"She never took first Communion," la Teuse said half-aloud. She shuddered.

"No, never," said Brother Archangias. "She must be sixteen. She's growing up like an animal. I saw her running on all fours in a thicket over by la Palud."

"On all fours," the servant whispered. She turned worriedly to the window.

Father Mouret wanted to voice a doubt, but the friar exploded. "Yes, on all fours! And she was jumping like a wildcat, her skirts up showing her thighs. I could have shot her down if I'd had a gun. People kill animals more pleasing to God. And besides, everybody knows she comes to Artauds every night to wail. She moans like a bitch in heat. If she ever got her claws in a man, she wouldn't leave any skin on his bones, not any skin at all."

And all his hatred of womankind came to the surface. He shook the table with his fist and shouted his usual insults: "They've got the devil in their flesh; they stink of the devil; they stink of him in their legs, in their arms, in their bellies, everywhere . . . That's what drives the fools mad."

The priest nodded agreement. Brother Archangias' violence and la Teuse's garrulous tyranny were like the strokes of a whip whose sting he often felt on his shoulders. He found pious joy in going down into such depths among these hands filled with accepted vulgarity. Heavenly peace seemed to wait at the end of this contempt for the world, of this debasement of all his being. It was a pleasurable insult to his body, a gutter where he liked to bathe his tenderness.

"There's nothing but filth," he muttered, folding his napkin.

La Teuse was clearing the table and wanted to pick up the plate where Désirée had put the blackbird's nest. "You're not going to sleep there, Miss," she said. "Get away from those awful animals."

But Désirée defended the plate. She covered the nest with her bare arms, no longer laughing, angry at being bothered.

"I hope you're not going to keep those birds," Brother Archangias exclaimed. "It'd be bad luck . . . You've got to wring their necks."

And he had already moved his massive hands forward. The girl stood up and recoiled, trembling and clasping the nest to her breast. Staring fixedly at the friar, her lips swollen, she looked like a she-wolf ready to bite.

"Don't touch the babies," she stammered. "You're ugly!"

She said the word with such vehement scorn that Father Mouret trembled, as if Brother Archangias' ugliness had struck him for the first time. The friar had simply growled. He felt deep hatred for Désirée, whose beautiful animal growth offended him. After she had backed out of the room without taking her eyes off him, he shrugged his shoulders and spit out an obscenity which no one heard.

"It's better for her to go to bed," said la Teuse. "She'd get in our way in church."

"Have they come?" asked Father Mouret.

"The girls have been outside for a good time now. They've got armfuls of leaves. I'm going to light the lamps. We can start whenever you're ready."

A few seconds later, they heard her swearing at the wet matches. Brother Archangias, alone with the priest, asked sullenly, "Is this for Mary's month?"

"Yes," replied Father Mouret. "For the last few days, the girls around here had so much work to do they couldn't come decorate the chapel of the Blessed Virgin as they usually do. We put the ceremony off until tonight."

"That's a nice custom," grumbled the friar. "When I see them all putting their branches down, I feel like throwing them to the floor so they can at least confess their foul sins before they touch the altar . . . It's an abomination to let women twitch their dresses so close to holy things."

The priest excused himself. He had been at Artauds only a short time and had to accept the customs.

"Whenever you're ready, Father," repeated la Teuse.

But Brother Archangias still detained him. "I'm going," he went on. "Religion is not a girl; you can't put it in flowers and lace." He was walking slowly to the door. He stopped again, raised one of his hairy fingers, and added, "Beware of your devotion to the Blessed Virgin."

◇◇◇◇◇◇◇◇◇◇◇◇◇◇◇◇◇◇◇◇◇◇◇◇◇◇◇◇◇◇◇◇◇◇◇◇

XIII In the church, father mouret found about ten girls holding branches of olive, laurel, and rosemary. Garden flowers did not grow on the Artauds rocks, so the custom was to decorate the altar of the Blessed Virgin with leaves hardy enough to last all month. La Teuse would add some wallflowers whose stems she could soak in old bottles.

"Do you want to let me do it, Father?" she asked. "You aren't used to it . . . Look, stand there, by the altar. You can tell me if you like what I'm doing."

He agreed, and she was the one who actually directed the ceremony. She had climbed a ladder and spoke roughly to the girls as they came up one after another with their leaves. "Not so fast there. Give me time to get the branches tied. We don't want all this wood to fall on the Father's head . . . All right, Babet, your turn. Don't look at me like that! . . . That's really pretty, your rosemary is. It's as yellow as thistle. Every dunce in the country must have peed on it. Now you, Rousse. Ah! That's pretty laurel at least. You got that in your Croix-Verte field."

The girls kissed the altar after laying their boughs on it. As they pressed against the cloth for an instant and passed the branches to la Teuse, they lost the wary slyness they had displayed while climbing the step. They began to laugh, bump knees, lean hips against the edge of the table, and stick breasts into the tabernacle. And, above them, the large Virgin of gilded plaster bent her painted face to smile with her pink lips at the naked Christ child she was carrying on her left arm.

"That's good, Lisa!" cried la Teuse. "Sit right down on the altar while you're at it. Would you be good enough to lower your skirts! Try not to show us everything you've got! . . . If I catch one of you lying down on something holy, I'll slap your face with a branch. Can't you even give me the things right?"

And, turning around, "Do you like that, Father? Do you think everything's all right?"

She was building a nest of greenery behind the Blessed Virgin, branches extended to form a cradle before falling back like palm. The priest gave his approval and risked one suggestion: "I think," he said softly, "we need a softer color at the top."

"Of course," grumbled la Teuse. "They don't bring me anything but laurel and rosemary. Who has the olive? Not one, just look! Those heathens are afraid of losing four olives."

But Catherine was climbing the step with an enormous olive branch which completely hid her. "Ah, you have some, brat," said the old servant.

"Sure she does," said a voice. "She stole it. I saw Vincent breaking the branch while she kept watch for him."

Furious, Catherine swore that it was all a lie. She had turned around without letting go of the branch and released her brown hair from the bush she was carrying. She lied with extraordinary poise, inventing a long story to show that the olive tree was really hers. "And besides," she concluded, "all trees belong to the Blessed Virgin."

Father Mouret wanted to intervene. But la Teuse asked if everybody was making fun of her by leaving her with her arms in the air. And she tightly tied up the olive branch while Catherine, who had climbed the ladder behind her, mocked the torturous way she turned her enormous body on her good leg. Even the priest smiled.

"There!" la Teuse said as she came down to examine her work. "The high part's done . . . Now we're going to put bundles between the candlesticks—unless you prefer a garland running along the seats."

The priest decided for large bundles. "Let's go, come on," the servant said after climbing the ladder again. "We don't want to spend the night here . . . Would you be good enough to kiss the altar, Miette! You think you're in a barn? . . . Father, see what they're doing down there. I can hear them laughing."

They raised one of the two lamps to light the dark end of the church. Three girls were pushing each other playfully under the gallery; one of them had her head in the holy-water font, and this made the others laugh so hard they collapsed on the floor. They came back, staring at the priest below, apparently glad to be scolded, their hands dangling and hitting against their thighs.

But what especially angered la Teuse was the sudden sight of Rosalie following the others to bring her boughs to the altar. "Would you be good enough to get out of here!" she yelled. "What nerve! . . . Let's see, hurry up, bring me your bundle."

"Hey, why?" Rosalie asked bravely. "Nobody can say I stole it."

The girls came up, playing games, exchanging winks. "Because you don't belong here! Go away! Do you understand?" Then, losing the little patience she had, she brutally released an awful word which made the peasant girls laugh.

"So?" said Rosalie. "How do you know what other people do? You didn't go watch, did you?" And she felt she had to burst into sobs. She threw her branches down and let herself be led a few paces away by Father Mouret, who spoke to her very sternly. He had tried to make la Teuse be quiet. He was beginning to feel ill at ease among these brazen girls filling the church with their armloads of greenery. They pushed up the steps to the altar and surrounded it with a section of living forest, brought to it the insistent perfume of scented wood, like a breath rising from their strong workers' limbs.

"Let's hurry, let's hurry," he said, lightly clapping his hands.

"I wouldn't mind going to bed," la Teuse muttered. "I hope you don't think it's fun, tying up all this wood." She had finished tying tufts of leaves between the candlesticks and folded up the ladder, which Catherine stored behind the main altar. All she had to do now was place arrangements on both sides of the table. The last bits of greenery were enough for this little garden; there were even some branches left, which the girls spread on the floor before the wooden railing. The altar of the Blessed Virgin was a grove, a copse, with a green lawn before it.

La Teuse then agreed to yield her place to Father Mouret. He went to the altar and lightly clapped his hands again. "Ladies," he said, "we shall continue the services of the month of the Blessed Virgin Mary tomorrow. Those who are unable to come should at least say their rosary at home."

He knelt while the peasants, with a great noise of skirts, sat on their heels. They responded to his prayer with an embarrassed mumble broken by fits of laughter. One of them felt her fanny being pinched and released a cry which she tried to conceal by a coughing fit; this amused the others so much that they had to hold their sides for a while after the *Amen*. They were unable to stand up; their noses remained on the tiles.

La Teuse sent these hussies away while the priest, who had crossed himself, remained at the altar, completely absorbed, apparently unaware of what was going on behind him.

"Come on, now, clear out," growled la Teuse. "You're a pack of good-for-nothing pigs; you don't even know how to respect the good Lord. It's an abomination, it's never been seen, girls in a church rolling around on the ground like animals in a field. What are you doing there, Rousse? If I see you pinch somebody, I'll tell the Father. Outside, outside, you boy-crazy hussies." She was slowly trotting around them to herd them to the door, her limp grossly accentuated. She thought she had succeeded in getting the last one out when she saw Catherine sitting peacefully in the confessional with Vincent, eating something and apparently having a marvelous time. She chased them away. And as she put her head out the door before closing it, she saw Rosalie hanging on to big Fortuné, who had been waiting for her. They disappeared into the darkness by the cemetery, and she heard the small sound of a kiss.

"And that shows itself at the altar of the Blessed Virgin," she spluttered as she shot the bolts. "It's not as if the others were any better. All those sluts came tonight with their branches to laugh and get kissed by their men when they left. Tomorrow, not a single one will bother to come. The Father can say his *Ave* alone. We won't see anybody but sluts out to meet somebody."

She bumped against the benches as she put them back into place and searched one last time for something suspicious before going to bed. In the confessional, she picked up a handful of apple skins which she threw behind the main altar. She also found a piece of ribbon ripped off a bonnet, and a lock of black hair. She wrapped it up to use as evidence in an investigation. With this one exception, the church seemed to be in order. The lamp had enough oil for the night, and the choir loft could last until Saturday without being washed.

"It's almost ten o'clock, Father," she said as she approached the still-kneeling priest. "You'd better come on up to bed, too."

He nodded his head without replying. "I know what that means," la Teuse continued. "In an hour he'll still be here, catching a cold on the stone floor . . . I'm leaving. I'm bothering him; it doesn't make sense, eat lunch at a time when other people are eating dinner, go to bed when the chickens are getting up . . . I'm bothering you, aren't I, Father? Good night. You're just not reasonable."

She was about to leave, but she came back to put out one of the two lamps, muttering that to pray so late "was murder on the oil." She finally left. Her sleeve brushed the altarcloth, which seemed to her to be gray with dust. Father Mouret, his eyes raised, his arms folded on his chest, was alone.

❖❖❖❖❖❖❖❖❖❖❖❖❖❖❖❖❖❖❖❖❖❖❖❖❖❖❖❖❖❖❖

XIV A SINGLE LAMP, BURNING AMONG THE GREENERY ON THE altar of the Blessed Virgin, filled both sides of the church with great floating shadows and made the pulpit a mass of shade reaching to the ceiling. Under the gallery, the confessional was a black lump resembling the weird silhouette of a gutted sentry box. All the light, softened, made green by the boughs, was drowsily focused on the large gilded Virgin; she seemed to be descending regally, carried by the cloud on which played winged heads of angels. The round lamp shining through the leaves seemed to be a pale moon rising over the edge of a wood, illuminating some sovereign apparition, a heavenly princess crowned with gold, dressed in gold, parading her Child's nakedness through the mystery of secret paths. Between the leaves, along the tall bundles, in the wide cradle of the arch, even on the branches strewn along the floor, starry beams flowed sleepily, like that milky rain which pierces the bushes on clear nights. Indistinct cracks came from the two dark ends of the church; the big clock to the left of the choir beat slowly in the heavy breathing of a sleeping machine. And the radiant Vision, the Mother, her light-brown hair parted in the middle, came closer, as if the nave's nocturnal peace had reassured her. The gentle flight of her cloud sent tremors through the grass in the grove.

Father Mouret was staring at her. This was when he loved the church. He forgot the pitiful Christ, the tortured man splattered with ocher and lake, dying behind him in the Chapel of the Dead. He was no longer distracted by the window's insistently raw light, the joys of morning coming in with the sun, outside life, sparrows and limbs invading the nave through the broken window panes. At this time of night, nature was dead; the shadows draped the whitewashed walls with crepe, the coolness laid a soothing hairshirt on his shoulders. He could vanish in absolute love. The games of the light, the caresses of a breeze or an odor, the beating of an insect wing no longer took him away from the joy of loving. His morning Mass never furnished the superhuman delights of his evening prayers.

Father Mouret's lips moved as he watched the large Virgin. He saw her leave her green nest and come to him in growing splendor. It was no longer moonlight streaming through the tops of the trees; she seemed to be dressed in sunlight. Her movement was majestic; she was glorious, colossal, so all-powerful that he was tempted to bury his face in the ground to escape the flaming light of this door open to heaven. All his being was consumed in adoration, words died in his mouth, and he remembered Brother Archangias' parting admonition as utterly blasphemous. The friar often reproached him for this particular devotion to the Blessed Virgin, which, according to him, was a theft of devotion due to God. He said such adoration softened souls, put skirts on religion, created a pious sentimentality unworthy of strong men. He had a grudge against the Blessed Virgin because she was a woman, because she was beautiful and a mother; always on his guard against her, he was seized by the hollow fear of being tempted by her grace and succumbing to this sweet seductress. "She'll lead you astray," he had cried to the young priest one day. He saw in her a beginning of human passion, an inclination to the delights of beautiful light-brown hair, large, limpid eyes, and the mystery of dresses falling from neck to feet. It was the revolt of a saint who radically separated the Mother from the Son, asking like the latter, "Woman, what can there be in common between you and me?" But Father Mouret resisted, prostrating himself. When, alone before the large gilded Virgin, he succeeded so well in creating hallucinations that he saw her lean forward and give him her tresses to kiss, he again became very young, very good, very strong, very just, his whole being infused with a life of tenderness.

Father Mouret's devotion to the Blessed Virgin Mary dated from his early youth. As a slightly rebellious child hiding in corners, he liked to imagine that a beautiful woman was protecting him, that two gentle blue eyes smilingly followed his every move. Often, at night, when he felt a breeze blow through his hair, he said that the Blessed Virgin had come to kiss him. He had grown up under this woman's caress, in this air filled with the rustle of a divine dress. From the age of seven, he satisfied his need for affection by spending all his money on holy images, which he jealously hid and enjoyed in solitude. And never was he tempted by Jesuses carrying the Lamb, Christs on the cross, or bearded God the Fathers perching on the edge of a cloud; he always came back to the gentle images of Mary and her thin, laughing mouth, her slender, outstretched hands. Little by little, he had collected them all: Mary between a lily and a distaff, Mary carrying the Child like an older sister, Mary crowned with roses, Mary crowned with stars. They were for him a family of beautiful girls endowed with something like grace. Every one had the same look of goodness, the same smooth face; they were all so young under their veils that despite their name of Mother of God, he was not afraid of them as he was of other grownups. They seemed to him to be his age, to be little girls he would have liked to meet, the heavenly little girls with whom little boys who died at the age of seven played forever in a corner of paradise. But he was already becoming serious; he grew into the exquisite modesty of adolescence and still kept the secret of his religious love. Mary grew up with him; she always remained one or two years older, just the right age for a sovereign friend. She was twenty when he was eighteen. She no longer kissed his forehead at night; she kept her distance, her arms crossed, her smile chaste and adorably gentle. He now spoke her name very softly; his heart seemed to stop beating each time his prayers brought the beloved name to his lips. He no longer dreamed of childish games in heavenly gardens, but of continuous contemplation before this white face, so pure that he could not imagine touching it even with his breath. His mother herself did not know how much he loved the Blessed Virgin Mary.

Then, some years later, when he was in seminary, his beautiful love for Mary, so upright, so natural, began to give rise to strange worries. Was the cult of Mary necessary for salvation? Did it not steal from God by giving Mary a portion of his love, the greatest portion, his thoughts, his heart, his all? Disturbing questions, inner struggle which impassioned him, which bound him tighter to her. So he buried himself in the subtleties of his affections and gave himself undreamed-of raptures by debating the legitimacy of his emotion. The books devoted to Mary excused him, delighted him, filled him with logic which he contemplated like prayers. This was how he learned to be the slave of Jesus in Mary. He came to Jesus through Mary. And he quoted all kinds of proofs, he made distinctions, he drew consequences: Mary, whom Jesus had obeyed on earth, was to be obeyed by all men; Mary retained the power of a mother in heaven, where she was the great dispenser of God's treasures, the only one who could implore Him, the only one who meted out thrones; Mary, a simple creature compared to God, was raised to his level to become the human link between heaven and earth, the intermediary of all grace and mercy; and the conclusion of his reasoning was always that he must love her above all else, in God Himself. Moreover, there were more twisted theological curiosities: the marriage of the Heavenly Bridegroom, the Holy Ghost sealing the chosen vessel, bringing the Virgin Mother into an eternal miracle, giving to the devotion of man her inviolate purity. She was the Virgin victorious over all heresy, the irreconcilable enemy to Satan, the new Eve announced as come to crush the serpent's head, the august Portal of Grace through which the Saviour once entered, through which he would enter again on the last day, an imprecise prophecy, sign of a larger role for Mary which gave Serge a dream of some immense expansion of love. This entry of woman into the jealous and cruel heaven of the Old Testament, this white figure set at the foot of the awesome Trinity, was for him religious grace itself, his consolation under the shock of faith, the refuge for a man lost in the mysteries of dogma. And when he had proved to himself, point by point, at great length, that she was the easy, short, perfect, certain road to Christ, he yielded to her again, completely, without qualms; he wanted to be her true worshiper, wanted to die to himself and plunge into the depths of submission.

Hour of divine bliss. The pious books celebrating the Virgin burned in his hands. They spoke to him in a language of love which smoked like incense. Mary was no longer the adolescent veiled in white, her arms crossed, standing a few feet from his pillow; she came in splendor, and he saw her as John had seen her, dressed in sunlight, crowned by twelve stars, the moon under her feet. Her perfume permeated him; she enflamed him with desire for heaven, delighted him with even the heat of the stars blazing on her forehead. He threw himself before her, shouted that he was her slave; and nothing was sweeter than this word "slave," which he repeated, which his stuttering mouth tasted more fully the more he collapsed at her feet to become her plaything, her trifle, the dust touched by her blue robe. He said with David, "Mary was made for me." He added with the Evangelist, "I have taken her for all my goods." He called her "my dear mistress." He could find no words and finally babbled like a child and like a lover, as only the short breath of passion passed his lips. She was the Blessed Virgin, the Queen of Heaven celebrated by the nine choirs of angels, the Mother of beautiful love, the Lord's Treasure. Vivid images multiplied to compare her to an earthly paradise of untilled land, acres of virtuous flowers, plains green with hope, impregnable towers, houses charming and secure. Again, she was a fountain on which the Holy Ghost had set His seal, a sanctuary where the Holy Trinity rested, the throne of God, the city of God, the altar of God, the temple of God, the world of God. And, under the greenery's enchantment, he wandered in this garden, in shadow and in sunlight; he sighed for the water of this fountain; he lived in Mary's beauty, was supported, hidden, lost without fear, left to drink milk of infinite love which fell drop by drop from this virgin breast.

Every morning in the seminary, he greeted Mary with a hundred bows as soon as he awoke, and his face turned to the section of heaven visible through his window; at night, he bid her farewell by bending the same number of times, his eyes on the stars. Often, on peaceful nights, when Venus shone blond and dreamy through the warm air, he gave himself up to contemplation, the *Ave maris stella* dropped from his lips as an emotional hymn revealing distant blue strands, gentle seas barely rippled by the shiver of a caress, lit by a smiling star as large as a sun. Again, he would recite the *Salve Regina,* the *Regina coeli,* the *O gloriosa domina,* all the prayers, all the hymns. He would read the Office of the Virgin, the sacred books in her honor, the small Psalter of St. Bonaventura, his devotion so acute that tears prevented him from turning the pages. He fasted, he mortified himself in order to offer her his ravaged body. At the age of ten, he took her livery, the holy scapular, the double image of the Blessed Virgin Mary sewed in cloth, whose heat sent shivers of happiness across the naked skin of his back and chest. Later, he took the chain to show his slavery in love. But his great act always remained the angelic greeting, the *Ave Maria,* the perfect prayer for his heart. "Hail Mary," and he saw her come to him, full of grace, blessed among women; he threw his heart before her gentle feet for her to walk on. He multiplied this greeting, he repeated it in a hundred ways, straining his wits to make it more effective. He said twelve *Aves* to remind him of the crown with twelve stars around Mary's forehead; he said fourteen in memory of her fourteen delights; he said ten seven times in honor of the years she was on earth. He fingered his beads for hours. Then, slowly, on certain days of mystical reunion, he undertook the infinite whispering of the greater rosary.

When alone in his cell and with time to love, kneeling on the floor, he saw all the tall, chaste flowers of Mary's garden bloom round him. The rosary's garland of *Aves* spaced by *Paters* flowed through his fingers like a garland of white roses, mingled with the lilies of the Annunciation, the bleeding flowers of Calvary, the stars of the Coronation. He walked slowly through the perfumed paths, stopping at each of the fifteen decades of *Aves,* finding repose in the Mystery to which each corresponded. He was lost in joy, sorrow, and glory as he passed through the three groups of Mysteries, the joyful, the sorrowful, the glorious. Incomparable legend, story of Mary, complete human life, with all its smiles, tears, triumph, which he relived from beginning to end in an instant. And first he entered joy, the five happy Mysteries, bathed in the serenity of dawn: the greeting of the archangel, a ray of fertility sliding from heaven, bringing the adorable swoon of union without sin; the visit to Elizabeth, on a clear morning of hope, when the fruit of her womb was for the first time giving Mary that kick which makes mothers grow pale; the labor in a Bethlehem stable and the long line of shepherds coming to pay their respects to divine maternity; the newborn child taken to the temple in the arms of the smiling woman who had just given birth, who, still fatigued, was already happy to offer her child to God's justice, to Simeon's embraces, to the world's desires; finally, Jesus as a young man, revealing himself before the sages, among whom his worried mother finds herself again, is comforted and made proud. Then, after that morning filled with such tender light, it seemed to Serge that the sky suddenly grew overcast. He now walked only on thistles, he scraped his fingers on the rosary beads as he bent low beneath the terror of the five Mysteries of sorrow: Mary suffering in her son in Gethsemane, receiving with him the lashes of the flagellation, feeling on her own forehead the rending crown of thorns, bearing the horrible weight of the cross, dying at his feet on Calvary. These necessary sufferings, this atrocious martyrdom of an adored Queen, for whom, he, like Jesus, would have given his blood, created in him horror which ten years of the same prayers and exercises had been unable to still. But the beads were still flowing, a sudden break appeared in the shadow of the Crucifixion, the shining glory of the final five Mysteries burst over him with the joy of a free star. Mary, transfigured, was singing the Alleluia of Resurrection, victory over death, eternity of life; consumed by wonder, stretching out her hands, she was present at the triumph of the Son rising to heaven among golden clouds fringed in purple; she gathered the Apostles around her, and the same burning spirit of love which had been hers on the day of conception was given her once more; returned to earth in ardent flames, she was in her turn taken up by a band of angels, borne on white wings forming an immaculate ark, put gently down into the splendor of the heavenly thrones; and there, as supreme glory, in light so dazzling it put out the sun, God crowned her with the stars of the firmament. Passion has only one word. In saying the hundred and fifty *Aves* Serge had repeated nothing. This monotonous muttering, this unvarying word which returned like a lover's "I love you," acquired ever deeper meaning. He lingered, spoke forever with the help of this one Latin sentence, knew Mary in her entirety, until the last bead of the rosary escaped his hands and the thought of separation made him faint.

The young man had spent many nights in this way, beginning the decades twenty times in succession, always putting off the moment when he had to take leave of his beloved mistress. Dawn would break while he whispered. He tried to tell himself that it was the moon making the stars grow pale. His superiors criticized him for these vigils, which left him weak, his face so white that he seemed to have lost a great deal of blood. For a long time, he had kept a colored engraving of the Sacred Heart of the Blessed Virgin on his cell wall. Smiling serenely, Mary opened her dress to show her heart burning through a red hole in her breast pierced by a sword crowned with white roses. This sword threw him into despair, waking in him such intolerable fear of seeing a woman suffer that the mere thought of such suffering drew him out of all pious submission. He blotted it out, saw only the crowned and flaming heart, half-torn from that exquisite flesh to offer itself to him. It was then that he felt he was loved. Mary gave him her heart, her living heart, just as it beat in her breast, with the pink drops of her blood. It became not an image of devout passion but a material thing, a prodigy of emotion, which, when he prayed before the engraving, made him open his hands to receive in awe the heart leaping from the spotless breast. He saw it, he heard it beat. And he was loved; the heart was beating for him! It was as if his whole being dissolved into his need to kiss that heart, to melt into it, to sleep nestled in this open chest. She loved him actively, and she wanted him to be eternally near her, to be always hers. She loved him effectively, always thinking of him, following him everywhere, never unfaithful to him. She loved him tenderly, more than all women together, with a blue, deep love, as infinite as the heavens. Where could he ever have found such a desirable mistress? What earthly caress was comparable to the blessed breath of Mary in which he walked? What miserable coupling, what filthy pleasure could be weighed against this eternal flower of desire, forever growing but never blooming? Then he exhaled the incense of the *Magnificat*. He sang the hymn of Mary's delight, her quiver of joy at the approach of the Divine Bridegroom. He glorified the Lord who overthrew the mighty on their thrones and who sent Mary to him, to the poor naked child dying of love on the icy floor of his cell.

And when he had given everything to Mary, his body, his soul, his earthly goods, his spiritual goods, when he was naked before her, with no more prayers to offer, the repeated, stubborn, dogging calls of the litanies of the Blessed Virgin gushed from his burned lips in a supreme plea for celestial help. It seemed to him that he was climbing a staircase of desire; he went up a step with each leap of his heart. First, he said she was Holy. Then he called her Mother, most pure, most chaste, most amiable, most admirable. And his strength restored, he shouted her virginity to her six times, his mouth increasingly cooled by the word "Virgin," to which he linked ideas of power, goodness, faith. As his heart bore him higher in degrees of light, a strange voice spoke in his veins, burst into ever-expanding bloom. He wanted to melt into perfume, to explode into light, to expire in a musical sigh. As he named her Mirror of Justice, Seat of Wisdom, Spring of his joy, he could see himself pale with ecstasy in that mirror; he knelt on the warm tiles of that seat; he drank long draughts from that intoxicating spring. And still he had not finished transforming her; he gave rein to his insane desire in order to be ever more closely united with her. She became a Vessel of Honor chosen by God, the elected Bosom into which he wanted to pour his being and sleep forever more. She was the mystical Rose, a great flower blossoming in paradise, composed of angels surrounding their Queen, so pure, so sweet, that the depths of his unworthiness inhaled her odor in an expansion of joy which cracked his ribs. She became the House of Gold, Tower of David, Tower of Ivory, of unfathomable richness, of purity envied by swans, a tall, strong, firm body which he longed to clasp with his outstretched hands so as to make a belt of submission. She stood on the horizon: she was the Gate of Heaven, which he glimpsed over her shoulders when a breath of wind blew the folds of her veil. She grew behind the mountain at the hour when night grew pale: she was the Morning Star, the Friend of lost travelers, the Dawn of Love. Here, out of breath, still unsatisfied, with nothing but words to betray the forces of his heart, he could glorify her only with the title of Queen, which he threw to her nine times like nine strokes of the censer. His hymn died of happiness in these final triumphant cries: Queen of Virgins, Queen of all the saints, Queen conceived without sin! She shone, ever higher. He himself was on the last step, the step which only those beloved of Mary attain, and he remained there a moment, swooning in the thin air which numbed him, still too far away to kiss the hem of her blue garment, already feeling himself roll back, with the eternal desire to climb again, to test once more this superhuman joy.

How often, when the entire seminary was in chapel to recite the litanies of the Blessed Virgin, had he been left in this condition, his knees broken, his head empty, as if he had fallen from a great height! Father Mouret had learned to love the Virgin still more since completing his studies. He devoted to her that impassioned cult in which Brother Archangias sniffed the odor of heresy. It was she who was to save the church by some grand prodigy, she whose coming appearance would cast a spell on the earth. She was the only miracle of an impious age, the blue lady revealing herself to the little shepherds, the nocturnal whiteness seen between two clouds, trailing the hem of her garment on the peasants' roofs. When Brother Archangias asked him roughly if he had ever seen her, he only smiled and pinched his lips, as if to keep his secret from escaping. The truth was that he saw her every night. She now appeared to him neither as a happy sister nor as a beautiful, fervent girl: she wore the dress of a bride; she had white flowers in her hair, her lowered eyes wet with hope, her expression illuminating her cheeks. And he felt that she was coming to him, that she was promising him to tarry no more, that she was saying, "Here I am, take me." Three times each day, when the Angelus rang, at dawn's awakening, at noon's maturity, at dusk's tender fall, he bared his head, said an *Ave,* and looked around to see if this were finally the bell announcing Mary's return. He was twenty-five years old. He was waiting.

In the month of May, the young priest's wait was filled with glad hope. He did not even worry about la Teuse's scolding. If he prayed so late in the church, it was with the insane idea that the large gilded Virgin would at last come down to him. And he was nevertheless afraid of her, afraid of this Virgin who resembled a princess. He did not love all Virgins in the same way. This one filled him with sovereign respect. She was the Mother of God and had the fecund figure, the august face, the strong arms of the Divine Bride carrying Jesus. This was how he imagined her in the heavenly court, the train of her royal robes trailing among the stars, too high for him, so powerful that he would crumble into dust if she deigned to lower her eyes to his. She was the Virgin of his days of weakness, the stern Virgin who created an awesome vision of paradise, through which he regained his inner peace.

That night, Father Mouret knelt more than an hour in the

empty church. His hands clasped, his eyes fixed on the golden Virgin rising like a star among the greenery, he tried to calm in the slumber of ecstasy the strange uneasiness he had felt during the day. But he could not slide into prayer's half-sleep with his customary joyous ease. Mary's maternity, glorious and pure as she revealed herself, this round body of a mature woman carrying her naked child on one arm, upset him profoundly; she seemed to be a heavenly continuation of the overflowing outburst of generation through which he had been walking since morning. Like the vines on the rocky hillsides, like the Paradou trees, like the human flock of Artauds, Mary gave birth, engendered life. And prayer died on his lips; he was distracted and lost his train of thought; he saw things he had never seen before: the soft curve of her light-brown hair, the slight swelling of her chin and its pink drops. So she had to make herself sterner; she had to bury him under the brilliance of her omnipotence to bring him back to his place in the interrupted prayer. It was finally by her golden crown, by her golden cloak, by all the gold which transformed her into a terrible princess, that she succeeded in crushing him to a slave's submission; prayer flowed evenly from his mouth, his mind was lost in the depths of unique adoration. Until eleven o'clock, he slept while this ecstatic numbness awakened him. He could now feel only his knees; he thought he was held and rocked like a child being put to sleep; he abandoned himself to repose without losing his awareness of a heavy weight on his heart. Shadows filled the church around him, the lamp was smoking, the tall foliage was darkening the large Virgin's green face.

When the clock's rough voice grated before striking the hour, Father Mouret gave a start. He had not felt the church's coolness fall on his shoulders. Now he was shivering. As he crossed himself, a sudden memory passed through the stupor of his awakening: the chattering of his teeth reminded him of the nights spent on the floor of his cell before the Sacred Heart of the Blessed Virgin, the nights when his body shook with fever. He rose painfully, unhappy with himself. Ordinarily, his flesh was serene and Mary's sweet breath was on his forehead when he left the altar. That night, when he took the lamp to go up to his room, it seemed to him that his temples were splitting; prayer had had no effect. After a brief respite, he found that the heat which had been in his heart all day had now spread to his brain. When he was about to go through the sacristy door, he turned around and raised the lamp mechanically, trying to see the large Virgin one last time. She was drowned under the shadows descending from the beams; she had been thrust into foliage, which revealed only the golden cross of her crown.

◇◇

XV FATHER MOURET'S BEDROOM WAS IN A CORNER OF THE presbytery. Each of the two outside walls was broken by an immense rectangular window, one opening over Désirée's barnyard, the other overlooking the village of Artauds and, in the distance, the valley and hills on the horizon. The bed, its yellow curtains, the walnut chest, and the three wicker chairs were all lost under the high ceiling with its whitewashed rafters. The red-tiled floor shone like a mirror and emitted the faintly bitter, acrid odor associated with old frame houses in the country. On the chest, a large statuette of the Immaculate Conception introduced a note of sweet grayness between the two clay pots which la Teuse had filled with white lilacs.

Father Mouret put the lamp on the edge of the chest, next to the virgin. He felt so sick he decided to light the dried vine stems already laid in the fireplace. And he stood with the tongs in his hands, watching the kindling burn, feeling it light his face. He could hear the house's heavy sleep below him. The silence rumbling in his ears began to sound like whispering voices. Slowly, invincibly, these voices invaded him, redoubling the anxiety which had clutched his neck several times that day. Where could this anguish have come from? What was this unknown trouble which had softly grown until it became intolerable? He had not sinned. It seemed to him only yesterday that he had left the seminary, with all the ardor of his faith, set so strongly against the world that he walked among men and saw only God.

He thought he was in his cell one morning at five o'clock: time to get up. The deacon of the day was knocking on his door with a stick and crying the prescribed words, *"Benedicamus Domino."*

"Deo gratias," he replied, only half-awake, his eyes swollen with sleep. And he jumped to the narrow rug, washed his face, made his bed, swept his room, replaced the water in his basin. The morning chill running over his skin made these housekeeping chores a joy. A deafening noise of wings and song came from the plane trees in the courtyard as the sparrows began to wake up with him, and he thought they too were saying their prayers. He went down to the Meditation Room and knelt for thirty minutes after prayers, meditating on this thought of Loyola: "What does it profit a man to gain the whole world if he loses his soul?" It was a subject pregnant with good resolutions, which made him renounce all earthly goods and dream his cherished dream of a life in the desert under his only possession, the vast blue sky. After ten minutes, his knees, bruised by the tile, hurt so much that he began to feel his entire being swoon, began to experience the ecstasy of seeing himself as a great conqueror, as the master of an immense empire, who throws away his crown, breaks his scepter, crushes beneath his feet unheard-of wealth, caskets of gold, rivers of jewels, cloth sewed with gems, to put on rough garments which tear his skin, to bury himself in Theban depths. But Mass drew him out of these fantasies; he left them as if they were beautiful, true stories of something which had happened to him in olden times. He took Communion and sang very ardently the psalm of the day, hearing no voice but his own, pure as crystal, so clear that he could feel it fly to the ears of the Lord. And when he went back to his room, he took only one step at a time, as St. Bonaventura and St. Thomas Aquinas recommend. He walked slowly, looked preoccupied, his head lowered, finding indescribable joy in obeying the least important rule. It was now time for breakfast. At the refectory, he was charmed by the rows of bread beside glasses of white

wine; he had a good appetite and was naturally gay. For example, he liked to say that the wine was most Christian wine, an extremely daring allusion to the water which the steward was suspected of mixing with it. His jokes did not prevent him from becoming his serious self again when it was time for class. He took notes on his knees as the professor, his fists on the edge of the rostrum, spoke Latin broken by French words when he could think of nothing better. A discussion arose; the students argued in a strange jargon and never laughed. At ten o'clock, Scripture was read for twenty minutes. He went to get the richly bound, gilt-edged Holy Book, kissed it with particular veneration, read it bareheaded, and bowed whenever he came to the names of Jesus, Mary, or Joseph. The second meditation found him, for the love of God, completely ready to bear another period of kneeling even longer than the first. He never rested on his heels; he relished this forty-five minute examination of his conscience, trying hard to discover sins in himself, coming to believe himself damned for forgetting to kiss the two images of his scapular the night before or for going to sleep on his left side; abominable sins which he wanted to expiate by torturing his knees all day, fortunate sins which occupied his thoughts, without which he would not have known how to examine the guileless heart which his white life almost put to sleep. He entered the refectory as completely relieved as if he had made retribution for a frightful crime. The seminarians on duty, the sleeves of their cassocks rolled up, aprons of blue twill tied to their belts, served vermicelli soup, little squares of boiled beef, portions of lamb and beans. The awesome noise of hard-working jaws and furious forks broke the gluttonous silence; the seminarians cast envious glances at the iron table where the directors were eating more tender meat and drinking redder wines. And over this raging hunger the thick voice of some peasant's son with strong lungs and a complete disregard for periods and commas hemmed and hawed through some pious reading—letters from missionaries, bishops' pronouncements, articles from religious newspapers. He listened between mouthfuls. These bits of polemic, these descriptions of distant voyages, surprised him, even frightened him, by revealing the turmoil of an immense horizon beyond the seminary walls of which he had never dreamed. The students were still eating when a rattle announced recreation period. The courtyard was sandy and contained eight large plane trees which furnished cool shade in the summer. To the south was a wall five meters high, topped with broken glass, hiding all Plassans except the tip of St. Mark's steeple, a short stone needle in the blue sky. He and a group of friends would form a line and walk slowly from one end of the courtyard to the other. Each time he faced the wall, he would look at the steeple which was for him the entire town, the entire world under the free-flying clouds. Noisy discussions arose under the plane trees, friends broke off, two by two, into the corners, always spied on by some director hidden behind the curtains of his window. Violent games of ninepins and tennis were organized and disturbed the peaceful lotto players lying over their cards with the sand kicked up by stray balls. A hush fell when the bell rang, a cloud of sparrows flew out of the plane trees, and the still-panting students went to their class in plainsong, arms crossed, necks very serious. And the day ended in this peace; he went back to class; he was glad when four o'clock came and he could begin once more his eternal walk under St. Mark's spire; he dined amid the same chewing noise, under the heavy voice finishing the morning's reading; he went up to the chapel to recite the evening prayers; he retired at quarter past eight, after sprinkling his bed with holy water to ward off bad dreams.

How many such beautiful days had he spent in the old Plassans convent saturated with the odor of centuries of devotion! For five years, days had flowed after days to the same murmur of clear water. He remembered a thousand touching details: going with his mother to buy his first set of school clothes, two cassocks, two belts, six clerical bands, eight pairs of black socks, one surplice, one three-cornered hat. And how his heart had pounded on that warm October evening when the seminary door had closed behind him! He had come at the age of twenty, after his other studies were completed, directed by a need to believe and to love. The next day he had forgotten everything; it was as if he were asleep in the depths of this big, silent house. Again he saw the narrow cell where he had spent his two philosophy years, a cubbyhole furnished with bed, table, and chair, a poorly constructed partition separating this cubbyhole from its neighbors, dividing an immense room into fifty identical crannies. Again he saw his theologian's cell, where he lived for three more years; this room was larger, had an armchair, a dressing table, a library—a happy room filled with the dream of his faith. In the endless corridors, on the stone stairs, in certain corners, he had had sudden revelations, had found unhoped-for succor. The high ceilings dropped the voices of guardian angels. Not one tile of the rooms, not one stone in the walls, not one limb of the plane trees but spoke to him of the pleasures of his contemplative life, of his emotional stammering, of his slow initiation, of the caresses received in return for the gift of his being, of all this joy of the first Divine Lover. One day, he had awakened to see a bright light which bathed him in joy. Closing the door of his room one night, he had felt his neck grasped by warm hands so tenderly that he regained consciousness to find himself sobbing heavily on the floor. Moreover, at times, especially when under the little vault on the way to chapel, he had completely relaxed to let supple hands support him. All heaven was then concerned with him, walked around him, put into the least important of his acts, into the fulfillment of his most vulgar needs, a certain sense, a surprising perfume whose faint odor seemed destined to remain forever on his clothes, on his skin itself. Again, he remembered the Thursday walks. They left at two o'clock for some green spot a few miles from Plassans. It was most often on the edge of the Viorne, at the end of a meadow, where knotty willows soaked their leaves in the running water. He saw nothing, not the meadow's large yellow flowers, not the swallows drinking in flight, skimming their wings across the surface of the little river. He and his comrades would sit under the willows until six o'clock, reciting the Office of the Virgin or pairing off to read the *Petites Heures,* the young seminarian's facultative breviary.

Father Mouret was smiling as he poked the fire. He could

find nothing but great purity and perfect obedience in his past life. He was a lily whose sweet smell charmed his teachers. He did not recall one evil act. He never took advantage of the absolute freedom of the walks, when the two directors on duty went to chat with a neighborhood priest, to smoke behind a hedge or to drink beer with a friend. He never hid novels under his mattress, never put bottles of anisette far back in his night stand. For a long time he had not even suspected the sins surrounding him, chicken wings and cakes smuggled in during Lent, clandestine letters brought by servants, abominable whispered conversations in certain corners of the yard. He had shed hot tears the day he learned that few of his schoolmates loved God for Himself alone. He found peasants' sons who took orders to avoid conscription, lazy boys dreaming of an idle life, ambitious boys already possessed by a vision of the cross and miter. And the discovery of mundane filth at the very base of the altar had made him turn even more into himself; he gave himself more completely to God to console Him for being abandoned by men.

But the priest remembered that he had once crossed his legs in class. When the professor criticized him, he turned as red as if he were guilty of something indecent. He was one of the best students, never quibbling, simply learning the texts by heart. He proved God's existence and eternity by proofs taken from Holy Scripture, by the opinion of the Fathers of the Church, and by the universal consent of all peoples. Reasoning of this sort filled him with unshakable certainty. During his first philosophy year, he worked in his logic course with such assiduity that his professor had stopped him, saying that wisdom is not holiness. Thus, in his second year, he completed his study of metaphysics as if it were an onerous duty, entering very feebly into the day's exercises. He began to hold knowledge in contempt; he wanted to remain ignorant in order to retain the humility of his faith. Later, in theology, he followed the course in Rorbacher's *Ecclesiastical History* only as an act of submission. He moved on to Gousset's arguments, to Bouvier's *Theological Instruction,* without daring to touch Bellarmine, Liguori, Sanchez, Thomas Aquinas. Only Holy Scripture moved him. Here he found desirable knowledge, a story of infinite love which must be enough learning for all men of goodwill. He accepted only his teachers' affirmations and left to them all concern with questioning. He did not need this mumbo jumbo to love; he accused books of stealing time from prayer. He had even succeeded in forgetting his previous instruction. He no longer knew; he was now complete ingenuousness, a child stammering through catechism.

Thus, step by step, he had risen to the priesthood. His memories began to crowd against each other, each one unbearably moving, still warm with heavenly joy. Every year had brought him closer to God. He spent his vacations in sanctity at an uncle's house, confessing every day and taking Communion twice a week. He imposed fasts on himself, hid coarse salt blocks deep in his trunk and, his knees bare, knelt on them for hours at a time. He remained in the chapel during recreation or went to hear a director tell extraordinary pious anecdotes. Then, when the day of the Holy Trinity drew near, he was compensated beyond all measure, invaded by that emotion which fills seminaries on the eves of ordinations. It was the great celebration; heaven was opening to allow the elect to climb another step. He put himself on bread and water two weeks before the great day. He closed his curtains so as not to see even the light, prostrating himself in the shadows, begging Christ to accept his sacrifice. For the last four days, he was seized by anguish, by awful scruples which, in the middle of the night, took him out of his bed to knock on the door of an outside priest who was directing the retreat, some barefooted Carmelite, often a converted Protestant, who supposedly had an amazing history. He made at great length the general confession of his life, his voice broken by sobs. Only absolution tranquilized him, refreshed him as if he had been bathed in grace. He was all white on the morning of the great day, so acutely conscious of this whiteness that he felt he was radiating light. And the clear tones of the seminary bell rang out as the June smells of blooming stocks, mignonettes, and heliotrope came over the high courtyard wall. In the chapel, the waiting, well-dressed parents were so moved that the women were sobbing behind their veils. It was time for the procession: the deacons who were to enter the priesthood in gold chasubles; the underdeacons in dalmatics; the underclassmen, those who had just been tonsured, their surplices floating from their shoulders, their black bars in their hands. The organ boomed and spread about the flutelike notes of a psalm of holy joy. At the altar, the bishop, his crook in his hand, was officiating, assisted by two canons. The chapter was there, the priests from all the parishes pressing closer, amid an unheard-of luxury of dress, a blaze of gold lit by the large sunbeam falling from one of the nave windows. After the text, the ordination began.

Father Mouret still remembered the cold scissors which had tonsured him at the beginning of his first theology year. He had shivered slightly. But the tonsure was at that time very small, scarcely as large as a small coin. It had grown each time he entered a new order, always growing until it crowned him with a white spot as wide as a large wafer. And the organ grew softer; the silver noise of chains was heard as the censers released a cloud of white smoke which unfolded like lace. He saw himself in a surplice, recently tonsured, being led to the altar by the master of the ceremony; he knelt and bowed his head for the bishop to cut three locks of his hair with golden scissors, one over his forehead, the two others near his ears. He saw himself again one year later, in the chapel filled with incense, receiving the four minor orders. Led by an arch-deacon, he went to slam shut and reopen the large door to show that he was committed to guarding the church; he was ringing a bell in his right hand, thus announcing that he had the duty to call the faithful to services; he was returning to the altar, where the bishop conferred new privileges on him, those of singing the lesson, blessing bread, lighting and extinguishing candles, hearing children's catechism, exorcising the devil, serving deacons. Then the memory of the following ordination came back to him, more solemn, more awesome, surrounded by the song of the organs, whose rolling tones seemed to be the very thunder of God. That day, he had the dalmatic of an underdeacon on his shoulders; he was binding himself forever by the vow of chastity; despite his faith, all his flesh trembled at the bishop's terrible *"Accedite,"* which put to flight two of his comrades, who had been growing pale at his side. His new duties were to assist the priest at the altar, prepare the cruets, sing the psalm, rub the chalice, carry the cross in processions. And, finally, he filed one last time into the chapel under the rays of the June sun; but, this time, he walked at the head of the procession; he had the alb tied to his belt, the stole crossed on his chest, the chasuble falling from his neck; fainting from extreme emotion, he saw the pale face of the bishop who was to give him priesthood, the fullness of the ministry, by a triple laying on of hands. After the vow of ecclesiastical obedience, he felt as if he were being lifted from the floor as the prelate's full voice said the Latin sentence, *"Accipe Spiritum sanctum; quorum remiseris peccata, remittuntur eis, et quorum retineris, retenta sunt."*

◇◇◇◇◇◇◇◇◇◇◇◇◇◇◇◇◇◇◇◇◇◇◇◇◇◇◇◇◇◇◇◇◇◇

XVI EVOKING THE GREAT HAPPINESS OF HIS YOUTH HAD GIVEN Father Mouret a slight fever. He no longer felt the cold. He dropped the tongs, approached the bed as if to retire, then returned to lean his forehead against a window and stare with unseeing eyes at the night. Was he sick then, that his limbs were languid while his blood was burning his veins? At the seminary, he had twice had such an indisposition, a kind of physical anxiety which made him very ill; once he had even been delirious. And he thought of a possessed girl whom Brother Archangias said he had cured by a simple sign of the cross when she fell stiff before him. That made him think of the spiritual exercises one of his teachers had recommended: prayer, general confession, frequent Communion, the choice of a wise confessor with great power over his penitent's mind. And, with no transition, with a suddenness which astounded him, he saw at the back of his mind the round face of one of his friends, a peasant, a choirboy at eight, whose seminary expenses were paid by a lady who had taken him under her protection. He was always laughing; he openly enjoyed in advance the trade's little benefits: the twelve-hundred-franc stipend, the presbytery behind a garden, the gifts, the dinner invitations, the small profit from marriages, baptisms, burials. That one must be happy in his parish.

The melancholy regret awakened by this memory was a great surprise to the priest. Was he not happy as well? Until that day, he had regretted nothing, wanted nothing, envied nothing. And even now, his self-examination could uncover no reason for his bitterness. He thought he was exactly what he had been early in his deaconate, when the obligation to read his breviary at fixed times had filled his days with continuous prayer. From that time on, weeks, months, years flowed by without his having leisure for an evil thought. Doubt did not torment him in any way; he yielded before the mysteries he could not understand; he easily made the sacrifice of his reason, which he scorned. On leaving the seminary, he had been delighted to find that he was a stranger to other men, that he did not walk like them, that he carried his head differently, that he had the gestures, words, and feelings of a being apart. He felt feminized, drawn closer to the angels, washed free of sex, of his manly smell. It made him almost proud to be no longer part of the species, to have been raised for God, carefully purged of human filth by a jealous education. It seemed to him that he had for years been immersed in holy oil, prepared according to the rites, which had penetrated his flesh with the beginning of beatification. Certain organs had disappeared, dissolving away little by little; his limbs, his brain, had lost matter to be filled with spirit, with a subtle air which could make him so intoxicatingly dizzy that it seemed the earth had suddenly opened beneath his feet. He had the fears, ignorance, and candor of a cloistered girl. He sometimes smilingly said that he had never left childhood; he thought of himself as a very small boy with puerile sensations, ideas, and judgments; thus, at the age of six, he knew God as intimately as at twenty-five; the tones and inflections of his prayers had not changed; he still found the same joy in folding his hands just so. The world seemed to be like the world he saw when his mother held his hand to take him for a walk. He was born a priest, he had grown up as a priest. When he revealed some striking ignorance of life before la Teuse, she looked him in the eyes, stupefied, and said with a peculiar smile that he was "really Miss Désirée's brother." He could remember only one shameful shock in his whole life: during the last six months of seminary, between the deaconate and priesthood, they had made him read the work of Father Craisson, Father Superior at the large Valence seminary, *De rebus veneris ad usum confessariorum*. He was jolted and sobbing when he laid the book down. This sophisticated casuistry of vice, this revelation of man's abomination, descending to the most monstrous instances of unnatural passions, brutally raped his physical and mental virginity. He remained forever dirtied, like a bride painfully initiated into the violence of lust. And he fatally returned to that questionnaire of shame each time he heard confession. If dogma's obscurity, the priesthood's duties, the death of all free will, left him serene and smiling at being nothing but God's child, he retained despite himself the carnal shock of these obscenities he had been required to sift through; he was aware of an ineradicable spot somewhere in the depths of his being which could one day grow and cover him with mud.

The moon was rising behind the Garrigues. Father Mouret's fever burned hotter; he opened the window and leaned on his elbows to offer his face to the cool night. He no longer knew exactly when he had first felt ill. He remembered, however, that he had felt very calm, very rested, while saying the Mass that morning. It must have been later, perhaps during his long walk in the sun or under the quivering trees in Paradou or in the stifling barnyard with Désirée. And he relived the day.

The vast plain spread out before him, more tragic under the moon's oblique paleness. Olive trees, almond trees, slender trees, stood as gray spots amid the chaos of the great rocks stretching to the dark line of the hills on the horizon, large splotches of shadow, broken ridges, bloody spots of ground where the red stars appeared to be staring at one another; white chalk spots became the scattered clothes of rejected women whose flesh was drowned in shade as they lay dormant in the country's hollows. At night, this ardent country assumed the tortured arch of a woman consumed by lust. She slept, but the covers had been thrown aside; she swayed, twisted, passionately spread her legs, exhaled in great warm breaths the powerful smell of a beautiful, sleeping woman dripping with sweat. It was like some strong Cybele fallen on her back, her breasts outthrust, her belly under the moon, drunk with the sun's heat, forever dreaming of impregnation. Farther along this great body, Father Mouret's eyes followed the Olivettes road, a thin, pale ribbon hanging loose like the trailing string of a corset. He heard Brother Archangias raising the skirts of his girls before whipping them until blood flowed and spitting in their faces, and he breathed in the stench of this man who smelled like a billy goat whose desires could never be satisfied. He saw Rosalie laughing to herself like a lascivious animal while old Bambousse was throwing dirt clods at her back. And he thought he had still been well when he was with them, his neck barely warmed by the beautiful morning. At that time, he had felt only a rustling behind his back, this confused mutter of life, which he had first heard vaguely during morning Mass, when the sun came in through the smashed windows. Never had this country disturbed him so much as now, with its giant breasts, soft shadows, shining, perfumed skin, all this nakedness of a goddess barely hidden under the silvery muslin cast by the moon.

The young priest lowered his eyes to the village of Artauds. Heavy with fatigue, the town had collapsed into sleep, into the void which is peasant sleep. Not one light. The hovels formed black spots cut by the white stripes of the roads raked by the moon. The dogs themselves must be snoring on the sills of the closed doors. Perhaps the Artauds had poisoned the presbytery with some abominable scourge? He listened to the breathing come up behind him, growing ever louder, moving closer, filling him with anguish. Now he could distinguish something like a marching flock, a thick cloud of dust raised by a herd of animals. His thoughts of the morning came back to him: this handful of men beginning time again, growing among the bald rocks like a handful of thistles sown by the winds; he felt that he was witnessing the slow birth of a race. When he was a child, nothing surprised or frightened him more than those myriads of insects which he saw well up from a crack when he raised certain wet rocks. Even sleeping, exhausted in the shadows, the Artauds perturbed him; he found their smell in the air he was breathing. He would have liked to have nothing but rocks under his window. The village was not dead enough; the thatched roofs rose and fell like chests; the cracks in the doors let escape sighs, tiny noises, living silences, revealed the presence in this hole of a swarming litter cradled in black night. The smell was undoubtedly all that was nauseating him. And yet he had often breathed just as strong a smell without feeling any need other than that of refreshing himself in prayer.

His temples sweating, he went to open the other window in a quest for moving air. The cemetery stretched below, off to the left, surmounted by the tall bar of the Hermit, whose shadow was not disturbed by any breeze. The scent of new-mown grass rose from the empty field. The big gray church wall, this wall crawling with lizards, planted with wallflowers, was growing cold under the moon, while the panes of one of the wide windows shone like steel sheets. The sleeping church could live at this hour only with the extrahuman life of the God of the Host, enclosed in the tabernacle. He thought of the shadows eating the lamp's yellow spot and was tempted to go back down to relieve his sick head among these pure shadows free from every blemish. But a strange terror held him back; his eyes fixed on the panes lit by the moon, he suddenly thought he saw the inside of the church begin to glow like a bursting furnace, glow with the brilliance of an infernal celebration where the month of May, the plants, the animals, the daughters of the Artauds, frenetically grasping whole trees in their bare arms, all whirled in insane dance. Then, leaning over, he saw Désirée's barnyard, now completely black, smoking below him. He could not clearly distinguish the rabbits' boxes, hens' perches, duck's hut. It was one single pile of stench, the sleep of the same pestilential breath. The goat's bitter smell came from under the stable door, while the piglet, wallowing on its back, puffed heavily next to an empty basin. From his brass throat, the great wild rooster Alexander released a cry which awoke one by one the distant, passionate calls of every rooster in the village.

Suddenly, Father Mouret remembered. The fever whose pursuit he heard at his back had first struck him in Désirée's barnyard, with the hens still warm from their laying and the mother rabbits tearing fur from their bellies. Then the sensation of something breathing on his neck was so clear that he turned around to see at last who could be grasping him. And he remembered Albine leaping out of Paradou before the door slammed on the vision of an enchanted garden; he remembered her galloping along the endless wall, following the carriage, throwing birch leaves to the wind like so many kisses; he remembered her again at dusk, laughing at Brother Archangias' curses, her skirts fleeing down the road like a small cloud of dust rolled along by the evening breeze. She was sixteen; she was strange, her face a little too long; she smelled of the open air, grass, earth. And he had so precise a memory of her that he saw a scratch on one of her supple hands, showing pink against her white skin. Why was she laughing like that while she looked at him with her blue eyes? He was caught up in her laugher as in a deep wave which resounded against every part of his flesh; he breathed her, felt her vibrate inside him. Yes, all his trouble came from drinking that laughter.

Both windows were open; he was shivering in the middle of the room, in the grip of fear so overpowering that he hid his face in his hands. So the entire day was to end in this evocation of a blond girl with blue eyes whose face was a little too long? And the entire day came in through the two open windows. In the distance was the heat of the red land, the passion of the great rocks, of olive trees growing in stones, of vines twisting their arms around the edges of roads; nearer was the human sweat carried by the wind from Artauds, the flat smells of the cemetery, the odors of incense from the church, perverted by the odors of girls with thick hair; manure vapor, barnyard steam, suffocating fermentation of bacteria. And all these breaths thronged together in a single asphyxiating gust, so rough, building with such violence, that he could not breathe at all. He closed his senses, tried to annihilate them. But Albine reappeared before him like a large flower, growing and made beautiful on this dung heap. She was the natural flower of this filth, delicately opening the young bud of her white shoulders to the sun, so happy to be alive that she leaped from her stem, flew to his mouth, and perfumed him with her long laughter.

The priest cried out in pain. His lips had been burned; an ardent stream seemed to have flowed into his veins. Then he sought sanctuary by throwing himself to his knees before the figure of the Immaculate Conception, shouting, his hands clasped, "Holy Virgin of Virgins, pray for me!"

◇◇◇◇◇◇◇◇◇◇◇◇◇◇◇◇◇◇◇◇◇◇◇◇◇◇◇◇◇◇◇◇

XVII THE IMMACULATE CONCEPTION ON THE WALNUT CHEST smiled tenderly from the corner of thin lips indicated by a carmine stroke. She was small, all white; the long white veil falling from her head to her feet had only one imperceptible gold thread on its hem. The long straight folds of her dress covered her sexless body so completely that only her supple neck was revealed. Not one lock of her light-brown hair was visible. Her face pink, her clear eyes turned to heaven, she clasped pink hands, childish hands, whose fingertips came out of the folds just over the blue kerchief which seemed to tie two floating bits of firmament to her body. None of the seductive parts of the female body was bare, except her feet, feet adorably bare to press the mystical rosebush. And golden roses grew on the nakedness of her feet as the natural blossoms of her twice-pure flesh.

"Faithful Virgin, pray for me," repeated the priest desperately.

This one had never bothered him; she was not yet a mother; her arms did not hold Jesus out to him; her body did not have the rounded lines of fertility. She was not the Queen of Heaven descending crowned with gold, dressed in gold, like an earthly princess, triumphantly borne by a flock of cherubs. This one had never been awesome, had never talked to him with the sternness of an all-powerful mistress whose sight alone makes men bury their heads in the dust. He dared to look at her, to love her without fear of responding to the soft curve of her light-brown hair. Only her bare feet aroused his desire, feet of love blooming like a garden of chastity, blooming too miraculously for him to gratify his wish to fondle them. She perfumed the room with the odor of a lily. She was the silver lily set in a golden vase, precious, eternal, impeccable purity. In her white veil, clinging so tightly to her body, there was nothing human, nothing but a virgin fire burning in a never-diminishing flame. On going to bed at night, on arising in the morning, he found her there, the same ecstatic smile on her lips. Without embarrassment, he undressed before her as if nothing but his own modesty were in the room.

"Most pure Mother, most chaste Mother, Mother eternally virginal, pray for me!" he stammered in terror, seizing the Virgin's feet as if he heard Albine's echoing trot behind his back. "You are my refuge, cause of my joy, temple of my wisdom, tower of ivory where I have consigned my purity. I put myself in your spotless hands. I beg you to take me, to cover me with a corner of your veil, to hide me under your innocence, behind the sacred rampart of your garment, where no carnal breath can reach me. I need you; without you I die; we must be separated forever if you do not take me away. I beg you to enfold me in the succor of your arms, to take me far from here, take me to the burning whiteness in which you live. Mary conceived without sin, destroy me in the immaculate snow falling from each of your limbs. You are the prodigy of eternal chastity. Your race was born on a ray, like a marvelous tree grown from no seed. Your son Jesus was born of the breath of God; you yourself were born without your mother's womb being defiled, and I must believe that this virginity goes from age to age in endless ignorance of the flesh. Oh, to live, to grow, outside the shame of the senses! Oh, to multiply, to have children, without the abominable necessity of sex, under the simple approach of a heavenly kiss!"

This desperate appeal, this cry purified of desire, reassured the young priest. The Virgin, completely white, her eyes to heaven, seemed to smile more sweetly with her thin pink lips. He began again with even more feeling. "I want to be a child again. I want never to be anything but a child walking in the shadow of your dress. When I was very small, I folded my hands to say the name of Mary. My cradle was white, my body was white, all my thoughts were white. I saw you distinctly, I heard you call me, I went to you in a smile of rose petals. And nothing else. I did not feel, I did not think, I lived barely enough to be a flower at your feet. Men should not grow up. Only blond heads should surround you, only a race of children who love you, their hands pure, their lips healthy, their limbs tender, without dirt, as if they were slipping out of a bath of milk. You kiss a child's soul on his cheek. Only a child can say your name without making it dirty. Later, the mouth is spoiled and poisons all passions. Even I, who love you so much, who have given myself to you, even I do not dare call you. I must not force you to touch my male impurity. I have prayed, I have chastised my flesh, I have slept under your guard, I have lived chaste; and I am crying, I see today that I am not yet dead enough to the world to be your betrothed. O Mary, adorable Virgin, why am I not five years old, why did I not remain the child who pressed his lips against your picture? I would take you to my heart, I would lay you by my side, I would kiss you like a friend, like a girl my own age. I would possess your clinging dress, your childish veil, your blue kerchief, all this childhood which makes you my big sister. I would not try to kiss your hair, for hair is naked; no one should see it. But I would kiss your bare feet one after the other, for whole nights at a time, until my lips had plucked all the petals from the golden roses, from the mystical roses of your veins."

He stopped to wait for the Blessed Virgin to lower her blue eyes and touch his forehead with the edge of her veil. The Blessed Virgin was still covered by muslin to her neck, to her fingernails, to her toes. She belonged entirely to heaven; her body rose like a thing without weight, released from earth.

"Please," he cried, more desperate now, "make me a child again, kind Virgin, powerful Virgin. Make me five years old. Take my senses, take my virility. Let a miracle destroy the man which has grown in me. You reign in heaven; nothing is so easy for you as to strike me down, dry up my organs, leave me sexless, incapable of evil, so deprived of strength that I cannot raise even my little finger without your consent. I want to be open with this openness which is yours, which no human spasm can disturb. I do not want to feel my nerves, or my muscles, or the beating of my heart, or the labor of my desires. I want to be a thing, a white stone at your feet, into which you will allow but one perfume, a stone which will not budge from the place where you have thrown it, a stone without ears, without eyes, completely satisfied to be under your heel, to be as incapable of thinking filth as other stones of the field. Oh, what a blessed state! My first attempt will allow me to attain effortlessly the perfection I dream of. I will finally proclaim myself your true priest. I will be what my studies, my prayers, my five years of slow initiation, could not make me. Yes, I deny life; I say that the death of the species is preferable to the continuous abomination which propagates it. Sin makes everything dirty. Universal stench spoiling love, spoiling the bridal chamber, spoiling the newborn baby's cradle, spoiling even the flowers swooning under the sun, even the trees sprouting their buds. Earth bathes in this impurity whose smallest drops spew forth shameful growths. But for me to be perfect, O Queen of Angels, Queen of Virgins, hear my cry, answer it! Make me one of those angels who have only two big wings behind their cheeks; I would not have trunk or limbs; I should fly to you if you called me; I shall be only a mouth singing your praise, a pair of spotless wings cradling your voyages in the heavens. Oh, death, death, venerable Virgin, give me death to all things. I will love you in the death of my body, in the death of that which lives and propagates. I will consummate with you the only marriage my heart desires; I will go higher, always higher, until I have reached the fire where you shine resplendently. The great star, the immense white rose whose every petal burns like a moon, silver throne from which you radiate with such glowing innocence that all paradise is lit by the light from your veil alone. All that is white in the world, the dawn, the snow of inaccessible peaks, the barely open lilies, the milk of plants revered by the sun, the smiles of virgins, the souls of children who died in their cradles, all these rain on your white feet. Then I will rise to your lips like a subtle flame, I will enter you through your half-open mouth, and the wedding will take place while archangels tremble at our gladness. To be a virgin, to love as a virgin, to retain virginal whiteness in the sweetest kisses! To possess all love has to offer, lying on the wings of swans, in a cloud of purity, in the arms of a mistress of light whose caresses are joys to the soul! Perfection, superhuman dream, desire cracking my bones, delights transporting me to heaven! O Mary, chosen Vessel, castrate the humanity in me, make me a eunuch among men, and deliver fearlessly unto me the treasure of your virginity."

And Father Mouret, his teeth chattering wildly, was struck down by his fever and fainted on the floor.

BOOK TWO

◇◇◇

I THE DAWN LIGHT, FILTERED THROUGH THE CAREFULLY DRAWN calico curtains on the two wide windows, lit the spacious bedroom with its high ceilings and old wooden Louis XV furniture, painted white and decorated by red flowers and scattered foliage. In the recesses above the doors on both sides of the alcove, paintings still displayed the pink bellies and rumps of little cupids flying in groups, playing at games obscured by time; the wainscoting surrounded oval panels, double doors, a round ceiling once painted sky blue, and held framed scrolls, medals, knots of flesh-colored ribbon, all of which was deteriorating into a very gentle gray, a gray which retained something of the emotion of this faded paradise. Across from the windows, the large alcove opened under fluffy clouds spread apart by plaster cupids, leaning forward, tumbling over in a brazen attempt to see the bed; like the windows, it was enclosed by calico curtains, woven so primitively that they suggested a peculiar innocence in this room still redolent with a remote odor of sensuality.

Seated by a table on which a kettle was heating over a kerosene lamp, Albine attentively studied the alcove curtains. Dressed in white, her hair tucked into an old lace kerchief, her hands by her sides, she kept watch with the gravity of a woman. Weak breathing, the breath of a feeble child, could be heard in the great silence. But, after a few minutes, she became worried and could not restrain herself from tiptoeing over to raise a corner of the curtain. Serge lay apparently sleeping on the enormous bed, his head on one of his folded arms. His hair and beard had grown during his illness. Very pale, his eyes sunken, his lips white, he had the grace of a convalescent girl.

Albine, moved by this sight, was about to drop the curtain. "I'm not asleep," Serge said in a very tired voice. And he did not move his head, did not move at all, as if he were prostrated by happy fatigue. His eyes had slowly opened, his breath was lightly hitting one of his bare hands and raising the hairs on

99

his pale skin. "I heard you," he muttered again. "You were walking very quietly." He used the familiar *tu* with her, and she was overjoyed. She came and crouched by the bed to bring her face level with his. "How are you?" she asked, using *tu* in her turn and relishing the sweetness of this new means of address passing her lips for the first time. "Oh, you're well now," she went on. "Do you know that I cried all the way home when I went down to your place and they had bad news for me? They told me you were delirious; they said this awful fever would ruin your mind if it spared your life . . . How I kissed your uncle Pascal when he brought you to get well here!"

She was tucking in the covers as if she were his mother. "You see, those scorched rocks down there weren't good for you. You need trees, coolness, peace . . . The doctor didn't even tell anyone he was hiding you here. It's a secret between him and those who love you. He thought there was no hope . . . Now, nobody will bother you. Uncle Jeanbernat smokes his pipe by his greens. The others will come on the sly to see how you're doing. And even the doctor himself won't come back anymore because, from now on, I'm your doctor . . . It looks like you don't need drugs anymore. You need to be loved, do you understand?"

He gave no sign that he heard; his brain was still empty. Without moving his head, he looked around the room, and she thought he was worried about waking up in a strange place.

"It's my room," she said. "I've given it to you. It's nice, isn't it? I took the best furniture from the attic, then I made these calico curtains so the light wouldn't blind you . . . And you're not any bother at all. I'll sleep on the third floor. There are still three or four rooms empty."

But he was still worried. "Are you alone?" he asked.

"Yes. Why do you want to know that?"

He made no reply but simply muttered anxiously, "I was dreaming; I'm always dreaming. I hear bells, and that's what makes me tired." After a silence, he went on: "Go close the door and latch it. I want you to be alone, completely alone."

When she came back with a chair and sat at the head of the

bed, he was as happy as a child and kept repeating, "Now nobody can come in. I won't hear the bells anymore. I'm not tired when you talk."

"Do you want anything to drink?" she asked.

He gestured to show that he was not thirsty. He was watching Albine's hands and looked so surprised, so charmed to see them, that she smiled and put one next to the pillow. Then he let his head slide down and leaned his cheek against that small, cool hand. He laughed softly and said, "Ah, it's soft as silk. It feels like it's fanning my hair. Don't take it away. Please!"

Then they were both silent for a long time. They were looking into each other's eyes with great friendliness. Albine could see herself in her patient's vacant eyes. Serge seemed to be listening to something indistinct being whispered in his ear by the small, cool hand.

"It's really good, your hand," he said. "You can't imagine how good it is for me. It feels like it's going deep into me to take away the pain in my limbs. It's a caress everywhere, a great relief, a cure." He gently rubbed her cheek and became alive again. "Promise you won't give me something awful to drink, you won't torture me with all kinds of medicine. Your hand's enough, you know. I came for you to put it there, under my head."

"My good Serge," Albine whispered, "you've suffered a lot, haven't you?"

"Suffered? Yes, yes, but it was long ago. I couldn't sleep, I had frightful dreams. I'd tell you all about it if I could." He closed his eyes for a while in a great attempt to remember. "All I see is darkness," he stammered. "It's strange. I'm ending a long trip. I don't know where I left from. I had a fever, a fever running through my veins like an animal . . . It was like that, I remember now. Always the same nightmare; it made me crawl alone in an endless cavern. And then I would be in great pain and the cavern would suddenly be walled up; a pile of rocks would fall from the ceiling, the walls would come to get me. I panted with rage because I wanted to go beyond. So I flung myself against the obstacle, I struggled with my feet, my fists, my skull, and all the time I knew with more and more certainty that I would never get out of that cavern. But often, all I had to do was touch it with my finger; everything disappeared, and I walked freely in a wider passage. I was fatigued only because of the emotion I felt."

Albine tried to put her hand on his mouth.

"No, I can talk without getting tired. You see, I'm talking in your ear. It's as if I'm only thinking and you understand me. The funniest thing in my cavern was that it never occurred to me to go back. I just got more stubborn, even when I realized it would take thousands of years to clear just one of the cave-ins. It was a task assigned by fate that I had to accomplish or be punished even more. My knees bled; my forehead beat against the rocks; I was both conscientious and terrified as I worked as hard as I could to get there as soon as possible. Get where? I don't know, I don't know."

He closed his eyes, dreaming, searching. Then he pouted nonchalantly and again abandoned himself to Albine's hand, saying with a laugh, "It's just dumb. I'm like a baby."

But to see if he were really all hers, the girl questioned him, brought him back to the tangled memories he was trying to evoke. He remembered nothing; he was truly in happy childhood. He felt he had been born the day before.

"Oh, I'm not well yet. You see, the farthest back I can remember is being in a bed which burned my whole body; my head rolled on the pillow as if it were a forge. I wore the skin off my fists by rubbing them against each other all the time. Oh, I was really sick. It seemed people were exchanging my body for another one, that they were taking everything from me, that they were repairing me like a broken machine."

This conceit made him laugh again, and he went on: "I'm going to be all new. Being sick was really a way to cleanse me. But what did you say? No, no one was there. I was suffering all alone deep in a black hole. No one, no one. And, beyond that, there's nothing, I see nothing . . . I'm your child, is that all right? You'll teach me to walk. I see you and nothing else now. I don't care about anything that's not you. I tell you I don't remember now. I came, you took me, and that's all."

And he calmed down a little and said again, caressingly,

"Your hand is warm now; it's as nice as sunlight. Let's don't talk anymore. I'm getting hot."

In the spacious room a shimmering silence fell from the blue ceiling. The kerosene lamp had just gone out, leaving the kettle spewing a smaller and smaller jet of steam. Albine and Serge, their heads on the same pillow, were watching the large calico curtains drawn before the windows. Serge's eyes especially focused on them, as if he were seeing the white source of all light. He bathed himself there as if this were daylight adjusted particularly to his convalescent strength. He found the sun behind a yellow spot in the calico—that was enough to cure him. He listened to a deep rustling of leaves in the distance while the greenish shadow of a tall branch, clearly drawn on the right-hand window, held him with disturbing dreams of the forest he felt so near.

"Do you want me to open the curtains?" Albine asked, mistakenly interpreting the meaning of his gaze.

"No, no," he replied hurriedly.

"It's lovely out. You could have the sun. You could see the trees."

"No, please, I beg you. I don't want anything from outside. That branch there makes me tired by moving and growing like something alive. Leave me your hand, I want to sleep. Everything is white . . . That's good." And he went trustingly to sleep, watched over by Albine, who blew on his face to cool his slumber.

❖❖❖❖❖❖❖❖❖❖❖❖❖❖❖❖❖❖❖❖❖❖❖❖❖❖❖❖❖❖❖

II THE NEXT DAY, THE FAIR WEATHER HAD DISAPPEARED. IT was raining. Serge's fever returned; he suffered all day, his eyes desperately fixed on the curtains, from which came only a cavernous, sinister light, gray as ashes. He could no longer find the sun; he searched for that shadow which had made him afraid, that tall limb which, drowned in the dark blur of the downpour, seemed to have made the entire forest vanish with itself. Toward evening, shaken by a slight convulsion, he sobbed and cried to Albine that the sun had died, that he heard all heaven and earth weeping to mourn the sun's death. She had to console him like a child, promise him the sun, assure him that it would come back, that she would give it to him. He pitied the plants as well. The seeds must be in agony underground, waiting for the sun. They shared his nightmares, they dreamed that they were crawling along a cavern blocked by cave-ins, that they were struggling furiously to reach the sun. And he began to weep more softly, saying that winter was a disease of the earth, that he was going to die with the earth if spring did not come to cure them both.

The weather was frightful for three more days. Heavy showers burst against the trees with the distant noise of a river in flood; gusts of wind rolled and crashed against the windows with the fury of enormous waves. Serge had insisted that Albine seal the shutters hermetically. With the lamp lit, those pale curtains no longer seemed to be in mourning; he no longer felt the gray sky come in through the thinnest cracks and flow to his bed, like dust burying him. He gave himself up, his arms thin, his face pale, growing weaker as the countryside grew sicker. Under certain ink-black clouds, when the twisted trees cracked and the earth let its plants trail under the rain like the hair of a drowned woman, he lost even his power to breathe; he expired, defeated by the hurricane. Then, at the first sign of a clear sky, at the least bit of blue between two clouds, he breathed again, relishing the relaxation of the cleansed leaves, the whitened paths, and the fields gulping their last swallow of water. Now Albine too began to implore the sun; she went to the landing window twenty times a day to question the horizon, overjoyed at the smallest white spots, distressed at the lurid masses of shadow, loaded with hail, continuously afraid of some overly dark cloud that would kill her beloved invalid. She talked of sending for Dr. Pascal. But Serge wanted no one and said, "Tomorrow the sun will be on the curtains, and I shall be cured."

One night, when he was weakest, Albine gave him her hand to put his cheek on. And she cried to see herself impotent when her hand had no effect. Since he had sunk back into the dead of winter, she had not felt strong enough to pull him out of the nightmare in which he was floundering. She needed the complicity of spring. She herself was wasting away, her arms icy, her breath short, no longer knowing how to breathe life into him. For hours she paced the spacious, saddened room. When she passed the mirror, she saw herself black and believed herself ugly.

Then, one morning, as she was fluffing up the pillows without daring to try the broken magic of her hands, the tips of her fingers brushed against his neck, and she thought she saw the smile of the first day on Serge's lips.

"Open the shutters," he muttered.

She thought he was delirious; one hour earlier, she had seen only a mournful sky from the landing window. "Go back to sleep," she said sadly. "I promised to wake you at the first ray of sun. Sleep some more, the sun isn't there."

"Yes, I feel it, the sun is there. Open the shutters."

III AND THE SUN WAS THERE. WHEN ALBINE OPENED THE shutters behind the wide curtains, the good yellow light again warmed a section of the cloth's whiteness. But what made Serge sit up in bed was to see once more the shadow of the branch, of the bough which proclaimed a return to life. All the resuscitated countryside, with its vegetation, its waters, its wide circle of hills, was there for him in this greenish spot quivering at the slightest breath of air. It no longer perturbed him. He avidly followed it as it swayed; he needed the strength of sap which it announced. Albine, supporting him in her arms, said joyously, "Ah, my good Serge, winter is over—we're saved now."

He lay down again, his eyes already shining, his voice firmer. "Tomorrow," he said, "I shall be stronger. You will open the curtains. I want to see it all."

But the next day he was gripped by childish fear. He never consented to have the windows opened wide. He muttered, "In a little while, later," and remained anxious, fearful of receiving the first burst of light in his eyes. Night came, and he had still not been able to make up his mind to have the sun full on him once more. He had kept his face turned to the curtains, following on the transparent cloth the pale morning, the burning noon, the violet dusk, all the sky's colors and emotions. There he saw painted the shiver sent through the warm air by a bird beating its wings, the joy of the smells shimmering in a sunbeam. Behind this veil, behind this emotional dream of the powerful life outside, he listened to spring rising. And at times he even felt stifled when the rush of the earth's new blood came to him too roughly, despite the obstacle of the curtains.

And, the following morning, he was still asleep when Albine, rushing his cure, shouted to him, "Serge, Serge! Here is the sun!"

She rapidly drew the curtains and opened the windows wide. He sat up, knelt in bed, suffocating, collapsing, his hands clasped to his chest to stop his heart from bursting. The big sky was before him, nothing but blue, an infinite blue; he washed away his suffering in it, gave himself up to it as to gentle, cradling arms, drank sweetness, purity, and youth from it. Only the branch whose shadow he had seen rose past the window to spot the blue sea with vigorous green; and the flow was already too strong; his invalid weakness was wounded by the stain of swallows flying on the horizon. He was being born. Short, involuntary cries burst from his lips; he was drowned in light, beaten by waves of warm air, and he felt a vast gulf of life pour over him and into him. His hands stretched out as he collapsed on his pillow in a faint.

What a happy, moving day! The sun entered from the right, far from the alcove. All morning long, Serge watched it advance little by little, saw it come to him, yellow as gold, chipping the old furniture, playing games in the corners, sometimes sliding across the floor like a bale of cloth unrolling. It was a slow, confident march, the approach of a lover stretching her fair limbs, moving rhythmically to reach the alcove, displaying voluptuous slowness which created an insane desire to possess her. Finally, around two o'clock, the square of sunlight left the last chair, climbed along the covers, and lay on the bed like hair hanging loose. Serge gave his thin, convalescent hands to this hot caress; his eyes half-closed, he felt kisses of fire run across each of his fingers; clasped by a star, he was in a bath of light. And when Albine came to lean over and smile, "Go away," he stammered, his eyes completely closed, "don't hold me so tight. How do you manage to hold me that way, all of me in your arms?"

Then the sun retraced its steps down the bed, marching slowly away on the left. And Serge watched it turn again, sit on one chair after another, sorrowful that he could not keep it on his chest. Albine had remained at the edge of the bed. Their arms around each other's neck, they both watched the sky grow paler and paler. An immense shudder occasionally seemed to whiten it with sudden emotion. Serge's languor played at ease there, found exquisite subtleties which he had never suspected. It was not all blue, but pinkish blue, lilac blue, yellowish blue, living flesh, a vast, immaculate nakedness, palpitating with each breath like a woman's breasts. Whenever he looked into the distance, he was surprised to see unknown corners of the air, discreet smiles, adorable curves, gauze hiding the superb, great bodies of goddesses deep in occasionally glimpsed paradises. And he flew away, his limbs lightened by suffering, amid this changing silk, in this innocent down of azure, his sensations floating above his failing being. The sun sank, the blue melted into pure gold, the sky's living flesh grew even lighter, slowly drowned by all the shade of night. Not one cloud, the retreat of a virgin going to bed, undressing, but revealing only a stripe of modesty on the horizon. The big sky was asleep.

"Oh, the dear baby," Albine said as she watched Serge, who had, at the same time as the sky, gone to sleep on her shoulder. She put him to bed and closed the windows. But at dawn the next morning they were open. Serge could no longer live without the sun. He gathered strength, grew accustomed to the puffs of air which made the alcove curtains fly. Even the blue, the eternal blue, was beginning to be insipid. It tired him to be a swan, a spot of white swimming forever on the clear lake of the sky. He finally wished for the arrival of black clouds, some destructive clouds to break the monotony of this vast purity.

As his health returned, he came to need stronger sensations. Now he spent hours watching the green limb; he wanted to see it grow, expand, send shoots all the way to his bed. It was not enough; it only awakened his desires by speaking to him of other trees, whose deep calls he heard without being able to make out their tops. There was infinite whispering of leaves, conversations of running waters, beating of wings, a complete high, prolonged, vibrating voice.

"When you can get up," Albine said, "you can sit by the window. You can look at the beautiful garden."

He closed his eyes and murmured, "Oh, I see it, I listen to it. I know where the trees are, where the streams are, where the violets grow." Then he went on, "But I see them dimly, I see them without light. I must grow stronger and go to the window."

Sometimes, when she thought he was asleep, Albine dis-appeared for hours. And, when she returned, she found him eaten by impatience, his eyes shining from curiosity. He shouted to her, "Where have you been?"

And he took her arms, smelled her skirts, her shirt, her cheeks. "You smell of all good things," he repeated, delighted. "I knew it. When you came in, you seemed to be a great flower. You bring me all the garden in your dress." He kept her near him, breathing her in like a bouquet. Sometimes she returned with thorns, leaves, and twigs stuck to her clothes. Then he picked these things off and hid them under his pillow like relics. One day she brought him a cluster of roses. He was so moved that he began to cry. He kissed the flowers and went to bed with them clasped in his arms. But when they faded, he was so upset that he forbade Albine to pick more. He preferred her, just as fresh, just as perfumed; and she did not fade; she always kept the odor of her hands, the odor of her hair, the odor of her cheeks. He finally sent her to the garden himself, telling her not to return for an hour.

"You see, that way," he said, "I have sun, I have air, I have roses until the next day." Often, seeing her come in out of breath, he would question her. Which walk had she taken? Had she gone under the trees or had she stayed on the edge of the meadows? Had she seen any birds' nests? Had she sat down behind a wild rosebush or under an oak or in the shade of a group of poplars? Then, when she answered, when she tried to explain the garden to him, he put his hand on her mouth. "No, no, keep quiet," he muttered. "I'm wrong. I don't want to know. I prefer to see for myself."

And he fell back into his favorite dream of this greenery he felt near him, two steps away. For several days, he lived only on this dream. At first, he said, he had seen the garden more clearly. As he gathered strength, his dream was agitated by the rush of blood warming his veins. He felt increasing uncertainty. Now he could not say if the trees were on the right, if the streams flowed at the back, if great rocks were not piled beneath his windows. He spoke to himself about it, very softly. On the slightest evidence, he erected marvelous designs which a bird's song, a limb's crack, a flower's perfume made him modify, to plant there a clump of lilacs, to replace a lawn farther on with flower beds. Each hour he would outline another garden, to the sound of Albine's laughter. When she surprised him, she would say, "That's not it, I assure you. You can't imagine. It's more beautiful than all the beautiful things you've ever seen. So don't crack your skull over it. The garden is mine, and I'll give it to you. Don't worry, it won't go away."

Serge, who had already been afraid of the light, was again worried when he felt strong enough to lean on the windowsill. Once more he said "Tomorrow" every evening. He turned to the wall, trembling, when Albine cried to him that she smelled the hawthorn, that she had scratched her hands by hollowing out a hole in the hedge to bring him all its scent. One morning, she suddenly took him in her arms and almost carried him to the window, holding him up, forcing him to see.

"Are you ever a coward!" she said in her lovely deep voice. And she waved one of her hands to all points of the compass, repeating in a triumphant voice filled with tender promises, "Paradou! Paradou!" Speechless, Serge looked at it.

IV A SEA OF GREENERY, STRAIGHT AHEAD, TO THE RIGHT, TO
the left, everywhere. A sea whose surging leaves rolled to the
horizon without the obstacle of a house, a wall, or a dusty road.
A deserted sea, virginal, sacred, spreading its wild sweetness in
the innocence of solitude. Only the sun was allowed in, to
gambol like a golden cover in the meadows, to file through the
walks in the wild race of its beams, to let its fine flaming hair
hang across the trees, to drink at the springs, its pale lip touching the water with a shudder, Under this powder of flames, the
vast garden was as exuberantly alive as a happy animal released
at the end of the world, far from everything, free from everything. There was such an orgy of foliage, such an overflowing
tide of plants, that it was as if he were emptied from head to
toe, inundated, drowned. Nothing but green slopes, shoots
springing up like fountains, frothing masses, forest curtains
hermetically drawn, cloaks of trailing plants spread over the
ground, flocks of gigantic branches pushing against each other
from all sides.

Under this awesome invasion of sap, it was difficult to recognize the old plan of Paradou. Straight ahead, in a kind of
immense amphitheater, was what must have been the flower
garden, with its crushed pools, broken steps, buckled stairs,
overturned statues, whose whiteness could be seen at the rear of
the dark lawns. Farther on, behind the blue line of a pool of
water, was spread a jumble of fruit trees; still farther, a high
wood hid its violet undergrowth shot by stripes of sunshine, a
forest become virgin again, whose treetops, spotted with yellowish green, pale green, green strong from all smells, thrust
up like breasts. On the right, the forest scaled heights, planted
small pines, died in thin scrubs on an enormous slope of bare
rocks, a collapsed mountain barring the horizon, where ardent
vegetation cracked the earth and monstrous plants lay immobile in the sun like reptiles relaxing. A stream of silver, a
spattering which from the distance resembled a dust cloud of
pearls, indicated the waterfall, the source of these calm waters

running so indolently along the flower beds. Finally, on the left, the river flowed through a vast meadow and divided into four streams, whose capricious wandering took them under the reeds, between the willows, behind the great trees; as far as the eye could see, clumps of greenery increased the coolness of the low land: landscape washed in bluish vapor, light of day melting little by little into the greenish blue of dusk. Paradou, flower garden, forest, rocks, waters, meadows, held the vastness of the sky.

"Paradou!" stammered Serge, opening his arms as if to clasp all the garden to his chest. He staggered. Albine had to help him into an armchair. There he remained, without speaking, for two hours. His chin in his hands, he was watching. At times his eyelids flickered and a flush rose to his cheeks. He was watching slowly, with profound astonishment. It was too vast, too complex, too strong. "I don't see, I don't understand," he cried as he held his hands out to Albine in a gesture of supreme fatigue.

Then the girl leaned against the back of the chair. She took his head, forced him to look again, and told him in a soft voice, "It's ours. No one will come. When you're well, we'll take walks. We have enough to walk in all our life. We'll go where you want to . . . Where do you want to go?"

He smiled and murmured, "Oh, not far. The first day, two steps from the door. You see, I would fall. Look, I'll go there, under that tree near the window."

She said softly, "Do you want to go into the flower garden? You'd see the rosebushes, the big flowers that have eaten everything, even the old paths where they sow new clumps. Or would you rather see the orchard, where the fruit makes the limbs hang so low I have to lie flat on my belly to move around. We'll go even farther if you feel strong enough. We'll go to the forest, into the shade, very far away, so far we'll sleep outside when night comes and surprises us. Or one morning we'll climb up on the rocks. You'll see plants that frighten me. You'll see the springs, a rain of water, and we'll have fun letting its tiny drops hit our faces. But if you'd rather walk along the hedges by a stream, we'll have to go to the meadow.

It's nice under the willows at night, when the sun goes down. You stretch out in the grass, you watch little green frogs jump on rushes."

"No, no," Serge said. "You're making me tired. I don't want to see so far. I'll go a couple of steps. That'll be an awful lot."

"Even I," she went on, "even I haven't been able to go everywhere yet. There're a lot of places I don't know about. I've been taking walks for years, and I still feel unknown holes around me, places where the shade must be cooler, the grass softer . . . Listen, I've always thought there must be one place especially, where I'd like to live forever. It's certainly somewhere; I must have passed by it, or maybe it's hidden so far away that I haven't come to it yet, despite the way I've been wandering all the time. Okay, Serge? We'll look for it together, we'll live there."

"No, no, keep quiet," stammered the young man. "I don't understand what you're saying to me. You're making me die."

She let him cry in her arms for a while, upset, distressed at not finding the words to calm him. "Isn't Paradou as nice as your dreams?" she asked again.

He pulled his face away and replied, "I don't know anymore. It was very small, and now it grows and grows. Take me away, hide me!"

She led him to his bed, soothing him like a baby, cradling him with a lie. "Well, all right, no, it's not true, there isn't any garden. It's just a story I made up to tell you. Sleep well."

◇◇◇◇◇◇◇◇◇◇◇◇◇◇◇◇◇◇◇◇◇◇◇◇◇◇◇◇◇◇◇◇◇◇◇◇◇

V EVERY DAY, SHE MADE HIM SIT THUS BY THE WINDOW IN the cool of the day. Using the furniture to support himself, he even risked taking a few steps. His cheeks were touched with pink, his hands lost their wax transparency. But, in this convalescence, he was gripped by a stupor of his senses, which carried him back to the vegetative life of a poor thing born the day before. He was nothing but a plant, felt nothing but the air in which he was growing. He remained turned in on himself, his blood still too poor for him to spend himself outside, touching the ground, letting all his body's sap be drunk. It was a second conception, a slow hatching in the warm egg of spring. Albine, who remembered some of Dr. Pascal's words, was very much afraid to see him remain a little boy, innocent, stupefied. She had heard that certain diseases leave behind them insanity as their cure. And she forgot herself for hours, watching him, striving like a mother to smile at him in order to make him smile back. He still did not laugh. When she passed her hand before his eyes, he did not see, he did not follow its shadow. When she talked to him, he scarcely turned his head toward the noise. She had only one consolation: he was really growing, he was a handsome child.

Then came a week of delicate care. She patiently waited for him to grow up. She noticed certain signs of awakening and reassured herself, believing that age would still make a man out of this. First, there was a slight trembling when she touched him. Then, one night, he gave a feeble laugh. The next day, after putting him by the window, she went down to the garden and began to run and call to him. She disappeared under the trees, ran through patches of sunlight, and returned, out of breath, to clap her hands. At first, his eyes flickering, he did not see her. But as she was starting her race again, playing peek-a-boo once more, leaping behind every bush while shouting to him, his eyes finally began to follow the white spot of the skirt she was wearing. And when she suddenly stood beneath the window, her face raised, he held out his arms and seemed to want to go to her. She came back up and kissed him, as proud as could be.

"Ah, you saw me, you saw me," she cried. "You want to come to the garden with me, don't you? If you knew how you've upset me the past few days, acting like an animal, not seeing me, not hearing me!" He seemed to be listening to her with an effort which bent his neck in frightening motions. "Still, you're better," she added. "Now you're strong enough to go down when you want to. Why don't you tell me anything now? Cat got your tongue? Oh, what a brat! You'll see, I'll have to teach him to speak."

And, in fact, she amused herself by telling him the name of

the objects he touched. He only babbled; he doubled the number of syllables in every word, pronounced nothing clearly. Nevertheless, she began to walk him about the room. She held him up, led him from the bed to the window. It was a great trip. He almost fell two or three times on the way, which made her laugh. One day, he sat on the floor, and it was a lot of trouble to get him back up. Then she made him walk around the room, helped him rest on the sofa, armchairs, and straight-backed chairs, a walk around this little world which required a full hour. Finally, he could try a few steps all alone. She stood in front of him, called him as she walked backward, so that he had to cross the room to regain the support of her arms. When he was stubborn, when he refused to walk, she took out her comb and held it to him like a toy. Then he came to get it and remained peacefully in a corner, playing with it for hours, gently scratching his hands.

One morning, Albine found Serge already up. He had succeeded in opening a shutter and was trying to walk without leaning on the furniture. "Just look at him, what a big strong man," she said happily. "Tomorrow he'll jump out the window if we leave him alone . . . So we're all strong again now?"

Serge replied with a boyish laugh. His limbs had regained the health of adolescence, but no more conscious sensation had been awakened in him. He stared at Paradou for hours on end, on his face the expression of a child who sees nothing but white, who hears only the vibration of noises. He kept his infant ignorance, his sense of touch still so innocent that it did not allow him to distinguish between Albine's dress and the material covering the old armchairs. And there was always the astonishment of wide-open eyes which do not understand, hesitating movements not knowing how to go where they want, a beginning of existence, purely instinctive outside knowledge of his surroundings. The man was not born.

"Fine, fine, be an animal," Albine muttered. "We'll see." She took out her comb and offered it to him. "Do you want my comb?" she said. "Come get it." Then, when she had backed up so far that he was out of the bedroom, she put her arm around him and supported him on every step. She amused him even while putting her comb back into place, tickled his neck with her hair, and thus prevented him from realizing that he was going downstairs. But, at the bottom of the steps, before she had opened the door, the hall shadows frightened him.

"Have a look, just have a look!" she cried. And she opened the door wide.

It was a sudden dawn, a curtain of shadow abruptly drawn, revealing the day in its morning joy. The park opened, spread in green clarity, cool and deep as a spring. Charmed, Serge remained in the doorway with the hesitant desire to dip his foot in this lake of light.

"It looks like you're afraid of getting wet," said Albine. "Come on, the ground is solid."

He had risked one step, surprised at the sand's soft resistance. This first contact with the earth gave him a shock, a new upsurge of life, which infused his body and made him stand erect, grow tall, breathe hard.

"Come on, be brave," repeated Albine. "You know you promised me to go five steps. We'll go to that mulberry tree under the window. You can rest there."

It took him a quarter of an hour to take the five steps. He stopped after each effort, as if he had had to pull up the roots holding him to the ground. The girl, who was pushing him, said laughingly, "You look like a tree walking."

And she put his back against the mulberry tree, under the rain of sun falling from its branches. Then she left him; she leaped away, telling him not to move. Serge, his hands at his sides, slowly turned his head to face the park. It was childhood. The pale greenery was drowning in milk of childhood, bathing in pale light. The trees remained boyish, the flowers had a baby's flesh, the waters were blue with the trusting blue of beautiful eyes opened wide. There was everywhere, even under each leaf, a charming awakening.

Serge had stopped at a yellow gap which the walk opened in the middle of the thick mass of foliage before him; at the very end, to the east, meadows soaked in gold seemed to be the field of light where the sun set; and he waited for the morning to take this walk and flow to him. He felt it come in a warm breath, very weak at first, barely touching his skin, then expanding little by little, so sharp that his whole body shuddered. He tasted it coming, its flavor gradually more distinct, bringing him the healthy tang of open air, putting to his lips the feast of sweet spices, bitter fruits, fragrant woods. He smelled it coming with the perfumes which he picked as they ran, the smell of warm plants, the smell of living animals, a complete bouquet of smells whose violence made him dizzy. He heard it coming with the graceful flight of a bird, skimming the plants, pulling the entire garden out if its silence, giving voices to all it touched, making the music of things and beings ring in his ears. He saw it coming from the end of the walk, from the meadow soaked in gold, pink air, so happy it lit his way with a smile, so large in the distance it seemed a part of the day itself, becoming in a few leaps the sun's very glory, And the morning came to beat against the mulberry where Serge was leaning. Serge was born in the morning's childhood.

"Serge! Serge!" called Albine's voice, lost behind the tall bushes in the flower garden. "Don't be afraid. I'm right here."

But Serge was no longer afraid. He was being born in the sun, in this pure bath of light inundating him. He was being born at the age of twenty-five; his senses were abruptly opened, delighted with the big sky, the happy earth, the prodigy of the horizon spread around him. The garden which he had not known the day before caused him extraordinary joy. Everything filled his being with ecstasy, each blade of grass, each stone in the walks, each breath which he did not see as it passed across his cheeks. His entire body took possession of this bit of nature, clasped it with its limbs; his lips drank it, his nostrils breathed it, he carried it away in his ears, hid it deep in his eyes. It was his own. The roses of the garden, the tall branches of the wood, the rocks ringing the waterfall from the springs, the meadows where the sun planted its blades of light, were all his own. Then he closed his eyes and gave himself the joy of opening them slowly to gain a second dazzling awakening.

"The birds have eaten all the strawberries," Albine said as

she ran up, distressed. "Here, these two are all I could find." But she stopped a few steps away, touched to the heart, to look at Serge with delight and astonishment. "How beautiful you are!" she cried. And she came closer, she remained there, drowning in him, murmuring, "I'd never seen you before."

He had unquestionably grown. Dressed in a loose garment, he was standing up straight, still a little thin, his limbs slender, his chest full, his shoulders rounded. His white neck, tanned on its nape, turned freely and threw his head slightly back. Health, strength, and power were visible in his face. He was not smiling, he was at rest, with a serious and gentle mouth, firm cheeks, a big nose, gray eyes, very clear and regal. His long hair, which hid his whole skull, fell in black curls to his shoulders. His light beard showed on his upper lip and chin, revealing the whiteness of his skin.

"You're beautiful, you're beautiful!" Albine repeated slowly, crouching before him, raising her caressing eyes. "But why are you sulking now? Why don't you talk to me?"

He stood still without replying. His eyes were focused on distant spots; he did not see this child at his feet. He spoke to himself. He said, in the sun, "How good light is!"

And it seemed that these words were vibrations from the sun itself. Scarcely said aloud, they fell like a musical breath, like a shudder of heat and life. Albine had not heard Serge's voice for a few days. She found it as changed as the rest of his being. It seemed to her that it was expanding in the park more sweetly than the voices of the birds, more magisterially than the wind bending the branches. It was a queen, it commanded. All the garden heard it even though it had passed like a sigh; all the garden trembled with the gladness it brought.

"Talk to me," begged Albine. "You've never talked to me that way. Up there, in the bedroom, before, you were dumb, you babbled like a child. Why don't I recognize your voice anymore? Just now I thought your voice was coming from the trees. It came to me from the whole garden; it was one of the deep sighs that used to bother me at night, before you came . . . Listen, everything is being still, to hear you speak again!"

But he still did not know she was there. And she became

more gentle: "No, don't talk if it makes you tired. Sit here by me. We'll stay in the grass till the sun goes away. And look, I found two strawberries. It was awfully hard. The birds eat everything. There's one for you, both of them if you want. Or we can share them so we can both taste each one. You'll tell me thank you, and I'll hear you."

He did not want to sit down; he refused the strawberries, and Albine spitefully threw them away. She herself did not say another word. She preferred him when he was ill, as on the first few days, when she gave him her hand for a pillow and felt him be reborn under the breath with which she cooled his face. She cursed the health which now stood him erect in the light like an indifferent young god. Was he going to remain this way, without thinking of her? Would he not be cured even more, so he would come to see her and to love her? And she dreamed of becoming his cure again, of completing with only the power of her little hands her care for this second childhood. She could easily see that his eyes lacked fire, that his beauty was pale, like that of the statues which had fallen into the nettles in the flower garden. Then she stood up and came to put her arm around him again, blowing on the back of his neck to animate him. But, on this morning, Serge did not even feel the breath ruffling his silky beard. The sun had gone; it was time to go back in. In the room, Albine cried.

From that morning on, the convalescent took a short walk in the garden every day. He went beyond the mulberry to the edge of the terrace, to the wide staircase whose broken steps descended to the flower garden. He grew accustomed to the fresh air; each sunbath made him bloom more. A young chestnut tree, sprouted from a nut fallen between two of the stones in the balustrade, split the casing around its buds and spread its fanning leaves with less vigor than Serge. One day, he had even wanted to go down the stairs, but his strength betrayed him; and he sat on a step among pellitories growing through cracks in the stones. He had seen a small clump of roses below, to the left. That was where he dreamed of going.

"Wait a little while," Albine said. "The scent of roses is still too strong for you. I've never been able to sit under the rosebushes without feeling very tired. My mind goes wild; I get a very nice feeling that makes me want to cry. All right, I'll take you under the rosebushes. And I shall cry, for you make me very sad."

◇◇◇◇◇◇◇◇◇◇◇◇◇◇◇◇◇◇◇◇◇◇◇◇◇◇◇◇◇◇◇◇◇

VI FINALLY CAME THE MORNING WHEN, WITH HER HELP, HE could go all the way down the stairs; she pushed her feet through the plants, clearing a path for him through the dog-rose thorns whose flexible arms barred the last few steps. And they slowly entered the forest of roses. It was a forest composed of thick clusters of tall rose stems, spreading foliage as heavy as that of trees, of enormous bushes standing like impenetrable clumps of scrub oak. This garden had contained the most admirable collection of plants imaginable. But everything had run wild since the abandonment of the flower garden; the virgin forest had grown up, the rose forest invading paths, drowning in wild shoots, mixing species until it seemed that roses of all scents and all colors were blooming on the same stems. Rambling roses formed a thick carpet on the ground, climbing roses clung to other bushes like ivy, climbed in bursts of greenery, dropped the rain of their shedding petals at the slightest breath of wind. And natural walks had formed through the wood; narrow paths, wide avenues, adorable covered walks where strollers passed through shadow and scent. These walks led to crossroads, to bright clearings cradled by small red roses, huddled between walls spotted with small yellow roses. Sunny spots shone like green silk overlaid with spangles; shady spots induced contemplation like an alcove and were imbued with the smell of love and the moist warmth of a bouquet wilted on a woman's bosom. The bushes had whispering voices. The bushes were full of singing nests.

"Let's be careful not to get lost," said Albine, leading the way through the forest. "I was lost once. The sun was already down before I could get away from the rosebushes. They held my skirts every time I took a step."

But they had been walking only a few minutes when Serge,

broken by fatigue, wanted to rest. He lay down and fell into a deep sleep. Albine, seated by him, was dreaming. They were in the clearing, next to the beginning of a path which, striped by sunbeams, led a long way before opening to the sky in a narrow passage, round and blue. Other small roads stopped in green dead ends. The clearing was made of tiers of rosebushes, rising in an orgy of branches, a jumble of thorny creepers so arranged that thick squares of foliage held on to the air, hung suspended, stretched the sides of a living tent from one shrub to another. These bits of green cloth seemed to have been cut through like flimsy lace to let pass only imperceptible streams of light, an azure sieve admitting only a microscopic dust of sun. And from the vault, from each cluster of blooms, hung loose branches, heavy tufts held by the green thread of a stem, armloads of flowers hanging to the ground along some rip in the ceiling, like a strip torn from a curtain.

Albine was watching Serge sleep. She had never before seen his body so exhausted, his hands open on the grass, his face dead. He was dead to her as well, and she thought she could kiss him without his feeling it. And, sad and distraught, she occupied her idle hands by picking the petals off the roses within reach. Above her head hung an enormous bunch, just touching her, putting roses in her hair, behind her ears, around her neck, throwing a cloak of roses over her shoulders. Higher, under her fingers, it was raining roses, wide tender petals possessing the exquisite roundness and barely blushing purity of a virgin's breast. Like a living snowfall, the roses already hid her feet crossed in the grass. Roses came to her knees, covering her skirts, drowning her to her waist; while three stray rose petals, blown to the beginning of the valley of her bust, seemed to be three bits of her adorable nudity.

"Oh, the lazy boy!" she muttered, bored, gathering two handfuls of petals and throwing them in Serge's face to wake him up.

He remained stupefied; roses blocked his eyes and mouth. That made Albine laugh. She leaned over, With all her heart she kissed both his eyes, she kissed his mouth, breathing out as she kissed him to make the petals fly away; but the petals stayed on his lips, and she gave a deeper laugh, amused by this flowery caress.

Serge had slowly raised himself. He looked at her, astonished, as if frightened to find her there. He asked her, "Who are you, where do you come from, what are you doing at my side?"

She was still smiling, delighted to see him wake up like this. Then he seemed to remember, and, with a movement of happy confidence, he continued, "I know, you are my love, you came from my flesh, you're waiting for me to take you in my arms so we two can become one. I was dreaming of you. You were in my chest, and I was giving you my blood, my muscles, my bones. It didn't hurt. You took half my heart, so gently that it gave me pleasure to share myself that way. I looked for the best I had, the most beautiful I had, to give it to you. You could have taken everything. I would have thanked you. And I woke up when you came out of me. You came out through my eyes and mouth. I felt it. You were all warm, all perfumed; you caressed me so that it was the first tremor of your body that made me sit up."

Ecstatic, Albine listened to him talk. Finally, he saw her; finally, he completed his birth, he was cured. Her hands outstretched, she begged him to go on.

"How did I manage to live without you?" he muttered. "But I was not living. I was like a sleeping beast. And you're mine now! And you're nothing else but me! Listen, you must never leave me; for you are my breath, you would take life away from me. You will be in my flesh as I shall be in yours. If I ever leave you, may I be damned, may my body dry up like a useless, evil plant!" He took her hands, repeating in a voice shimmering with wonder, "How beautiful you are!"

Albine, in the falling dust of sunbeams, had milk-white skin, barely gilded by a reflected ray. The rain of roses around her, on her, drowned her in red. Her blond hair, poorly contained by her comb, gave her a setting star as headdress, covered her neck with the riot of its last flaming locks. She wore white, her dress so alive on her, revealing so much of her arms, breast, and knees, that it left her naked. She showed her innocent skin, blooming like a flower, without shame, perfumed with its own scent. She lay at full length, not too tall, supple as a snake, soft curves, voluptuous mounds, the full grace of a body being born, still bathed in childhood, already swollen by puberty. Her long face with its narrow forehead and its mouth a little too strong was laughing with all the tender life of her blue eyes. And, with her simple cheeks and plump chin, she was still serious and as naturally beautiful as the trees.

"And how I love you," said Serge, pulling her to him.

They remained clasped in one another's arms. They did not kiss; they had taken each other's waist, putting cheek to cheek, united, mute, charmed at being only one creature. The rosebushes bloomed around them. It was the insane flowering of a lover, filled with red laughter, pink laughter, white laughter. The living flowers opened like naked flesh, like bodices revealing the treasures of breasts. There were yellow roses shedding the gilded skin of savage girls, straw roses, lemon roses, roses the color of the sun, all the subtle shades of necks bronzed by burning skies. Then the flesh softened, tea-colored roses hinted at exquisite moistness, spread hidden modesty, displayed the parts of the body which are not shown, possessing silken smoothness, made slightly blue by the body's veins. Next the laughing rose-life blossomed out: rose white, barely tinted by a spot of lake, white like a virgin's foot dipping into the water of a spring; pale rose, more discreet than the hot whiteness of a half-glimpsed knee, than the light with which a young arm illumines a wide sleeve; frank rose, blood under satin, naked shoulders, naked hips, all woman's nakedness caressed by light; lively rosebuds of a woman's breasts, half-open flowers of her lips, exhaling the smell of warm breath. And climbing rosebushes, large bushes raining white petals, dressed all these roses, all this flesh, in the lace of their clusters, in the innocence of their thin chiffon; while here and there, wine roses, almost black, bleeding, broke into this bridal purity with a passionate wound. Marriage of the scented forest leading May's virginity to the fertility of July and August; first ignorant kiss, picked like a flower on the wedding morning. Even in the grass, the moss roses, with their long dresses of green linen, waited for love. Along the path striped by sunbeams strolled flowers, their faces bent forward, calling the gentle winds as they passed. Under the open tent of the clearing, all the smiles were shining. No two blooms were alike. The roses had their ways of loving. Some, very timid, their hearts blushing, agreed only to half-open their buds; while others, their corsets unlaced, panting, opened as wide as possible, seemed to have thrown their honor away, their bodies so insane that they could die. There were little, alert, happy roses, filing away, a cockade in their hats; there were enormous roses, bursting with sexual enticements, showing the curves of sleek Oriental queens; brazen roses, like whores, coquettishly meretricious, offering petals whitened by makeup; virtuous roses, dressed like correct housewives; aristocratic roses, endowed with supple elegance, offering accepted nonconformity, inventing new revelations. The roses blooming like a cup seemed to offer their perfume in a precious crystal vessel; the roses falling backward to form an urn let it fall out drop by drop; the round roses, resembling cabbages, exhaled it in the regular breaths of sleeping flowers; the rosebuds clasped their petals, emitting only the vague breath of their virginity.

"I love you, I love you," Serge repeated softly.

And Albine was a great rose, one of the pale roses opened only that morning. Her feet were white, her knees and arms pink, her neck blond, her bosom adorably veined, pale, endowed with exquisite moistness. She smelled good, she extended her lips and offered their still-weak perfume in a coral cup. And Serge breathed it in, clasped it to his chest.

"Oh," she said with a laugh, "you're not hurting me, you can take all of me."

Serge was delighted with her laughter, which sounded like the cadenced song of a bird. "You're the one who has this song," he said. "I've never heard anything so sweet. You are my delight."

And she laughed louder in pearly scales of high flute notes, very sharp, slowly drowned in stately sounds. It was an endless laugh, cooing in the throat, resounding, triumphant music celebrating the pleasures of awakening. Everything laughed in this laugh of a woman being born to beauty and to love, roses, scented wood, all Paradou laughed. Until this moment, the great garden had lacked one charm, a Grace's voice to be the living gladness of the trees, waters, and sun. Now the great garden was given this charm of laughter.

"How old are you?" asked Albine, after extinguishing her song on a long dying note.

"I'll soon be twenty-six," replied Serge.

She was astonished. What! He was twenty-six! He himself was surprised at having said that so easily. It seemed to him that he was not one day old, not one hour old.

"And you, how old are you?" he asked in turn.

"I'm sixteen." And she went on, vibrantly repeating her age, singing her age. She laughed at being sixteen, releasing a very fine laugh flowing like a stream of water in the tremolo rhythm of her voice. Serge watched her closely, marveling at the life of laughter which made this child's face shine. He scarcely recognized her, with her cheeks dimpled, her lips arched, showing the wet pink of her mouth, her eyes like bits of blue lit by a rising star. When she threw her head back, she warmed him by leaning her chin, swollen with laughter, on his shoulder.

He held out his hand and mechanically felt the back of her neck. "What do you want?" she asked. And, remembering, she shouted, "You want my comb! You want my comb!" And she gave him the comb and let the heavy braids of her hair fall loose. It was like a bale of golden cloth being unrolled. Her hair clothed her to her waist. Locks flowing on her breast completed decking her in royal robes. Serge had cried aloud on seeing this sudden blaze. He kissed each lock, burned his lips on these rays of the setting sun.

But now Albine was making up for her long silence. She chattered, questioned, stopped no more. "Ah, how you hurt me! I was nothing to you, useless and powerless; I spent my days licking my wounds like a good-for-nothing . . . But still, at first, I had helped you some. You saw me, you spoke to me. Don't you remember, when you were in bed and went to sleep on my shoulder, muttering that I was good for you?"

"No," said Serge, "no, I don't remember. I had never seen you, I've just seen you for the first time, beautiful, shiny, unforgettable."

She clapped her hands and cried impatiently, "And my comb? You must remember how I gave you my comb to get a little peace when you became a baby again. You were just looking for it."

"No, I don't remember. Your hair is fine silk. I had never kissed your hair."

She became angry, gave precise details, told him all about his convalescence in the room with the blue ceiling. But, still laughing, he finally put his hand on her lips and said in a tired and worried voice, "No, keep quiet, I don't know now, I don't want to know now. I have just awakened and I found you there, full of roses. That's enough."

And he took her in his arms again, held her for a long time, dreaming aloud: "Maybe I've already lived. It must be a very long time ago. I loved you in a painful dream. You had your blue eyes, your face a little too long, your childish airs. But you hid your hair under cloth, very carefully; and I did not dare move the cloth because your hair was awesome and would have made me die. Now, today, your hair is the very sweetness of your person. It's what keeps your smell, what delivers your softened beauty to me, puts all your beauty in my hands. When I kiss it, when I thrust my face into it, I drink your life."

He was rolling her long curls in his hands, pressing them to his lips, as if to make all Albine's blood come out through her hair. After a time he said, "It's strange, before being born you dream of being born. I was buried somewhere. I was cold. I heard outside life moving above me. But I stopped up my ears, desperately. I was used to my shadowy hold; I tasted terrible joys there; I didn't even try to get out from under the pile of dirt weighing heavily on my chest. Where was I? Who finally brought me into the light?"

He was trying to remember, and Albine, anxious now, was afraid he was going to succeed. Smiling, she took a handful of her hair, tied it to the young man's neck, and attached him to her. This game brought him out of his reverie. "You're right," he said, "I'm yours. What does anything else matter? You're the one who took me out of the ground, aren't you? I must have been under this garden. What I heard was your steps on the gravel paths. You were looking for me; over my head you were bringing the songs of birds, the smell of carnations, the heat of the sun. And I suspected you would finally find me. You know I've been waiting for you for a long time. But I did not even dare hope you would give yourself to me without your veil, with your hair hanging free, your awesome hair, which has become so gentle." He took her to him, laid her on his knees, put his face next to hers. "Let's don't talk anymore. We're alone forever. We love each other."

They stayed innocently in one another's arms. They forgot everything for a long time. The sun was rising; rays of a warmer day were falling from the high branches. Yellow roses, white roses, red roses, were now only a radiation of their joy, one of their ways of smiling. They had made the buds around them bloom. The roses crowned their heads, threw garlands over their bodies, and the perfume of the roses became so penetrating, so strong in loving tenderness, that it seemed to be the perfume of their breath.

Then it was Serge who rearranged Albine's hair. With charming clumsiness, he took a handful and laid the comb across it, into the enormous bun piled on her head. Now her hair was delightfully arranged. Then he stood up, held his hands out to her, and held her waist to help her stand up. They were both smiling silently. Softly they walked down the path.

◇◇◇◇◇◇◇◇◇◇◇◇◇◇◇◇◇◇◇◇◇◇◇◇◇◇◇◇◇◇◇◇◇◇

VII ALBINE AND SERGE ENTERED THE FLOWER GARDEN. SHE was worriedly studying him, afraid that he would be fatigued. But he reassured her with a gentle laugh. He felt strong enough to carry her wherever she wanted to go; he sighed from joy to find himself in the bright sun. At last he was living, he was no longer that plant subject to winter's death agonies. And what emotional gratitude! He would have liked to preserve Albine's little feet from the rough walk; he dreamed of her hanging around his neck like a child being put to sleep by its mother. Already he protected her like a jealous guardian, pushed aside rocks and thorns, took care that the wind did not steal from her worshiped hair caresses which belonged to him alone. She had nestled against his shoulder; filled with peace, she gave herself up to him.

It was thus that Albine and Serge walked in the sun for the first time. The couple left a good smell behind them. They made the path shudder as the sun rolled a golden carpet under their feet. They moved ecstatically between big flowering shrubs, so desirable that the many walks all called them from afar, greeted them with murmuring admiration, as crowds greet long-awaited kings. They were only one being, regally beautiful. Albine's white skin was nothing but the whiteness of Serge's brown skin. They passed slowly, dressed in sunlight; they were the sun itself. The flowers bowed down and worshiped them.

Slow, drawn-out emotion awaited them in the flower garden. The old garden served as their escort. A vast field growing freely for a century, a bit of paradise where the wind sowed the rarest flowers. The happy peace of Paradou, asleep in the sun, prevented the hybridization of species by furnishing a constant temperature, a piece of earth where each plant had long ago enriched the soil in order to live there in the silence of its strength. The vegetation was enormous, splendid, proud, powerfully untrimmed, full of chance encounters spreading monstrous flowers unknown to spade and gardener's sprinkler. Left to herself, free to grow without shame deep in this solitude protected by ancient shelters, nature abandoned herself more with each new spring, frolicked wildly, delighted in offering herself strange bouquets, destined to be picked by no hand, at all times of the year. And she seemed bent on overturning what human efforts had created; she rebelled, released stampedes of flowers into the walks, attacked the artistically arranged rocks with the rising tide of her moss, lassoed the necks of marble statues and pulled them over with the help of her climbing plants; she broke the tiles in pools, on stairs, on terraces, by thrusting shrubs through them; she crawled about until she possessed every cultivated spot and had shaped them as she chose, had planted there the rebel flag of some seed gathered on the road, a humble green thing which she made into a gigantic green thing. The flower garden, kept for a master passionately devoted to flowers, had once displayed a marvelous selection of plants in neat beds and manicured rows. Today the same plants were found, but perpetuated, enlarged into families so innumerable, gamboling about all parts of the garden with such exuberance, that it was now nothing but a riot, a bushy mob beating against the walls, a suspicious place where intoxicated nature hiccoughed verbena and carnations.

Albine was actually leading Serge, although she seemed to be giving herself to him, to be supported by his shoulder. First, she led him to the grotto. Nestled in a grove of poplars and willows, a hollowed rock had been eroded, blocks of stone had fallen into a fountain, streams of water flowed across the rocks; the grotto was disappearing under the plants' assault. Below, tiers of hollyhock seemed to block the entry with a gate of red, yellow, mauve, and white flowers, twigs drowning in colossal nettles, green as bronze, peacefully sweating their burning poison. Then came a prodigious thrust rising all the way up in a few leaps; jasmine, made starry by soft flowers; wisteria, petals of delicate lace; dense ivy, leaves cut like japanned iron; flexible honeysuckle, riddled with blades of pale coral; loving clematis, arms extending, adorned with tiny white blossoms. And other, frailer plants were intertwined among these to bind them more tightly and weave an odorous woof into their warp. Nasturtiums, their flesh green and bared, opened mouths of red gold. Scarlet runners, strong as thin rope, lit various places with the flame of their living sparks. Convolvulus, spreading the slashed heart of its petals, rang a silent carillon of exquisite colors with thousands of tiny bells. Sweet peas, like bands of stately butterflies, folded tawny wings, pink wings, ready to let themselves be carried farther by the first breath of wind. An immense green head of hair, ornamented by a storm of flowers, whose locks fell everywhere, escaped in insane dishevelment, created dreams of a swooning young giantess thrusting her head backward in the convulsions of her orgasm, a stream of gorgeous hair rising like a pond of perfumes.

"I've never dared go into that darkness," Albine whispered in Serge's ear. He gave her courage, carried her over the nettles; and when a stone blocked the entrance to the grotto, he held her in his arms so she could lean over the hole yawning a few feet below.

"There's a marble woman," she muttered, "who fell full length into the flowing water. The water has eaten her face." Then he pulled himself up so he too could see. A cool breath struck his cheeks; in the rushes and duckweed, under the ray of light sliding from the hole, the woman was on her back, naked to the waist, a cloth draped over her thighs. Some woman who had been drowning for a hundred years, the slow suicide of a statue whose troubles had sent her to the bottom of this spring. The transparent glass flowing over her had made her face smooth stone, whiteness without features, while her two breasts, as if raised out of the water by the muscular strength of her neck, remained unmarred, still alive, swollen with ancient passion.

"She's not dead," said Serge as he came down. "We'll have to come get her out of there one day."

But Albine, shuddering, led him away; they returned to the sunlight filling the licentious abandon of angular and round flower beds. They crossed a meadow of flowers, going where they chose, following no path. Their feet had charming plants for a carpet, dwarf plants which once lined the walks but now stretched in endless sheets. Sometimes their feet disappeared in the speckled silk of pink silenes, in the plumed satin of garden pinks, in the blue velvet of forget-me-nots, spotted with tiny, melancholy eyes. Farther along, they passed through gigantic mignonettes rising to their knees, like a mounting bath of perfumes; they cut through a field of lily of the valley to spare a neighboring field of violets, so gentle and soft that they trembled to think of bruising the smallest cluster; then, surrounded on all sides, having nothing but violets around them, they were forced to pass through the very breath of spring. Beyond the violets unfolded the green linen of lobelias, slightly rough, shot with clear mauve; subtle stars of selaginellas, blue cups of nemophilas, yellow crosses of soapworts, pink and white crosses of rockets, wove rich tapestries, spread before the couple a royal luxury of color, so the young people could move without fatigue in the joy of their first walk together. And the violets always returned, a sea of violets flowing everywhere, pouring precious balm on their feet, accompanying them with the breath of leaf-hidden flowers.

Albine and Serge were losing their way. A thousand plants formed hedges, arranged narrow paths, which they amused themselves by following. The paths led deeper, made abrupt turns, ran into one another, led to impassable thickets: ageratums, sky-blue blossoms; woodruffs, light smell of musk; mimuluses, showing bronzed throats, underscored by vermilion spots; magnificent scarlet and violet phlox, raising spikes of flowers waving in the wind; red flax, blades as fine as hair; chrysanthemums, resembling full moons, golden moons throwing off short, muted rays, white, violet, and pink. The couple simply stepped over obstacles, continuing the happy walk between two green hedges. To the right rose light fraxinellas, centranthus falling like purest snow, gray hound's-tongues, a drop of dew in each tiny cup of their flowers. To the left was a long avenue of columbine, every variety of columbine, white, light pink, dark violet, the last almost black, dressed in sad mourning, hanging from high stems, petals folded and crimped like crepe. And as they continued to walk, the hedges changed, formed flowery limbs of enormous larkspur, lost in curling leaves; admitted the open mouths of wild snapdragon; raised thin schizanthus leaves, filled with a flowery nation of butterflies, whose sulfur wings bore spots of soft blue. Campanula ran with them, furiously throwing bluebells to the top of huge asphodel, whose golden stems served as bell towers. In one section, a giant fennel seemed to be a lady dressed in transparent lace, opening her blue-green parasol. Then the couple suddenly came to a dead end; they could go no farther, a hill of living flowers blocked the path, an eruption of plants forming a stone gate topped with a triumphant plume. Near the ground, acanthuses erected a foundation from which sprang scarlet bennet and rhodantia, whose dry petals cracked like painted paper; clarkia, large white crosses, hand-worked, reminiscent of the crosses of a barbarian sect. Higher bloomed pink viscaria, yellow leptosiphon, white colinsia, lagurus, twining its tufts of green ashes through all these vivid colors. Still higher, red digitalis and blue lupin rose in slender columns to support a Byzantine rotunda, savagely streaked with purple and azure; at the very top, the bleeding leaves of a colossal ricinus seemed to raise a dome of burnished copper.

Serge was already stretching out his hands to pass through when Albine begged him not to hurt the flowers. "You'd break the branches; you'd crush the leaves," she said. "In all the years I've lived here, I've been very careful not to kill anyone. Come on, I'll show you the pansies."

She forced him to backtrack and led him down the narrow paths to the middle of the garden, where the large pools had once been. The filled-in pools were now only vast flowerpots formed by crushed and broken marble. In one of the widest, the wind had sown a marvelous bed of pansies. The velvet flowers seemed alive, violet hair, yellow eyes, pale mouths, delicate, flesh-colored chins. "When I was little I was afraid of them," muttered Albine. "Just look at them. Don't they look like thousands of little faces watching you from the ground? And they all turn their faces together. They look like buried dolls sticking their heads out."

She pulled him away again. They walked around the other pools. In the next basin had grown amaranth, bristling with monstrous combs, which Albine did not dare touch. They reminded her of immense caterpillars with blood oozing through their fur. Balsam, yellow as straw, peach colored, gray as flax, white dipped in pink, filled another basin; their elastic pods popped with a small dry noise. Then, nestled in the ruins of a fountain, came a group of splendid carnations: white carnations, spilling out of the mossy basin; flamboyant carnations, planting gaudy ruching of pierced muslin in the cracks of the stones, while deep in the throat of the lion which formerly spit out water bloomed a huge red carnation, sending out such vigorous shoots that the old wounded lion now seemed to be spitting out his life's blood. And, on one side, the main ornamental pool, an old lake where swans had swum, had become a grove of lilac shading forty-day stocks, verbenas, morning-glories, half-asleep, all moist with perfume, their delicate colors protected by the larger flowers around them.

"And we haven't even seen half the garden yet," Albine said proudly. "The big flowers are down there, fields where I disappear completely, like a partridge in a wheat field." They went there. They walked down a wide staircase whose overturned vases still blazed with the tall violet flames of iris. A stream of wallflowers flowed over the steps like a sheet of liquid gold. On both sides, thistles raised slender candelabra of green bronze, bristling and curved like the beaks of fantastic birds, created by a strange art to display the elegance of Chinese censers. Sedum hung blond tresses between the rods of broken banisters, greenish hair, like river weeds, revealing spots of mold. A second garden stretched below, broken by box trees strong as oaks, old, proper box trees once trimmed into balls, pyramids, octagonal towers, now magnificently untrimmed, sporting great rags of dark greenery whose holes revealed bits of blue sky.

And Albine led Serge to the right, into a field which seemed to serve as the garden's cemetery. Here scabious brought out deep mourning. Brigades of poppies marched in formation, reeking of death, blossoming in heavy flowers, brightly febrile. Tragic anemones formed afflicted mobs of bruised colors, their faces ashy from some pestilential wind. Squat daturas opened violet trumpets, where insects tired of living came to drink the poison of suicide. Marigolds buried their blossoms under choked leaves, burst into the bodies of dying stars, already releasing the plague of their decomposition. And there was still more sadness; fleshy ranunculuses, showing the dull color of rusted metal; hyacinths and tuberoses, breathing poison gas, dying in their own perfume. But the cinerarias were dominant, a great growth of cinerarias parading the half-mourning of violet and white dresses, dresses of striped velvet, dresses of solid velvet, rich in their sternness. In the middle of the melancholy field stood a marble cupid, wounded, the arm holding his bow fallen into the nettles, still smiling under the lichen chilling his childish nakedness.

Then Albine and Serge were waist-deep in a field of peonies. The white flowers released a rain of wide petals, cooled their hands like the big drops of a summer storm. The red flowers had apopleptic faces whose enormous laugh made them uneasy. On the left, they encountered a field of fuchsias, a jumble of supple shrubs growing free, delighting them like Japanese toys decorated with a million tinkling bells. Then they crossed fields of veronicas, lavender clusters of blooms, fields of geraniums and pelargoniums, on which seemed to play burning sparks, the incandescent red, pink, and white of a forge, made to glow even brighter by the slightest puff of wind. They had to go around curtains of gladiolas as tall as reeds, brandishing stems of flowers burning in the light with the rich flames of ignited torches. They were lost in a grove of sunflowers, a forest of stems as thick as Albine's waist, veiled by crude leaves wide enough to cradle a baby, inhabited by giant faces, starlike faces as resplendent as so many suns. And they finally came to another rhododendron grove, so filled with flowers that the branches and leaves could not be seen, offering for their view monstrous bouquets, baskets of tender calices swelling to the horizon.

"Come on, we're not finished yet," cried Albine. "Let's walk some more, let's keep walking." But Serge stopped her; they were in the center of ruins of an old colonnade. The column shafts formed benches among tufts of primroses and periwinkles. In the distance, more fields of flowers stretched between standing columns: fields of tulips, displaying the bright decorations of painted pottery; fields of calceolarias, slight blisters spotted with blood and gold; fields of zinnias, huge angry daisies; fields of petunias, petals soft as a woman's negligee, showing pink skin; still more fields, fields stretching infinitely, whose flowers could not be identified, whose carpets stretched under the sun in a confused motley of violent clusters drowned in soft plant greens.

"We'll never be able to see everything," said Serge, smiling and offering his hand. "It must be good to sit down here in the rising scent." Beside them was a field of heliotropes, exhaling vanilla breath so sweet that it gave the wind a velvet caress. Then they sat on one of the overturned columns in a clump of superb lilies. They had been walking for more than an hour. They had come from the roses to the lilies through all the other flowers. Lilies offered them a guileless asylum after their lovers' walk amid the ardent concern of sweet honeysuckle, musk-scented violets, verbenas exhaling the cool smell of a kiss, tuberoses releasing the swoon of fatal seduction. With their extended stems, the lilies put them in a white pavilion under the snowy roof of their calices, brightened only by the subtle golden drop of their pistils. And, like engaged children, royally chaste, they seemed to be in the center of a tower of purity, of an impregnable tower of ivory, where they loved each other with all the charm of their innocence.

Albine and Serge remained with the lilies until it began to grow dark. They were comfortable there; they completed their births there. Serge lost the last fever of his hands. Albine became completely white, with a milky whiteness which no blush tinted with pink. They no longer saw that their arms were bare, their necks bare, their shoulders bare. Their hair no longer troubled them like brazenly displayed nakedness. One against the other, they gave a clear laugh and found that it refreshed them to cling to each other. Their eyes kept the clear calm of spring water; nothing impure rose from their flesh to dirty its limpid crystal. Their cheeks were barely-ripened downy fruits, which they did not dream of biting. When they left the lilies, they were not even ten years old. It seemed to them that they had just met, alone deep in the vast garden, to live there in eternal friendship and games. And as they were crossing the flower garden once more, going home at dusk, the flowers seemed to become discreet, happy to see them so young, not wanting to corrupt these children. The groves of peonies, beds of carnations, carpets of forget-me-nots, tapestries of clematis, no longer raised a lovers' alcove before them. They were now drowned in the evening air, asleep in childhood as pure as their own. The pansies turned their tiny open faces to watch them like friends. The mignonettes, languorous, brushed by Albine's white skirt, seemed to be gripped by pity and avoided hastening their fever with a breath.

◇◇◇◇◇◇◇◇◇◇◇◇◇◇◇◇◇◇◇◇◇◇◇◇◇◇◇◇◇◇◇◇◇◇◇◇◇

VIII THE NEXT DAY, IT WAS SERGE WHO CALLED ALBINE. HE was up at dawn. She slept on the floor above him, and he did not intend to go up. Immediately after he arose, he leaned out the window and saw her opening her shutters. And they both laughed to see each other like this.

"Today you won't go out," said Albine, after coming down to join him. "We have to rest. Tomorrow I'm going to take you far away, very far, where we'll be awfully happy."

"But we'll be bored," complained Serge.

"Oh, of course not! I'm going to tell you stories."

They had a charming day. The windows were wide open; Paradou came into their room to laugh with them. Serge finally took possession of this happy room, where he imagined he had been born. He wanted to see everything, to have everything explained to him. The plaster cupids tumbling over the side of the alcove made him so happy that he climbed up on a chair to tie Albine's belt around the neck of the smallest one, a tiny bit of a man, acting lewd, his rump in the air and his head below. Albine clapped her hands, said he looked like a June bug on a string. Then, as if gripped by pity, "No, no, untie him. He can't fly like that."

But it was, above all, the cupids painted above the doors that seized Serge's attention. He became angry because the paintings were so faded he could not understand what games they were playing. With Albine's help, he brought a table, and they both clambered up on it. Albine explained: "Look, these are strewing flowers. Under the flowers you can't see anything but three naked legs. I seem to remember that when I first came I could still make out a lady lying down. But she's gone away since then."

They visited all the panels without anything impure coming to them from these pretty bedroom obscenities. The paintings, crumbling like a rouged eighteenth-century face, were dead enough to leave only the knees and elbows of bodies swooning in amorous luxury. The too-stark details, which must have pleased the ancient love whose distant smell lingered in the alcove, had disappeared, eaten by fresh air; so that, like the park, the bedroom had naturally become virginal again, under the peaceful glory of the sun.

"Bah, these are kids having fun!" said Serge as he climbed down from the table. "Do you know how to play hot cockles?"

Albine knew how to play any game. But there had to be three people to play hot cockles. That made them laugh. But Serge exclaimed that they were quite well off with only two, and they swore to be always only two.

"You're really at home here. You don't hear anything," the young man went on as he stretched out on the sofa. "And the furniture smells good because it's so old. It's as cozy as a nest. This is a room where happiness is."

The girl was seriously nodding her head. "If I scared easy," she muttered, "I'd really have been afraid at first. That's the story I want to tell you. I heard it from the peasants. They might be lying. So what, it'll be fun." And she sat down beside Serge.

"Years and years ago, Paradou belonged to a rich lord who came here to shut himself up with a very beautiful lady. The chateau doors were so tightly closed, the garden walls so high, that no one ever saw the smallest trace of the lady's skirts."

"I know," interrupted Serge, "the lady never came out."

As Albine, caught by surprise, angry to see he knew her story, was watching him, he went on, half-aloud, as astonished as she: "You've already told me about it, about this lady."

She denied it. Then she seemed to change her mind and let herself be convinced. Which did not prevent her from ending her tale in this way: "When the lord went away, his hair was white. He had every opening barricaded, so nobody could go disturb the lady . . . The lady died in this room."

"In this room!" exclaimed Serge. "You didn't tell me that. Are you sure she died in this room?"

Albine was peeved. She said everyone knew it. The lord had

built the summer house to lodge this unknown woman who looked like a princess. The chateau servants later told everyone that he spent each day and night there. Moreover, they often glimpsed him in a walk leading the lady's tiny feet deep into the darkest thickets. But for nothing in the world would they have risked spying on the couple as they traveled through the park for weeks at a time.

"And that's where she died," repeated Serge, struck by this idea. "You took her bedroom, you use her furniture, you sleep in her bed."

Albine was smiling. "You know I don't scare easy," he said. "Besides, all that was so long ago. And you thought the room was filled with happiness." They fell silent. They looked at the alcove for a while, at the high ceilings, at the gray shadows in the corners. There was something like tender love in the faded colors of the furniture. It was a discreet sigh from the past, so submissive that it still resembled the warm gratitude of a worshiped woman.

"Yes," murmured Serge, "you can't be scared. It's too peaceful."

And Albine continued to speak as she came closer to him. "What only a few people know is that they had discovered a place of perfect bliss in the garden, and they finally lived there all the time. I heard that from a certain source. A corner of cool shade hidden deep in impenetrable thickets, so marvelously beautiful it makes you forget the whole world. The lady must have been buried there."

"Is it in the flower garden?" Serge asked curiously.

"Oh, I don't know," said the girl with a discouraged gesture. "I've looked everywhere; I still haven't been able to find that blessed clearing. It's not in the roses or the lilies or on the violet carpet."

"Maybe it's that section of sad flowers where you showed me a standing boy with an arm broken off."

"No, no."

Albine thought a minute. Then she went on, as if speaking to herself. "I started to look for it soon after I got here. If I spent whole days in Paradou, if I pushed aside the smallest bits of greenery, it was just to sit for one hour in the clearing. How many mornings I wasted sliding under thorns, visiting the most distant corners of the park! Oh, I would have known it right away, this enchanted retreat, the immense tree which must cover it with a leafy roof, grass soft as a silk cover, walls of green bushes which not even the birds can get through."

She threw an arm around Serge's neck and raised her voice to beg. "All right! There're two of us now, we'll look, we'll find it. You, you're strong, you'll push aside the heavy branches in front of me, so I can go to the back of the thickets. You'll carry me when I'm tired; you'll help me jump over the streams; you'll climb trees to look if we lose our way. And what happiness when we can sit side by side under the leafy roof in the center of the clearing! They told me that you live a whole lifetime in one minute there. All right! My good Serge, we'll leave tomorrow, we'll look through every thicket in the park until we've satisfied our desire."

Serge shrugged his shoulders and smiled. "What good will it do?" he said. "Aren't we happy in the garden? We have to stay with the flowers, don't you see, without looking far away for more happiness."

"That's where the dead woman is buried," muttered Albine, falling into her dreams again. "It was the joy of sitting there that killed her. As for me, I'd be happy to die like that. We'd sleep in each other's arms; we'd be dead; no one would ever find us again."

"No, keep quiet. I don't like that," Serge broke in. "I want us to live in the sun, far from that fatal shade. What you're saying worries me; it's as if you were pushing us to some final catastrophe. It must be forbidden to sit under a tree whose shade makes you shiver that way."

"Yes, it's forbidden," Albine declared seriously. "Everybody in the country told me it was forbidden."

Silence fell. Serge left the sofa, where he had still been lying. He laughed and said he did not like that kind of story. The sun was going down when Albine finally agreed to go into the garden for a while. She led him to the left, along the dividing wall, to a field of ruins bristling with thorns. It was the old chateau site, still black from the fire which had destroyed its walls. Under the thorns, charred stones were cracking, collapsed beams were rotting. It looked like a section of sterile rock, filled with cracks and gullies, dressed in rough grass with creepers slithering into each split like snakes. And they played at running all over this trap, going down to the bottom of holes, sniffing the waste to see if they could guess something about this past lying in ashes. They did not admit their curiosity; they chased each other through collapsed floors and overturned walls; but in reality they were thinking only of these ruins, of that lady more beautiful than the day, whose silk skirt had trailed on these steps, where now only big lizards paraded lazily.

Serge finally stopped on the highest pile of ruins, looking at the park which was unfolding its immense green sheets, looking in the trees for the gray spot of the summer house. Standing beside him, Albine was silent and grave once again. "The house is there, to the right," she said without being asked. "It's all that's left of the buildings. Do you see it, right past those lindens?" They were silent again. And as if continuing aloud the silent reflections they both were making mentally, she went on: "When he went to see her, he had to go down this walk; then he went around the big chestnuts and in through the lindens. It barely took him fifteen minutes."

Serge said not a word. When they returned, they went down the walk, around the chestnuts, and in through the lindens. It was a road of love. They seemed to be looking for footprints on the grass, for a fallen piece of ribbon, a whiff of old perfume, some sign to show them unmistakably that they were on the path leading to the joy of being together. Night was falling; the park was a great dying voice calling them deep into its foliage.

"Wait," said Albine when they had come to the summer house. "Don't come up for three minutes." She gaily ran away and shut herself up in the room with the blue ceiling. Then, after letting Serge knock twice, she discreetly cracked the door and received him with an old-fashioned curtsey.

"Good day, my dear lord," she said as she kissed him.

They thought this was great fun. They played lovers with the abandon of small children, stammered through the passion which had once died there. They studied it like a lesson which they recited in an adorable way, ignorant of how to kiss one another's lips, fumbling around their cheeks, finally dancing before each other and bursting into laughter, not knowing how else to show the pleasure they found in love.

◇◇◇◇◇◇◇◇◇◇◇◇◇◇◇◇◇◇◇◇◇◇◇◇◇◇◇◇◇◇◇◇◇◇◇◇

IX THE NEXT MORNING, ALBINE WANTED TO LEAVE AS SOON AS the sun was up, to start the great walk she had been planning since the day before. She tapped her feet happily and said they would not be back that day.

"So where are you taking me?" asked Serge.

"You'll see! You'll see!"

But he took her wrists and looked in her eyes. "We're going to be good, aren't we? I don't want you to look for your clearing or your tree or your grass where people die. You know it's forbidden."

She blushed a little, protested, said that she was not even dreaming of such things. Then she added, "Still, if we found it without looking, just by chance, wouldn't you sit down? So you don't love me very much!"

They left. They went straight through the flower garden without stopping to watch the flowers as they awoke, naked in their bath of dew. The morning had the smile and pink complexion of a beautiful child opening his eyes to the whiteness of his pillow.

"Where are you taking me?" Serge asked again.

And Albine laughed, unwilling to answer. But as they approached the sheet of water dividing the end of the garden, she was quite upset. The river was still swollen from the last rain. "We'll never be able to cross," she murmured. "I usually just take off my shoes and raise my skirts. But today the water would come to our waists."

They walked along the river for a while, looking for a ford. The girl said it was useless, that she knew all the holes. There was once a bridge there, a bridge whose collapse had strewn huge stones in the river, between which the water flowed in frothing whirlpools. "Get on my back," said Serge.

"No, no, I don't want to. If you slipped, we'd both take a terrific fall. You don't know how treacherous those rocks are."

"Will you get on my back?"

That tempted her. She took a running start and leaped like a boy, so high that she straddled Serge's neck. And, on feeling him tremble, she cried that he was still not strong enough, that she wanted down. Then she jumped again, twice. This game delighted them.

"Whenever you're through," said the laughing young man. "Now hold tight. Here comes the big step." And in three light leaps he crossed the river, his toes barely getting wet. When they were in the middle of the stream, Albine thought he was slipping. She cried out and seized his chin with both hands. But, galloping like a horse, he was already carrying her to the fine sand of the other bank.

"Giddyap, giddyap," she cried, reassured, amused by this new game. He ran as much as she wanted, tapping his feet, imitating the sound of hooves. She clucked with her tongue. She had gripped two locks of his hair and pulled them like reins to send him to the right or left.

"There, there, we're here," she said, slapping him gently on the cheeks. She jumped to the ground while he, all sweaty, leaned against a tree to catch his breath. Then she scolded him and threatened not to take care of him if he got sick again.

"Cut it out! That's good for me," he replied. "When I've got all my strength back, I'll carry you all morning . . . Where are you taking me?"

"Here," she said, as she sat under a gigantic pear tree.

They were in the old park orchard. A living hedge of hawthorn, a huge green wall breached in several places, created a separate part of the garden, a forest of fruit trees unpruned for a century. Certain powerfully warped trunks grew askew under the stormy gusts which had bent them; others, twisted by enormous knots, hollowed by deep holes, seemed to be held to the ground only by the giant ruins of their bark. High branches, bent every year by the weight of their fruit, spread far and wide their immoderate clusters; even those limbs most heavily laden, those which had split and now touched the ground, did not stop producing: they were simply glued to the trunk by layer upon layer of oozed sap. Trees lent one another natural props, were now nothing but twisted pillars supporting a vault of leaves forming long galleries, abruptly expanding into airy halls, bending almost to the ground like collapsed garrets. Around each colossus, wild shoots made thickets, contributed the tangle of their young stems, whose small berries were exquisitely bitter. In the greenish light flowing like clear water, the great silence of the moss was broken only by the hollow fall of fruit being picked by the wind.

And there were patriarchal apricot trees blithely bearing their great age, already paralyzed on one side, a forest of dead wood, like scaffolding around a cathedral; but so alive on the other side, so young, that tender shoots everywhere broke their rough bark. Venerable plum trees, hoary with moss, still grew to drink the burning sun. Not one of their leaves had faded. Cherry trees built entire cities, several-story houses, threw down staircases, created ceilings of branches wide enough to cover ten families. Then came the apple trees, their strength gone, their limbs twisted by arthritis, looking like huge invalids, their scaly skin spotted by green rust; lissome pear trees, raising masts of tall slender stems, immense, resembling the entry to a port, scoring the horizon with brown bars; pink peach trees, making room for themselves in the crush of their neighbors by lovable laughter and the slow movement of beautiful girls lost in a crowd. Certain trees, abandoned while being trained flat, had broken through the low walls restraining them; now they gamboled about, free of the trellises whose split remains still hung from their arms; they grew as they pleased, retained of their special size only the vague appearance of properly polite trees trailing the tatters of their formal dress. And on each trunk, on each branch, from one tree to another, ran riots of vines; rising like insane laughter, they gripped some high knot for a while, then left again in a new outburst of more insistent laughter, splattering under the foliage in happy intoxication, tender green gilded by the sun, lighting with a hint of drunkenness the gray heads of the orchard's great old men.

Then, to the left, trees spaced farther apart, almond trees, their thin foliage letting the sun pass through to the ground to ripen gourds like fallen moons. On the banks of a stream crossing the orchard were melons decorated by warts, lost in the profusion of crawling leaves, varnished ellipses, as perfectly oval as ostrich eggs. Currant bushes blocked the former walks every step of the way, displaying the shy clusters of their fruit, rubies whose every facet was highlighted by a drop of sun; rows of raspberries extended like wild thorns; and the ground was nothing but a carpet of strawberry vines, a lawn sown throughout with ripe strawberries, their smell a hint of vanilla.

But the enchanted part of the orchard was still more to the left, next to the slope of rocks which began rising to the horizon there, truly ardent earth, a natural greenhouse where the sun shone all the time. It was first necessary to pass awkwardly gigantic fig trees, stretching their branches like the gray arms of an awakening monster, so choked with the hairy leather of their leaves that, in order to pass, the couple had to break many young shoots growing from stumps dried by age. They then walked among groves of crab apple, green as giant box trees, whose red berries made them look like maypoles decorated with balls of scarlet silk. Next came a forest of service trees, medlars, and jujubes, surrounded by the eternally green tufts of a border of pomegranates, whose fruit was slowly ripening, barely as large as a child's fist; purple flowers, poised on the tips of branches, seemed to be beating their wings like exotic island birds who do not bend the plants on which they live. And they finally came to a grove of orange and lemon trees, growing vigorously in the uncultivated ground. Straight trunks stood like files of brown columns; shining leaves spotted the blue of the sky with the gaiety of clear paintings, expertly carved the shade into thin pointed blades, which seemed to draw on the ground the palms of Indian cloth. It was a shady spot whose charm was unique, beside which ordinary European shade became insipid: humid joy of light filtered into a cloud of living gold, creating certainty of

perpetual greenery, strength of continuous perfume, the penetrating perfume of the blossom, the more serious perfume of
the fruit, giving the trees' limbs the languid suppleness of
torrid zones.

"And we're going to eat!" shouted Albine, clapping her
hands. "It's at least nine o'clock. I'm awfully hungry." She had
stood up. Serge admitted that he would not mind eating a little
something himself. "You old bear!" she said. "Don't you see
that I was taking you to eat? Huh? We won't starve here. It's
all for us."

They went under the trees, spreading branches to reach the
fattest fruits. Albine went first, her skirts tucked up; she turned
around, asked her companion in her high voice, "What do you
like? Pears, apricots, cherries, currants? I warn you, the pears
are still green—but they're awfully good."

Serge chose cherries, and Albine said it was all right to start
with them. But as he was ignorantly going to climb the nearest
cherry tree, she made him walk at least ten minutes more
through a frightful tangle of limbs. That cherry tree had puny
little worthless cherries; this one's were bitter; that other one's
would be ripe in a week. She knew all the trees. "Here, climb
this one," she said finally, stopping by a tree so laden with fruit
that clusters hung to the ground like coral necklaces draped on
its branches

Serge made himself comfortable in a fork and began to eat.
He did not hear Albine and thought she was in another tree a
few paces away until he lowered his gaze and saw her lying
peacefully on her back below him. There she was, eating
without using her hands; she could have all the cherries she
wanted simply by pulling off those held to her lips by the tree.
When she saw she was discovered, she laughed for a long time
and flopped on the grass like a white fish out of water, turning
on her stomach, crawling on her elbows, going completely
around the tree, without ceasing to pull off the fattest cherries.

"Just imagine, they're tickling me," she cried. "Look, there's
another one that fell down my neck. They're really good. I've
got them in my ears, in my eyes, in my nose, everywhere! If I

felt like it, I'd crush one to make me a moustache. They're sweeter down here than up high."

"Hah," said Serge laughingly. "You're just not brave enough to come up."

She was so insulted she could not speak. "Me! Me!" she stammered.

And, grabbing her skirt and tucking it into her belt, without noticing that her thighs were revealed, she grabbed the tree and shinnied up the trunk with one pull of her wrists. She ran along the branches, avoiding any use of her hands; long and lithe as a squirrel, she turned around the knots, kicked her feet, kept her balance only by the bend in her waist. When she was at the very top, at the end of a thin limb, furiously shaken by her weight, she yelled, "All right! Am I brave enough to come up?"

"Please, hurry down," begged Serge, in the grip of fear. "Please, please, you're going to hurt yourself."

But she triumphantly climbed still higher, straddled the very tip of the limb, inching out over the abyss, grabbing tufts of leaves with both hands. "The limb's going to break!" said Serge, stunned.

"So what, let it break," she answered with a great laugh. "It'd save me the trouble of climbing down."

And the limb did break: but slowly, with such a long crack that it fell bit by bit, as if to set Albine very gently on the ground. She was not at all afraid; she leaned back and shook her half-naked thighs, repeating, "It's awfully nice. It feels like a carriage."

Serge had jumped from the tree to catch her in his arms. She teased him when she saw how pale he was: "But people fall out of trees every day! It never hurts. So laugh, you old bear. Here, put a little spit on my neck. I got scratched."

He put a little spit on her with the tip of his finger. "There, it's well," she said, and she ran away like a jumping child. "Let's play hide-and-seek, okay?"

She made him look for her. She disappeared, cried "Cuckoo! Cuckoo!" from deep in plants known only to her, places where

Serge could not hope to find her. But this game of hide-and-seek could not occur without a terrible hail of fruit. The meal went on as the two big children chased each other. Even as she was running under trees, Albine put out her hand to pop off a green pear or filled her skirt with apricots. Moreover, in certain places she found things that made her sit down and forget the game to do some serious eating. Suddenly, she could not hear Serge, and it was her turn to look for him. And she was surprised, almost angered, to find him under a plum tree which she herself did not know about whose ripe plums had a light odor of musk. She scolded him in a charming way. So he wanted to eat them all and hadn't said a word about it! He was being stupid, but he had a good nose; he smelled good things from a long way off. She was especially furious with the plum tree, a sly tree, hiding well, which must have grown overnight just to upset people. While she was complaining, Serge, refusing to pick a single plum, was vigorously shaking the tree. A rain, a hail of plums fell. Albine, caught in the storm, received plums on her arms, plums down her neck, plums on the very tip of her nose. Then she could not keep from laughing; she stayed in the flood, shouting "More! More!" amused by the round balls bouncing off her, offering her mouth and hands, her eyes closed, crouching on the ground to make herself very small.

Children's morning, pranks of kids let loose in Paradou. Albine and Serge spent boyish hours at this bushy school, running, shouting, tagging each other, without any tremor running across their innocent flesh. It was still the friendship of two little scamps who might one day, when the trees had no more dessert to offer them, think of kissing one another on the cheeks. And what a happy bit of nature for this first escapade! A section of foliage with excellent hiding places. Paths along which it was impossible to be serious because of the fat laughter continuously emitted by the hedges. In this happy orchard, the park possessed a gang of prankish bushes running free, cool shady spots inviting people to eat, great old grandfather trees, their pockets filled with sweets. Deep in green mossy retreats, under fallen trunks which made them crawl one after the other through leafy halls so narrow that Serge laughingly bumped into Albine's bare legs, even here they never encountered a dangerous, dreamy silence. The grove was at play and hinted at nothing which the two children did not understand.

And when they tired of apricot, plum, and cherry trees, they ran under thin almond trees and ate the green nuts, scarcely as large as peas; they looked for strawberries in the grassy carpet, became angry at the watermelons for not being ripe. Albine finally ran as fast as she could, chased by Serge, who could not catch her. She went to the fig trees, jumped over thick branches, grabbed leaves and threw them into her companion's face behind her. In a few leaps, she crossed the crab-apple grove, tasting red berries in passing; and it was in the forest of service trees, medlars, and jujubes that Serge lost her. At first he thought she was hiding behind a pomegranate tree; but he was mistaking two flower buds for her two pink wrists. Then he searched the orange grove, delighted with the lovely weather there, imagining he was visiting the sun-fairies' palace; he saw Albine in the middle of the grove. She did not think he was so close and was agitatedly prying about, searching the green depths with her eyes.

"What are you looking for?" he exclaimed. "You know it's forbidden."

She started and blushed a little for the first time that day. And, sitting by Serge, she told him of the happy days when the oranges were ripe. Then the grove was all gilded, illuminated by round stars piercing the green vault with yellow eyes.

Then, when they finally left, she stopped at every wild shoot to fill her pockets with small bitter pears, small acid plums, saying these were to eat on the way, that they were a hundred times better than anything else they had tasted. Serge had to swallow some, despite the faces he made each time he took a bite. They returned, exhausted and happy, after laughing so much that their sides ached. Albine did not even feel like going to her room that night; she went to sleep at Serge's feet, lying across the bed, dreaming she was climbing trees, munching, as she slept, the wild fruit she had hidden under the covers beside her.

X A WEEK LATER, THERE WAS ANOTHER LONG TRIP INTO THE park. They wanted to go past the orchard, to the left, on the path leading to the wide meadows crossed by four streams. They would walk through several miles of grass; they could live by catching fish if they got lost.

"I'll take my knife," said Albine, showing a peasant's knife with a long blade.

She put almost everything into her pockets, string, bread, matches, a small bottle of wine, rags, a comb, needles. Serge was to take a bedroll, but it was so much trouble that he hid it under a fallen wall after they had passed the lindens and come to the ruins of the chateau.

The sun was brighter. Albine had been delayed by her preparations. Almost reasonable, they walked side by side through the warm morning air, able to take twenty steps at a time without pushing one another and laughing. They were talking.

"I don't ever wake up," said Albine. "I really slept well last night. What about you?"

"Me, too," replied Serge.

She continued. "What does it mean when you dream about a bird talking to you?"

"I don't know. And what did your bird say?"

"Oh, I've forgotten. He said nice things, a lot of things I thought were funny. Hey, look at that big poppy. You can't have it, you can't have it!"

She was off, but Serge, thanks to his long legs, outran her, picked the poppy, and shook it furiously. Then, almost crying, she pinched her lips without saying a word. All he could think of was to throw down the flower. Then, to have peace, "Do you want to get on my back? I'll carry you like the other day."

"No, no." She was pouting. But she had not taken thirty steps when she turned around, all smiles. A thorn had caught her skirt. "Hey, I thought you were trying to step on my dress. It just doesn't want to let go. Help me get loose."

And when he had released her, they again walked side by side like good little children. Albine said it was more fun to walk this way, like serious people. They had just come to the meadows. Before them, all the way to the horizon, unrolled wide patches of grass, occasionally broken by the tender foliage of a curtain of willow trees, grass, fluffy as pieces of velvet, dark green slowly paling in the distance, drowning in bright yellow on the horizon, under the fiery sun. The willow groves and everything around them seemed to be pure gold in the shimmering heat. Dancing dust gave rushing light to the tips of the grass blades; certain puffs of wind, passing freely across this naked solitude, made the grass sway in the shiver of caressed plants. And, along the closest fields, crowds of small white daisies, piled up, scattered about, grouped together like people milling through the streets for some celebration, populated the dark lawns with their open joy. Golden buds displayed the gladness of tiny burnished brass bells, about to begin tinkling from the light touch of a fly's wing; huge, solitary poppies burst like red bombs, went farther, now joined into bands to spread joyous liquid, the purple bottoms of wine tubs; large bluebottles balanced their small peasant hats, quilled in blue, threatening with each puff to fly away over the windmills. Then carpets of velvet grass, vernal grass, hairy trefoil, sheets of fescue, dogstail, bent, spear grass. Sainfoin presented long thin hairs, clovers showed molded leaves, plantains brandished forests of blades, lucerne created soft beds, eiderdowns of sea-green satin, brocaded with violet flowers. All this, to the right, to the left, straight ahead, everywhere, rolling over the flat ground, swelling the mossy surface of a still sea, sleeping under the sky which seemed even more vast. The immensity of grasses was in places clear blue, as if reflecting the blue of the sky.

Albine and Serge were wading through green rising to their knees. It seemed to them that they were in cool water lapping against their calves. There were moments when they struggled against real crosscurrents, heard the high blades streaming rapidly between their legs. They saw calm lakes dozing, pools of short grasses which barely wet their ankles. They played games as they walked, trying not to break everything as they had in the orchard, trying to go slowly instead; their feet were tied by the plants' supple fingers; they felt purity, the caress of a stream calming their youthful brutality. Albine ran into a patch of giant grass reaching to her chin. Only her head was visible. She stood very still and called to Serge: "Come on! It's like a bath. There's green water everywhere."

Then she bounded away without even waiting for him, and they followed the first river which blocked their way. It was calm, shallow water, flowing between two banks of watercress, moving gently, leisurely twisting back and forth, so pure and clear that it reflected the smallest reed like a mirror. Albine and Serge had to walk with the current, moving more slowly than they, for a long time before they found a tree whose shadow was falling on the lazy stream. As far as the eye could see, the naked water, lying on its grassy bed, was stretching pure limbs, sleeping in the sun like a pliant, half-relaxed blue snake. Finally they came to a grove of three willows; two had their feet in the water, the other stood a little to the rear; their trunks had been struck by lightning and crumbled by age, but they were still topped with the blond hair of a child. Their shadow was so light that it barely gave a different tint to the sunny bank. The water, so smooth upstream and downstream, gave a brief shudder here, the disturbance of its clear skin expressing its surprise at feeling the touch of this veil. The meadow sloped imperceptibly down to the three willows to put poppies in the holes of the old blasted trunks, and they seemed to be facing a green tent erected on three stakes, by the edge of the water, in a rolling desert of grasses.

"Here it is, here it is," exclaimed Albine as she slipped under the willows. Serge sat beside her, his feet almost in the water, looked around, and murmured, "You know everything; you know the best places. It's like an island about ten-square-feet big that we found on the high seas."

"Yes, we're home now," she continued, so gay she struck the grass with her fist. "It's a house for us. We're going to do everything." Then, as if caught up by a marvelous idea, she threw herself on him and, with an explosion of joy, said in his face, "Do you want to be my husband? I'll be your wife."

The idea charmed him. Caught even more than she, he replied that he certainly wanted to be the husband. Then, all of a sudden, she became serious; she pretended to be a housewife in a hurry: "You know," she said, "I'm the boss. We'll eat when you finish setting the table."

And she ordered him about like a queen. He had to put everything she took from her pockets into a hole in one of the willows, which she called the "cupboard." The rags were their linen, the comb represented what they needed to be neat, the needles and thread were to be used to sew up the explorers' clothes. As for victuals, they consisted of the small bottle of wine and the leftover crusts. In reality, there were still some matches to cook the fish they would catch.

As he finished setting the table, with the bottle in the middle and the three crusts around it, he risked saying that the feast was rather skimpy. But she shrugged her shoulders with womanly superiority, put her feet in the water, and said sternly, "I'm the fisherman. You can watch."

For thirty minutes she took infinite pains in an attempt to catch tiny fish with her hands. She had raised her skirts and tied them with string. She moved cautiously and was extremely careful not to disturb the water; then, when she was very near a fish hiding between two stones, she reached with her bare arm, made a terrible racket, and caught only a handful of gravel. Serge burst out laughing, and she stormed angrily to shore, shouting that he had no right to laugh.

"But," he said finally, "what will you cook your fish with? There's no wood." That discouraged her. Besides, that fish didn't really look like anything to brag about. Without thinking of putting her stockings back on, she left the water and ran through the grass, legs bare, to dry herself. And she began to laugh again because some grass was tickling the soles of her feet.

"Oh! Bloodwort!" she said abruptly as she fell to her knees. "Now that's what's good! We're going to have a real feast." Serge had to put a pile of bloodwort on the table. They ate bloodwort with bread, Albine maintaining it was better than nut butter. She served like the lady of the house and cut the bread for Serge, to whom she would never entrust the knife. "I'm the wife," was her serious reply to all his rebellious objections.

Then she had him put back into the cupboard the few drops of wine at the bottom of the bottle. He even had to sweep the grass, so they could go from the dining room to the bedroom. Albine lay down first and said, "You understand, we're going to sleep now. You have to lie down beside me and snuggle up."

He stretched out as she had ordered him. They were both very stiff. They were touching from shoulders to feet; their hands were empty, and they put them over their heads; their hands bothered them more than anything else. They were completely serious. They looked at the sky with their big, open eyes and said that they were asleep and that they were comfortable.

"You see," murmured Albine, "when you're married you stay warm. Don't you feel me?"

"Yes, you're like eiderdown. But we mustn't talk if we're asleep. It's better not to talk."

They were silent for a long time, always quite serious. They had imperceptibly moved their heads farther apart, as if the heat of their breath bothered them. Then, in this great silence, Serge added one thing, "I like you very much."

It was love before sex, the loving instinct which sends ten-year-old men to stand in front of young girls in white dresses. Around them the meadows opened wide to calm their slight fear of one another; they knew that they were visible to the grasses, visible to the blue sky watching them through slender leaves, and that did not blow to the couple the languor of deep thickets, the hot worries of hidden holes and green alcoves. A healthy wind of free air blew to them from the horizon, bringing the coolness of that sea of greenery swollen by waves of flowers; and the river at their feet was one more bit of childhood, candor whose cool, flowing voice seemed to be the distant cries of a laughing playmate. Happy solitude, filled with peace, exposing its nudity with the charming brazenness of ignorance! Immense field where the narrow lawn serving as their bed took on the openness of a cradle.

"Okay, it's over," said Albine as she stood up. "We've slept." He was a little surprised that it was over so soon. He stretched out his arm and pulled her skirt as if to bring her next to him again. And she fell on her knees, laughing and repeating, "What? What?"

He did not know. He looked at her and took her elbows; he grabbed her hair for an instant, which made her yell. Then, when she was up again, he buried his face in the grass holding the warmth of her body. "Okay, it's over," he said, standing in his turn.

They ran through the meadows until dark, darting far ahead to look. They visited the garden. Albine walked in front, scurrying about like a puppy, saying nothing but always looking for the happy clearing, even though the big tree she dreamed about was nowhere around. Serge was awkwardly gallant in all sorts of ways: he ran ahead so clumsily to spread the tall grass that he almost made her fall; when he wanted to help her across the streams, he lifted her body with one arm in a clasp that bruised her. Their greatest joy was reaching the three other rivers. The first followed a bed of pebbles between two endless lines of willows, their leaves so thick that the couple had to feel their way through the water and ran the risk of falling in a deep hole; but Serge, who went in first, found the water reached only to his knees, so he caught Albine in his arms and carried her to the other side to prevent her from getting wet. The next river was black with shadows falling from the tall trees on its banks. It listlessly passed under them with the slight rustle and white folds of a satin skirt trailing behind a woman dreaming in a forest: deep water, icy, disturbing, which they were lucky enough to be able to cross on a tree fallen from one bank to the other. They straddled the trunk and inched their way across, playing at dipping toes into the mirror of burnished steel, then going faster, frightened, frightened by the strange eyes opened by every drop they raised in the sleep of the current. And the last river held them longer than any other. This one was as playful as they; it slowed at certain bends to speed off again in pearly laughter, surrounded by big rocks, calmed in the shelter of a clump of arbutus, out of breath but still quivering; it displayed every mood, used for its bed fine sand, flat rocks, clear gravel, rich soil, from which leaping frogs raised puffs of yellow smoke. Albine and Serge were adorable as they wallowed there. Their feet bare, they went up the river to go home, preferring the watery road to the grassy road, dawdling at every island blocking their way. They disembarked on them, conquered barbarian hordes, rested in huge rushes, large reeds which seemed to build huts expressly for the shipwrecked couple. Charming return, made happy by the banks unfolding their spectacle, cheered by the good moods of living waters.

But as they were leaving the river, Serge realized that Albine was always looking for something, along the banks, on the islands, even in the plants sleeping in the stream. He had to pick her up in the middle of a patch of water lilies, whose wide leaves gave her legs the collars of Renaissance nobility. He said nothing, threatened her with his finger, and they finally returned home, arm in arm, all excited by the day's happiness, like a young married couple returning from some lark. They looked at each other and found that they were stronger and more beautiful; their laughter was undoubtedly different from what it had been in the morning.

◇◇◇◇◇◇◇◇◇◇◇◇◇◇◇◇◇◇◇◇◇◇◇◇◇◇◇◇◇◇◇◇◇◇◇◇◇◇

XI "AREN'T WE GOING OUT ANYMORE?" ASKED SERGE A FEW days later. And, on seeing her shrug her shoulders and look bored, he added, as if to make fun of her, "So you've given up looking for your tree?"

They made that a joke to last all day. The tree did not exist; it was an old wives' tale. Nevertheless, they shivered a little while speaking of it. And, the next day, they decided they would take a walk deep in the park, under the tall trees which Serge did not yet know. Albine did not want to take anything the morning they left; she was preoccupied, even a little sad, and her smile was very gentle. They had breakfast and did not leave until very late. The sun, already hot, softened them, made them walk slowly, near one another, looking for bits of shade. Neither the flower garden nor the orchard, both of which they had to cross, held them. When they reached the coolness of the forest shadows, they walked still more slowly, buried themselves in the trees' moving meditation without a word, with a long sigh, as if relieved to escape the sun. Then, when there was nothing but leaves around them, when no hole was left to show them the sun on the distant park, they looked at one another and smiled, vaguely perturbed.

"How nice it is!" muttered Serge. Albine nodded her head, her throat so tight she was unable to answer. They did not put their arms around each other as was their custom. Arms swinging, hands open, heads lowered, they walked without touching.

But Serge stopped when he saw tears fall from Albine's cheeks and drown in her smile. "What is it?" he cried. "Are you sick? Did you hurt yourself?"

"No, I'm laughing. I really am," she said. "I don't know, it's the smell of all these trees that's making me cry." She looked at him and added, "You're crying, too. You see, it's all right."

"Yes," he murmured. "All this shade shocks you. It feels like we're going into something so incredibly sweet it'll hurt us. But you'd have to tell me if you were sad about something. I wasn't mean; you're not mad at me?"

She swore that she was not, that she was really happy. "Then why aren't you having fun? Do you want to chase me?"

"Oh, no, let's don't chase each other," she replied, pouting like a big girl.

And when he mentioned other games, climbing trees for birds' nests, looking for strawberries or violets, she finally said impatiently, "We're too old. It's stupid to play games all the time. Wouldn't you rather walk like this, by my side, everything peaceful?"

She was in fact walking so agreeably that he took great pleasure from hearing her little boots click against the hard earth of the walk. He had never noticed the swaying of her body, the living trail of her skirt, rustling behind her like a serpent. He found so many new charms in the slightest curve of her limbs that he felt he could never exhaust his joy in seeing her walk staidly beside him.

"You're right," he cried. "It's more fun than anything. I'd go with you to the end of the world if you wanted me to." A few paces farther he asked if she was tired. Then he let her know that he would be happy to rest a little himself. "We could sit down," he stammered.

"No," she replied, "I don't want to."

"You know, we'd lie down like the other day, in the meadow. We'd be warm, we'd be comfortable."

"I don't want to! I don't want to!"

She had leaped away, terrified by these male arms stretching toward her. He called her stupid, tried to catch her. But when he barely touched her with the tips of his fingers, she screamed so desperately that he stopped, trembling all over.

"Did I hurt you?" But she did not answer at once, herself astonished by her scream, already smiling at her fear.

"No, let me go, don't torture me. What would we do if we sat down? I like walking better." And she added in a serious voice, pretending to joke, "You know I'm looking for my tree."

Then he began to laugh and offered to look with her. He was very kind; he did not want to frighten her anymore. He saw she was still quivering even though she had again begun walking slowly at his side. It was forbidden, what they were going to do there; it would bring bad luck; and he felt the same delicious terror affecting her. Each distant sigh of the forest shook him; the smell of trees, the greenish light falling from high branches, the whispering silence of underbrush, filled him with anguish. It was as if, at the first turn in the path, they were to find awesome happiness.

And they walked through the trees for hours, moving at the same speed. They barely exchanged a word; they were never apart for a minute; one followed the other through the darkest places. At first they went into thickets whose young trunks were not as large as a child's arm. They had to spread them apart to open a path between the tender shoots blinding them with the flying lace of their leaves. Their wake disappeared behind them, the opened path closed again, and they moved haphazardly, lost, confused, leaving no sign of their passing beyond high swinging branches. Albine, tired of not seeing three feet in front of her, was happy when she could jump out of this enormous clump of bushes whose end they had been seeking for a long time. They were in a glade of tiny paths; on all sides narrow walks went through the hedges, reversed themselves, crossed themselves, twisted, extended whimsically. They climbed up to look over the hedges, but they were not pressed; they would have been happy to remain there, forgetting everything to wander continuously, relishing the joy of always walking without ever arriving, if only the proud line of the forest had not been before them. They finally entered the forest, religiously, with something like awe, as the faithful enter a high church. Straight trunks, whitened by lichen, the grayish cold of old stone, rose out of all proportion, fell into infinitely long columns. Far away, naves and side aisles were formed; strangely daring naves, borne by thin pillars, covered with lace, hand-worked, so fine that they admitted everywhere the blue of the sky. Religious silence fell from the giant arches; severe nudity hardened the soil into worn tile. There was no grass; the earth was sown only with the brown powder of fallen leaves. And, penetrated by the grand solitude of this temple, they listened to their echoing steps.

It was unquestionably here that they would find the tree for which they had been looking for so long, the tree whose shade granted perfect bliss. They felt that it was near from the magic flowing in them, from the half-light of the high vaults. The trees seemed to be beneficient beings, full of strength, full of silence, full of happy immobility. They looked at them one after another; they loved each of them; they expected from their sovereign tranquillity some secret which would make them, too, grow tall in the joy of powerful life. Maple, ash, hornbeam, and dogwood were colossal people, a proudly gentle mob, heroic comrades living in peace, even though the fall of one of them would be enough to wound and kill a whole section of the wood. The elms had enormous bodies, swollen limbs injected with sap, barely hidden by small clusters of tiny leaves. The girlish whiteness of birch and alder curved into slender bodies, let fly in the wind the hair of huge goddesses already half-metamorphosed into trees. The regular torsos of plane trees stood erect, their smooth skin tattooed red, apparently dropping flakes from cracked paintings. Larch trees came down a hill like a barbarian army, their loincloths of woven greenery streaming behind them, a balm of resin and incense rubbed into their skin. And the oaks were kings, immense oaks, square, stocky bodies opening dominating arms, taking all space from the sun; titan trees, thunderstruck, overthrown into poses of unconquered warriors, whose far-flung limbs alone created an entire forest.

Was it not one of these gigantic oaks? Or maybe one of those lovely planes, one of those birches white as a woman, one of those elms straining its muscles? Albine and Serge went still deeper, no longer conscious, drowned in this mob. For an instant, they thought they had found it; they were in a ring of walnut trees, in shade so cold they began to shiver. Later, they felt a different emotion: they entered a small grove of chestnuts, all green with moss, bizarre patterns of spreading branches, large enough to hang a village from. Still deeper, Albine discovered a clearing, and they both ran to it, panting. In the center of a carpet of soft grass stood a carob tree spreading a riot of greenery, a Babel of foliage, ruins covered with extraordinary plants. Stones were enclosed in the wood, ripped from the ground by the rising stream of sap. The high branches bent back on themselves to touch the earth behind, surrounded the trunk with deep arches, a nation of new trunks multiplying endlessly. And in the bleeding cuts of the bark ripened carob beans; even the fruit of this monster was a struggle which wounded its skin. They walked slowly around it, went under spreading branches where the streets of a city were laid out, looked searchingly at yawning holes between naked roots. Then they went away, not having felt there the superhuman happiness for which they were searching.

"Where are we?" asked Serge. Albine did not know. She had never been in this section of the park. They were then in a grove of laburnums and acacias, whose racemes emitted a very sweet, almost sugary smell.

"We're lost," she murmured with a laugh. "I'm sure I don't know these trees."

"But," he said, "the garden has an end. You know the end of the garden?"

She gestured broadly. "No," she said.

They were silent, for they had never before had such a happy sensation of the park's immensity. They were delighted to be lost in a kingdom so large that they themselves could not hope to know its limits. "All right, we're lost," repeated Serge happily. "It's better when we don't know where we're going." He came closer to her, humbly. "You're not afraid?"

"Oh, no, there's only the two of us in the garden. What should I be afraid of? The walls are too tall. We don't see them, but they're guarding us."

He was very close to her. He murmured, "A little while ago you were afraid of me."

But, without blinking, she looked serenely in his eyes. "You were hurting me," she said. "Now you're being very good. Why should I be afraid of you?"

"Then you'll let me take you like that? We can go back under the trees."

"Yes, you can hold me, I like for you to. And let's go slow, okay, so we don't find our way too fast."

He had put his arm around her. It was thus that they went back under the tall trees, where the majesty of the vaults again slowed their walk of older children awakening to love. She said she was a little tired and leaned her head on Serge's shoulder. However, neither mentioned sitting down. They did not think of it; it would have disturbed them. What pleasure could they get from resting on the grass which could be even compared to the joy they tasted in walking forever side by side? The legendary tree was forgotten. They now wanted only to bring their faces closer together to smile. And it was the trees, maples, elms, and oaks, which whispered to them their first tender words, in their clear shade.

"I love you," said Serge in a soft voice which blew the thin golden hair on Albine's temples. He wanted to say something more; he repeated, "I love you! I love you!"

Albine was listening with a lovely smile. She was learning this music. "I love you! I love you!" she sighed, still more sweetly, with her pearly girlish voice. Then, raising her blue eyes, where a dawn of light was expanding, she asked, "How do you love me?"

Serge thought deeply. The trees were solemnly gentle, the deep naves retained the quiver of the couple's dull steps. "I love you more than anything," he replied. "You're more beautiful than anything I see in the morning when I open my window. When I look at you, you're all I need. All by yourself, you're enough to make me happy."

She lowered her eyes and rolled her head as if it were in a cradle.

"I love you," he continued. "I don't know you, I don't know who you are, I don't know where you come from; you're neither my mother nor my sister. And I love you enough to give you my whole heart, to keep none of it for the rest of the world . . . Listen, I love your cheeks; they're as smooth as satin. I love your mouth; it smells like a rose. I love your eyes, where I see me and my love. I love even your eyelashes, even those tiny blue veins on your pale temples. That's to say that I love you, I love you, Albine."

"Yes, I love you," she said. "You have a very soft beard which doesn't hurt me when I lean my forehead on your neck. You're strong, you're big, you're handsome. I love you, Serge."

They were silent for a moment, delighted with each other. They felt that a flute was preceding them, that their words came to them from a marvelous orchestra which they could not see. They were now taking very short steps, leaning against one another, making endless detours among the giant trunks. In the distance, along the colonnades, was the light of the setting sun, a line of girls in white dresses entering church for a wedding, listening to the deep tones of the organ. "And why do you love me?" asked Albine again.

He smiled and did not reply at first. Then he said, "I love you because you came to me. That says it all. Now we're together; we love each other. It seems to me that I could not live if I did not love you. You are my breath." He lowered his voice and spoke in a dream. "You don't know it at first. It grows in you with your heart. You have to grow, you have to be strong. You remember how we loved each other! But we didn't say it. People are stupid when they're children. Then, one fine day, it gets too bright, it goes away. Come on, there's nothing else to do: we love each other because our life is to love each other."

Albine, head thrown back, eyes completely closed, was holding her breath, relishing the still-warm silence of this caress of words. "Do you love me? Do you love me?" she stammered, without opening her eyes.

He was silent, extremely unhappy because he had nothing else to say to show her how he loved her. He looked slowly at her pink face, as relaxed as if she were asleep: her eyelids had the delicacy of living silk; her mouth was an adorable fold wet by a smile; her forehead was purity drowning in a golden line at the roots of her hair. And he wanted to put all her being into the word he could feel on his lips without being able to pronounce it. Then he leaned closer to her; he seemed to be trying to decide where on this exquisite face to place the supreme words. He said nothing, he only sighed. He kissed Albine's lips.

"Albine, I love you!"

"I love you, Serge!"

And they stopped, trembling with this first kiss. She had opened her eyes very wide. He remained with his lips slightly extended. They looked at each other without blushing; something powerful, something sovereign was invading them. It was like a long-awaited meeting in which they saw themselves grown up, made for each other, tied forever. Stunned for an instant, they raised their eyes to the religious vault of the foliage, apparently searching the peaceful nation of trees for the echo of their kiss. But before the serene complicity of the forest, they felt the gaiety of unpunished lovers, a prolonged, resounding gaiety, filled with the chattering birth of their desire.

"Ah, count the days when you loved me. Tell me everything.

Did you love me when you slept on my hand? Did you love me the time I fell out of the cherry tree and you were on the ground, so pale, stretching out your arms? Did you love me in the meadows when you took my waist to help me cross the streams?"

Until dark, they lived on this word "love," which ceaselessly returned with new sweetness. They searched for it, brought it into every sentence, said it without reason for the sheer joy of saying it. Serge did not think of kissing Albine's lips a second time. In their ignorance, it was enough to keep the smell of the first kiss. Without thinking at all about the paths, they had found their way again. It was dusk when they left the forest, the moon was rising, shining yellow through black trees. And it was a childlike return through the middle of the park, with that discreet star watching them through all the holes in the great trees. Albine said the moon was following them. The night was very sweet and warm with stars. Far away the trees were whispering; Serge listened and thought, "They're talking about us."

When they crossed the flower garden, they walked in extraordinarily sweet perfume, that perfume which flowers have at night, more languid, more caressing, perfume which might be the very breath of their sleep.

"Good night, Serge."

"Good night, Albine."

They had taken one another's hand on the first landing without going into the bedroom, where they usually said good night. They did not embrace. When he was alone, sitting on the edge of the bed, Serge listened for a long time as Albine went to bed over his head. He was weak from happiness putting his body to sleep.

◇◇◇◇◇◇◇◇◇◇◇◇◇◇◇◇◇◇◇◇◇◇◇◇◇◇◇◇◇◇◇◇◇◇

XII BUT ALBINE AND SERGE WERE NOT AT EASE WITH ONE AN-
other for the next few days. They avoided any reference to their walk under the trees. They had not kissed, they had not pledged their love. It was in no way shame which kept them

from speaking, but fear, fear of spoiling their joy. And when they were not together, they lived on nothing but the beautiful memory: they buried themselves in it, relived the hours they had spent with each one's arms around the other, each one's breath caressing the other's face. It had finally made them ill. Their eyes pale, very sad, they chatted of things which did not interest them. Then, after a long silence, Serge asked Albine in a worried voice, "Are you sick?"

But she shook her head and replied, "No, no, you're the one who doesn't look well. Your hands are burning."

The park gave rise to profound worries which they did not attempt to understand. At a bend in some path, there was danger which was watching for them, which would seize their necks to throw them to the ground and hurt them. They never opened their mouths to speak of these things; but, by certain cowardly looks, they confessed their anxiety and cut themselves off like enemies. One morning, Albine, after a long hiatus, risked saying, "You're wrong to stay shut up. You'll get sick again."

Serge laughed in an irritated way. "Bah!" he muttered. "We went everywhere. We know the whole garden."

She shook her head and repeated very softly, "No, no, we don't know the rocks; we didn't go to the springs. That's where I get warm in the winter. There're places where the stones themselves seem alive."

The next day, without saying another word, they went out. They went to the left, behind the grotto where the marble lady was sleeping. As they were stepping on the first stones, Serge said, "It made us worry. It's just that we have to look everywhere. Maybe then we can find peace."

The weather was stifling and threatened to storm. They had not dared put their arms around each other. They were walking single file, burning in the heat. She used a wide spot in the path to let him pass her, for she was bothered by his breath; it hurt to feel it on her back, so near her skirts. Around them the rocks rose in wide layers. A gentle slope was created by immense slabs bristling with rough plants. First they met golden broom, patches of thyme, patches of sage, patches of lavender, all kinds of aromatic plants, bitter juniper and rosemary, so strong they became dizzy. At intervals on both sides of the path stood hedges of hops, resembling the delicate creations of ironworkers, ornamental gates of black bronze, cast iron, polished brass, very ornate, very flowery. Then they had to pass through a grove of pines to reach the springs, the thin shade weighing on their shoulders like lead. Dry needles cracked under their feet and released a small resinous cloud to burn their lips even more.

"This isn't the easiest part of the garden," said Serge as he turned to Albine.

They smiled; they were on the banks of the springs. Clear waters offered them relief, although they were not hidden under greenery like those flatland springs which plant thick bushes all around so they can doze lazily in the shade. These springs were born in the sun, from a hole in the rock, without one blade of grass to make their blue water green. They looked like silver soaking in the light. The sun shone on the sand at their bottoms in a dust of living, breathing light. And the waters left the first pool to extend arms of pure whiteness, bounced along like a playful, naked child, suddenly fell over a cliff in a waterfall whose soft curve seemed to be the fair torso of a woman's body.

"Put your hands in," said Albine. "The water's like ice at the bottom."

They could in fact cool their hands. They splashed water in each other's face, in the rain rising from the flowing sheets. The sun seemed to be wet.

"Hey, look!" cried Albine again. "There's the flower garden, and the meadows, and the forest." They looked at Paradou stretched out below them. "And, you see," she continued, "you can't see any trace of a wall. The whole country is ours, all the way to where the sky begins."

They had finally put their arms around each other, without being aware of it, in a reassuring and confident gesture. The springs cooled their fever. But as they were going away, Albine seemed to remember something; she took Serge back and said, "There, at the bottom of the rocks, I saw the wall once."

"But you can't see anything," muttered Serge, a little pale.

"Yes, yes, it must be behind the chestnut avenue, beyond that underbrush." Then, on feeling Serge grip her arm more nervously, she added, "I may be wrong. Still, I remember finding it in front of me all of a sudden when I left the walk. It blocked my way; it was so tall I was afraid. And, a few steps away, I was really surprised. There was a huge hole in it; you could see everything through it."

Serge looked at her and begged silently with his eyes. She shrugged her shoulders to reassure him. "Oh, but I stopped up the hole. Look, I told you, we're all alone. I stopped it up right away. I had my knife and I just cut some thorns. I pushed over big rocks. I dare a sparrow to get through. If you want to we'll go see one day. It'll make you feel better."

He shook his head and they walked away, arms around each other. But they were worried again. Serge looked down at Albine's face beside him. Her eyelids flickered; it upset her to be watched in that way. Both wanted to go back, to avoid the troubles of a longer walk. And, despite themselves, yielding to some force driving them, they went around a rock and climbed up to a plateau, where the intoxication of the bright sun was awaiting them. They no longer found the happy languor of aromatic plants, the musk of thyme, the incense of lavender. They were crushing stinkweeds; the bitter alcoholic breath of wormwood, the rotting flesh smell of rue; burning valerian, dripping its aphrodisiac sweat; mandrake, hemlock, setterwort, and belladonna sent dizziness to their temples, weakened them, made them tremble in one another's arms, their hearts on their lips.

"Do you want me to carry you?" Serge asked Albine when she leaned heavily against him; he was already holding her with both arms. But she pulled away, breathing rapidly.

"No, you're choking me," she said. "Let go. I don't know what's wrong. The earth is trembling under my feet. Look, that's where I hurt." She took his hand and put it on her heart. He blanched. He was nearer collapse than she was. And tears welled in both their eyes to see themselves like this without being able to find a cure for their great unhappiness. Were they going to die there from this unknown disease?

"Come in the shade, come sit down," said Serge. "It's the plants that are killing us; it's their smell."

He guided her with the tips of his fingers, for she trembled when he touched even her wrist. The grove of green trees they sought was made of lovely cedars spreading the flat roofs of their branches for more than ten yards around. Behind them grew the strange scents of conifers: cypresses whose soft, flat foliage resembled thick lace; firs straight and stern as ancient sacred stones, still black from sacrificial blood; yews whose dark dresses showed silver hems; all the evergreens, stocky plants whose leaves looked like shiny leather spattered by yellow and red paint, so strong that the sun slid off them and could never make them wilt. A monkey puzzle was especially strange, its huge, symmetrical arms a maze of intertwined reptiles, bristling with overlapping leaves, like the scales of angry snakes. The heat was drowsily voluptuous in this heavy shade; without moving at all, the air was dozing in a humid alcove. A perfume of Oriental love, the perfume of the painted lips of the woman of Salamis, wafted from the aromatic woods.

"Aren't you going to sit down?" said Albine. And she moved over a little to make room for him; but he started and remained standing. Then she invited him again, and he dropped to his knees a few feet away, muttering, "No, my fever is higher than yours, I'd burn you. Listen, if I wasn't afraid of hurting you, I'd hold you in my arms, so tight, so tight we could not feel our pains."

He came a little closer to her, walking on his knees. "Oh, to have you in my arms, to have you in my flesh. I don't think of anything else. At night I wake up and hug the void, I hug your dream. I want to take just the tip of your little finger at first, then I would slowly take all of you, until nothing was left, until you'd become mine, from your feet to your smallest eyelash. I would keep you forever. It must be a wonderful good to possess what you love that way. My heart would melt into your heart."

He came still closer; he could have touched the edge of her

skirt if he had stretched out his hand. "But I don't know, I feel far away from you. There's some wall between us that my fists can't beat down. But I'm strong today; I could bind you with my arms, throw you on my shoulders, and carry you away like one of my toys. And it's not that. I would not have you enough. When my hands take you, they hold nothing of your being. Where are you with all of you? Tell me, so I can go look for you."

He had fallen to his elbows, prostrate in a crushed position of worship. He placed a kiss on the hem of Albine's skirt; then, as if she had received this kiss on her skin, she stood up straight, put her hands to her temples, wild, stammering.

"No, I beg you, let's walk some more."

She was not fleeing. She let Serge slowly follow her, her feet stupidly tripping against the roots, her hands still grasping her head to silence the riotous clamor rising inside her. And when they left the little grove, they took a few steps on tiers of rocks teeming with ardent tribes of thick-leaved plants, a crawling stream of nameless beasts glimpsed in a nightmare, monsters composed of spiders, caterpillars, lice, amazingly huge, skin bare and green, skin bristling with terrifying hair, dragging injured limbs, deformed legs, broken arms, some swollen like obscene bellies, some bearing the expanded spines of a pullulating swarm of hunchbacks, some awkwardly strewn about like bones from a pillaged tomb. Nipple cacti piled pustules; they were swarming vermin, greenish turtles terribly bearded with long hairs harder than steel spikes. Echinocacti showed more skin, looked like nests of young vipers knotted together. Globe thistles were only one bush, a red-haired excrescence inducing nightmares of some giant insect rolling itself into a ball. Opuntias raised pulpy leaves as tall as trees, powdered with reddish needles like swarms of microscopic bees, like purses bursting at their seams from the vermin filling them. Gasterias extended paws, huge spiders struggling on their backs; their limbs were black, spotted, striped, damasked. Cereus planted shameful vegetation, enormous polyp trees, disease of this too-hot earth, sinful offspring of the orgy of poison sap. But the aloes especially spread the myriad hearts of fainting plants: all shades of green, soft, strong, yellowish, grayish, brown speckled with rust, deep green lined with pale gold; all shapes: wide leaves like hearts, thin leaves like sword blades, some laced with pimples, others finely stitched; enormous leaves holding away from their bodies the tall stick of their flowers, draped with necklaces of pink coral; tiny leaves growing in groups on a stem like pulpy blooms, flitting their deft serpents' tongues in all directions.

"Let's go back to the shade," begged Serge. "You can sit down like a while ago, and I'll get on my knees, and I'll speak to you."

Huge drops of sun were raining all around. The star conquered, seized bare ground, and pressed it to its burning breast. Albine staggered under the oppressive heat and turned to Serge. "Take me," she said in a dying voice.

The instant they touched, they fell into each other's arms, lips upon lips, without making a sound. They felt as if they were falling forever, as if the rock had sunk beneath them into a bottomless pit. Wandering hands searched face and neck, passed over all their clothes. But it was an approach so filled with anxiety that they moved away almost at once, exasperated, unable to move closer toward satisfaction of their desires. And they ran away by different paths. Serge ran to the house and threw himself on his bed, his head on fire, his heart despairing. Albine did not come home until that night, after crying herself out in a corner of the garden. For the first time, they did not return together, sharing the joyous fatigue of their long walks. They were in a bad mood for three days. They were terribly unhappy.

◇◇◇◇◇◇◇◇◇◇◇◇◇◇◇◇◇◇◇◇◇◇◇◇◇◇◇◇◇◇◇◇◇◇◇

XIII MEANWHILE, THE ENTIRE PARK HAD BECOME THEIR OWN. They had taken possession of it like a king and queen; not one bit of ground but belonged to them. It was for them that the rosebushes bloomed, that the flower garden had sweet and languorous smells which wafted their way through their open windows to put them to sleep at night. The orchard fed them, filled Albine's skirts with fruit, cooled them with the musky shade of its branches, under which it was so pleasant to have breakfast after sunrise. In the meadows, they had plants and waters: plants which extended the couple's kingdom by unrolling endless silk carpets before them, waters which were the best of their joys, their great purity, their great innocence, the cool stream where they loved to dip their youth. They owned the forest, from the enormous oaks which the arms of ten men could not encircle to the slender birches which a child could have broken, the forest with all its trees, all its shade, avenues, clearings, hidden greenery unknown to the birds themselves, the forest which they used as they pleased, as if it were a giant tent where they could shelter at noon the emotion born in the morning. They reigned everywhere, even over the rocks, over the springs, over that terrible ground with its monstrous plants, ground which had trembled under the weight of their bodies, which they loved more than the garden's soft beds because of the strange shiver they had felt there. Thus, now, straight ahead, to the left, to the right, they were the masters; they had conquered their domain; they walked through a friendly nature which knew them, which greeted them with laughter as they walked by, offering itself to their pleasure like a submissive servant. And they also enjoyed the sky, the wide blue patch above their heads; the walls did not enclose it, but it belonged to their eyes; it was part of their happy life, during the day with its triumphant sun, during the night with its warm rain of stars. It delighted them every minute of the day, changing like living flesh, in the morning whiter than a girl getting out of bed, at noon gilded by desire for fertility, in the evening swooning in the happy fatigue of its emotions. It never had the same face twice. It especially amazed them in the evenings, at the hour of good-byes. The sun sliding behind the horizon always found a new smile: sometimes it went away in serene peace, without a cloud, drowning little by little in a bath of gold; at other times it burst into purple rays, crushed its airy dress, escaped in waves of flames striping the sky with the tails of gigantic comets, whose flowing hair inflamed tops of the tall forest trees. There were also days when the tender star went to sleep on beaches of red sand, long shores of pink coral, after blowing its rays out one by one; or again, a discreet retirement behind some big cloud hanging like the gray silk curtain of an alcove, showing only the redness of a lamp, in the growing shadows; or a passionate retirement, proffered whiteness beginning little by little to bleed under the fiery disk biting it, finally rolling behind the horizon in the chaos of intertwined limbs collapsing into light.

Only the plants had not performed their rite of submission. Albine and Serge walked royally through the crowd of animals displaying their obedience. When they passed through the flower garden, flocks of butterflies rose for the pleasure of their eyes, fanned them with beating wings, followed them like a living shiver of the sun, like flowers flying up to shake out their scent. In the orchard, they found themselves sharing the tops of the trees with gluttonous birds: sparrows, finches, orioles, and bullfinches showed them the ripest fruits, scarred by their pecking beaks; and there was also a riot of pupils out for recess, a gay turbulence of petty thievery, bold bands coming to steal cherries from under their feet while they straddled the branches to eat. Albine had even more fun in the meadows, catching the small frogs crouching among the rushes, with their golden eyes and the gentleness of ruminative beasts; while she played with them, Serge used a straw to drive crickets from their holes, to tickle cicadas' bellies and make them sing, to catch blue insects, pink insects, yellow insects, and put them on his sleeve like buttons of sapphire, ruby, and topaz. They had moreover the mysterious life of the rivers, dark-backed fish darting through underwater half-light, eels hinting at their presence by rustling water grasses, small fry flitting away at the slightest sound, like a puff of dark sand, flies balanced on water skates, wrinkling the dead sheet with wide silver circles, all that silent swarm which planted them on the banks and often made them want to stand bare-legged in the middle of the stream to feel these millions of existences glide endlessly by. On other days, days of soft laziness, they went into the deep shade under the forest trees to listen to the serenades of their musicians, the crystal flute of nightingales, the thin silvery trumpet of bluetits, the distant accompaniment of cuckoos; they wondered at the sudden flight of pheasants, whose tails seemed to stripe the trees with sunlight; they stopped, smiling, to let a playful band of fawns pass a few feet away or to return the stare of a pair of serious deer slowing to watch them. On other days, when the sky was burning, they climbed the rocks, took pleasure from the clouds of grasshoppers which their feet kicked up in patches of thyme, grasshoppers crackling like a fire under the bellows; serpents stretching out beside reddish bushes, lizards on hot white rocks, followed them with a friendly eye; pink flamingos dipping their feet in spring water did not fly away from them, and their confident gravity reassured the water hens relaxing in the middle of the pool.

Albine and Serge had not recognized the growth of this park life around them until the day they felt themselves live in a kiss. Now they were stunned by it at times: it spoke to them in a tongue they could not understand; it communicated worries to which they did not know how to react. It was this life, all these animal voices and animal heat, all these plant smells and plant shade, which, even though they found only affectionate familiarity in the park, worried them and made them angry with one another. Each blade of grass, each tiny beast, became their friend. Paradou was a huge caress. Until they came, the sun had reigned alone for more than a hundred years, an absolute master hanging his splendor from every branch. The garden then knew only him: each morning it saw him leap over the wall with his oblique rays, sit right above the swooning earth at noon, and depart at night, on the other side, his farewell kiss grazing the foliage. Thus the garden had no shame now: it welcomed Albine and Serge, acting like good children who bother no one, as it had for so long welcomed the sun. Animals, trees, waters, stones, kept their lovable extravagance, spoke out loud, lived completely naked with no secrets, displayed innocent effrontery and the beautiful tenderness of the world when it was newborn. This bit of nature discreetly laughed at the fears of Albine and Serge, was moved by them, unfolded the softest beds of grass under their feet, expertly arranged its plants to make paths for them. If it had not yet thrown them into each other's arms, it was because it enjoyed playing with their desires and hearing their awkward kisses resound through the shadows like cries of angry birds. But, suffering from the great sensuality surrounding them, they cursed the garden. The afternoon after their walk among the rocks, when Albine had cried so much, she had shouted to the Paradou she felt alive and burning around her, "If you're our friend, why do you make us so unhappy?"

◇◇◇◇◇◇◇◇◇◇◇◇◇◇◇◇◇◇◇◇◇◇◇◇◇◇◇◇◇◇◇◇◇

XIV THE NEXT DAY, SERGE LOCKED HIMSELF IN HIS ROOM. The smell of the flower garden exasperated him; he drew the calico curtains so as not to see the park, so as to keep it from coming into his home. Perhaps, far from this greenery whose shade was like gentle fingers on his skin, he could find his childhood peace once more. Moreover, in the long hours of their conversations, he and Albine did not speak of the rocks, waters, trees, or sky. Paradou no longer existed. They tried to forget it. And they still felt it there, all-powerful and enormous behind the thin curtains; the smell of grass penetrated through the cracks in the boards; prolonged cries made the windows vibrate; all the outside life laughed and whispered as it lay in ambush under the windows. They grew pale and raised their voices, searching for some distraction which would allow them not to hear.

"Didn't you see it?" asked Serge one morning during one of these difficult hours. "There's a painting of a woman who looks like you over the door." He laughed raucously. And they went back to the painting; once again they dragged the table along the walls, trying to find something to keep them busy.

"Oh, no," muttered Albine. "She's a lot bigger than I am. Besides, you really can't tell; she's lying such a funny way, with her head at the bottom."

They were silent. From the painting, faded and eaten by time, rose a scene which they had never noticed. A resurrection of soft flesh coming out of the gray wall, a picture with new life, whose details seemed to reappear one by one in the summer heat; the supine woman was arched backward in the embrace of a goat-footed faun. They clearly saw the extended arms, yielding breast, and rolling torso of this huge naked girl, surprised in a bed of flowers being cut by tiny cupids who, their scythes in their hands, were ceaselessly adding new handfuls of roses to the soft couch. They could also make out the struggles of the faun, his panting chest, his attack on the girl. The other side showed only the woman's two feet thrown high in the air, flying away like two pink doves.

"No," said Albine again, "she does not look like me. She's ugly."

Serge said nothing. He seemed to be comparing the woman and Albine, looking fixedly at one, then at the other. The young girl pushed one of her sleeves up to her shoulders to show that her skin was whiter. And they fell silent again; they returned to the painting, questions they were unwilling to ask hovering on their lips. Albine's big blue eyes stopped for a while, focused on Serge's gray eyes, where a flame was burning. "So you've repainted the whole room!" she exclaimed as she jumped down from the table. "It looks like all these people are waking up."

They began to laugh, but in a worried way, glancing at the frolicsome cupids and at the huge nakedness of nearly whole bodies. They wanted to see everything again, to show that they could. Every panel astounded them, and they called one another to point out limbs which had certainly not been there the month before, supple limbs bent to shaking arms, legs displaying their entire length from feet to hips, women reappearing in the arms of men who had formerly clasped only emptiness. Even the plaster cupids in the alcove seemed to be tumbling with more brazenness. And Albine no longer spoke of children at their games, Serge no longer dared explain things aloud. They became serious; they tarried before each scene, wanting the painting to recover its original brightness in one stroke, even more upset and fearful because of the few veils hiding the paintings' crudities. These remnants of sensuality completed their indoctrination into the science of love.

But Albine was frightened. She ran away from Serge, whose breath was growing hotter in her hair, went to sit on the end of the sofa, and muttered, "They scare me, I don't like them. The men look like bandits, the women have the dying eyes of people being killed."

Serge sat in an armchair a few feet away from her and spoke of other things. They were both very tired, as if they had run a long race. And they were ill at ease because they thought the paintings were looking at them. Clusters of cupids rolled out of panels with the noise of loving flesh, with the clamor of shameless children, throwing flowers to them, threatening to tie them together with the blue ribbons they used to link two lovers in a corner of the ceiling. Couples came alive, unfolded the story of this large naked girl loved by a faun, from the time the faun crouched behind a rosebush to spy on her to the girl's surrender amid a pile of rose petals. Were they all about to descend? Were they not already panting, did not their breath fill the room with the smell of bygone sensuality?

"I'm stifling, aren't you?" said Albine. "It doesn't do a bit of good to air it out, this room still smells old."

"The other night," Serge began, "I was awakened by a perfume so penetrating that I called your name. I thought you had come into the room. It was like the warm smell of your hair when you put sprigs of heliotrope in it. At first it came from far away, like the memory of a smell. But now I can't sleep; the smell grows until it suffocates me. In the evenings especially, the alcove is so warm I'll end up sleeping on the sofa."

Albine put a finger to her lips and whispered, "It's the dead woman, you know, the one who lived here."

They went to sniff around the alcove, pretending to joke but actually very serious. It was certain that the alcove had never emitted such a disturbing smell. The walls seemed to be still trembling from the touch of a musky skirt; the floor had kept the scented sweetness of two satin slippers dropped beside the bed. And, on the bed itself, against the headboard, Serge said he found the impression of a small hand which had left its persistent violet perfume there. From every piece of furniture now arose the dead woman's scented ghost.

"Hey! That's the chair she must have used," cried Albine. "You can feel her shoulders on the back." And she sat down herself; she told Serge to get on his knees to kiss her hand. "Do you remember the day I admitted you and said, 'Good day, my dear lord'? But that wasn't all, was it? He kissed her hands after they closed the door. There they are, my hands. They belong to you."

Then they tried to play their old games again in order to forget Paradou and the great laugh coming louder and louder to their ears; they wanted to hide the paintings, to yield no more to the languorous alcove. Serge looked so stupid at her feet that Albine laughed and bent over backward. "You big bear, take my waist, tell me things like a lover, that's what you're supposed to be. So you don't know how to love me?"

But the instant he took her and began brutally to pick her up, she fought back and ran away, very angry. "No, leave me alone, I don't want to . . . You could die in this room!"

From that day on, they were as afraid of the bedroom as of the garden. Their last sanctuary became a frightening place where they could not be together without staring guiltily at each other. Albine hardly ever came in now. She stayed on the threshold, kept the door wide open behind her, as if to assure a swift retreat. Serge lived alone, in painful anxiety, stifling even more, sleeping on the sofa, trying to escape the sighs of the park and the smell of the old furniture. At night, he had insane dreams based on the paintings' nakedness, but he retained only a nervous half-memory of them when he awoke. He thought he was ill again; his health needed one more thing to be completely restored, a sense of supreme fullness, of absolute satisfaction. And he did not know where to look for it. He spent his days silently, his eyes heavy, starting awake only when Albine came to see him. They faced each other gravely, exchanged rare words of tenderness, which only upset them more. Albine's eyes, even heavier than Serge's, were begging him.

Then, after a week of this, Albine began to remain only a few minutes. She seemed to be avoiding him; she came fretfully, remained standing, was in a hurry to leave. When he questioned her, when he reproached her for no longer being his friend, she turned her head so as not to have to answer. She never wanted to tell him how she spent her mornings away from him; she shook her head in an irritated way and said how lazy she was. If he insisted, she would jump away and say nothing more to him beyond a formal good night as she passed his door that evening. But he could see that she was crying a great deal; he read on her face phases of hope always frustrated, continual revolt of a desire which had to be gratified. On certain days, she was fatally sad; her face showed utter discouragement; she walked slowly and seemed to doubt whether her search for joy was worthwhile. On other days, she seemed to be containing laughter; her face shone with thoughts of a victory which she did not yet want to mention; her feet were nervous and would not be still, eager to run to the last certainty. And, the next day, she was absolutely sad again, only to recover her hope a day after that. But what she soon could not hide at all was her immense fatigue, which seemed to be breaking her tired limbs. Even on her confident days, she buckled, she fell asleep with her eyes open.

Serge no longer questioned her after he understood that she would not answer. Now, when she came in, he watched her anxiously, afraid that the evening would come when she lacked the strength to return to him. Where could she be growing so tired? What constant struggle made her so distressed and so happy? One morning, he was startled by a light step beneath his windows. No fawn would run the risk of going there. He knew too well that rhythmic step which did not even hurt the grass: Albine was roaming through Paradou without him. It was from Paradou that she brought discouragement to him, that she brought hope to him, all that struggle, all that fatigue from which she was dying. And he quickly suspected what she was looking for alone, deep in the dense growth, silently, with the mute stubbornness of a woman who has sworn to find it. From that time on, he listened for her steps; he did not dare open the curtain to watch her, far away in the branches, but he experienced a singular, almost painful feeling to know that she was near him or far away, that she was burying herself in the flower garden. The park's noisy life, the trees' rolling voice, the waters' flow, the animals' continuous song, could not prevent him from recognizing her footfall, so clear that he could tell whether she was walking on river gravel, loose forest soil, or tiles of bare rocks. He could even judge whether she had found joy or sadness by the nervous click of her heels as she returned. As soon as she started up the stairs, he left the window; he did not admit that he had been with her everywhere. But she must have guessed his complicity, for, with a knowing look, she began to tell him about her quests.

"Stay here, don't go out anymore," he said one morning, his hands folded, when he saw her still out of breath from the day before. "You're worrying me too much."

She ran away, irritated. He began to suffer still more because of this garden resounding with Albine's steps; the small noise of her boots was another calling voice, a dominant voice whose echoes swelled in him. He stopped his ears; he did not want to hear, and the distant step pounded in the beating of his heart. Then, when she came back in the evenings, the whole park trooped behind her, bearing memories of their walks, the long awakening of their emotion, surrounded by their accomplice, all of nature. She seemed to be older, more serious, as if she were being ripened by her lonely walks. Nothing of the playful child remained, and his teeth sometimes chattered when he saw her so desirable.

One day, around noon, Serge heard Albine running back. When she left, he had promised himself not to listen. Usually it was late when she returned, and he was surprised to hear her leap as if she were running in a perfectly straight line, breaking the limbs in her path.

Below, under the windows, she was laughing. When she reached the stairs, she was breathing so hard that he thought he could feel her warm breath on his face. And she opened the door wide and shouted, "I found it!"

She had sat down, and she repeated softly, in a panting voice, "I found it. I found it." But Serge, stunned, put his hand on her lips and stammered, "I beg you, don't tell me anything about it. I don't want to know anything. It would kill me if you spoke."

Then she was silent, her eyes burning, pinching her lips together so the words could not spurt out despite her. And she remained in the room until evening, trying to meet Serge's eyes, telling him a little of what she knew as soon as his gaze encountered hers. There was something like light on her face. She smelled so good, she was so infused with life, that he breathed her in, that she entered him as much by his hearing as by his sight. All his senses drank her. And he tried desperately to defend himself against this slow conquest of his being.

When she came down the next day, she again sat in his room. "Aren't you going out?" he asked, feeling that he would be conquered if she remained. She said she was not, that she would go out no more. As she lost her fatigue, he felt her stronger, more glorious. Soon she would be able to grip his little finger and lead him to the grassy bed whose sweetness was so eloquently described in her silence. That day she did not speak; she was content to pull him to a cushion at her feet. It was only the day after that she risked talking. "Why are you poisoning yourself here? It's so nice under the trees."

He stood up, his arms outstretched, like a suppliant. But she laughed. "No, no, we won't go if you don't want to. It's just that this room has such a strange smell! We'd be better off in the garden, more at ease, more sheltered. You're wrong not to want to go to the garden." He had mutely stood up again, his eyes lowered, spasms running across his face. "We won't go," she continued, "don't get mad. But don't you like the grass in the park better than these paintings? You remember what we saw together. The paintings are what make us sad. They're bad, the way they watch us all the time."

And as he was relaxing against her little by little, she put an arm around his neck and laid his head on her knees, murmuring again, very softly, "That's how nice it would be in a place I know. Nothing would bother us there. The park air would cure your fever."

She was silent when she felt him tremble, afraid that too naked a word would reawaken his terror. She conquered him slowly by simply passing the blue caress of her gaze across his face. He had opened his eyes; he was resting without nervous trembling; he was completely hers.

"Ah, if you only knew," she whispered in his ear. She grew bolder on seeing that he continued to smile. "It's a lie, it's not forbidden," she murmured softly. "You're a man, you should not be afraid. If we went and there was something dangerous, you'd protect me, wouldn't you? You could carry me away on your back. I'm not scared when I'm with you. Just look how strong your arms are. Can a man with arms that strong be afraid of anything?"

She slowly rubbed his hair, neck, and shoulders with one hand. "No, it's not forbidden," she went on. "That story doesn't make sense. The people that used to spread it about just didn't want anybody to come bother them in the most delicious spot in the garden. Just say to yourself that you'll be perfectly happy as soon as you sit on that grass carpet. Only then will we know everything, will we be the real masters . . . Listen, come with me."

He shook his head, but without anger, like a man amused by this game. Then, after a time, distressed to see her pouting, wanting her to caress him again, he finally opened his lips and asked, "Where is it?"

She did not reply immediately. She seemed to be looking at something in the distance. "It's down there," she muttered. "I can't point it out. You have to go down the long walk, turn left, and turn left again. We must have passed it twenty times. It wouldn't do you any good to look; you couldn't find it unless I took your hand to guide you. I can go right to it even if I can't teach you the way."

"And how did you find it?"

"I don't know. That morning, the plants seemed to be pushing me that way. The long limbs whipped me from behind, the grass sloped to it, the paths opened up by themselves. And I think the animals had a hand in it, too. I saw a stag running in front of me, inviting me to follow him, and a flock of bullfinches went from tree to tree and warned me by little cries when I was about to go wrong."

"And it's very beautiful?"

Again, she did not reply, her eyes drowned in profound ecstasy. And, when she could speak, "More beautiful than I know how to tell you. Such delight penetrated me that I was aware only of nameless joy falling from the boughs, sleeping on the grass. And I ran back here to get you, so I would not taste the happiness of sitting in that shade all alone." She took his neck in her arms once again, ardently begging him, her lips almost on his, "Oh, you'll come," she blurted. "Just think how awful it would be if you didn't come. It's a feeling I have, a great need which got bigger every day, until it began to hurt me terribly. You can't want me to be hurt? And even if you were to die from it, even if that shade were to kill us both, would you hesitate, would you have any regrets? We would lie together forever at the foot of the tree; we would sleep forever against each other. It would be very nice, wouldn't it?"

"Yes, yes," he stammered, won over by the insanity of this passion vibrating with desire.

"But we shall not die," she continued, her voice rising in the laughter of a victorious woman. "We shall live to love each other. It's a tree of life, a tree under which we shall be stronger, healthier, perfect. You'll see, everything will be cozy for us. You'll be able to take me as you dreamed of doing, so tightly that no part of my body will be outside you. Then—I see it now—something heavenly will come down to enter us. Do you want to?"

He grew pale and blinked his eyes as if a great light were shining on him.

"Do you want to? Do you want to?" she repeated more ardently, already half-standing.

He stood up and followed her, trembling at first, then attached to her waist, unable to separate himself from her. He went where she went, pulled along by the warm air flowing from her hair. And when he fell slightly behind, she turned to him, her face shining with love, the temptation of her mouth and eyes calling him so regally that, like a faithful dog, he would have gone anywhere with her.

XV THEY WENT OUT AND WALKED THROUGH THE MIDDLE OF
the gardens; Serge continued to smile. He saw the greenery
only in the bright mirrors of Albine's eyes. The garden seemed
to laugh long on seeing them; a satisfied murmur flew from
leaf to leaf, reaching to the end of the deepest avenues. For days
it had had to wait for them to come thus, tied to each other's
waist, reconciled to the trees, seeking their lost love on the
grassy beds. A solemn hush fell over the boughs; the two-
o'clock sky was hot and limp; plants stood on tiptoe to watch
them pass.

"Do you hear them?" asked Albine, half-aloud. "They fall
silent when we approach. But, far away, they're waiting for us;
they're passing the word about which path to show us. I told
you we shouldn't worry about finding our way. The trees are
pointing with their arms to show me the road."

The entire park was gently pushing them. It seemed that a
wall of bushes was being continuously erected behind them to
prevent their turning back, while, before them, the grassy
carpet rolled out so effortlessly that they did not even look to
see where they were stepping. They gave themselves to the
earth's gentle slope.

"And the birds are going with us," Albine went on. "It's the
tits this time. Do you see them? They're flying along the
hedges and stopping at every turn to make sure we don't get
lost. Ah, if we understood their song, we'd hear them urging
us to hurry." And she added, "Every animal in the park is with
us. Don't you feel them? There's a great rustle behind us: it's
the birds in the trees, the insects in the grass, the does and stags
in the thickets, and even the fish are stirring the silent waters as
they swim. Don't turn around, you'd scare them; but I'm certain that we have a lovely procession behind us."

During all this time, they had continued to walk without
fatigue. Albine spoke only to charm Serge with the music in her
voice; Serge obeyed the slightest pressure from Albine's hand.
Neither knew where they were, but both were certain that they

were going in the right direction. As they went farther, the garden became more discreet, it muted the breath of its shadows, the chattering of its waters, the ardent life of its animals. There was now only great shimmering silence, religious expectation.

Then, instinctively, Albine and Serge raised their heads. Before them was a colossal mass of green. And as they hesitated, a doe watching them with its lovely, gentle eyes leaped into the underbrush.

"There it is," said Albine. She went in first, her head turned to pull Serge to her. They disappeared behind trembling leaves, and everything became calm. They were entering delicious peace.

In the center was a tree drowned in such heavy shade that its shape could not be discerned. It had a giant body, a trunk breathing like a chest, branches extending like arms raised in defense. It seemed kind, robust, powerful, fruitful; it was the dean of the garden, the father of the forest, the pride of the grass, the friend of the sun, which every day rose and set over it. From its green vault fell all the joy of creation: flower smells, bird songs, drops of light, cool, awakening dawns, warm, sleepy dusks. Its sap was so powerful that it flowed through its bark, bathing the tree in a vapor of fertility, making it the very manhood of the earth. And this tree was enough to enchant the clearing. The other trees around it built the impregnable wall isolating it deep in a temple of silence and half-light; there was nothing but green, no bit of sky, no sign of the pale horizon, nothing but a rotunda draped all around with the soft silk of leaves, hung with the satiny silk of moss. It was like entering the icy crystal of a spring surrounded by limpid greenery, a silvery sheet dozing under reflected reeds. Colors, smells, sounds, tremors, all was vague, transported, unnamed, swooning from happiness so great that inanimate things were made to faint. The languor of an alcove, the glow of a summer's night fading on the bare shoulder of a woman in love, a barely audible exchange of lovers' moans abruptly becoming a great mute climax of passion, all this hung from the immobile branches unrustled by any breeze. The solitude of a wedding night filled with embracing beings, an empty bedroom where one felt, behind curtains drawn somewhere in the darkness, nature satisfying her desires in the arms of the sun. The tree's loins sometimes cracked; its arms stiffened like those of a woman in labor; the sweat of life flowing from its bark rained harder on the surrounding grass, exuding the softness of desire, drowning the air with its surrender, dimming the clearing with its pleasure. Then the tree collapsed with its shadows, grassy carpets, and belt of dense thickets. It became nothing but sensual delight.

Albine and Serge were under its spell. The moment the tree took them into the sweetness of its shade, they knew themselves to be cured of their intolerable anguish. They no longer felt that fear which made them flee one another, no longer felt those hot, desperate struggles in which they were hurt without knowing what enemy they were resisting so fiercely. Now, absolute trust, supreme serenity, filled them; they gave themselves up to each other, slid slowly into the pleasure of being together, far away, deep in a miraculously hidden retreat. Still not suspecting what the garden required of them, they gave it freedom to dispose of their emotion; they were calmly waiting for the tree to speak to them. The tree created such amorous blindness that the immense and royal clearing disappeared to leave its perfume as their only support. They had stopped, gripped by musky coolness, and they gave a light sigh. "The air tastes like a piece of fruit," muttered Albine.

Serge, in his turn, said very softly, "The grass is so alive it feels like I'm walking on the hem of your dress."

Religious awe lowered their voices. They had no curiosity and did not even look up to see the tree. Its majesty weighed too heavily on their shoulders. Albine looked at Serge to ask if she had exaggerated the magic of the greenery. Serge answered with two clear tears on his cheeks. Their joy at finally being there could not be put into words. "Come," she said in his ear, her voice softer than a breath.

And she went first to lie down at the very foot of the tree. With a smile, she held her hands out to him; still standing, he too was smiling as he gave his hands to hers. When she had them, she pulled him to her slowly, and he fell next to her. He immediately clasped her to his chest. This embrace gave them both an easy joy.

"Oh, you remember," he said, "that wall which seemed to separate us. Now I feel you, nothing is between us now. Are you all right?"

"Yes, yes," she replied. "It feels good."

They fell silent without releasing one another, invaded by a delicious, smooth emotion, sweet as a spreading sheet of milk. Serge rubbed his hands over Albine's body. He kept repeating, "Your face is mine, your eyes, your mouth, your cheeks, your arms are mine, from your fingernails to your shoulders. Your feet are mine, your knees are mine, all of you is mine."

And he kissed her face, her eyes, her mouth, her cheeks. From her fingers to her shoulders, he covered her arms with short kisses. He kissed her feet, he kissed her knees. He bathed her in a rain of kisses, falling in big drops, warm as the drops of a summer shower, falling everywhere, beating on her neck, her breasts, her hips, her ribs. He took possession; without haste but never stopping he conquered the smallest blue veins on her pink skin. "It is in order to give myself that I take you," he said. "I want to give you all of me, forever, because, I truly know it now, you are my mistress, my sovereign, the woman I must worship on my knees. I am here only to obey you, to remain at your feet, to foresee your needs, to protect you with my outstretched arms, to blow away the falling leaves which could disturb your peace. Oh, deign to permit me to vanish, to be absorbed in your being! Let me be the water which you drink, the bread which you eat. You are my goal. Since I woke up in this garden, I have been walking toward you. I have grown for you. Always I have seen your grace as my aim and compensation. You walked through sunlight with your golden hair; you were a promise announcing that you would one day show me the necessity of this creation, of this earth, these trees, these waters, this sky, all this, whose final purpose I do not yet know. I belong to you, I am a slave, I shall listen to you, my lips on your feet."

He said these things bent to earth, worshiping woman.

Albine, proud, let herself be adored. She offered her fingers, breasts, lips, to Serge's devout kisses. Seeing him so strong and so humble before her made her feel she was a queen. She had conquered him; she held him at her mercy; she could dispose of him with a single word. And what made her all-powerful was to hear the garden around them rejoice in her triumph and help her with a slightly louder noise.

Serge was only mumbling now; his kisses had no direction or design. He murmured again, "Ah, I want to know, I want to take you, to keep you, to die perhaps, or to fly away with you, I cannot say."

They both remained silent, panting for air, their heads spinning. Albine had the strength to raise a finger as if to invite Serge to listen.

It was the garden which had wanted the sin. For weeks it had lent itself to the slow apprenticeship of their desire; then, on the last day, it came to lead them into the green alcove. Now it was the tempter whose many voices all taught love: from the flower garden came smells of swooning flowers, a long whisper telling of the roses' wedding night, the violets' sensuality; and never had the heliotropes' entreaties had more carnal a heat. From the orchard, the wind brought clouds of ripe fruits, a heavy smell of fertility, apricots' vanilla, oranges' musk. The meadows raised a deeper voice, composed of sighs of millions of grasses being kissed by the sun, widespread cry of an innumerable multitude in heat, being inflamed by the river's cool caresses: running water's nakedness flowing through the willows, dreaming aloud of desire. The forest breathed the giant passion of oaks, the organ songs of tall woods, solemn music accompanying the marriage, deep in leafy sanctuaries, of ashes, birches, hornbeams, and planes; bushes and young thickets were filled with adorable sexual games, a racket of lovers pursuing each other, throwing each other down next to a ditch to steal sexual pleasure and vigorously shake the boughs around them. And, in the mating of the entire park, the roughest embraces were heard in the distance, on the rocks, where heat burst stones swelling with passion, where spring plants loved tragically without the neighboring springs being able to relieve them, springs which were themselves aflame with the star entering their bed.

"What are they saying?" asked Serge, shocked. "What do they want from us to make them beg that way?" Without replying, Albine clasped him to her.

The voices had become clearer. The garden animals were also shouting for them to love. Cicadas sang of emotion until they seemed about to die; butterflies spread kisses as they beat their wings; sparrows had momentary affairs, the caresses of a sultan hurrying through his harem. In the clear waters, fish were fainting as they dropped their fry in the sunlight, frogs were emitting ardent and melancholy cries, mysterious passion was monstrously satisfying itself in the insipid green of the reeds. Deep in the woods, nightingales threw out pearly laughs of sensual creatures, stags troated, drunk with such lust that they died of fatigue beside females which they had almost eviscerated. And, on the tiles of the rocks, beside the scrawny bushes, serpents, tied two by two, kissed gently, huge lizards sat on their eggs, their spines quivering in their small ecstasy. From the most distant places, from patches of sun and of shade, rose an animal smell warmed by universal heat. All this swarming life trembled as if giving birth. An insect was conceiving under each leaf, a family was growing in each tuft of grass. In the air, flies clung to each other, unable to wait until landing to be impregnated. The invisible parts of life which inhabit matter, the atoms of matter themselves, loved, copulated, gave a sensual quiver to the soil, and made the park a huge fornication.

Then Albine and Serge heard. He said nothing; he held her ever more tightly in his arms. The necessity of procreation surrounded them, and they yielded to the demands of the garden. It was the tree which whispered in Albine's ear what mothers tell brides on their wedding night.

Albine surrendered. Serge possessed her.

And the entire garden shared the couple's orgasm in one last cry of passion. Trunks bent as before a great wind; grasses released drunken sobs; flowers fainted, their lips open, and exhaled their soul; the sky itself, all burning from the retiring sun, showed immobile clouds, swooning clouds, from which fell superhuman rapture. And it was a victory for the animals, the plants, all the things which had wanted these two children to enter everlasting life. The park applauded ecstatically.

◇◇◇◇◇◇◇◇◇◇◇◇◇◇◇◇◇◇◇◇◇◇◇◇◇◇◇◇◇◇◇◇◇◇◇

XVI ALBINE AND SERGE SMILED AT EACH OTHER WHEN THEY recovered from the stupor of their bliss. They were returning from a country of light; they were descending from a great height. Then they clasped hands to thank each other. Each recognized the other, and they said, "I love you, Albine"; "Serge, I love you."

And never had the words "I love you" contained such sovereign meaning for them. They signified everything, they explained everything. For a length of time which they could not judge, they remained there, deliciously resting, holding each other even closer. They felt absolute perfection of their being. The joy of creation bathed them and made them the equals of the first forces in the world, made them the earth's strength itself. And in their happiness was the certainty of a law obeyed, the peace of a goal logically discovered step by step.

As he took her in his strong arms, Serge said, "Look, I'm cured. You gave me all your health." Albine surrendered herself to him and answered, "Take all of me, take my life."

They were filled with life to their lips. In possessing Albine, Serge had found his male sex, the energy of his muscles, the courage of his heart, the final health which his long adolescence had thus far lacked. Now he felt complete. He had clearer senses, broader thoughts. It was is if he had suddenly awakened as a lion ruling the plain under a free sky. When he stood up, his feet planted themselves firmly on the ground, his body expanded in the pride of his limbs. He took Albine's hand and pulled her up. She trembled a little, and he had to support her.

"Don't be afraid," he said. "You're the one I love." Now she was the servant. She put her head on his shoulder and gave him a look of worried gratitude. Would he not always dislike her because she had led him there? Would he not one day reproach her for that hour of worship when he had called himself her slave?

"You're not angry?" she asked humbly. He smiled, arranged her hair, and stroked her with his fingers as if she were a child. She continued, "Oh, you'll see, I'll be very small. You won't even know I'm here. But you'll let me stay in your arms, won't you, for I need you to teach me to walk. It seems to me that I have forgotten how to walk." Then she became very serious. "You must love me forever, and I shall be obedient. I shall work for your joy; I shall give you everything, even my most secret desires."

Serge's strength seemed to double when he saw her so submissive and affectionate. He asked, "Why are you trembling? What should I be angry at myself for?"

She did not reply. She was looking almost sadly at the trees, the greenery, the grass they had crushed. "Baby!" he said, laughing. "So you're afraid I'm mad at you for what you did to me? Come on, this can't be a sin. We loved as we had to love. I want to kiss the prints left by your feet when you led me here, as I kiss your lips which tempted me, as I kiss your breasts which have just completed the cure which your small cool hands began."

She shook her head. And she averted her eyes to avoid seeing the tree and said in a soft voice, "Take me away."

Serge slowly took her away. He looked one last time at the tree. He thanked it. The shadows were growing darker in the clearing; the shivers of a woman startled while retiring for the night fell from the greenery. When, on leaving the foliage, they saw once more the sun whose splendor still filled one part of the horizon, they were reassured; especially Serge, who found new meaning in each being, in each plant. Everything around him bowed, everything did homage to his love. The garden was now only a serf of Albine's beauty, and it seemed to have grown and become more lovely in the embrace of its masters. But Albine's joy was still troubled. She interrupted her laughter to start abruptly and cock her ear.

"What is it?" asked Serge.

"Nothing," she replied, glancing furtively behind her.

They did not know the lost section of the park they were in. Usually it made them happy to be uncertain where their whims had taken them; this time, they were worried and strangely upset. They gradually quickened their pace; they were going deeper and deeper into a labyrinth of bushes.

"Didn't you hear it?" said Albine fearfully as she stopped, out of breath. And, as he listened, caught up in his turn by the anxiety which she could not hide, she added, "The thickets are filled with voices. They sound like people making fun. There, isn't that laughter coming from that tree? And, over there, didn't that grass mutter something when I touched it with my dress?"

"No, no," he said, wanting to reassure her. "The garden loves us. If it spoke, it would never be to frighten you. Don't you remember all the good words whispered in the leaves? You're nervous, you're imagining things."

But she shook her head and said, "I know the garden is our friend. So it must be someone who has come in. I tell you I hear someone, I'm trembling too much. Oh, I beg you, take me away, hide me." They began to walk again, carefully studying the thickets, thinking they saw faces appear behind every trunk. Albine swore she heard a distant step searching for them. "Let's hide, let's hide," she repeated, desperately begging him to do something.

And she turned completely pink. It was the birth of modesty, shame gripping her like disease, spotting the open whiteness of her skin, which had never before displayed a blush. Serge was frightened to see her completely pink, her cheeks flushed, her eyes brimming with tears. He wanted to take her in his arms again, to calm her with a caress; but she ran away, she made a desperate sign to show him that they were not alone. Blushing even more, she looked at the open dress revealing her naked-ness, her arms, her neck, her bosom. The insane locks of her hair made her shoulders tremble. She tried to adjust her comb; then she was afraid of displaying too much of her neck. Now the rustle of a limb, the light sound of an insect's wing, the smallest breath of wind, made her jump, as if she were under the lascivious touch of an invisible hand.

"Be calm," begged Serge. "There's nobody here. You're red with fever. Let's rest for a minute. Please, let's rest."

She had no fever; she wanted to return home at once, so that no one could look at her and laugh; and, walking faster and faster, she picked leaves to hide her nakedness along the way. She tied a sprig of mulberry in her hair; she twined convolvulus around her arms and tied it to her wrists; around her neck she put a collar of clematis stems, so long they covered her breast with a leafy veil.

"Are you going to a costume ball?" Serge asked in an attempt to make her laugh.

But she threw the leaves she had just picked in his face. In a soft voice, quivering with alarm, she said, "Can you not see that we are naked?"

And he was also ashamed; he tied leaves to his disordered clothes.

They could not find their way out of the bushes. Suddenly, they came to the end of a path and met an obstacle, a gray mass, tall and stern. It was the wall.

"Come here! Come here!" yelled Albine.

She wanted to pull him away. But they had gone less than twenty steps before finding the wall again. Then they panicked and began to run along beside it. It was dark; there was no crack opening to the outside, but suddenly, on the edge of a meadow, it seemed to collapse. A breach opened a window of light to the neighboring valley; it must have been the hole Albine mentioned one day, the hole she said she had closed with rocks and thorns. The thorns were strewn all about like slashed rope; the rocks were thrown far away; the hole seemed to have been enlarged by some vengeful hand.

◇◇◇◇◇◇◇◇◇◇◇◇◇◇◇◇◇◇◇◇◇◇◇◇◇◇◇◇◇◇◇◇◇◇◇◇

XVII "OH, I KNEW IT," ALBINE SAID, WITH A CRY OF ULTI-mate despair. "I begged you to take me away. Serge, if you have pity, don't look!"

Serge looked despite himself. It was as if he were nailed before the breach. Below, at the back of the plain, the setting sun sent a golden glow to the village of Artauds, which was like a vision springing from the dusk already drowning the neighboring fields. It was easy to make out the huts scattered helter-skelter along the road, the little courtyards filled with dung, the narrow vegetable gardens. Farther away, the huge cemetery cypress raised its dark profile. And the red tiles on the church roof seemed to be a furnace, above which the black bell tower was a hastily sketched face; the old presbytery beside the church opened its doors and windows to the evening air.

"As you have pity," Albine said again, sobbing, "don't look, Serge. Remember, you promised to love me forever. Oh, will you ever love me enough now? Here, let me put my hands over your eyes. You know that my hands are what cured you. You cannot push me away."

But he did push her away, slowly. Then, as she was embracing his knees, he passed his hands in front of his face, as if to banish from his eyes and mind the dregs of sleep. So that was the unknown world, the strange land which he could not imagine without hollow fear. Where had he seen that land? From what dream was he awakening to feel such gripping agony rise from his loins and expand in his chest until he felt he must suffocate? The village was alive with the people's return from the fields. The men were going home, their coats thrown over their shoulders, walking like harried animals; on the thresholds of the houses, the women gestured to them; bands of children chased hens with rocks. Two children were slipping into the cemetery, a boy and a girl. They crawled along behind the tiny wall so as not to be seen. Flocks of sparrows were going to bed under the tiles on the church roof. A blue printed skirt, so wide it blocked the door, had just appeared on the presbytery steps.

"Oh, help me," stammered Albine. "He's looking, he's looking. Listen to me. You swore to obey me a little while ago. I beg you, turn around, look at the garden. Weren't you happy in the garden? It gave me to you. And how many happy days it still has for us, now that we know all the bliss of the shade. But death will come in through that hole if you don't run away, if you don't take me away. Look, those are the others; it's the world coming between us. The garden is our love. Look at the garden, I'm begging you on my knees."

But Serge was shaking. He was remembering. The past was reborn; he had clearly heard the village live. Those peasants, those women, those children, they were Mayor Bambousse coming home from his Olivettes field, calculating his profits from the coming harvest; they were the Brichets, the man dragging his feet, the woman groaning under her poverty; they were Rosalie behind a wall, being embraced by big Fortuné. He also recognized the two children in the cemetery, that good-for-nothing Vincent and that shameless Catherine, watching the fat flying grasshoppers among the tombs; they even had the black dog Voriau helping them; he sniffed the dry grass, smelled every crack in the old tombstones. Under the tiles on the church roof, the sparrows were fighting before going to bed; the boldest flew in through the broken panes; and in watching them he remembered the uproar they created next to the pulpit and on the altar steps, where there was always bread for them. And, on the presbytery steps, la Teuse, in her blue-printed dress, seemed to have grown still fatter; she was turning her head to smile at Désirée, who was leaving the barnyard, laughing loudly, her flock behind her. Then they both disappeared.

"It's too late," Albine muttered, as she fell into the slashed thorns. "You will never love me enough."

She was sobbing. He listened frantically, trying to seize the slightest distant noise, waiting for a voice to awaken him completely. The bell had jerked a little; and, through the drowsy evening air, the three strokes of the Angelus came slowly to Paradou. Silvery breaths, soft, regular calls. Now the bell seemed alive.

"My God!" shouted Serge. He fell to his knees, the tiny breaths of the bell had knocked him down. He prostrated himself and felt the three strokes of the Angelus pass over his neck and grip his heart. The bell had a louder voice; it returned again and again for minutes which seemed to be years. It evoked all his past life, his pious childhood, his seminary joys, his first Masses in the burning valley of Artauds, where he dreamed of the solitude of the saints. It had always spoken to him like this. He recognized the smallest inflections of this voice of the church, which had endlessly risen to his ears like the voice of a serious and gentle mother. Why had he not heard it? Once it promised him the coming of Mary. Was it Mary who had led him deep into happy greenery where the bell's voice could not penetrate? He would never have forgotten if the bell had not stopped ringing. And, as he bent lower, the caress which his beard gave to his folded hands frightened him. He did not know this long fur, this silky fur which gave him the beauty of an animal. He twisted his beard, put both hands in his hair to seek the naked spot of the tonsure; but his hair had grown powerfully; the tonsure was drowned in a virile flood of large curls stretching from his forehead to the nape of his neck. All his once-shaven flesh bristled like the flesh of a wild beast.

"Ah, you were right," he said, looking desperately at Albine. "We have sinned. We deserve some terrible punishment. I reassured you; I did not hear the threats flying through the boughs."

Albine tried to take him in her arms once more. She begged, "Hurry, get up, let us flee together. There may still be time for us to love."

"No, I'm not strong enough now; the smallest piece of gravel would make me fall. Listen, I'm horrified by myself. I don't know what man is in me. I have killed myself, and my blood covers my hands. If you took me away, my eyes would show nothing but tears, forever."

She lowered her weeping eyes, shouting furiously, "That doesn't matter. Do you love me?"

He was terrified and could not answer. A heavy step was dislodging the pebbles behind the wall; it was like the slow approach of snarling anger. Albine had not been mistaken; there was someone there, disturbing the bushes' peace with his jealous breath. Then they both wanted to hide behind a thicket. Their shame increased as they listened. But, from his stand on the threshold of the breach, Brother Archangias had already spied them.

The friar, his fists clenched, did not speak for some time. He was looking at the couple, at Albine trying to find sanctuary by grasping Serge's neck, with the disgust of a man who recognizes dung beside a ditch. "I thought so," he said between his teeth. "They had to hide him here." He took a few steps and shouted, "I see you, I know that you are naked. It is an abomination. Are you a beast that you run through the forest with this female? She took you a long way, admit it; she dragged you through filth, and here you are all covered with hair like a goat! Tear off a limb and break it on her back."

In a voice burning with feeling, Albine said very softly, "Do you love me? Do you love me?"

Serge, his head bowed, was silent. He did not push her farther away.

"Fortunately, I have found you," Brother Archangias continued. "I have discovered this hole. You have disobeyed God, you have killed your peace. Temptation will bite you with its flaming tooth forever, and from this time forward you will not have your ignorance to combat it. This slut tempted you, didn't she? Do you not see the serpent's tail twining through the locks of her hair. She has shoulders whose sight alone makes men vomit. Leave her, touch her no more, for she is the beginning of hell. In the name of God, come out of that garden!"

Albine kept saying, "Do you love me? Do you love me?"

But Serge had walked away from her as if he were actually burned by her naked arms, by her naked shoulders.

"In the name of God! In the name of God!" yelled Brother Archangias.

Serge was moving irresistibly toward the breach. When Brother Archangias had brutally pulled him out of Paradou, Albine, who had slid to the ground and stretched her hands to her departing lover like an insane woman, stood up, her chest crushed by sobs. She fled, vanishing into the trees, and her flowing hair beat against their trunks.

BOOK THREE

❖❖❖❖❖❖❖❖❖❖❖❖❖❖❖❖❖❖❖❖❖❖❖❖❖❖❖❖❖❖

I   AFTER THE PATER, FATHER MOURET HAD BOWED BEFORE THE
altar and gone to the epistle side. Then he returned to make the
sign of the cross over big Fortuné and Rosalie, kneeling side
by side at the rail.

"*Ego conjungo vos in matrimonium, in nomine Patris, et
Filii, et Spiritus Sancti.*"

"*Amen,*" responded Vincent, curiously studying his brother's
face out of the corner of his eye while serving Mass.

Fortuné and Rosalie lowered their chins. Despite the fact
that they had laughed and nudged one another while kneeling,
they were moved a little. Vincent had gone for the holy-water
stoup and sprinkler. Fortuné put the ring, a heavy, solid-silver
circle, in the stoup. When the priest had blessed it by making
the sign of the cross and sprinkling it, he returned it to Fortuné, to be slipped onto Rosalie's ring finger. Her hand was
green from grass stains which soap had been unable to remove.

"*In nomine Patris, et Filii, et Spiritus sancti.*" Father Mouret
murmured again, giving them a final blessing.

"*Amen,*" responded Vincent.

It was early in the morning. The sun was not yet coming in
through the church's wide windows. Outside, on the limbs of
the service tree, whose green seemed to have broken through
the windows, the sparrows were noisily awaking. La Teuse had
not had time to do the good Lord's housekeeping; she was
dusting the altars, stretching on her good leg to wipe the feet of
the Christ splattered with ocher and lake, arranging the chairs
as discreetly as possible, bowing, crossing herself, beating her
chest, listening to Mass, all this without missing a single stroke
of her feather duster. Alone at the foot of the pulpit, a few feet
from the bride and groom, Mother Brichet was attending the
marriage; she prayed immoderately, remained on her knees,
mumbled so loudly that the nave seemed to be full of buzzing
flies. And, on the other side, by the confessional, Catherine held
in her arms a diapered baby; the child had begun to cry, and

she had had to turn her back to the altar, bounce it, and try to entertain it with the bell cord hanging above its nose.

"*Dominus vobiscum,*" said the priest as he turned around, his hands open.

"*Et cum spiritu tuo,*" responded Vincent.

At that moment, three big girls came in. Without daring to go too close, they shoved one another in an attempt to see. They were three of Rosalie's friends who had run off on the way to the fields, curious to hear what the priest would say to the newlyweds; huge scissors hung from their belts. They finally hid behind the baptistry, pinching each other, twisting and swaying like enticing women, stifling laughter in clenched fists.

"Oh, well," said la Rousse, a magnificent girl whose hair and skin were like brass, "at least we won't have to fight a crowd to get out when it's over!"

"Well, old Bambousse is right," muttered Lisa, small and black, her eyes aflame. "You take care of your own vines; the priest insisted Rosalie get married, so he can just do it all by himself."

The other one, Babet, hunchbacked, her eyes too large for her face, was making jokes. "Still, there's Mother Brichet," she said. "She's religious enough for the whole family. Hey, just listen to her snore! For her that's a good day's work. She knows she'll get paid for it."

"She's the organist," said la Rousse. And all three began to laugh. La Teuse threatened them with her duster. At the altar, Father Mouret was offering Communion; when he went to the epistle side to have Vincent pour the water and wine of ablution over his thumb and index finger, Lisa said more softly, "It'll soon be over. He'll talk to them in a minute."

"Big Fortuné can still go to the fields," la Rousse pointed out. "And Rosalie won't lose a day's harvesting. It's handy to have your wedding in the morning . . . He looks stupid, Fortuné does."

"Sure!" whispered Babet. "That boy has an awful lot of trouble staying on his knees so long. You can bet he hasn't done that since he took first Communion."

But they were suddenly distracted by the baby Catherine was trying to entertain. He wanted the bell cord and was stretching out his hands, blue with anger, crying so hard he was choking. "Hey, the brat's here," said la Rousse.

The child cried louder and twisted like a dervish. "Put him on his stomach and give him the teat," Babet whispered to Catherine, who reared her head and began to laugh hysterically, with the brazenness of a ten-year-old. "I don't like this at all," she said as she shook the child. "Will you shut up, pig! My sister dropped him on my knees."

"Of course," Babet said cruelly. "She couldn't give him to the priest to hold, now could she?" This time la Rousse laughed so hard she almost fell over backward. She collapsed against the wall, her hands pressing her sides, laughing until she felt she would burst. Lisa had thrown herself against her to seek relief by pinching her shoulders and hips. Babet laughed like a hunchback, her chortles passing between her teeth and making a noise like a saw.

"If it hadn't been for the brat," she continued, "the good Father would have lost his holy water. Old Bambousse had decided to marry Rosalie to the Laurent boy from the Siguières section."

"Right," said la Rousse, during a lull in her laughter. "Do you know what he did, old Bambousse? He threw dirt clods at Rosalie's back to keep the baby from coming."

"Still, he's awfully fat," muttered Lisa. "The clods must have done him good." At that all three fell against one another in a fit of insane laughter, and la Teuse came limping up. She had gone behind the altar to get her broom. The three girls were frightened; they withdrew and remained silent.

"Sluts!" la Teuse managed to say. "You have the gall to say dirty things here! Aren't you ashamed, you, Rousse. Your place should be over there, on your knees in front of the altar, like Rosalie. I'll throw you out if you budge, understand?"

Rosalie's copper cheeks blushed a little, while Babet looked at her waist and chuckled. "And you," continued la Teuse, turning to Catherine, "will you leave that child alone! You're pinching him to make him cry. Don't lie to me! Give him here."

She took him, rocked him an instant, and put him on a chair, where he slept as peacefully as a cherub. The church regained its sad calm, broken only by the cries of the sparrows in the service tree. At the altar, Vincent had taken the missal back to the right, and Father Mouret had folded the corporal and slipped it into the burse. Now he was saying the final prayers, caught up in stern meditation which neither the baby's cries nor the farm girls' laughter had been able to disturb. He seemed to hear nothing, to be entirely given over to the supplications he was sending to heaven for the happiness of the couple he had blessed. That morning the sky was gray with a summer haze drowning the sun. Only gingery steam announcing a stormy day came in through the broken panes. Along the walls, the violently illuminated paintings of the Stations of the Cross displayed the dark brutality of their yellow, blue, and red spots. At the rear of the nave cracked the dried planks of the gallery, while the grass in the steps, grown to gigantic size, sent under the main door long ripe chaff teeming with tiny brown grasshoppers. The clock in its wooden frame grated mechanical lungs, as if to clear its throat, and struck half-past six.

"*Ite, missa est,*" said the priest, turning to the sanctuary.

"*Deo gratias,*" responded Vincent.

Then, after kissing the altar, Father Mouret turned again, mumbling the final prayer over the back of the newlyweds' bowed heads. "*Deus Abraham, Deus Isaac, et Deus Jacob sit vobiscum.*" His voice was lost in monotonous sweetness.

"Now he's going to talk to them," whispered Babet to her two friends.

"He's all pale," Lisa pointed out. "He's not like Father Caffin, that one's fat face always looked like he was laughing . . . My little sister Rose says she doesn't tell him anything at confession."

"That doesn't matter," murmured la Rousse. "He's not a mean man. His disease made him a little older, but on him it looks good. His eyes are bigger, he's got two wrinkles at the corners of his mouth that make him look like a man. He was too much like a girl before his fever."

"I think he's sad about something," said Babet. "It's like he was pining away. His face looks dead, but his eyes are shining! Don't you see him when he closes his eyes slowly like he was trying to snuff them out?" La Teuse shook her broom. "Hush!" she whispered, so energetically that it seemed a blast of wind had passed through the church.

Father Mouret had collected his thoughts, and he began in a voice which was almost a whisper: "My beloved brother, my beloved sister, you are united in Christ. The estate of marriage is the symbol of the holy union between Christ and His Church. It is a bond which nothing can sever, which God wants to be eternal, so that man cannot put asunder what heaven has joined together. In making you the bones of your bones, God has taught you that you have the duty to walk side by side in faith and trust, following in the way prepared by His omnipotence. And you must love one another in the very love of God. The slightest bitterness between you would be dis-obedience to the Creator who drew you from a single body. Remain forever united, as the image of the Church which Jesus wed by giving all of his flesh and all of his blood."

Big Fortuné and Rosalie, their noses raised curiously, were listening.

"What did he say?" asked Lisa, who was hard of hearing.

"Heavens, he said what they always say," replied la Rousse. "He's got a gift of gab, like any other priest."

Meanwhile, Father Mouret was still speaking, his eyes dim, looking over the heads of the newlyweds, staring at a hidden corner of the church. And, little by little, his voice grew softer; he put feeling into the words which he had long ago memo-rized with the help of a manual for young priests. He had turned to Rosalie, adding emotional sentences when memory failed him.

"My beloved sister, submit to your husband as the Church submits to Christ. Remember that you must leave everything to follow him like a faithful servant. You shall abandon your father and mother to bind yourself to your husband; you shall obey him in order to obey God Himself. And your yoke shall be a yoke of love and peace. Be his rest, his faithfulness, the reward of his good works, the salvation of his hours of weakness. Let him find you always at his side, like divine grace. Let him need only to extend his hand to find you. Thus will you both walk without becoming lost; thus will you find happiness in accomplishing the divine commandments. Oh, my beloved sister, my beloved daughter, your humility is filled with soft fruits; it will make domestic virtues, hearthside joys, pious prosperity grow in you. Have for your husband the tenderness of Rachel, the wisdom of Rebecca, the long faith of Sarah. Say to yourself that a pure life leads to all good things. Ask God each morning for the strength to live as a woman who respects her duties; for the punishment would be terrible, you would lose your love. Oh, to live without love, to rip your flesh from his flesh, to belong no longer to him who is your other half, to die far from what you loved! You would hold out your arms and he would turn away from you. You would seek your joys and find only shame in your heart. Hear me, my daughter, it is in you, in submission, in purity, in love, that God has put the strength of your marriage."

At that moment there was a laugh at the other end of the church. The baby had just awakened on the chair where la Teuse had laid him. But he was not naughty now; he was laughing, all alone. He had kicked off his blanket and was waving his tiny pink feet in the air. And it was his tiny feet which were making him laugh. Rosalie, bored by the priest's oration, quickly turned her head to smile at the child. But when she saw him kicking about on the chair, she was frightened and gave Catherine a terrible look. "Okay, you can look at me all you want," muttered her sister. "I'm not picking him up anymore!" And she walked under the gallery to study an ant hole in the corner of a broken tile.

"Father Caffin didn't talk so long," said la Rousse. "When he married pretty Miette, he just gave her two taps on the cheek and told her to be good."

"My beloved brother," Father Mouret said, half-turned to big

Fortuné, "it is God who grants you a companion today. For He did not want man to live alone. But if He decided that she would be your servant, He requires that you be a master filled with gentleness and affection. You shall protect her because God gave you strong arms only to spread them over her head when she is in danger. Remember that she is entrusted to you, she is submission and weakness which you cannot abuse without committing a serious crime. Oh, my beloved brother, what happy pride you must be feeling! From this day forth you will not live in the egoism of solitude. At all times you will have an adorable duty. Nothing is better than to love, except perhaps to protect what you love. Your heart will expand, your male strength will be increased a hundredfold. Oh, to be a support, to receive tenderness in trust, to see a child give herself entirely to you and say, 'Take me, make me what you will, I trust you!' And may you be damned if you ever fail her. That would be the most cowardly desertion which God ever punished. The minute she gave herself, she became yours forever. Better to carry her in your arms and put her on the ground only when she is safe. Leave everything, my beloved brother . . ."

Father Mouret, his voice profoundly altered, was now muttering indistinctly. He had completely closed his eyes, his face white, speaking with an emotion so painful that even big Fortuné was crying, uncomprehendingly.

"He's not all well yet," said Lisa. "He's wrong to tire himself out. Look! Fortuné's crying."

"Men are softer than women," whispered Babet.

"Still, he spoke well," concluded la Rousse. "These priests say a lot of things nobody else even thinks about."

"Hush!" cried la Teuse, already preparing to snuff the candles.

But Father Mouret was haltingly attempting to find the concluding sentences. "That is why, my beloved brother, my beloved sister, you must live in the Catholic faith, which alone can guarantee the peace of your home. Your families have certainly taught you to love God, to pray to Him morning and evening, to rely only on the gifts of His mercy . . ."

He could not finish. He turned around to pick up the chalice on the altar and returned to the sacristy, preceded by Vincent, who was trying so hard to see what Catherine was doing in the back of the church that he almost dropped the cruets and towel.

"Oh, what a heartless girl," said Rosalie, who had abruptly left her husband to come enfold her child in her arms. The baby was laughing. She kissed it and arranged its blanket, brandishing her fist at Catherine. Big Fortuné waddled up, and the three girls gathered around, pinching their lips.

"Look how proud he is now," Babet whispered in the others' ears. "That rat has earned all old Bambousse's money in the hay, out behind the mill. I saw him every night when he crawled along the little wall with Rosalie."

They cackled. Big Fortuné stood in front of them and cackled louder. He pinched la Rousse and let Lisa call him names. He was a solid lad who cared not a whit for anyone else. The priest had bored him. "Hey, Mother!" he called in his thick voice.

But Mother Brichet was begging at the presbytery door. She stood there, lachrymose and emaciated, as la Teuse dropped eggs into her apron pockets. Fortuné felt no shame; he winked and said, "She's sharp, my mother is . . . Why not? If the priest wants people in his church."

Rosalie had calmed down. Before leaving, she asked Fortuné if he had asked the priest to come bless their bedroom that evening, according to the local custom. Then Fortuné ran to the presbytery, stomping across the nave as he would have crossed a field. And he reappeared shouting that the priest would come. La Teuse was scandalized by the racket these people made; they seemed to think they were in an open road. She clapped her hands and pushed them to the door. "It's over," she said, "go away, go to work."

And she thought they were all outside when she spied Catherine, who had been joined by Vincent. They were both leaning anxiously over the ant hole. Catherine was using a long straw to dig around, so roughly that a wave of frightened ants was flowing across the floor. And Vincent was saying she had to go to the very bottom to find the queen.

"Oh, you lice!" yelled la Teuse. "What're you doing there? Will you be good enough to leave those animals alone! That's Miss Désirée's ant hole. She'd be happy to see you doing that, I don't think."

The children ran away.

◇◇◇◇◇◇◇◇◇◇◇◇◇◇◇◇◇◇◇◇◇◇◇◇◇◇◇◇◇◇◇◇◇◇◇

II FATHER MOURET, BAREHEADED OVER HIS CASSOCK, HAD RE- turned to kneel at the altar. In the gray light falling from the windows, his tonsure made a wide, pale spot in his hair, and the slight tremors on his skin seemed to come from the cold he must be feeling there. He was praying ardently, his hands folded, so lost in supplication that he did not hear la Teuse's heavy steps as she walked around him, without daring to inter- rupt. She was apparently suffering to see him like this, crushed, his knees cracking; once she thought he was crying and went behind the altar to get a better view. She had been unwilling to leave him alone in the church since his return, for one night she had found him passed out on the floor, his teeth clenched, his cheeks icy, as if he were dead.

"Come on, Missy," she said to Désirée, who was pushing her head through the sacristy door. "He's still there, hurting him- self. You know you're the only one he listens to."

Désirée smiled. "Heavens, we have to eat," she said. "I'm very hungry." And she crept over to the priest like a wolf. When she was very near him, she took his neck and kissed him. "Good morning, brother," she said. "So you want me to starve today."

He raised such a sorrowful face that she kissed him on both cheeks. He was emerging from a death agony. When he recog- nized her, he gently tried to push her aside; but she had one of his hands and would not release it. She barely allowed him to cross himself before leading him away. "Come on, I'm hungry, you're hungry, too."

La Teuse had laid breakfast in the small garden, under two large mulberry trees creating a leafy roof with their out- stretched branches. The sun, finally victorious over the stormy morning haze, warmed the vegetable patches, while the mulberry threw a wide cover of shade over the rickety table and its two cups of milk and thick slices of bread and butter. "You see, it's nice here," said Désirée, delighted to be eating in the open air. She was already cutting enormous pieces and devouring them with a huge appetite. When la Teuse remained standing, she said, "Aren't you going to eat anything?"

"In a minute," replied the old servant. "My soup is warming up." And, a short while later, marveling at the busy teeth of this big child, she said to the priest, "It's a pleasure to watch. Doesn't that make you hungry, Father? You have to force yourself."

Father Mouret looked at his sister and smiled. "Oh, she's a healthy kid. She gets bigger every day."

"It's because I eat," she exclaimed. "If you ate, you'd get big and fat. Are you still sick? You look very sad. I don't want that to start again, okay? I was too worried while you were off somewhere being cured."

"She's right," said la Teuse. "You don't have any common sense, Father; that's no way to live, eating two or three crumbs a day, just like a bird. How do you expect to make any blood? That's what makes you pale. Aren't you ashamed to be as thin as a rail when we're so fat, all us women? People must be saying we don't leave you anything to eat." And, bursting with health, they both scolded him in a friendly way. His eyes were very big and clear; something like a void was visible behind them. Still smiling, he replied, "I'm not sick, I've almost finished my milk."

He had drunk two swallows without touching the bread. "Animals," Désirée said dreamily, "are healthier than people."

"Well, that's not a very nice thing to say about us, what you just said," la Teuse exclaimed with a laugh. But that dear innocent twenty-year-old had no trace of malice in her.

"Of course," she continued, "hens don't have headaches, do they? You can make rabbits as fat as you like. And my pig, you can't say he ever looks sad." Then, turning to her brother, she said in an excited voice, "I named him Matthew because he looks like that fat man who brings the mail. He's really strong now. It's not very nice of you to say all the time you don't want to see him. One day, you'll want me to show him to you, right?"

While thus being nice to her brother, she had taken his bread and was chewing it with her beautiful teeth. She had finished one slice and was biting into another when la Teuse saw her. "But that's not yours! So you're taking bread from his mouth now!"

"Leave her alone," Father Mouret said gently. "I wouldn't have touched it. Eat, eat it all, my darling."

Désirée, slightly embarrassed for a while, looked at the bread and tried to hold back her tears. Then she began to laugh and finished the bread. And she said, "My cow isn't sad like you either. You weren't here when Uncle Pascal gave her to me and made me promise to be good. Otherwise you would have seen how happy she was when I hugged her for the first time."

She cocked her ears. A rooster's crow was coming from the barnyard, an uproar arose, the beating of wings, groans, harsh cries, the panic of terrified animals. "Oh, you don't know," she said abruptly, clapping her hands, "she must be pregnant. I took her to the bull ten miles away in Béage. You don't find bulls everywhere. Then I stayed to watch while she was being serviced."

La Teuse shrugged her shoulders and looked irritatedly at the priest. "You'd be better off if you went to make peace among the hens," she said. "They're all killing each other."

But Désirée continued her story. "He mounted her and took her between his hooves. People laughed. But there's nothing to laugh about, it's natural. The mothers have to make babies, don't they? Tell me, do you think she'll have a baby?"

Father Mouret made an indefinite gesture. His eyes had lowered before the girl's steady gaze. "Go, run!" cried la Teuse. "They're eating one another up."

The quarrel in the barnyard was becoming so violent that she was leaving with a great noise of rustling skirts when the priest called her back. "And the milk, darling, aren't you going to finish the milk?" He held out his cup, which he had hardly touched. She returned and drank the milk without scruples despite la Teuse's angry gaze. Then she rushed away again and ran to the barnyard, where they heard her making peace. She must have sat down among her animals; she was softly humming a lullaby to them.

◇◇◇◇◇◇◇◇◇◇◇◇◇◇◇◇◇◇◇◇◇◇◇◇◇◇◇◇◇◇◇◇◇◇◇

III "Now MY SOUP'S TOO HOT," GRUMBLED LA TEUSE AS SHE returned from the kitchen with a bowl containing a wooden spoon. She stood before Father Mouret and carefully began to eat from the end of the spoon. She hoped to cheer him up, to draw him out of his overwhelming silence. Since his return from Paradou, he had been saying he was cured and never complained. Often he even smiled so tenderly that the Artauds said his illness had done him good. But he was sometimes gripped by crises of silence, racked by torture which he would not admit, even though he had to use all his strength to keep it hidden; and mute agony was breaking him, it made him remain dumb for hours, prey to some abominable internal struggle whose violence could be guessed only by the anguished perspiration on his brow. At such times, la Teuse did not leave him; she numbed him with a flood of words until he gradually began to look kind again, as if he had put down the revolt of his blood. That morning, the old servant was mounting an attack even rougher than usual. She began to release words even while giving full attention to the spoon burning her tongue.

"Really, you have to live in a terrible place to see things like that. Do people in nice villages ever get married by candlelight? That's enough to show that all these Artauds aren't worth a hill of beans . . . In Normandy, I saw weddings that made everybody for five miles around drunk as lords. People ate for three days. The priest came, so did the mayor; at one of my cousins' wedding, even the firemen came. And what fun everybody had! But to get a priest up before the sun so you can get married while the chickens are still in bed, that doesn't make sense! If I were you, Father, I'd have refused. Heavens, you haven't slept enough as it is; you might have caught a chill in church. That's what made you relapse. Besides, we'd all rather marry animals than that Rosalie and her pimp, with their brat right there—he peed on a chair, by the way . . . You really should tell me where you hurt. I'd make you something hot . . . Father, answer me!"

He said weakly that he was all right, that all he needed was a little air. He had leaned against one of the mulberries, out of breath. He was giving up.

"All right, all right, it's your funeral," said la Teuse. "Marry people when you're not strong enough and it'll make you sick. I thought as much, I said so yesterday. Like now, if you listened to me, you wouldn't stay here, the barnyard smell makes you sick. It's really stinking now! I don't know what Miss Désirée can be stirring up. She's singing, she doesn't care a bit, it puts color in her cheek . . . Oh, I meant to tell you. You know I did all I could to keep her from staying to watch the bull service her cow. But she's just like you, stubborn as a mule. It's a good thing it doesn't mean anything to her. She finds joy in animals with their babies . . . Please, Father, be reasonable. Let me take you to your room. You could lie down and rest a little . . . No, you don't want to. All right, too bad, I tried to help. People shouldn't keep things bottled up until they choke on them, the way you do."

And her anger made her swallow a whole spoonful of soup, at the risk of burning out her throat. She tapped the wooden handle against her bowl, grumbling to herself: "There's never been such a man. He'd drop dead before he'd say a word . . . Okay, let him keep quiet. I know enough about it. It's not hard to guess the rest. Yes, yes, let him keep quiet. It's better this way."

La Teuse was jealous. Dr. Pascal had had to struggle valiantly to take her patient away when he thought the young priest was lost if left at the presbytery. He had to explain that the bell increased his fever, that the saints' pictures filling his room haunted his mind with hallucinations, that he needed to forget everything, needed different surroundings, some place where he could be reborn into the peace of a new life. And she shook her head, she said that there was no place where the "dear child" could find a nurse superior to her. Still, she had finally consented; she had even resigned herself to seeing him go to Paradou, although she kept protesting against the doctor's incomprehensible choice. But she retained burning hatred against Paradou, and she was especially wounded by Father Mouret's silence concerning his life there. She had often strained her wits vainly in an attempt to make him talk. That morning, exasperated at seeing him so pale, suffering so stubbornly without complaints, she began to shake her spoon like a stick and shout, "You'd better go back up there, Father, if you were so well off. There's somebody there who'll take better care of you than I do."

It was the first time she had risked a direct allusion. The blow was so cruel that the priest cried out and raised his sorrowful face. La Teuse's good soul felt instant regret. "Besides," she muttered, "it's your Uncle Pascal's fault. I told him enough about it. But those educated men don't ever change their minds. Some of them make you die so they can look into your body. He made me so mad I couldn't talk about it to anybody. Yes, Father, it's thanks to me that nobody knew where you were. I thought it was too awful. When Father Guizot, from Saint-Estampe, the one who took your place while you were away, came to say Mass here on Sundays, I told him stories, I swore you were in Switzerland. I don't even know where Switzerland is . . . I don't want to hurt you, but I'm sure that's where you caught this disease. So you're cured in a very strange way. It would have been better if they had left you with me. I wouldn't have thought it was a good idea to drive you insane."

Father Mouret, his head bowed again, did not interrupt her. She had sat on the ground a few feet from him in an attempt to meet his gaze. She was speaking maternally, delighted with the attentive way he seemed to be listening. "You never wanted to know Father Caffin's story. As soon as I mention it, you make me be quiet. Well, Father Caffin, in our hometown of Canteleu, had troubles. He was a very holy man, however, and he had a golden character. But, you see, he was awfully finicky, he loved delicate things. So a young lady hung around him, a miller's daughter boarding with us. To cut it short, what had to happen happened, you understand, don't you? Then, when people found out, everyone got mad at the priest. They wanted to stone him to death, so he ran to Rouen; he went to moan with the archbishop. And they sent him here. The poor man was punished enough by having to live in this hole . . . Later, I found out something about the girl. She married a beef trader. She's very happy."

La Teuse, enchanted at finally being able to tell her story, was encouraged by the priest's immobility. She came closer and continued. "Good Father Caffin! He wasn't proud with me; he often spoke to me about his sin. That doesn't keep him from being in heaven, and I'll answer for what I say! He can sleep peacefully over there under the grass. He never wronged anyone. I don't understand why people get so mad at a priest when he loses control. It's so natural! It's not pretty, of course, it's a sin which must make God angry. But it's better to do that than to go steal something. You can confess and wipe the slate clean. That's right, isn't it, Father, when people truly repent they earn their salvation anyway?"

Father Mouret had slowly become rigid. By a supreme effort, he had broken through his anguish. Still pale, he said firmly, "We must never sin, never, never!"

"Oh, now," the old servant exclaimed, "you're too proud, sir! That's not pretty either, pride. If I were you, I wouldn't be so stiff about it. People talk about their troubles, they don't suddenly slice their heart to pieces; they get used to separation. It goes away bit by bit. But as for you, why you even avoid saying people's names. You forbid others to mention them, it's as if they were dead. Since you came back, I haven't dared give you the smallest bit of news. All right, I'll talk now; I'll tell what I know because I see that all this silence is eating away at your heart."

He looked at her sternly and raised a finger to make her be quiet.

"Yes, yes," she continued, "I've got news about that place, and I'll tell it to you. First, the person is no happier than you are."

"Shut up," said Father Mouret, who found the strength to

get up and run away from her. La Teuse also stood up and blocked his way with her enormous body. She was growing angry and cried, "There, you're running away. But you'll listen to me. You know I don't like those people up there, don't you? If I talk about them, it's for your own good. People say I'm jealous. All right, I dream of taking you up there one day. You'd be with me, you wouldn't be afraid of doing wrong . . . Do you want to?"

He gestured for her to leave. His face had calmed, and he said, "I want nothing, I know nothing. We have high Mass tomorrow. We have to prepare the altar." After beginning to walk away, he added with a smile, "Don't worry, my good Teuse. I'm stronger than you think. I'll cure myself alone."

And he walked off, looking strong, his head held high; he had won. His cassock rustled very gently along the thyme bordering the walk. La Teuse, who had remained fixed to the same place, gathered up her bowl and wooden spoon and began to gripe. She said things between her teeth and shrugged her huge shoulders. "He acts strong, he thinks he's not built like other men because he's a priest. The truth is that that man is awfully hard. I've known men you didn't have to torment so long. And he's able to crush his heart like I crush a flea. It's the good Lord he talks about that gives him that strength."

She was returning to the kitchen when she saw Father Mouret standing by the barnyard gate. Désirée had stopped him to make him heft a capon she had been fattening for a few weeks; he agreeably said that it was very heavy and made the big child laugh.

"Capons crush their hearts like fleas, too," la Teuse spit out, completely furious. "They have reasons for it. There's no glory in them living right."

IV   FATHER MOURET SPENT HIS DAYS IN THE PRESBYTERY. HE avoided the long walks he had taken before his illness. The scorched earth of Artauds, the fires of this valley where grew nothing but twisted vines, disturbed him. Twice he had tried to go out in the morning to walk along the roads and read his breviary, but he had not passed the village, he had returned home, troubled by the smells, bright sun, and wide horizon. Only in the evening, in the coolness of approaching night, did he risk a few steps in front of the church, on the path leading to the cemetery. He had been seized by a need for activity which he did not know how to satisfy, so, in order to keep busy in the afternoon, he had given himself the task of pasting squares of paper in the nave's broken windows. For a week, this had kept him on a ladder, very attentive to properly placing the squares, cutting the paper with the care of a seamstress, spreading paste so there were no smudges. La Teuse watched over him from the foot of the ladder; Désirée cried that he must not stop up all the holes, that he had to leave a place for the sparrows to come in. And, so she would not cry, the priest forgot two or three panes in each window. Then, when these repairs were done, his ambition led him to beautify the entire church, without using mason, carpenter, or painter: he would do it all himself. He said this manual labor amused him, gave his strength back to him. Uncle Pascal encouraged him whenever he visited the presbytery, assuring everyone that this fatigue was better than all the drugs in the world. Father Mouret filled the holes in the walls with handfuls of plaster, nailed the altars with heavy blows of his hammer, ground colors to give a coat of paint to the pulpit and confessional. People talked about it five miles away. Peasants came, their hands behind their backs, to see the Father work. A blue apron tied around his waist, his fists bruised, absorbed by this rough job, he had a pretext for never going out. He lived his days among workmen's debris; more peaceful, almost smiling, he forgot the world outside, sun, trees, warm breezes which troubled him.

"The good Father can do whatever he wants if it doesn't cost the commune anything," old Bambousse said with a cackle. He dropped by every evening to see how the job was progressing.

Father Mouret spent on repairs the money he had saved while in seminary. The beautification project presented an awkward, almost laughable naïveté. Masonry quickly repelled him; he was satisfied to replaster the walls only to the level of a man's head. La Teuse mixed the plaster. When she spoke of also repairing the presbytery, which, she still maintained, might one day fall on their heads, he explained that he could not do it, that they would need a workman, and this gave rise to a terrible quarrel. She shouted that it didn't make good sense to have so beautiful a church where no one slept when right there they had bedrooms where they themselves would surely be found dead one fine morning, crushed by the ceilings. "What I can do," she grumbled, "is come make my bed here, behind the altar. I'm too scared at night."

Since it was undeniable that they lacked plaster, however, she referred no more to the presbytery. Besides, seeing the freshly painted church charmed her, was the great appeal of all this labor. The priest, who had replaced boards everywhere, amused himself by taking a brush and spreading a beautiful yellow color over the wood. The brush had a very gentle back-and-forth movement, which almost rocked him to sleep, which left him without any thought for hours as he followed the paint's thick trail. When everything was yellow, confessional, pulpit, gallery, even the outside of the clock, he risked veining and marbling the high altar to brighten it. And he grew even bolder, he repainted the whole thing, making it white, yellow, and blue: it was magnificent. People who had not come to Mass for fifty years lined up to see it.

The paint was now dry; Father Mouret had nothing left to do except edge the panels with brown stripes. He started that very afternoon, wanting everything to be completed by night-fall, since, as he had told la Teuse, there was a high Mass the next day. She was waiting to groom the altar; she had already put on the credence the silver crucifix, the candlesticks, the porcelain vases filled with artificial roses, and the lace cloth reserved for especially holy days. But it was so difficult to get the stripes exactly right that the priest worked until nightfall. It was dark when he finished the last panel.

"It's going to be too pretty," a rough voice said from the gray evening haze filling the church.

La Teuse, who had knelt in order to make sure that the brush was holding to a straight line, started in fright. "Ah, it's

Brother Archangias," she said, as she turned to look. "So you came in through the sacristy? My heart skipped a beat. I thought your voice was coming from under the floor."

After greeting the friar with a nod, Father Mouret continued working. The visitor stood silently, his big hands together in front of his cassock; then, after shrugging his shoulders on seeing how carefully the priest was attempting to get the stripes absolutely straight, he said again, "It's going to be too pretty."

La Teuse, almost hysterical, started a second time. "Goodness," she cried, "I'd already forgotten you were there. You could at least cough before you say something. Your voice comes on as suddenly as a corpse's." She had stood up and moved back to admire the work. "Why too pretty?" she said. "Nothing that has to do with the good Lord is too pretty. If the Father had had any gold, he would have used gold!"

The priest had finished, and she rushed to change the cloth, being very careful not to tangle the strings, before arranging crucifix, candlesticks, and vases in a symmetrical pattern. Father Mouret had moved to Brother Archangias' side and was leaning against the wooden barrier separating the choir from the nave. They said nothing to each other. They were looking at the silver crucifix which, in the growing shadow, still reflected the drops of light falling on the Saviour's feet, right temple, and left side. When la Teuse had finished, she came gloriously over to them.

"Well," she said, "it's nice. You'll really see people tomorrow. These heathens don't come visit God unless they think He's rich. Now, Father, we'll have to do the same thing to the altar of the Blessed Virgin."

"Throwing money away," grunted Brother Archangias.

But that made la Teuse angry. And since Father Mouret said nothing, she led both of them to the altar of the Blessed Virgin, pushing and pulling them in turn. "But just look! It clashes too much now that the high altar is so nice. It doesn't do a bit of good to rub it every morning, the dust just won't come off the wood. It's black, it's ugly. Don't you know what people will say, Father? Sure as you're born, they'll say you don't love the Blessed Virgin."

"So what?" said Brother Archangias.

La Teuse almost choked. "So that would be a sin, for heaven's sake! This altar's like a forgotten tomb in the cemetery. It it weren't for me, there'd be spider webs and moss all over it. Sometimes, when I can save some flowers, I give them to the Virgin. Every flower in our garden used to be hers." She had gone to the altar and picked up two forgotten dry bouquets. "See?" she added, "it's just like in the cemetery"; and she threw the flowers at Father Mouret's feet.

He picked them up without saying a word. It was now completely dark. Brother Archangias was having trouble walking among the chairs and almost fell. He swore, he said terrible things, often using the names of Jesus and Mary. When la Teuse, who had gone to get a lamp, came back into the church, she asked the priest, "So it's all right to put the buckets and brushes in the attic?"

"Yes," he replied. "It's done. We'll see about the rest later."

She walked in front of them, carrying everything. She kept quiet because she was afraid of saying too much. Father Mouret still held the two bouquets in his hand, and as they were passing the barnyard, Brother Archangias yelled, "Throw that stuff away!"

The priest took a few more steps, his head bowed; then he threw the flowers over the gate and into the dung heap.

◇◇◇◇◇◇◇◇◇◇◇◇◇◇◇◇◇◇◇◇◇◇◇◇◇◇◇◇◇◇◇◇◇

V AFTER EATING, THE FRIAR STRADDLED A CHAIR TO WAIT FOR the priest to finish his dinner. Since the latter's return to Artauds, the friar had come to the presbytery almost every night; never before had he forced his company on them so roughly. His huge shoes crushed the floor; his voice thundered; his fists struck the furniture as he chatted about the little girls he had whipped that morning or as he summarized his morality in formulas as hard as blows from a stick. As a remedy against his boredom, he thought of card games with la Teuse; they played Battle interminably, for la Teuse was unable to learn any other game. Father Mouret, who smiled when the first cards were thrown violently to the table, slipped little by little into a deep reverie, and he forgot everything for hours; he escaped despite Brother Archangias' defiant glances.

That night, la Teuse was in such a foul mood that she talked of going to bed as soon as the table was cleared, but the friar wanted to play. He tapped her shoulders and finally made her sit down, so roughly that the chair cracked when she hit it. Désirée, who loathed their guest, had disappeared to eat her dessert in bed, as she did almost every night.

"I want the red cards," said la Teuse. And the struggle began. At first la Teuse won some of the friar's good cards. Then two aces fell to the table together. "Battle!" she shouted with extraordinary feeling. She dropped a nine and was thrown into consternation, but when the friar dropped a seven, she triumphantly pulled in her booty. After half an hour she was back to two aces, the odds were even again; after forty-five minutes, it was her turn to lose an ace. Winning and losing jacks, queens, and kings presented the fury of a massacre.

"It's a great game, isn't it?" Brother Archangias said as he turned to Father Mouret. But he saw him so lost, so far away, with such an unconscious smile on his lips, that he brutally raised his voice. "Okay, Father, why aren't you watching us? That's not very polite. We're just playing to keep you entertained. We want to cheer you up. Come on, watch the game. It'd be better for you than daydreaming. What were you thinking about?"

The priest was startled. He did not reply; he forced himself to follow the game, his eyelids heavy. The contest continued relentlessly; la Teuse won her ace back, then lost it again. There were evenings when they fought over aces in this way for four hours, and often they even went to bed, livid, without either being able to win.

"But I just thought of something," suddenly cried la Teuse, who was now afraid she might lose. "The Father was supposed to go out tonight. He promised big Fortuné and Rosalie to come bless their bedroom, according to the custom. Hurry, Father, the friar can go with you."

Father Mouret was already standing and looking for his hat. But, without letting his cards go, Brother Archangias said angrily, "Forget it! Does something like that need to be blessed? It's a pigsty. Just think of the nice things they're going to do there, in that bedroom. That's another custom you ought to get rid of. A priest has no business sticking his nose under the sheets on a marriage bed. Stay here. Let's finish the game, that's the best thing to do."

"No," said the priest, "I promised. Those good people might be hurt. You stay here, finish the game while I'm gone."

La Teuse, very worried now, looked at Brother Archangias. "All right, yes, I'll stay," he said. "It's just too stupid."

But Father Mouret had barely reached the door when the friar stood up to follow him and threw his cards all over the floor. He turned and said to la Teuse, "I was going to win. Try to leave the cards the way they are. We'll finish tomorrow."

"Oh, sure, everything's messed up now," the old servant replied after hurriedly mixing the cards. "If you think I'm going to preserve your hand under glass, you've got another think coming! Besides, I could have won, I still had an ace."

In a few big strides, Brother Archangias joined Father Mouret on the narrow path to Artauds. He had given himself the task of watching over him and surrounded him with spies every hour of the day, accompanied him everywhere, had a boy in his school follow him when he himself could not perform this task. He said, with his terrible laugh, that he was "God's policeman." And, in fact, the priest seemed to be a guilty man imprisoned in the black shadow of the friar's cassock, an untrustworthy convict considered weak enough to revert to the way of sin if let out of sight for an instant. The friar was as ruthless as a jealous old maid, as minutely conscientious as a jailer who extends his duty so far that he hides bits of sky visible from his prisoner's cell. He was always there, to block the light, to prevent smells from entering, to wall up the dungeon so thoroughly that nothing from outside could ever come there again. He watched for the least signs of weakness; he recognized the priest's tender thoughts by the light which came to his eyes, and, pitiless as a mad beast, he crushed them with a word. Silence, smiles, a pale forehead, a trembling limb, everything belonged to him. Moreover, he avoided all direct reference to the sin; his presence alone was a reproach. His tone of voice in saying certain things gave his words the sting of a whip. He concentrated into a single gesture all the filth he could spit out about weakness. Like betrayed husbands who crush their wives under bloody allusions whose cruelty they alone can gauge, he never spoke of what he had seen in Paradou; he was content to awaken thoughts of it with a word: that was enough to destroy the rebellious flesh at times of crisis. He too had been betrayed by this priest dripping with divine adultery, by the man who had neglected his vows. He too felt the forbidden caresses whose distant odor was enough to enflame his own continence, the continence of a billy goat which has never been satisfied.

It was almost ten. The village was asleep; but, at the other end of town, one of the hovels, brilliantly lit, was emitting loud noises. Old Bambousse, while keeping the best rooms for himself, had given his daughter and son-in-law a corner of his house. They were downing one last glass while waiting for the priest. "They're drunk," grunted Brother Archangias. "Do you hear them stomping around?"

Father Mouret did not reply. It was a marvelous night, all blue under moonlight transforming the distant valley into a sleeping lake. And he slowed his pace, as if this sweet light were bathing him in well-being; he even stopped in certain bright spots and felt a delicious chill, the same sensation he felt on stepping into cool water. The friar continued to take big strides and chided him: "So, come on. It's not healthy to be out at this time of night. You'd be better off in bed."

But, at the entrance to the village, he suddenly froze in the middle of the road. He was staring at the hills, at the point where the white lines of gullies were lost in the black spots of small pine groves. He growled like a dog who smells danger. "Who could be coming down so late?" he muttered.

The priest, hearing nothing, seeing nothing, was now the one to tell the other to hurry. "Leave me alone, here he is," said Brother Archangias animatedly. "He's just turned the corner.

Look, he's in the moonlight. You must see him now. It's a big man with a stick." Then, after a time, he went on, his voice hoarse, choked with fury, "It's him, it's the old bastard . . . I thought so."

The newcomer was now at the bottom of the slope, and Father Mouret recognized Jeanbernat. Despite his eighty years, the old man was walking so fast that the nails in his heavy shoes struck sparks on the flint road. He walked straight as an oak without using the stick he was carrying on his shoulder like a rifle.

"Oh, the damned old man," the friar managed to say. He seemed to be nailed in place. "The devil's burning his feet with every coal in hell."

The priest, extremely upset, despairing of inducing his companion to abandon his prey, turned his back to walk on, still hoping to avoid Jeanbernat, hurrying to reach the Bambousse house. But he had not gone five steps when the old man's mocking voice seemed to come from right behind him. "Hey, Priest, wait for me. Are you scared?" Father Mouret stopped and waited for him, and he added, "Hell, your cassocks get in the way, you can't run with one on. Besides, you can be recognized from a long way off no matter how dark it is. When I was way up the slope, I said, 'Hey, that's the little priest down there.' Oh, my eyes are still good. So you're not coming to see us anymore."

"I've had a lot of things to do," muttered the pale priest.

"Okay, okay, it's a free country. I just mentioned it to show that I don't hate you for being a priest. We don't even have to talk about your good Lord. I don't care one way or the other. The girl thinks I'm the one keeping you from coming. I told her, 'The priest is an idiot'; and I meant it. Did I bite you when you were sick? I didn't even come up to see you. It's a free country."

He was speaking with perfect indifference and pretended not to notice Brother Archangias. But when the latter growled more threateningly, he said, "Hey, Priest, are you walking your pig?"

"Just wait, louse," screamed the friar. His fists were clenched.

Jeanbernat, his stick raised, pretended to recognize him. "Lower your paws," he cried. "Ah, it's you, churchy. I should have known it from the smell. We've got something we have to settle. I swore in the middle of your class to cut your ears off. The girls you're poisoning will get a big kick out of that."

The friar recoiled before the menacing stick, his craw bulging with curses. He stuttered, he could not find words. "I'll send you to jail, murderer. You spit on the church, I saw you. You make poor people deathly sick just by passing their doors. At Saint-Eutrope you made a girl miscarry by forcing her to chew a consecrated wafer you had stolen. Everybody knows it, devil. You're the scandal of the area. The man who strangled you would earn immediate entry to paradise."

The old man listened, cackled, and twirled his stick. During a break in the other's insults, he repeated softly, "Go to it, go to it if it makes you feel better, snake. In a minute I'll break your head open."

Father Mouret tried to intervene, but Brother Archangias pushed him aside and shouted, "You're on his side! Didn't he make you walk on a crucifix? Just try to deny it!" And, turning to Jeanbernat again: "Ah, Satan, you must have really laughed when you had a priest in your clutches. May Heaven crush those who helped you in that blasphemy! What did you do at night when he was asleep? You came with your spit, didn't you, to wet his tonsure so his hair would grow faster. You breathed on his chin and cheeks so his beard would grow an inch every night. You rubbed his whole body with your evil charms, you breathed the rage of a mad dog into his mouth, you put him in heat. And that's how you made him an animal, Satan!"

"He's really dumb," said Jeanbernat as he laid his stick on his shoulder. "He's boring me."

The friar, braver now, came to put his fists under the other's nose. "And your slut!" he yelled. "You're the one who slid her naked into the priest's bed!"

But he screamed and jumped back. The old man's stick had

just broken across his back. He retreated farther and picked up a piece of flint as large as both fists from a pile of rocks beside the road; he threw it at Jeanbernat's head. It would have crushed his skull if he had not bent over. He ran to another pile of rocks, took cover, and began to gather stones himself. And, from one pile to the other, a terrible battle arose. It hailed flint. The bright moon clearly silhouetted the combatants.

"Yes, you slid her in his bed," repeated the raging friar. "And you put a crucifix under the mattress so the filth would fall on Christ. Ha, ha! You're wondering how I know everything. You're expecting some monster from their mating. Every morning, you make the thirteen signs of hell on your slut's belly so she'll give birth to Antichrist. You want Antichrist, thief. Here, I hope this gets you in the eye."

"And I hope this shuts you up for good, churchy," replied Jeanbernat, very calm again. "Is he ever dumb, that beast with his little stories! Am I going to have to break your head to go on? Is it your catechism that drove you insane?"

"Catechism! Do you want to know the catechism taught to damned people like you? Yes, I'll teach you to make the sign of the cross. This is for the Father, this for the Son, and this for the Holy Ghost. Ah! You're still standing. Just wait, just wait . . . So be it!" He threw a handful of pebbles which spread like buckshot. Jeanbernat, struck in the shoulder, dropped the rocks he was holding and walked peacefully over while Brother Archangias was picking up two more handfuls and stammering, "I shall destroy you! God desires it. God is in my arm!"

"Will you shut up!" the old man said as he seized the other's arm. There was a short struggle on the dusty road made silver and blue by the moon. The friar saw that he was the weaker and tried to bite. Jeanbernat's dry limbs were like rope tying him so tightly that he felt knots bite into his flesh. He was silent, suffocating, trying to think of some treacherous move. After gaining the upper hand, the old man said menacingly, "I'd like to break your arm so I could break your God. You must see He's not the strongest, your God. I'm the one who's destroying you. Now I'm going to cut your ears off. You've been too much trouble."

And he calmly took a knife from his pocket. Father Mouret, who had several times vainly thrown himself between the combatants, now intervened so insistently that the old man finally consented to put off that little operation.

"You're wrong, Priest," he muttered. "This hero needs to be bled. Still, if you're against it, I'll wait. I'm sure to meet him somewhere again." The friar growled and he broke off to shout, "Don't move or I cut 'em off right now!"

"But," said the priest, "you're sitting on his chest. Get off so he can breathe."

"No, no, he'd start horsing around again. I'll let him up when I'm ready to go . . . As I was saying, Priest, when this bastard interrupted us, we'd be pleased to have you come see us. The girl's the boss, you know. I don't contradict her any more than I do my greens. Everything grows. Only imbeciles like churchy here see any evil in it. Where did you find evil, hog! You're the one who invented evil!" He shook the friar again.

"Let him up!" begged Father Mouret.

"In a minute . . . The girl hasn't been herself for a long time. I didn't notice anything, but she told me about it. Now I'm going to Plassans to warn your Uncle Pascal. At night, everything's peaceful, you don't meet anybody . . . Yes, yes, the girl's not feeling well at all."

The priest could think of nothing to say. He was trembling, his head was bowed.

"She was so happy taking care of you," continued the old man. "I heard her laugh while I was smoking my pipe. That was enough for me. Girls are like hawthorns: when they make flowers, they make all they can. Okay, you'll come if you feel like it. It might cheer the girl up. Good night, Priest."

He had stood up slowly, holding the friar's hands, watching for a low blow. And he walked away without looking back, in the same hard, lengthy stride. The friar silently crawled to the rock pile; he waited for the old man to be some distance away.

Then he started again, furiously hurling stones with both hands. But they simply fell in the dusty road. Jeanbernat did not condescend to grow angry; he walked away, straight as a tree, into the calm night.

"The cursed man, Satan makes him strong!" stammered Brother Archangias, throwing one last rock. "An old man you ought to be able to knock down by just flicking your little finger. He's been tempered in the fires of hell. I felt his claws."

His impotent rage kicked at the scattered rocks and he suddenly turned against Father Mouret. "It's your fault," he yelled. "You should have helped me. The two of us could have strangled him."

At the other end of town, the noise in the Bambousse house had increased. They distinctly heard glasses rhythmically beating the table. The priest had begun to walk again, his head still bowed, heading for the lighted window which looked like the flame from a bonfire of dried vines. The friar gloomily followed him, his cassock covered with dust, bleeding from one cheek, where he had been grazed by a rock. Then, after a time, he asked in his hard voice, "Will you go?"

When Father Mouret did not reply, he added, "Be careful! You're going back to sin. All it took was for that man to pass by and all your flesh quivered. I saw you in the moonlight, pale as a girl. Be careful, understand? This time God will not forgive. You would fall into the last rotten filth. Ah, miserable mud, dirt is carrying you away."

Then the priest finally raised his head. He was silently shedding big tears, and he said with moving gentleness, "Why do you talk to me that way? You're always there; you know the struggles I have every minute of every day. Don't have doubts about me; leave me the strength to conquer myself."

These simple words, bathed in silent tears, acquired in the night such sublime sadness that, despite his roughness, Brother Archangias himself felt moved. He said nothing more, brushed his cassock, wiped his bleeding cheek. When they reached the Bambousse house, he refused to go in. He sat down a few feet away on the overturned frame of a broken cart and waited there with the patience of a watchdog.

"Here's the priest!" cried all the Bambousses and all the Brichets around the table. And they filled the glasses again. Father Mouret had to take one. There had been no wedding feast, but, in the evening, after dinner, they had put on the table a fifty-liter demijohn, which they were trying to empty before going to bed. There were ten of them, and old Bambousse could already tip the demijohn with one hand. Only a thin red stream flowed from it now. Rosalie, very gay, was dipping the baby's chin into her glass, while Fortuné was turning somersaults and picking up chairs with his teeth. Everyone entered the bedroom. The custom was for the priest to drink his wine there: that was what they called blessing the room. It brought happiness and kept the couple from fighting. In Father Caffin's day, it was a very happy time, the old priest loved to laugh; he had even acquired a reputation for emptying his glass without leaving a drop at the bottom. This was an especially important skill, for the Artaud women maintained that every drop left was one less year of happiness for the newlyweds. With Father Mouret, the jokes were not so loud. Still, he drank it all in one gulp, which seemed to be very flattering to old Bambousse. Mother Brichet frowned when she looked at the bottom of the glass and saw a little wine left. Next to the bed, an uncle in the militia was telling crude jokes which made Rosalie laugh. Big Fortuné had already pushed her to her stomach on the mattress as a kind of caress. And when everyone had thought of at least one crude thing to say, they returned to the dining room. Vincent and Catherine had remained there alone. Vincent had climbed on a chair and was tipping the enormous demijohn with both arms, emptying it into Catherine's open mouth.

"Thanks, Father," said Bambousse as he showed the priest out. "All right, they're married now. You're happy. Ah! The dirty kids! I hope you don't think they're going to be saying *Paters* and *Aves* in a little while. Good night, sleep well, Father."

Brother Archangias had slowly left the cart where he was sitting. "May the devil," he muttered, "throw shovelfuls of coals between their bellies to make them die in burning pain!" He said not another word. He walked with Father Mouret to the presbytery, where he waited until the door was closed before leaving; he even turned around twice to make certain the priest did not leave again. When Father Mouret was in his room, he threw himself fully clothed across the bed, his hands over his ears, his face in his pillow, so as to hear no more, to see no more. He erased himself and slept like a corpse.

◇◇◇◇◇◇◇◇◇◇◇◇◇◇◇◇◇◇◇◇◇◇◇◇◇◇◇◇◇◇◇◇◇◇◇◇◇◇

VI THE NEXT DAY WAS SUNDAY. SINCE THE EXALTATION OF the Holy Cross thus fell on the day of a high Mass, Father Mouret wanted to observe the feast in an especially brilliant way. He had begun to feel extraordinary devotion to the cross and had replaced the statuette of the Immaculate Conception in his room with a large crucifix made of black wood, before which he worshiped for hours. To exalt the cross, to plant it before him, above all other things, gave him the strength to suffer and to struggle. He dreamed of nailing himself up in place of Christ, of being crowned with thorns, of having his limbs pierced and his side opened. What kind of coward was he to complain of an illusory wound when his God was there, bleeding from His entire body, with the smile of mankind's redemption on His lips. And he offered his wound, petty as it was, as a sacrifice; he finally managed to slide into ecstasy, to believe that blood was really streaming from his forehead, limbs, chest. These were hours of relief, all impurity flowed out through his wounds. He stood tall and straight as a martyr, desiring frightful tortures so he could bear them without a murmur.

As soon as it was dawn, he knelt before the crucifix. And grace fell as abundantly as dew. He made no effort; all he had to do in order to feel it fill his heart was bend his knees; it soaked throughout his body, deliciously sweet. The day before, he had agonized without receiving it. For a long time it was deaf to the screams of his damned soul; it often helped him when he could do nothing but make the childish gesture of folding his hands. He was blessed this particular morning with absolute repose, with complete faith, and he forgot his anguish to give himself entirely to the triumphant joy of the cross. Armor rose to his shoulders, so impregnable that the world beat helplessly against it. When he went downstairs, he walked on a cloud of victory and peace. La Teuse marveled and went to get Désirée for him to kiss. They both clapped their hands and said he had not looked so well for six months.

In the church, during the high Mass, the priest completed his rediscovery of God. It had been a long time since he had approached the altar with such feeling. He had to force himself not to burst into tears when he glued his mouth to the altar cloth. It was a solemn high Mass. Rosalie's uncle, the militiaman, came to the singing desk and filled the crumbling church with the organ-like tones of his bass voice. Vincent, in a surplice formerly belonging to Father Caffin and much too big for him, swung an old silver censer, enormously amused by the noise of the chains. He lifted it very high to create a great deal of smoke and looked around to see if he could make anyone cough. The church was almost full: people wanted to see the Father's painting. Peasant women laughed because it smelled good, while their men, standing in the back under the gallery, shook their heads as the cantor's voice went lower and lower. The high ten-o'-clock sun, subdued by the paper panes, entered through the windows and spread moiré over the replastered walls. The shadows of the women's bonnets looked like flocks of giant butterflies, and the artificial flowers on the altar had the humid joy of real freshly picked flowers. When the priest turned around to bless the congregation, he felt even stronger emotion to see the church so full, so clean, so drowned in music, incense, and light.

After the Offertory, a murmur ran through the crowd of peasants. Vincent, who had curiously raised his head, almost dropped the coals in the censer on the priest's chasuble. And when the latter looked sternly at him, he tried to excuse himself by whispering, "Your uncle just came in."

Father Mouret saw Dr. Pascal at the back of the church, next to one of the thin wooden columns supporting the gallery. He did not have his customary smiling, almost mocking expression. He had removed his hat, serious, angry, following the

Mass with obvious impatience. The spectacle of the priest at the altar, of his concentration, his slow gestures, the perfect serenity on his face, seemed to irritate him more and more. He could not wait until the end of the Mass; he left and went to walk around his horse and buggy, which he had hitched to one of the presbytery shutters.

"Okay, when will that guy be through covering himself with incense?" he asked la Teuse, who was coming from the sacristy.

"It's over," she replied. "Go to the parlor. The Father is changing his clothes. He knows you're here."

"Of course, he does, unless he's blind!" said the doctor as he followed her into the cold room with hard furniture which she pompously called the parlor.

He paced back and forth for a few minutes. The room's gray sadness increased his bad humor. As he walked, he struck the worn fabric on the chairs with his cane, and it sounded as if he were striking rocks. Then he became tired and stopped by the chimney, where a big St. Joseph, done in abominable taste, stood in place of a clock.

"Well, it's about time," he said when he heard the door open. And he walked over to the priest. "Do you know you made me swallow half a Mass? That hasn't happened to me for a long time. I absolutely had to see you today. I wanted to talk to you."

He did not finish. He was startled by the priest's appearance. There was a brief silence. "Are you all right?" he said finally, in an altered voice.

"Yes, I'm much better," replied Father Mouret with a smile. "I didn't expect you until Thursday. Sunday's not your day. Do you have something to tell me?"

But Uncle Pascal did not reply at once; he was still examining the priest, who was soaked in the warmth of the church, who had the smell of incense in his hair and the joy of the cross in his eyes. His uncle shook his head at this triumphant peace.

"I've just come from Paradou," he said abruptly. "Jeanbernat came to get me last night. I saw Albine. I'm worried about her. She needs a lot of care." He continued to study the priest as he spoke and did not even see his eyes blink. "Well, she took care of you," he added, more roughly. "If it hadn't been for her, my boy, you might be in a padded cell in Tulettes, struggling against your straitjacket. I promised you would go see her. I'm taking you with me. To say good-bye. She wants to leave."

"I can do nothing but pray for the person you mention," Father Mouret said gently. And when the doctor furiously struck the couch with his cane, he added in a very firm voice, "I am a priest; prayers are all I have to give."

"Hey, you're right," cried Uncle Pascal as he collapsed into a chair. "It's just that I'm an old man and a fool. Yes, I cried all alone in my carriage when I was coming here, just like a baby. That's what happens when you live with books. You do nice experiments but you don't act right. Could I have suspected that all this would turn out so poorly?"

He stood up and began to walk again, a desperate look on his face. "Yes, yes, I should have suspected. It was logical. And with you it became awful. You're not like other men. But listen, I tell you you were done for. Only the air she created around you could have saved you from insanity. But you understand, I don't need to tell you how you were. It's one of my greatest successes. And I'm not proud of it, God knows I'm not, for now the poor girl's going to die of it."

Father Mouret was still standing calmly, glowing like a martyr whom nothing human can touch. "God will have mercy on her," he said.

"God! God!" the doctor muttered dully. "We'd be a lot better off if He weren't mixed up in it at all. We'd be able to fix everything." He raised his voice and added, "I had calculated everything. That's the worst part! You convalesced for a month. The trees' shade, the child's cool breath, all that youth put you back on your feet. On the other hand, the child lost her wildness, you humanized her. The two of us made her a little lady we could find a husband for. It was perfect. But could I have dreamed that that old philosopher Jeanbernat wouldn't have gone an inch away from his greens! It is true that I didn't leave my laboratory either. I was making some studies . . . And it's my fault, I'm a calloused man."

He was choking, he wanted to go outside. He looked everywhere for the hat on his head. "Good-bye," he stammered. "I'm leaving. So you refuse to come? Please, do it for me; you see how it hurts me. I swear to you she's leaving soon. It's understood. I've got my carriage . . . Please come, I'm begging you."

The priest made an exaggerated gesture, like those the doctor had made in church. "No," he said. "I can't." And as he was seeing his uncle out, he added, "Tell her to kneel and beg God for help. God will hear her as He heard me. He will give her relief as He gave it to me. There is no other salvation."

The doctor looked him in the eye and shrugged his shoulders menacingly. "Good-bye," he repeated. "You're well. You don't need me anymore."

But as he was untying his horse, Désirée, who had just heard his voice, ran up. She adored this uncle. When she was younger, he would listen to her girlish chatter for hours without growing tired. He still spoiled her, showed interest in her barnyard, was happy to spend an afternoon with her, among her hens and ducks, his astute, learned eyes smiling at her all the time. He called her the "big animal" in a tone of affectionate admiration. He seemed to set her far above other girls. She threw her arms around his neck in an outburst of emotion and cried, "You're staying? For lunch?"

But he kissed her and refused, disentangling himself churlishly from her arms. She laughed and hung on to his shoulders. "You're making a mistake," she said. "I've got some eggs that are still warm. I was watching the hens. They laid fourteen this morning. And we could have eaten a chicken, the white one, the one who beats up the others. You were here Thursday when he put out the speckled one's eye, weren't you?"

The uncle was still angry, irritated with a knot in the reins which he could not untie. Then she began to jump around him, clapping her hands and chanting in her flutelike voice, "Yes, yes, you're staying. We'll eat it, we'll eat it."

And the uncle's anger could not withstand such an attack. He raised his head and smiled. She was too healthy, too alive, too real, her gaiety was too large, as natural and fresh as the sunlight gilding her bare skin. "You big animal," he muttered, delighted. He took her wrists while she was still jumping and went on: "Listen, not today. I have to take care of a poor little sick girl. But I'll come another day. I promise."

"When? Thursday?" She pressed him. "You know the cow's pregnant. She hasn't looked like she was feeling good for two days. You're a doctor, maybe you could give her something."

Father Mouret, who had remained there, calmly listening, could not help laughing a little. The doctor happily entered his carriage and said, "Good idea, I'll take care of the cow . . . Come here and let me kiss you, you big animal. You smell good, you smell of health. And you're better than anybody else in the world. If everybody were like my big animal, this would be a great place to live."

He clicked softly to his horse and talked to himself as the carriage descended the slope. "Yes, brute animals, all we need is brute animals. We'd be beautiful, we'd be happy, we'd be strong. Ah, that's dreaming. It's turned out well for the girl, she's as happy as her cow. It's turned out poorly for the boy, he's dying inside his cassock. A little better blood, a little stronger nerves, then we'd see. But he's missing out on life. True Rougons and true Macquarts, those kids there. The tail end of the group, final degeneration." And, pressing his horse, he hurried up the hill leading to Paradou.

◇◇◇

VII SUNDAYS WERE VERY BUSY DAYS FOR FATHER MOURET. HE had vespers, which he generally said to empty chairs, since even Mother Brichet did not push devotion so far as to come to church in the afternoon. Then, at four o'clock, Brother Archangias brought his schoolchildren for Father Mouret to hear their catechism, and their recitation sometimes lasted until very late. When the children were too unruly, they called la Teuse, who frightened them with her broom.

That particular Sunday, Désirée was alone in the presbytery around four. She was bored, so she went to pull grass for her rabbits in the cemetery, where she could always find magnificent poppies adored by the rabbits. She crawled among the tombs, picked aprons full of lush grass, and watched the animals attack it ravenously. "Oh, what lovely plantains!" she exclaimed delightedly to herself as she crouched by Father Caffin's tombstone. There, growing in a crack in the stone, were indeed magnificent plantains, spreading their broad leaves. She had filled her apron when she thought she heard a strange noise. The sound of rustling branches and dislodged pebbles came from the ravine running along one side of the cemetery created by the Mascle, a stream whose source was in Paradou. The sides were so rough and steep that Désirée thought it must be some lost dog or runaway goat. She quickly walked to the edge, and, on leaning over, was stupefied to see a girl in the thorns, supporting herself with extraordinary agility in the smallest hollows in the rock. "Grab my hand!" she shouted. "You can break your neck there."

On seeing she was discovered, the girl gave a start and seemed about to go back down. But she raised her head and was brave enough to take the hand offered her.

"Oh, I know you," said Désirée, overjoyed, as she released her apron to grab the girl's waist in a childish caress. "You gave me the blackbirds. They died, bless their little hearts. I was really sad about it. Wait a minute, I know your name, I've heard it. La Teuse often says it when Serge isn't around. But she said I was not ever to say it . . . Wait a minute, I'll re-member." She tried hard to remember and became quite serious. Then, when she thought of it, she was happy once more; she wanted to hear the music of the name time and again. "Albine, Albine! What a sweet name! At first, I thought you were a tomtit, because I had a tomtit I called something like that, I'm not sure exactly what now."

Albine did not smile. She was very white, and the flame of fever was in her eyes. A few drops of blood oozed onto her hands. When she caught her breath, she said quickly, "No, let me go; you'll get your handkerchief dirty if I touch it. It's nothing, I just got stuck a few times. I didn't want to come on the road, somebody would have seen me. It was better to follow the stream. Is Serge here?"

It did not shock Désirée to hear that name pronounced so familiarly and with such ardor; she said he was in the church for catechism. "We mustn't talk loud," she added, putting a finger to her lips. "Serge forbids me to talk loud when he's hearing catechism. If we don't be quiet, they'll come scold us. We can go to the stable, okay? It's nice there, we can talk."

"I want to see Serge," said Albine simply.

The big child lowered her voice still more, glanced furtively at the church, and whispered, "Yes, yes, we'll really trap him. Come with me. We'll hide, we won't make any noise. Oh, this is a lot of fun!"

She had picked up the pile of grass which had fallen from her apron. She left the cemetery and returned to the buildings, using great care, telling Albine to be sure to hide behind her, to crouch down very low. As they were both running to the barnyard, they saw la Teuse walking through the presbytery; she seemed not to notice them.

"Hush! Hush!" said Désirée enchantedly when they were huddled deep in the stable. "Now nobody can find us. There's some straw, we can stretch out."

Albine had to sit on a pile of straw. "And Serge?" she asked with the stubbornness of a fixation.

"Listen, we can hear him . . . When he claps his hands, it'll be over, the children will go. Listen, he's telling them a story."

Father Mouret's voice could barely be heard through the sacristy door, which la Teuse had undoubtedly just opened. It was like a religious blast of air, a mumble where the name of Jesus appeared twice. Albine quivered. She was standing up to run to that beloved voice, in which she recognized her caresses, when the sound seemed to fly away, choked off by the door, which had been closed again. Then she sat down, apparently waiting, her hands clasped together, completely possessed by the thought burning deep in her bright eyes. Lying at her feet, Désirée looked at her with naïve admiration.

"Oh, you're beautiful," she said. "You look just like a statue Serge had in his room. She was all white, like you; she had big curls on her neck, and she showed her red heart here, where I feel yours beating. You aren't listening, you're sad. Do you want to play games?" But her voice broke off; she cried out between her teeth, keeping the noise low, "The dirty rats, they're going to get us caught."

She had not put down the grass in her apron, and her animals were taking her by storm. A flock of hens had run up, clucking and calling the others, pecking the visible blades of grass. The goat slyly stuck his head under her arm and bit the broad leaves; even the cow, tied to the wall, pulled against her rope, stretched her neck, and snorted her warm breath. "Ah, you thieves!" said Désirée. "This is for the rabbits! Would you please leave me alone? I'm going to bust you one. And you, if you don't get out of here, I'll give your tail a good twist . . . Dirty beasts, they'd eat my hands right off."

She slapped the goat, kicked at the hens until they dispersed, hit the cow's snout as hard as she could with both fists. But the animals simply shook themselves and came back hungrier than ever. They pounced on her like an invading army and almost pulled off her apron. And she winked and whispered in Albine's ear, as if she did not want the animals to hear, "Aren't they cute, the little darlings? Here, you can watch them eat."

Albine watched without looking any less serious.

"Come on, be good," said Désirée. "You'll all have some, but you have to wait your turn. Big Lisa first. Ha, you're crazy about plantain, aren't you?" Big Lisa was the cow. She slowly ground up a handful of the lush grass which had grown on Father Caffin's grave, a thin stream of saliva hanging from her mouth, her big brown eyes shining with gluttonous satisfaction. "Your turn now," continued Désirée, turning to the goat. "Oh, I know you want poppies. And you'd rather have them blooming, wouldn't you, with little buds that burst between your teeth like hot roasted nuts. Here, these are awfully nice. They come from the left-hand side, where they were burying people last year." And as she spoke she offered a bouquet of bleeding red flowers, on which the goat began to graze. When there was nothing but stems left in her hands, she put them between its teeth. The furious hens behind her were pecking at her skirts, and she threw them wild chicory and dandelions, which she had picked in the old stones along the church wall. The hens fought over the dandelions with such ferocity, with such a fury of wings and spurs, that the other barnyard animals heard them. Then came the real invasion. The big tawny rooster, Alexander, was the first to appear; he pecked at a dandelion and broke it in two without managing to get anything into his mouth. He crowed and called the hens still outside, stepping aside to invite them to eat. And a white hen entered the stable, followed by a black hen, then a line of hens bumping each other, climbing on each other, finally flowing like a pond of raging feathers. After the hens came the pigeons, and the ducks, and the geese, with the turkeys bringing up the rear. Désirée, drowned and lost in this living tide, laughed and said, "It's like this every time I bring grass from the cemetery. They'd kill each other to get some of it. It must taste really good."

And she struggled to lift the last few handfuls of greenery over her head in order to preserve them from these ravenous beaks raised toward her, repeating that they had to save some for the rabbits, that she was going to get mad, that she would put them all on bread and water. But she was weakening. The geese pulled the corners of her apron so roughly that she almost fell; the ducks were devouring her ankles; two pigeons had flown to her head; she had chickens on her shoulders. It was the ferocity of beasts who smell flesh, lush plantains, bleeding poppies, dandelions bursting with sap, containing something of the life of dead men. She was laughing too much, she felt herself on the verge of backsliding and dropping the last two handfuls, when a terrible snort threw everything around her into a panic. "It's you, my fat friend," she said, delighted. "Eat them, save me."

The pig came in. It was no longer the piglet, pink as a freshly painted toy, with a tail like a piece of string on his rump, but a strong pig, ready to be slaughtered, round as a cantor's gut, his back covered with rough bristles, exuding grease. His belly was amber-colored from his bed in the dung heap; his snout extended, rolling on his paws, he hurled himself among the animals, allowing Désirée to escape and give the rabbits the grass she had so valiantly defended. When she returned, peace was restored. The smug, stupid geese were softly swinging their necks, the ducks and turkeys were stealing away along the walls with the prudent sway of weaker animals, the hens were cackling softly as they pecked at invisible seeds in the stable's hard dirt floor, and the pig, goat, and big cow were blinking their eyes as if growing sleepier and sleepier. Outside, a storm was beginning.

"Oh, good, a real downpour," said Désirée as she sat on the straw and shivered. "You'd better stay here, my darlings, if you don't want to get soaked." She turned to Albine and added, "They look a lot like louts, huh? They don't wake up except to pounce on food, not a one of them does."

Albine had said nothing. The laughter of this pretty girl struggling with these voracious necks, these gluttonous beaks which tickled her, kissed her, and seemed bent on eating her flesh, had made her even whiter. So much happiness, so much health, so much life plunged her into despair. She clasped her hot arms, pressed the void to the breasts dried out by her abandonment. "And Serge?" she asked in the same clear and stubborn voice.

"Hush!" said Désirée. "I just heard him, he's not through yet. We made an awful lot of noise. La Teuse must be deaf tonight . . . Let's be quiet now. It's nice to listen to the rain fall."

The storm came in through the open door, beating the threshold with big drops. Some hens, perplexed after risking a step outside, had withdrawn to the back of the stable. All the animals sought refuge there, around the skirts of the two girls, except for three ducks walking peacefully through the rain. The coolness of the water flowing outside seemed to drive the burning air of the barnyard into the stable. It was very hot in the straw. Désirée made two fat piles, lay on them like pillows, and relaxed. She was absolutely comfortable, her whole body enjoyed the way she felt. "I like it, I like it," she whispered. "Lie down like me. I can dig myself in, I'm supported everywhere, the straws tickle my neck. And when you rub against it, it runs all over your skin, it feels like mice are running up to hide under your dress."

She rubbed against it and laughed silently; she hit the straw on both sides as if defending herself against the mice. Then she lifted her feet into the air and said, "Do you roll in the straw at your house? I don't know anything I like better. Sometimes I use it to tickle my feet. That's fun, too. Say, do you ever tickle yourself?"

But the big tawny rooster, who had walked sedately to her side when he saw her sprawled on the straw, had just jumped onto her bosom. "Get out of here, Alexander," she cried. "What a dumb thing he is! I can't lie down without him jumping on me like that. You're too rough, you're hurting me with your claws, do you hear me? You're welcome to stay, but you've got to be good, you can't pull my hair, okay?"

And she worried no more about him. The rooster held tightly to her skirt, seemed at times to be seriously studying the underside of her chin with his burning eye. The other animals gathered around her. After rolling over once more, she had relaxed completely in a blissful position, her limbs outstretched, her head thrown back. She said, "Ah, it feels so good. I get tired right away. Straw makes you sleepy, doesn't it? Serge doesn't like that. Maybe you don't either. Well, then, what do you like? Talk about it so I can find out."

She was slowly dozing off. One moment her eyes were wide open and she seemed to be searching for pleasures she did not know; the next moment she had closed her eyes with a peaceful smile, as if wholly satisfied. She was apparently asleep when, after a few minutes, she opened her eyes and said, "The cow's going to have a baby. That feels very good, too. It'll be more fun than anything."

And she fell into deep sleep. The animals had climbed all over her; she was covered by a tide of living feathers. Hens seemed to be brooding at her feet; geese stretched their downy necks along her thighs. On her left, the pig was warming her ribs while, on her right, the goat was nestling his bearded head in her armpit. Pigeons were sitting almost everywhere, in her opened hands, in the hollow of her stomach, behind her slumped shoulders. And she was all pink as she slept, caressed by the cow's stronger breath, smothered under the weight of the big crouching rooster, who had inched down from her breast, beating his wings, raising his crest, until his tawny belly burned through her skirts with a caress of flame.

The rain outside was falling in smaller drops. A patch of sunlight breaking through a cloud soaked the flying vapors in gold. Albine, still motionless, was watching Désirée sleep, watching this beautiful girl who satisfied her flesh by rolling on straw. She wanted to be this tired and relaxed; she wished that she too could be put to sleep by enjoyment; she wanted straws to tickle her neck as well. She envied those strong arms, that hard chest, that completely carnal life in the impregnating heat of a flock of animals, that purely bestial expansion which made the plump child a peaceful sister to the red and white cow. She dreamed of being loved by the tawny rooster and of loving as the trees grow, naturally, without shame, opening every one of her veins to spurts of sap. It was the earth which made Désirée drowsy when she lay on her back. The rain had now stopped completely. The three house cats were marching one behind the other into the barnyard, along the wall, being extremely careful not to get wet. They put their heads into the stable and came straight to the sleeping girl, purring, lying against her, their paws touching her skin. Moumou, the big black cat, huddled against one of her cheeks and began gently licking her chin.

"And Serge?" muttered Albine mechanically.

So what was the matter? Who was keeping her from satisfying herself in the same way, from being a happy child of nature? Why did she not love, why was she not loved under the sun, as freely as the trees grow? She did not know, she felt forever abandoned, forever bruised. And she was ferociously stubborn; she needed to have her treasure in her arms again, to hide it and enjoy it again. Then she stood up. The sacristy door had just been opened; she heard a light clap followed by the uproar of a group of children beating wooden shoes against the floor tiles: catechism was over. She quietly left the stable, where she had been waiting for an hour in the hot barnyard steam. As she slipped through the hall leading to the sacristy, she caught a glimpse of la Teuse, who went into the kitchen without turning around. And, certain that she had not been seen, she noiselessly pushed the door open and closed it behind her. She was in the church.

◇◇◇◇◇◇◇◇◇◇◇◇◇◇◇◇◇◇◇◇◇◇◇◇◇◇◇◇◇◇◇◇◇◇◇◇◇

VIII SHE SAW NO ONE AT FIRST. OUTSIDE, IT WAS RAINING again, a persistent drizzle. The church seemed completely gray to her. She went behind the high altar to the pulpit. The nave contained only benches scattered by children leaving catechism; the clock's pendulum was beating hollowly in this emptiness. Then she went to knock on the confessional which she saw at the other end. But, as she was passing the Chapel of the Dead, she found Father Mouret prostrate at the feet of the large bleeding Christ, not moving at all. He must have thought la Teuse was arranging the benches behind him. Albine put her hand on his shoulders. "Serge," she said, "I have come for you."

The priest, very pale, started and raised his head. He remained on his knees and crossed himself, his lips still trembling from his prayer.

"I waited," she continued. "Every morning, every evening, I watched to see if you were coming. I counted the days, then I didn't count anymore. It's been weeks. Then, when I realized that you would not come, I came myself. I said, 'I'll take him away.' Give me your hands. Let's go."

And she offered him her hands as if to help him up. He crossed himself again; still praying, he looked at her. He had quieted the first reaction of his flesh. He found superhuman strength in the grace which had been inundating him like a heavenly bath since morning. "You do not belong here," he said seriously. "Leave this place. You are increasing your pain."

"I'm not in pain now," she said with a smile. "I'm better, I'm cured, I see you . . . Listen, I pretended to be sicker than I was so they would go get you. I'm willing to admit it now. It was the same with that promise to go away, to leave this place after seeing you; you surely never imagined I would have kept it. Oh, no, I would have carried you away on my shoulders first.

The others don't know, but you know that now I can live only in your arms." She was almost happy again; she approached the priest with the caresses of an unfettered child, not noticing his cold stiffness. She grew impatient, joyously clapped her hands, and cried, "All right, make up your mind, Serge! We're losing time because of you. There's no need to think about it this much. I'm taking you away, for heaven's sake. It's simple. If you don't want to be seen we'll go up the Mascle. It's not a good road, but I took it all by myself; we can help each other if there're two of us. You know the way, don't you? We cross the cemetery and go down to the edge of the stream, and then all we have to do is follow it to the garden. And how nice it is down there at the bottom! There's not a soul around, nothing but bushes and lovely round stones. The bed is almost dry. When I was coming, I thought, 'When he's with me, in a little while, we'll walk softly while we hold each other.' Let's go, hurry up, I'm waiting for you, Serge."

The priest seemed not to hear. He had begun his prayers again and was asking heaven for the courage of the saints. Before the final battle, he was arming himself with the flaming swords of faith. For a moment he feared he would weaken. He had displayed a martyr's heroism in leaving his knees glued to the floor as Albine's every word was calling him; he felt his heart go to her, felt all his blood rise up to hurl him into her arms: the desire to kiss her hair was irresistible. With only the smell of her breath, she had awakened and made pass in a second all the memories of their affair, the big garden, the walks under the trees, the joy of their union. But grace soaked him in its more abundant dew; only the torture of a moment was emptying the blood from his veins. And there was nothing human left in him. He was now wholly God's.

Albine had to touch his shoulder again. She was becoming worried and angry. "Why don't you answer me? You can't refuse, you're going to come with me. You know I'd die if you refused. But no, it's just not possible. Remember. We were together, we were never to leave one another. And you gave yourself twenty times. You told me to take all of you, to take your limbs, to take your breath, to take your life. I don't think it was a dream. There's no part of your body which you did not surrender to me, not one of your hairs but I am its mistress. You have a birthmark on your left shoulder, I kissed it, it belongs to me. Your hands belong to me; I held them in mine for days. And your face, your lips, your eyes, your forehead, they all belong to me, I used them for my love . . . Do you hear me, Serge?" She stood up straight before him, regal, spreading her arms. She repeated in a louder voice, "Do you hear me, Serge? You belong to me."

Then, slowly, Father Mouret stood up. He leaned against the altar and said, "No, you're wrong. I belong to God."

He was filled with serene peace. His bare face was like the face of a stone saint untroubled by heat from his bowels; his cassock fell in perfect folds, like a black shroud which did not reveal even the shape of his body. Albine recoiled before the dark phantom of her love: she could not find his free beard, his free hair. Now she made out the pale spot in the middle of his cropped skull, his tonsure, and it worried her like an unknown disease, like some malignant sore growing there to devour the memory of happy days. She did not recognize his hands, once warm with caresses, or his limber neck, resonant with laughter, or his nervous feet, whose lope had carried him deep into green things. Could this be the boy with the strong muscles, with the open collar revealing the down on his chest, his skin expanded by the sun, his loins vibrating with life, in whose clasping arms she had lived a season? Now he seemed to have no flesh at all; his hair had shamefully fallen away from him. All his virility was drying up under this woman's dress which left him sexless.

"Oh," she muttered, "you're scaring me. Did you think I was dead? Is that why you're in mourning? Take off that black thing and get dressed. You'll roll up your sleeves and we'll fish for craydads again. Your arms were as light as mine."

She had put her hand on his cassock as if to rip it apart. He made a gesture that pushed her away without his being required to touch her. He looked at her, gathered his strength against temptation without taking his eyes off her. She seemed to him to have grown, to be no longer the tomboy of the wild groves, throwing her free laughter to the winds, nor the lover dressed in white skirts, bending her slender body, slowing her loving pace behind the hedges. Now the fuzz of a peach lightened her lip, her hips rolled freely, her breasts bloomed like a lush flower: she was a woman. Her long face gave her an unmistakable look of fertility, life slept in her widened trunk, the full maturity of her flesh showed on the skin of her cheeks. And the priest, completely enveloped in this passionate smell of a mature woman, derived bitter joy from braving the caress of her red mouth, the laughter in her eyes, the call of her bosom, the intoxication flowing from her every movement. He pushed his courage so far as to seek out on her body the parts he had once insanely kissed, the corners of her eyes, the corners of her lips, her narrow temples, soft as satin, the amber nape of her neck, smooth as velvet.

Never, not even in Albine's arms, had he tasted the bliss he felt in thus martyring himself, staring directly at the passion which he was refusing. When he was afraid that he might fall into some new fleshly trap, he lowered his eyes and said gently, "I cannot hear you here. Let's go outside if you insist on increasing both our sorrows. Our presence in this place is a scandal. We are in God's house."

"Who's that, God?" cried Albine, insane, become once more a girl released into nature. "I don't know Him, your God. I don't want to know Him if He steals you from me when I've never done anything to Him. My uncle Jeanbernat is right: he says your God is an invention of evil, a way to scare people and make them cry. You're lying, you don't love me anymore, your God does not exist."

"You're in His house," Father Mouret repeated emphatically. "You're blaspheming. With one breath He could crumble you to dust."

She released magnificently proud laughter, raised her voice, and defied heaven: "Then," she said, "you prefer your God to me! You believe He's stronger than I am. You think He will love you better than I do. You're a little baby. Give up those stupid dreams. We're going back to the garden together to love one another, to be happy and free. That's what life is all about." This time she had succeeded in putting her arm around his waist; she was pulling him away.

But he quivered and jerked out of her embrace; he went to lean against the altar again and forgot himself so far as to use the intimate *tu* with her as he had formerly done. "Go away," he blurted. "If you still love me, go away. Oh, Father, forgive her, forgive me for dirtying Your house. If I went out the door behind her, I might follow her. Here, in Your house, I am strong. Allow me to stay here to defend You."

Albine was silent for a moment. Then, in a quieter voice, she said, "That's fine, let's stay here. I want to speak to you. You can't be mean. You'll understand me. You won't let me go away by myself. No, there's no need to defend yourself. I won't take you now, it would hurt you. You see, I'm very calm. We're going to talk things over softly, the way we did when we got lost and didn't even try to find our way, so we could talk more." She smiled and continued, "Really, I don't know. My uncle forbade me to go to church. He said, 'Little idiot, you have a garden. What could you do in a shanty where everybody suffocates?' I grew up very happy. I looked into nests without touching the eggs. I didn't even pick flowers. I was afraid of making the plants bleed. You know that I never caught a bug to torture it. So why would God be angry with me?"

"You must know Him, pray to Him, give Him at all times the respect which is His by right," replied the priest.

"That would satisfy you, wouldn't it?" she said. "You would forgive me and love me again. All right, I want everything you want. Speak to me of God and I shall believe in Him, I shall worship Him. Each of your words will be a truth I shall hear on my knees. Have I ever had a thought that was not yours? We'll take our long walks once more. You can teach me and make me what you want. Oh, please say that's what we'll do!"

Father Mouret showed his cassock. "I cannot," he said simply. "I am a priest."

"A priest!" she repeated, no longer smiling. "Yes, my uncle

says that priests have no wife, no sister, no mother. So that's true. But why did you come? You're the one who took me for your sister, for your wife. So you were lying?"

He raised a pale face drenched in anguished perspiration. "I sinned," he whispered.

She continued. "When I saw you so free, I thought you were no longer a priest. I thought it was over and you would stay there forever, for me, with me. And what do you expect me to do now that you're taking my life away?"

"What I do," he replied. "Kneel, die on your knees, stand only when God has forgiven you."

"So you're a coward," she said, angry again, her lips curling in a contemptuous sneer.

He trembled and said nothing. Terrible pain gripped his throat, but he remained stronger than his suffering. He held his head high, his quivering mouth almost smiled. Albine defied him for a moment with her fixed stare. Then, in a new outburst, she said, "Look, answer me, accuse me, say that I'm the one who came to tempt you. That would be the last straw. You can beat me. I'd rather have your blows than this dead stiffness. Don't you have any blood now? Didn't you hear me call you a coward? Yes, you are a coward; you should not have loved me, for you cannot be a man. Is it your black dress that's bothering you? Rip it off. Maybe you'll remember when you're naked."

The priest slowly repeated the same words. "I sinned, I have no excuse. I am doing penance for my sin without hoping for forgiveness. If I ripped off my vestment, I would rip off my flesh, for I have given myself, I am wholly God's, I have given Him my soul and my bones. I am a priest."

"And what about me? What about me?" cried Albine one last time.

He did not lower his head. "May your pain be counted as my crime. May I be eternally punished for having to leave you. It would be just. Unworthy as I am, I pray for you every evening."

She shrugged her shoulders in a gesture of great discouragement. Her anger had left her; she was almost compassionate. "You're really crazy," she whispered. "Keep your prayers. I just want you . . . You'll never understand! I had so many things to tell you. And you stand there and make me mad with stories about another world. Let's wait until we've calmed down. Then we can talk some more. It's not possible for me to go away like this. I can't leave you here. It's because you're here that you seem to be dead, that your skin is so cold I don't dare touch it. Let's don't say anything. Let's wait."

She fell silent and walked a few steps, examining the small church. The rain was still streaming down the windows like fine ash; a cold light soaked in steam seemed to be permeating the walls. No noise came from outside beyond the shower's monotonous rumble. The sparrows must have been huddled under the tiles; the service tree extended its indistinct branches, drowned in vapor. The clock struck five, and each stroke seemed to be wrenched from its cracked chest; then the silence grew again, deafer, blinder, more desperate. The barely dried paint gave sad cleanliness to the high altar and wood paneling, made the church look like a convent chapel where the sun is not allowed. An awful death agony filled the nave splattered with the blood flowing from the limbs of the large Christ, while, along the walls, the fourteen Stations of the Cross displayed their atrocious drama, smeared in yellow and red, sweating in horror. It was life which was dying in this death tremor, on the altars resembling tombs in this bare burial cave. Everything spoke of massacres, of night, of terror, of repression, of nothingness. A whiff of incense still hovered like the last, moving breath of some corpse jealously strangled under the tile floor.

"Oh," said Albine at last, "how nice it was out in the sun, do you remember? One morning, it was on the left side of the flower garden, and we were walking by a hedge of big rosebushes. I remember the color of the grass; it was almost blue, with patches of watery green. When we got to the end of the hedge, the sun smelled so good we walked back on the same path. And that was our whole walk that morning, twenty steps up and twenty steps back, a stretch of happiness which you did not want to leave. The bees were buzzing; a tomtit stayed with us all the time, leaping from limb to limb; animals parading around us went about their business. You whispered, 'How good life is!' Life was the grass, the trees, the water, the sky, the sunlight, in which we were all blond with golden hair." She stopped to dream for a while, then added, "Life was Paradou. How big it seemed to us! We could never find the end of it. The leaves rolled freely to the horizon; they sounded like waves. And how much blue was over our heads! We could have grown; we could have flown away; we could have run like the clouds, encountering no more obstacles than they do. The air belonged to us."

She stopped and pointed to the church's collapsing walls. "And here you're in a dungeon. You can't stretch out your arms without hitting rocks and tearing the skin off your hands. The vault hides the sky from you and takes away your part of the sun. It's so cramped your limbs get stiff, as if you were buried alive underground."

"No," said the priest. "The church is as large as the world. God is in it."

She now pointed to the crosses, to the dying Christs, to the tortures of their Passions. "And you live in the midst of death. Grass, trees, water, sun, sky, everything dies around you."

"No, everything is reborn, everything is purified, everything goes back to the source of light." He had straightened up, a flame burning in his eyes. He left the altar, invincible now, burning with a faith so strong that he scorned the dangers of temptation. And he took Albine's hand, spoke to her like a sister, and took her to the sorrowful pictures of the road to Calvary.

"Look," he said, "this is what my God suffered . . . Jesus was scourged. You see, His shoulders are bare, His flesh is torn open, His blood flows to His loins . . . Jesus is crowned with thorns. Red tears flow from His pierced forehead. A great rip has opened His temple . . . Jesus is insulted by the soldiers. His tormentors have mockingly thrown a purple rag around His neck, and they are spitting in His face, they are slapping Him, they are using sticks to push His crown deeper into His flesh."

Albine turned her head so as not to see the crudely colored

pictures, where splotches of lake cut across Christ's ocher flesh. The purple mantle around His neck seemed to be a dangling strip of His mutilated skin.

"What good does it do to suffer; what good does it do to die?" was her answer. "Oh, Serge, if you would only remember! That day, you told me you were tired. And I knew you were lying, because it was cool, and we had been walking only fifteen minutes. But you wanted to sit down to take me in your arms. Deep in the orchard, you know it, there was a cherry tree growing beside a stream. You could never pass it without needing to kiss my hands, to plant quick kisses on my arms and shoulders until you came to my lips. The cherry season was over, you ate my lips. The fading flowers made us cry. One day you found a dead warbler in the grass and got all pale; you held me to your chest as if to keep the earth from taking me."

The priest pulled her to the other Stations. "Keep quiet," he shouted. "Look some more, listen some more. You must prostrate yourself in suffering and pity. Jesus falls under the weight of the cross. The road to Calvary is steep. He falls on His knees. He does not even wipe the sweat from His brow. He stands up again and keeps walking . . . Jesus falls again under the weight of His cross. He trembles with every step. This time He falls on His side, so roughly that the breath is knocked out of Him. His torn and bleeding hands drop the cross. His aching feet have left bloody prints behind Him. Terrible fatigue crushes Him, for He is bearing on His shoulders the sins of the world."

Albine had looked at Jesus in His blue loincloth, lying under the huge cross whose black color had run to dirty the gold of His halo. Then her eyes went out of focus and she murmured, "Oh, the paths through the meadows! Don't you have a memory anymore, Serge? You don't know the roads of soft grass running across the fields among great pools of green? The afternoon I'm talking about, we had gone out only for an hour. But we kept walking; we kept going straight through the grass, until the stars came out. It was so sweet, that endless carpet, smooth as silk. Our feet never met a stone. It was like a

245

green sea whose mossy water cradled us. And we knew perfectly well where we were being taken by those tender paths leading nowhere: they were taking us to our love, to the joy of living with our arms around each other, to the certainty of a day of happiness. When we came home, we were not tired. You were fresher than when you left, for you had given me your caresses and I was unable to return all of them."

Father Mouret pointed his anguished, trembling hands to the last pictures. He stammered, "And Jesus is nailed to the cross. The hammer blows drive the iron into His open hands. One nail is enough for His feet, whose bones are cracked. As His flesh is trembling, He raises His eyes to heaven and smiles . . . He is between the two thieves. The weight of His body enlarges his wounds horribly. From His brow, from His limbs, streams bloody sweat. The two thieves insult Him, the spectators mock Him, the soldiers cast lots for His clothing. And the shadows spread and the sun is hidden . . . Jesus dies on the cross. He cries out and gives up the ghost. O terrible death! The temple veil is rent asunder from top to bottom, the earth trembles, stones are split, tombs open."

He had fallen to his knees, his voice broken by sobs, his eyes on the three crosses on Calvary where three tortured bodies, made repulsively thin by crude artistry, were twisting in agony. Albine stood before the paintings so he could not see them.

"One evening," she said, "in a long-drawn-out twilight, I had put my head on your knees. It was in the forest, at the end of that big chestnut walk, and the setting sun pierced the trees with one final beam. Oh, what an affectionate good-bye! The sun lingered at our feet with a nice friendly smile to tell us he would see us later. The sky grew slowly dim. I laughed and told you it was taking off its blue dress and putting on its black dress with the gold flowers to go to a ball. You were studying the shadows, eager to be alone, without the sun to disturb you. And it was not darkness which was coming; it was discreet tenderness, hidden love, a mysterious place, like one of those very dark paths under the trees, where we went to hide for a while with the certainty of finding the joy of bright sunlight at the other end. That evening, the twilight's serene paleness promised a splendid morning. I pretended to go to sleep when I saw that the light was leaving too slowly for you. I can tell you now, I was not asleep while you were kissing my eyes; I tasted your kisses. It was all I could do to keep from laughing. I kept my breaths regular and you drank me in. Then, when it was dark, there was a long lullaby. You see, the trees weren't asleep any more than I was. At night, you remember, the flowers had a stronger smell."

And when he remained on his knees, his face bathed in tears, she took his wrists and pulled him up, passionately continuing her story. "Oh, if you knew, you would tell me to take you away; you would tie your arms around my neck so I could not possibly leave without you. Yesterday, I wanted to see the garden again. It's bigger, deeper, more unfathomable. I found new smells, so soft they made me cry. In the walks, I found showers of sunlight which cradled me with quivering desire. The roses spoke of you. The finches were astonished to see me alone. The whole garden sighed . . . Oh, come with me. The grass has never unrolled softer couches. I marked with a flower the secret place I want to take you. It's deep in the bushes, a green hole as wide as a big bed. From there you hear the garden live, with its trees, its water, its sky. The very breaths of the earth will rock us to sleep . . . Oh, come with me, we will love one another in the love of all things."

But he pushed her away. He had come back to the Chapel of the Dead, to the large Christ of painted cardboard, as tall as a ten-year-old child, dying with such frightening realism: nails imitated iron, wounds were still yawning horribly. "Christ who died for us," he cried, "tell her we are nothing! Tell her we are dust, filth, damnation. Ah, wait, let me cover my head with a hair shirt; let me rest my head on your feet and remain there, motionless, until death begins to make me rot. The earth will no longer exist, the sun will be extinguished. I shall not see, I shall not feel, I shall not hear. Nothing will come from this miserable world to turn my soul away from worshiping you."

He was growing more and more excited. He walked toward Albine, his hands raised. "You were right, death is what is here, death is what I want, death which delivers and which saves us from corruption. Do you hear me! I deny life, I refuse it, I spit on it! Your flowers stink, your sun blinds, your grass gives leprosy to everyone who lies on it, your garden is a charnel house where the cadavers of all things grow putrid and fall apart. The earth exudes abomination. You lie when you speak of love, of light, of a blissful life deep in your green palace. Nothing but shadow is in your home. Your trees drip poison which makes men into beasts; your thickets are black with the venom of vipers; your rivers roll pestilence along under their blue waters. If I ripped off your nature her shirt of sunlight and her belt of greenery, you would see that she is as hideous as a dried-up whore, with skeleton ribs devoured by vice. And even if you were telling the truth, even if your hands were filled with pleasures, even if you laid me on a bed of roses to give me a dream of paradise, I would defend myself against your embrace all the more desperately. There is war between us, an ancient war to the death. You see, the church is very tiny: it's ugly, it has a confessional and a pine pulpit, a plaster baptistry, altars made of four pieces of wood which I painted myself. And that doesn't matter! It is larger than your garden, than the valley, than the whole world! It is an awesome fortress which nothing can overturn. Winds, sun, forest, seas, everything which lives would find it futile to attack it. It will remain standing, it will not even be shaken. Yes, let the bushes grow, let them pound against the walls with their thorny arms, let swarms of insects come out of cracks to wear away the walls. The church, no matter how decrepit, can never be carried away by this flood of life. It is impregnable death! And do you want to know what is going to happen one day? The tiny church will become so colossal, it will cast such a shadow, that all nature will fall dead. Ah, death, death of all things, heaven opened wide to admit our souls, above the abominable ruins of the world!"

He was shouting; he was violently pushing Albine to the door. Very pale, she withdrew step by step. When he stopped, his voice choked off, she said seriously, "So it's over, you're sending me away? Still, I am your wife. You made me. After allowing that, God cannot punish us so much."

She was on the threshold. She added, "Listen, every day, at sunset, I'm going to the end of the garden, to the breach in the wall. I'll wait for you."

And she left. The sacristy door closed with a muffled sigh.

◇◇◇◇◇◇◇◇◇◇◇◇◇◇◇◇◇◇◇◇◇◇◇◇◇◇◇◇◇◇◇◇◇◇◇◇

IX THE CHURCH WAS SILENT EXCEPT FOR THE ORGAN-LIKE sound of the rain, falling harder now. The priest's anger fell away in this sudden calm; he was deeply moved. And, his face bathed in tears, his shoulders shaking with sobs, he came to throw himself to his knees before the large Christ. An act of burning gratitude flew from his lips.

"Oh, I thank You, my God, for the help You have sent to me. Without Your grace I would surely have listened to the voice of my flesh, I would have returned to my miserable sin. Your grace bound my loins like the belt of a soldier; Your grace was my armor, my courage, the internal support allowing me to stand without failing. Oh, my God, You were in me; it was You who spoke in me, for I no longer felt my creaturely cowardice. I felt strong enough to sever all the bonds of my heart. And here is my bleeding heart: it now belongs to no one, it belongs to You. For You I ripped it away from the world. But do not believe, oh, my God, that I draw vainglory from this victory. I know that I am nothing without You. I grovel at Your feet in my humility."

He had collapsed, half-sitting on the altar step, unable to find more words, letting his breath smoke like incense from his half-open lips. An abundance of grace bathed him in ineffable ecstasy. He turned in upon himself, sought Jesus in the depths of his being, in the sanctuary of love which he was at all times preparing in order to be worthy to receive Him. And Jesus was there; he felt Him in the extraordinary sweetness flowing over him. Then he began one of those internal conversations with Jesus which took him out of this world to let him speak mouth to mouth with his God. He stumbled through the verse of the Canticle of Canticles, "My beloved to me, and I to him who feedeth among the lilies, Till the day break, and the shadows retire." He meditated on the words of the *Imitation of Christ*, "It is a great skill to know how to speak with Jesus and a great safeguard to know how to keep Him with you." Then came charming familiarities. Jesus lowered Himself to him and chatted for hours about his needs, his joys, his hopes. And two friends who meet after a separation and withdraw to the bank of some lonely river exchange less tender confidences than they; for Jesus, in the hours of divine relaxation, condescended to be his friend, the best, most faithful friend, he who would never betray him, who gave him all the treasures of eternal life in return for a little affection. This time the priest wanted to possess Him for an especially long time. He was still listening, surrounded by the silence of all creatures, when the clock struck six in the muted church.

Confession of the whole being, free exchange of ideas, without the interference of a stumbling tongue, natural effusion of the heart flying to the other even before the thought is formed. Father Mouret told everything to Jesus as to a God who can hear everything, who has descended in the intimacy of affection. He admitted that he still loved Albine; he was amazed that he would have treated her so shabbily, that he could have chased her away without his bowels revolting within him; this astonished him, and he smiled serenely as if suddenly set in the presence of a miraculously strong deed performed by someone else. And Jesus said that he should not be amazed, that the greatest saints were often unconscious weapons in the hands of God. Then the priest voiced some doubt; was there not less merit in seeking refuge at the foot of the altar and even in the passion of his Lord? Was he not still weak at heart since he did not dare fight alone? But Jesus was tolerant. He explained that God is always concerned with man's weakness; He said He preferred suffering souls with whom He came to sit as a friend sits at the sickbed of a friend. Was he damned for loving Albine? No, not if that love went beyond the flesh, not if he added hope to the desire for another life. Then how must he love her? Without a word, without a step toward her, letting this completely pure emotion be exhaled like a good odor pleasing to heaven. Here Jesus chuckled to show his goodwill, inched closer in order to encourage more confessions; this worked so well that the priest gradually grew bold enough to give details of Albine's beauty. She had an angel's blond hair. She was all white with large gentle eyes, she was like haloed saints. Jesus said nothing but continued chuckling. And how she had grown! She looked like a queen now, with her full-blown body, her magnificent shoulders. Oh, to take her waist, if only for one second, to feel her shoulders fall back before his embrace. Jesus' chuckle grew pale and died like the rays of a star sinking below the horizon. Father Mouret was now talking to himself. Really, he had been too hard. Why chase Albine away without one tender word when heaven allowed love?

"I love her! I love her!" he cried aloud, in a wild voice which filled the church. He still saw her there. She was holding her arms out to him; she was desirable enough to make him break all his vows. And, showing no respect for the church, he threw himself on her breasts. He took her limbs and possessed her with a rain of kisses. It was before her that he was on his knees, begging for mercy, asking forgiveness for his brutality. He explained that there was at times a voice in him which was not his. Could he ever have mistreated her? Only that alien voice had spoken. It could not have been he, he who could never have touched a hair on her head without trembling. And he had chased her away; the church was actually empty! Where should he run to join her, to bring her back and wipe away her tears with his caresses? It was raining harder. The roads were lakes of mud. He saw her beaten by the storm, trembling in the ditches, her soaked skirts clinging to her skin. No, no, it was not he, it was the other, the jealous voice cruel enough to want his love to die.

"Oh, Jesus," he cried more desperately, "be kind, give her back to me!"

But Jesus was no longer there . . . Then Father Mouret, as if starting awake, grew horribly pale. He understood. He had not been able to keep Jesus with him; he had lost his friend; he was left defenseless against evil. Instead of that internal light illuminating his whole being, enabling him to receive his God, he now found in himself only shadows, a pestilential smoke irritating his flesh. Jesus had taken grace with him when he withdrew. He who had since morning been so strong in heavenly succor felt suddenly miserable, abandoned, weak as a child. And what an atrocious fall, what vast bitterness! To have fought heroically, to have remained standing, invincible, immovable, while temptation was there, alive in her full-blown body, magnificent shoulders, and smell of passion; then to succumb shamefully, to pant with abominable desire after temptation had departed, leaving behind her only the rustle of a skirt and a trace of perfume from the back of her neck. Now she returned as an all-powerful memory; she invaded the church.

"Jesus! Jesus!" the priest yelled one last time, "come back to me, speak to me again!" Jesus remained deaf. For an instant Father Mouret begged heaven with his insanely raised arms. His shoulders cracked from the extraordinary fervor of his prayers. And soon his discouraged hands fell to his sides. In heaven was only one of those hopeless silences which the saints know. He sat once more on the altar step, crushed, his face twisted by horror, pressing his elbows against his ribs as if to rub off his flesh. He shrank under the tooth of temptation.

"My God, Thou hast abandoned me," he murmured. "Thy will be done!" And he said not another word. He was panting like a hunted animal unable to move because of his fear of the dogs. He had been the plaything of the whims of grace since his sin. It refused his most ardent pleas; it descended, unexpected and charming, when he had not the least hope of possessing it for years. At first he had rebelled; he spoke like a betrayed lover and insisted on the immediate return of the consoler whose kiss made him so strong. Then, after a few sterile fits of anger, he had understood that humility bruised him less, was moreover the only thing that could help him bear his loneliness. Then, for hours, for days, he debased himself in the expectation of relief which did not come. It did no good to put himself in God's hands, to grovel before Him, to repeat as many times as he could the most effective prayers; he no longer felt God. His runaway flesh heaved with desire; the confused prayers on his lips ended in muttered obscenities. Slow death of temptation, during which the arms of faith fell one by one from his useless hands so that he became only an inert object in the clutches of his passions, watching his own ignominy without finding the courage to lift his little finger to chase away sin. This was now his life. He was familiar with all of sin's attacks. Not a day went by without his being tested. Sin took a thousand shapes, entered through his eyes, through his ears, seized his throat, treacherously jumped on his shoulders from behind, tortured the marrow of his bones. His sin was always there, Albine's nakedness, bursting like a sun to light the greenery of Paradou. Her figure left his field of vision only during those rare moments when grace was willing to close his eyes with its cool caresses. And he hid his disease as if it were shameful. He shut himself up in ghostly silences which no one could make him break, filling the presbytery with the martyrdom of his resignation, infuriating la Teuse, who brandished her fist at heaven behind his back.

This time, he was alone; he could writhe in agony without shame. Sin had just dealt him such a blow that he did not have the strength to leave the altar step where he had fallen. He stayed there, panting, burned dry by anguish, unable to shed a tear. And he thought of the peaceful life which had once been his. Oh, what serenity, what confidence when he had first come to Artauds! Salvation seemed to be a lovely road. He used to laugh when people mentioned temptation. He lived surrounded by evil without knowing it, without fearing it, in the certainty of discouraging it. He was a perfect priest, so chaste and ignorant before God that God held his hand to lead him about like a little child. Now all his boyishness had died. God visited him in the morning and immediately began to test him. His earthly life became temptation. With age, with the sin, he had undertaken the eternal struggle. Could it be that God loved him more now? The great saints had all left strips of their flesh hanging from the thorns along the painful way. He tried to console himself with this thought. With each gash in his flesh, with each crack of his bones, he promised himself extraordinary compensation. Never would heaven strike him enough. He went so far as to scorn his former serenity, the easy fervor which let him kneel in girlish delight without even feeling the floor bruise his knees. He tried to be clever enough to find some sensual pleasure in the throes of pain, so he could lie down and sleep. But his teeth chattered with terror even as he blessed the name of God; the voice of his rebellious blood shouted in his ear that all this was a lie, that the only real joy was to lie in Albine's arms, behind a flowering hedge in Paradou.

Meanwhile, he had left Mary for Jesus, sacrificed his heart in order to vanquish his flesh. He dreamed of bringing virility into his faith. Mary disturbed him too much with the narrow bands of her hair, with her outstretched hands and her woman's smile. He could not kneel before her without lowering his eyes out of fear of seeing the hem of her dress. Moreover, he accused her of having been too gentle with him; she had kept him nestled in her dress for so long that he had let himself slip from her arms into the arms of a creature without even noticing a change in the object of his adoration. And he remembered Brother Archangias' brutality, his refusal to worship Mary, the untrusting way he seemed to keep watch on her. He despaired of ever rising to this roughness; he simply let her go, hid her images, deserted her altar. But she remained deep in his heart like a secret, ever-present love. Sin, in a sacrilege so horrible it struck him down, used her to tempt him. Now, when he called her name at certain times of unconquerable emotion, it was Albine who came to him, in the same white veil, the same blue scarf tied to her belt, the same golden roses on her bare feet. All the Virgins, the Virgin in a royal golden cloak, the Virgin crowned with stars, the Virgin visited by the angel during the Annunciation, the Virgin serene between a lily and a distaff, awakened a new memory of Albine and her smiling eyes, or her delicate mouth, or the soft curve of her cheeks. His sin had deflowered Mary. So, by a supreme effort, he banished woman from religion and sought refuge in Christ, and even His gentleness irritated him at times. He had to have a jealous God, an implacable God, the God of the Bible, surrounded by thunderbolts, revealing Himself only to punish a terrified world. There were no more saints, no more angels, no more Mother of God: there was only God Himself, an omnipotent master requiring all souls for His own. He felt the hand of this God crush his loins, hold him at His mercy, like a guilty atom in space and time. To be nothing, to be damned, to dream of hell, to struggle fruitlessly against temptation's monsters, this was good. Of Christ he took only the cross. He had that fixation for the cross which has led so many lips to wear themselves away on crucifixes. He took up the cross and followed Christ. He weighed it down, made it overwhelming, had no greater joy than to succumb under it and carry it on his knees, his back breaking. He saw in it the strength of the soul, the joy of the spirit, the consummation of virtue, the perfection of holiness. Everything was in it, everything came to die on it. "Suffer," "die," these words rang ceaselessly in his ears as the end of human wisdom. And when he had nailed himself to the cross, he earned the limitless consolation of God's love. It was no longer Mary that he loved with the tenderness of a son and the passion of a lover. He loved in order to love with absolute love. He loved God more than himself, more than everything, loved him deep in expanding light. He was like a brand consumed in burning brightness. Death, when he wished for it, was in his eyes only a great explosion of love.

What was he neglecting that he must undergo such frightful testing? His hands wiped the sweat flowing from his brow; he thought that that very morning he had examined his conscience without finding any serious offense. Was he not leading a life of asceticism and maceration? Did he not love only God, and Him blindly? Ah, how he would have blessed His name if He had finally given him peace once more, after judging him punished enough for his sin. But perhaps this sin would never be expiated. And, in spite of himself, he came back to Albine, to Paradou, to his flaming memories. At first, he tried to find excuses. One evening he fell to the floor in his room, struck down by brain fever. For three weeks he belonged to this crisis of his flesh. His blood furiously washed his veins to the very tip of his limbs, groaning throughout his body with the noise of an unleashed torrent, everything from his skull to the bottom of his feet was cleansed, restored, and belabored by such frantic activity that in his delirium he often thought he heard workmen's hammers nailing his bones back together. Then he awoke one morning as a new man. He was born a second time, liberated from what twenty-five years of life had successively deposited in him. His childhood devotion, his seminary education, his young priest's faith, everything had gone away, had been submerged and carried off, to leave the slate clean. Certainly only hell had thus prepared him for sin, disarming him and making his bowels a bed of softness where evil could lie down and sleep. And he remained unconscious, he abandoned himself to his slow progress toward the sin. When he opened his eyes in Paradou, he felt himself bathed in childhood, with no memory of the past, with nothing left from his priesthood. His organs were surprised and delighted as they played the lovely game of beginning life anew, as if they did not know it and found great gladness in learning it. O delicious apprenticeship, charming encounters, adorable discoveries! This Paradou was one enormous joy. When it put him there, hell was fully aware that he would have no defense. Never during his first youth had growing up given him such sensual delight. That first youth, if he called it up now, seemed all black; tasteless, ungrateful, sickly, it had been spent far from the sun. Therefore, how he had welcomed the sun, how he had marveled at the first tree, the first flower, the smallest insect his eyes saw, the tiniest pebble his fingers touched! The stones themselves charmed him. The horizon was an extraordinary prodigy. A clear morning filling his eyes, the smell of jasmine in his nose, a lark's song in his ears—all his senses created emotions so strong that his legs grew limp. He had tasted long bliss in teaching himself life's slightest tremors. And the morning Albine was born at his side among the roses! He still laughed ecstatically at this memory. She rose like a star necessary to the sun itself. She illumined all, explained all. She completed him. Then he began again his walks with her to the four corners of Paradou, remembered the tiny hairs blowing on her neck when she ran in front of him. She smelled good. She swung warm skirts whose rustle was like a caress. Then she took him in her bare arms, supple as snakes; she was so slender he expected to see her curl upon his body and go to sleep glued to his skin. She was the one who led. She took him down a hidden path where they both lingered so as not to arrive too soon. She gave him the passion of the earth. He learned to love her by looking to see how the grass loves; emotion stumbling for a long time, whose great joy they had finally surprised one evening under the giant tree in the shadow sweating sap. There they came to the end of their road. Albine, lying on her back, her head rolling in her hair, stretched her arms out to him. He embraced her. Oh, to take her, to possess her again, to feel her body quiver with fertility, to make life and be God!

The priest suddenly groaned hollowly. He stiffened as if bitten by an invisible tooth, then he fell once more. Temptation had just attacked him. In what filth were his memories wandering? Did he not know that Satan has many ruses, that he profits even from the hours of inner examination to slip his serpent's head into man's soul? No, no, no excuse! Disease did not authorize sin. It was his duty to guard himself, to find God again when he emerged from his fever. On the contrary, however, he had enjoyed crouching in his flesh. And what unmistakable proof of his abominable appetites! He was unable to confess his sin without sliding despite himself into a great need to commit it again in his thoughts. Would he not silence that voice rising from the mud of his being! He dreamed of emptying his skull so he would think no more, of opening his veins so guilty blood would torture him no more. He remained for an instant, his face in his hands, trembling, hiding every bit of his skin, as if the beasts prowling around him had made his hair stand on end with their hot breath.

But he still thought, and the blood still beat in his heart. The eyes he was blocking with his fists saw the supple lines of Albine's body traced by a burning brand on the black shadows. She had a naked bosom as dazzling as the sun. Every effort to push in his eyes and chase this vision away made her more luminous. She accentuated her body by arching back, by calling to him with her outstretched arms, and the sight of her tore an anguished death rattle from the priest's throat. So God was abandoning him completely; so there was no sanctuary left for him? And, despite his rigid will, his sin was beginning again;

its every detail was still etched with frightful clarity. He saw once more the smallest blades of grass next to the hem of Albine's skirt. He found stuck in her hair the tiny flower of a thistle with which he remembered pricking her lips. Even the smells, the slightly acrid, sugary odors of crushed stems came back to him; even the distant sounds which he heard again, a repeated birdcall, a great silence, and then a sigh passing through the trees. Why had heaven not struck him down at once? He would have suffered less. He relished his abomination with the sensuality of a damned soul. He was shaken by rage when he heard the wicked words he had spoken at Albine's feet. They echoed now to accuse him before God. He had recognized woman as his sovereign. He had given himself to her as a slave; he had kissed her feet and dreamed of being the water she drank and the bread she ate. Now he understood why he could not pull himself together: God was leaving him to woman. But he would fight against her; he would break her limbs if she would not release him. She was the slave, the soiled flesh to which the Church should have refused a soul. Then he made himself hard and brandished his fists at Albine. And his fists opened, his hands flowed over her bare shoulders in a soft caress while the mouth filled with insults glued itself to her unfettered hair and stammered words of worship.

Father Mouret opened his eyes. The burning vision of Albine disappeared. Sudden, unhoped-for relief. He was able to cry. Sluggish tears cooled his cheeks as he took deep breaths, not yet daring to budge for fear of feeling his neck seized once more. He still heard a wild growl behind him. Then it was so sweet to be suffering less that he forgot everything to relish his well-being. Outside, the rain had stopped. The sun was setting in a great red light which seemed to hang pink silk curtains in the windows. The church was warm now, alive with this final breath of the sun. The priest distractedly thanked God for the respite He had seen fit to grant. A broad ray, a golden cloud of dust crossing the nave, lit the back of the church, clock, pulpit, and high altar. Perhaps grace was returning to him in this path of light descended from heaven. He was interested in the atoms moving along the ray with prodigious speed, like a band of busy messengers endlessly bearing news from heaven to earth. A thousand burning candles could not have filled the church with such splendor. Behind the high altar hung golden drapes, jewelry inlaid in gold streamed over the church, candelabra bloomed into showers of light, bejeweled coals burned in the censers, holy vessels grew little by little and glowed like comets; and everywhere luminous flowers rained on flying lace, pools, bouquets, garlands of roses, their hearts dropping stars as they opened. He had never even wished for such richness in his poor church. He smiled, dreamed of making this magnificence permanent, and arranged things as he chose. He would have preferred to see the golden drapes hung higher; the vessels too seemed to be scattered too negligently; he gathered the lost flowers, bound up the bouquets, gave a soft curve to the garlands. But how wonderful to see all this pomp spread before him! He became the pontiff of a golden church. Bishops, princes, women trailing royal robes, devout multitudes, their brows in the dust, visited it, pitched tents in the valley, waited at the door for weeks before being able to enter. Men kissed his feet because his feet too were golden; they could work miracles. Gold rose to his knees. A golden heart beat in his golden chest, with a musical sound so clear that the multitudes outside heard it. Then immense pride delighted him. He was an idol. The ray of sunlight was still rising; the high altar was aflame; the priest persuaded himself that it must actually be the return of grace giving him such inner joy. The wild growl behind him became a purr. He now felt on his neck only the softness of a velvet paw, as if some cat were caressing him.

And he continued his fantasy; he had never seen things in such a dazzling light. All seemed easy now that he considered himself so strong. Since Albine was waiting for him, he would join her. It was natural. That morning he had married big Fortuné and Rosalie. The Church did not forbid marriage. He saw them smiling and nudging one another under his hands blessing them. Then, that night, he had been shown their bed. Each of the words he had addressed to them resounded louder in his own ears. He was telling big Fortuné that God was sending him a companion because He did not want man to live alone; he was telling Rosalie that she must bind herself to her husband, never to leave him, and be his submissive servant. But he was also saying these things for himself and Albine. Was she not his companion, his submissive servant, she whom God sent him in order that his virility not dry up in loneliness? Moreover, they were bound. He could not understand why he had not known that right away; why he had not left with her as duty required. But his mind was made up, he would join her the next day. In half an hour, he would be near her. He would cross the village and take the road up the hill; it was by far the shortest. He could do anything, he was the master, no one would dare object. If people stared at him, he would simply gesture and all heads would bow low. Then he would live with Albine. He would call her his wife. They would be very happy. The gold rose and flowed between his fingers. He went back into this bath of gold, took the sacred vessels for his household needs, lived grandly, paid his help with bits of chalice, which he effortlessly twisted off with his fingers. He hung the altar's golden drapes on their wedding bed. For jewels, he gave his wife the golden hearts, golden beads, and golden crosses hanging from the necks of the Virgins and the saints. The church itself could serve as their palace if he added another floor to it. God would have no objections, after all; He allowed man to love. Besides, what did he care about God? Was not he himself God now? Did not his golden feet kissed by the multitude work miracles?

Father Mouret stood up. He made Jeanbernat's broad gesture, that gesture of negation embracing the universe. "There is nothing, nothing, nothing," he said. "God does not exist."

The church seemed to quake. The terrified priest, deathly pale once more, listened. Who could have spoken? Who could have blasphemed? Suddenly, the soft velvet caress on his neck became savage: claws ripped his flesh, his blood flowed again. He remained standing, however, struggling against his crisis. He insulted triumphant sin even as it laughed near his head, where all the hammers of evil were beginning to strike. Did he not know its treachery? Did he not know that it often plays cat-and-mouse, approaching its victims with soft paws in order to bury its knifelike claws bone-deep in their flesh? And his rage increased to think he had been caught like a child. So he would always be on the ground with sin squatting gloriously on his chest! Now here he was denying God. It was the fatal descent. Fornication killed faith. Then dogma collapsed. One doubt created by flesh pleading for its filth was enough to empty heaven. The divine law irritated man, the mysteries made him smile; in one corner of overthrown religion, man lay down to debate his sacrilege until, like a beast, he had hollowed a hole for himself where he could sleep off his foulness. Then came other temptations, sprawling on a bed of riches and pride. And man stole from God. He smashed monstrances to hang them from a woman's impurity. All right! He was damned. Nothing mattered to him. Sin could speak aloud. It was good to struggle no more. The monsters which had prowled behind his neck were now battling in his bowels. He expanded his chest so as to feel their teeth more acutely, abandoned himself to them with frightful joy. Rebellion made him brandish his fists at the church. No, he no longer believed in the divinity of Christ; he no longer believed in the Holy Trinity; he believed only in himself, in his muscles, in the appetitites of his organs. He wanted to live. He needed to be a man. Ah, to run in the open air, to be strong, to have no jealous master, to kill his enemies with stones, to carry away passing girls. He would arise from the grave where rough hands had laid him. He would awaken his virility; it must be only sleeping! And might he die of shame if he found his virility dead! And may God be damned if He had taken the priest out of the ranks of creatures by touching him with His finger to keep him for His service alone!

The priest was standing upright in the throes of hallucinations. He thought the church would collapse before this new blasphemy. The patch of sun soaking the high altar had slowly grown until it lit the walls in burning red. Spurts of flame rose still higher, licked the ceiling, died in the bloody light of glowing coals. The church suddenly became completely black. It seemed that the fire of this setting star had crushed the roof and beat down the walls, had everywhere opened yawning breaches to attacks from outside. The dark carcass shook in expectation of some great assault. Night was falling rapidly.

Then, from very far away, the priest heard a noise begin in the Artauds valley. There was a time when he did not understand the ardent language of this scorched earth where twisted only scrubs of knotty vines, scraggy almond trees, ancient olive trees swaying on diseased limbs. He could pass through all this passion in the serenity of his ignorance. But today, his flesh had been educated; he understood the softest sigh of leaves swooning under the sun. First, on the horizon, came the hills, still warm from the sun's good-bye, hills trembling and shaking with the dull tread of an army on the march. Then the scattered rocks, stones on the roads, every pebble in the valley, these too stood up, rolling and grumbling, as if thrust forward by a great need for movement. Then the patches of red earth, the rare fields conquered by the pick, began to flow and growl like flooding rivers, bearing in the tide of their blood conception and fertilization, sweeping along hatching roots and copulating plants. And soon everything was in motion: vines crawled like huge insects; thin wheat and scrawny grasses formed brigades armed with tall spears; trees ran in all directions and stretched their arms like wrestlers preparing for the struggle; fallen leaves marched; the dust in the roads marched. A vast multitude recruiting new strength with each step, a nation in heat whose sigh was drawing closer, a tempest of life whose breath seemed to come from an oven, carrying all before it in the confusion of a colossal lying-in. The attack was sudden. From the edge of the horizon the entire countryside swooped down on the church: hills, rocks, earth, trees. The church cracked under the first blow. Walls split, tiles blew off the roof. But the large Christ, though shaken, did not fall.

There was a brief respite. Outside, the voices rose in greater fury. Now the priest heard human sounds. The village, Artauds, this handful of bastards growing in the rocks with the stubborn persistence of thistles, was creating another wind laden with the swarm of being. The Artauds fornicated on the ground, planted a forest of men in one another, and their trunks took possession of all the earth around them. They climbed to the church and smashed in the door with one blow; they threatened to clog the nave with the invading branches of their family tree. Behind them the animals were running through the tangled underbrush to the church: bulls trying to beat down the walls with their horns; flocks of asses, goats, sheep, smashing against the ruins of the church like living waves; swarms of termites and crickets attacking the foundations, reducing them to dust with their saw teeth. And on the other side was Désirée's barnyard, whose dung heap sent out clouds of poison gas; the big rooster, Alexander, sounded the charge on his bugle; hens loosened stones with their beaks; rabbits dug tunnels under the altars in order to mine them and blow them up; the pig, so fat he could hardly move, snorted and waited for the sacred objects to be reduced to a handful of warm dust so he could lay his belly on them and wallow about. A frightening noise arose; it was time for the second assault. The village, the animals, all this tidal wave of life flowed over the church in a rage of bodies which bent the strongest beams. The females, in full melee, dropped from their bowels a continuous stream of fresh combatants. This time a section of the church wall was knocked out; the ceiling bent low; the frames were carried away from the windows; the twilight smoke grew darker and darker as it came in through the horrible breaches. The large Christ was held on the cross only by the nail through His left hand.

The collapse of a section of the wall produced great cheers. But, despite its wounds, the church still stood firm. It resisted stubbornly, ferociously, silently, darkly; it held tenaciously to the smallest stones in its foundation. It seemed that this ruin needed only one tiny pillar to remain standing; in a prodigious feat of balance, it still bore high its crushed roof. Then Father Mouret saw the tough mesa plants go to work, those terrible plants hardened by dry rocks, twisted like serpents, their wood hard and bulging with muscles. Rusty lichens, resembling a leper with inflamed sores, first ate the rough-cast plaster. Then thyme thrust its roots between the stones like crowbars. Lavender slid long crooked fingers under each stone and pulled it out, ripped it from the walls in a slow and unrelenting effort. Juniper, rosemary, and thorny hops climbed higher to push irresistibly against the edifice, and even the grass, the grass whose dried blades came under the main entrance, grew stiff as steel picks to disembowel the door and advance to the nave, where it pried up tiles with its powerful tongs. It was a victorious rout, revolutionary nature erecting barricades with overturned altars, demolishing the church which for centuries had been casting too large a shadow on it. The other combatants let the grass, thyme, lavender, and lichens work, settled back to watch these tiny things nibble more destructively than their strong hammer blows could ever do, this flaking away of the base whose hollow labor was to complete the collapse of the entire building. Then, abruptly, it was over. The service tree, whose tall branches were already penetrating the vault through the broken panes, rushed violently in with an awesome spurt of green. It stood in the middle of the nave and grew out of all proportion: the trunk became colossal until the church, like too small a belt, burst apart. The branches spread enormous knots in all directions, and each one carried off a piece of the wall or a strip of the roof; and they kept multiplying, each branch split infinitely; a new tree grew from every knot with such fury that the ruins of the church, pierced like an archery target, exploded and threw fine dust in all directions. Now the giant tree touched the stars. Its forest of branches was a forest of human limbs, legs, arms, torsos, bellies, all sweating sap. Women's hair streamed down, men's heads burst through the bark to laugh like new buds. At the very top, lovers, swooning in their nests, filled the air with the music of their delight and the smell of their fertility. The last puff of the hurricane which had blown away the church swept up the remaining dust, the powdery pulpit and confessional, the torn holy images, the crushed sacred vessels, all these ruins which the sparrows who once lived in the roof were now pecking avidly. The large Christ, ripped from His cross, was suspended for a moment in a mass of floating female hair, then was carried away to be lost in the depths of black night; He made a tiny sound when He hit bottom. The tree of life had just broken into heaven. And it rose higher than the stars.

Father Mouret applauded this vision wildly, as if he were damned. The church had been conquered. God no longer had a house. Now God would not bother him anymore. He could join the triumphant Albine. And how he laughed when he recalled that one hour before he had maintained that the shadow of the church would devour the earth! The earth had revenged itself by eating the church. His insane laugh startled him out of his hallucination. Stupefied, he looked at the slowly darkening nave; through the window, he could see bits of sky sprinkled with stars. And he was extending his arms to feel the walls when Désirée's voice called him from the sacristy hall: "Serge, are you in there? Answer me! I've been looking for you for thirty minutes."

She came in with a lamp. The priest saw that the church was still standing. He no longer understood; he was in terrible doubt, caught between the invincible Church rising from its ashes and all-powerful Albine, who made God tremble with one of her breaths.

◇◇◇◇◇◇◇◇◇◇◇◇◇◇◇◇◇◇◇◇◇◇◇◇◇◇◇◇◇◇◇◇◇◇◇

X Désirée brought her infectious gaiety with her. "There you are, there you are!" she cried. "Okay, so you want to play hide-and-seek. I called you ten times, as loud as I could. I thought you had gone for a walk." She looked curiously into the dark corners. She even went slyly over to the confessional, as if preparing to surprise someone hidden there. Disappointed, she returned and said, "So you're alone. Maybe you were asleep? What could you have been doing all by yourself when it's so dark? Well, come on, it's time to eat."

He wiped his brow with his hot hands to erase the thoughts which everyone was surely going to read. He mechanically tried to fasten his cassock, which seemed to him open, torn, in shameful disorder. Then he followed his sister, his face stern and immobile, stiffened by that will of a priest hiding the agony of his flesh under the dignity of his holy office. Désirée did not even notice his trouble. She simply said, as they were entering the dining room, "I had a fine nap. But you talked too much, you're all pale."

After dinner that evening, Brother Archangias came to play Battle with la Teuse. He was in a very good mood. When the friar was happy, he liked to punch la Teuse in the ribs, and she paid him back by slapping him as hard as she could. That made them laugh so much the ceiling shook. Moreover, he thought of extraordinary games: he broke plates on the table with his nose; he bet he could split the dining-room door by hitting it with his rump; he poured all the tobacco from his pouch into the old servant's coffee or brought in a handful of pebbles to drop down the front of her dress by pushing his hand in all the way to her belt. For no apparent reason, this happy joy burst out of his customary grouchiness; often something no one else laughed at gave him a fit of noisy guffaws, during which he stomped his feet, spun like a top, and held his belly.

"So tell me what's making you so happy," said la Teuse. He made no response. He had straddled a chair and was galloping around the table. "Fine, fine, play your stupid games," she continued. "Heavens! How dumb you are! If the good Lord is watching, He must be very pleased with you."

The friar had just fallen over backward, his spine on the floor and his legs in the air. Without getting up, he said seriously, "He sees me, He's pleased with what He sees. He's the one who wants me to be happy. When He's good enough to cheer me up, He rings a bell in my body. Then I go to it. It makes all paradise laugh." He bounced to the wall on his back; then, raising himself on his neck, he drummed his heels against the wall as high as he could reach. His cassock fell, revealing his black pants, mended at the knees with squares of green cloth. He went on, "Father, look how high I can reach. I bet you can't do it . . . Come on, it won't hurt you to laugh a little. It's better to crawl around on your back than to want a slut's skin for your mattress. You get what I'm driving at, don't you? Be silly for a while; scratch yourself to get rid of your vermin. It's relaxing. When I scratch, I like to imagine I'm God's dog, and that's what makes me say that all paradise is crowding around the windows and laughing at me . . . You can laugh, too, Father. I do it for the saints and for you. Here, a somersault for St. Joseph, another one for St. John, another for St. Michael, one for St. Mark, one for St. Matthew."

And he went through a whole rosary of saints as he somersaulted around the room. Father Mouret, still silently resting his fists on the table, had finally smiled. The friar's joy usually upset him. Then, as the acrobat came within reach of la Teuse, she kicked him. "Okay," she said, "are we ever going to play?"

Brother Archangias answered with a snarl. On all fours, he crawled straight to la Teuse, pretending to be a wolf. When he reached her, he buried his head under her skirts and bit her right knee.

"Will you please leave me alone!" she yelled. "Are you thinking dirty things now?"

"Me!" the frair exclaimed, so amused by this idea that he could not move. "Hey, look, I'm choking on one taste of your knee. It's too salty. I bite women, then I spit them out, understand?"

He used the familiar *tu* with her and spit on her skirts. When he succeeded in standing up, he puffed for a while and rubbed his sides. Bursts of gaiety still shook his belly as if it were a wineskin which someone was trying to empty. He finally said seriously, "Let's play . . . It's nobody's business if I laugh. You don't need to know why, Teuse."

And the game began. It was merciless. The frair hit the cards with his fists. When he yelled "Battle!" he shook the windows. La Teuse was winning. She had had three aces for a long time, and her eyes were shining as she sought the fourth. Brother Archangias was allowing himself more jokes. He lifted the table at the risk of breaking the lamp, cheated shamelessly, and defended himself with enormous lies, just for a joke, he said later. Suddenly he began to sing Vespers, in a voice so full he sounded like the cantor at the singing desk. And he did not stop his baleful rumbling; he accented the fall after each verse by tapping his cards against his left palm. When his gaiety was at its peak, when he could find no other way to express it, he sang Vespers for hours. La Teuse, who knew him well, leaned to him to shout over the roar filling the dining room, "Shut up, I can't stand any more. You're too happy tonight."

So the friar started the Compline. Father Mouret had gone to sit by the window. He seemed not to see or hear what was going on around him. During dinner, he had eaten as usual, had even managed to answer Désirée's endless questions. Now his strength was gone, he gave up; broken and destroyed, he was swept along by the furious quarrel continuing without quarter inside him. He lacked even the courage to stand up and go to his room. He was afraid the others would see the tears he could not hold back if he turned his face to the lamp. He leaned his brow against a pane and watched the shadows outside, growing more and more drowsy, slipping toward a nightmare stupor.

Brother Archangias, still chanting, winked and nodded in the direction of the sleeping priest. "What?" asked la Teuse. The friar repeated in an exaggerated form the game with his eyes. "Fine, fine, jerk your neck out of joint if you get a kick out of it!" the servant said. "But you have to talk if you want me to understand . . . Look, a king. Great, I get your queen."

He put his cards down, leaned over the table, and whispered in her face, "The girl was here."

"I know it," she replied. "I saw her in the barnyard with Dé-sirée."

He gave her a blistering look and brandished his fists. "You saw her, you let her in! You should have called me; we could have nailed her head to your kitchen door."

But she became angry even though she kept her voice low so as not to awaken the priest. "Oh, fine," she stammered, "you're really nice. Come kill somebody in my kitchen. Sure I saw her. And I even looked the other way when she went to see the Father in the church after catechism. They could have done anything they wanted to there. Is it my business? Didn't I have to put the beans on? I loathe her, I really hate that girl. But as soon as she makes the Father healthy—she can come every hour of the day and night. I'll lock them in a room together if they want me to."

"If you did that, Teuse," the friar said in a cold fury, "I'd strangle you."

She began to laugh. It was her turn to use the familiar *tu*. "Don't say stupid things, kid. You know women are as forbidden to you as the *Pater* is to jackasses. Just try to strangle me and watch what I do. Be good, let's finish the game. Hey, here's another king!"

He continued grumbling as he pulled out his card. "She must have come on some road only the devil knows about, or she wouldn't have escaped me today. I go stand guard up there near Paradou every afternoon. If I catch them together again, I'll introduce the girl to a dogwood stick I cut just for her. Now I'll watch the church, too."

He played, lost a jack to la Teuse, then leaned back in his chair, reconquered by his enormous laughter. He was unable to be really angry that night, and he murmured, "It doesn't matter if she saw him; she still fell flat on her face. I want to tell you about that anyway, Teuse. You know it was raining. I was at the school door when I saw her going down from the church. She was walking tall and proud despite the storm. And when she got to the road, wham! She fell right in the mud. Ah, I laughed and laughed, I clapped my hands. When she got up one of her wrists was bleeding. It made me happy enough to last a week. Every time I think of her lying on the ground, it tickles my throat and gut so much I feel like I'm going to bust."

And, now thinking only of the game, he puffed his cheeks and chanted *De Profundis*. Then he started again. The game ended in this lament which he made louder at times, as if to relish it more. He lost, but even defeat could not dampen his spirits. When la Teuse had let him out after awakening Father Mouret, they heard his voice die in the black night. He was repeating the last verse, *Et ipse redimet Israel ex omnibus iniquitatibus ejus*. Extraordinary jubilation rang in his voice.

XI FATHER MOURET SLEPT VERY SOUNDLY. WHEN, LATER THAN usual, he opened his eyes, he found his face and hands bathed in tears. He had cried in his sleep all night long. There was no Mass that morning. Despite his long rest, his fatigue from the previous evening had become so great that he remained in his room until noon, sitting on a chair at the foot of his bed. The stupor which was invading him more and more took away even his suffering. He felt only a great void; he was relieved, amputated, erased. It required a vast effort to read his breviary; the Latin verses seemed to be in a barbarous language whose words he could not even spell out. Then, when his book was thrown on the bed, he spent hours looking at the countryside through the open window without finding the strength to go lean on the sill. In the distance he could see the white wall around Paradou, a thin, pale line running over the heights among the dark spots made by small pine groves. The breach was on the left, behind one of those groves; he could not see it but he knew it was there; he remembered the smallest brambles spread among the stones. One day earlier he would not have dared lift his eyes to that awesome horizon. But now he could with impunity forget himself and seek the broken thread of the wall as it came into view behind the patches of green; it looked like the binding of a skirt which stuck to every bush it passed. His blood coursed no faster through his veins; temptation had abandoned his cowardly flesh as if it scorned his weak heart. He was left incapable of struggle, deprived of grace without even the passion of sin, ready to accept out of stupefaction everything he had furiously pushed away the day before.

He was surprised to find himself speaking aloud. Since the breach was still there, he would join Albine at sunset. He felt a little perplexed at this decision, but he did not see what else he could do. She was waiting for him, she was his wife. When he tried to call up her face, he saw her only as something very pale and distant. He was also worried about how they would live together. It would be hard for them to stay in the area; they would have to flee without anyone suspecting. Then, once they were hidden somewhere, they would need a lot of money to be happy. Twenty times he tried to arrange the elopement, to assure their life as happy lovers. He found nothing. Now that he was no longer driven mad by desire, he was terrified by the practical side of the situation; he stood with his feeble hands before a complicated task he knew nothing at all about. Where would they find their horses? If they walked, would they not be arrested as tramps? Besides, would he be capable of work, could he find a job, could he win bread for his wife? No one had ever taught him such things. He was ignorant of life; he searched his memory and found nothing but snatches of prayers, ceremonial details, pages of Bouvier's *Theological Instruction* memorized in the seminary. Even unimportant things were very difficult for him. He wondered if he would dare offer his wife his arm when they crossed the street. He would certainly not know how to walk with a woman on his arm. He would be so awkward that everyone would stare; people would guess he was a priest and insult Albine. All attempts to wash away his priesthood would be futile; he would always keep its sad paleness, its smell of incense. And what if he had children one day? He trembled at this unexpected thought and felt a strange repulsion. He felt he would not love them. There were two, a boy and a girl. He pushed them away from his knees; it hurt him to feel their hands on his clothes; he found nothing like other fathers' joy in bouncing them in the air. He could not get used to this flesh of his flesh, which seemed all sweaty with his man's impurity. The girl especially worried him with her big eyes already burning with a woman's loves. But no, he would have no children; he would avoid this horror which he felt at the idea of seeing his limbs grow and live forever. Then the hope of being impotent calmed him. All his virility must have left him during his long adolescence. His mind was made up. That night he would flee with Albine.

At night, however, Father Mouret felt too tired. He put his departure off until the next day. The next day he found another excuse: he could not let his sister stay alone with la Teuse; he would leave a letter for her to be taken to his Uncle

Pascal. For three days he promised himself to write that letter; paper, pen, and ink were standing ready on the table in his room. And the third day he left without writing it.

He had suddenly picked up his hat and set out for Paradou out of stupidity. He was obsessed, he resigned himself, he walked as if bound for an awful task he could not avoid. Albine's face was still dim; he saw her no more; he was obeying ancient desires now lying dead within him, but whose thrust persisted in the great silence of his being.

Once outside, he made no attempt to hide. He stopped in the village to chat for a while with Rosalie; she told him that her child was having convulsions, but she still laughed out of the corner of her mouth. Then he marched straight through the rocks to the breach. Out of habit, he had taken his breviary. Since the road was long, he grew bored, opened his book, and read the prayers for that day. When he put it back under his arm, he had forgotten Paradou. He still walked ahead, dreaming of a new chasuble which he wanted to buy to replace the chasuble of golden cloth which was definitely crumbling into dust; for some time he had been hiding his small change, and he calculated that he would have enough money in seven months. He was on the heights when a peasant's song in the distance reminded him of a song he had once learned in the seminary. He tried without success to remember the first few verses. It upset him to have such a bad memory. So, when it finally came back to him, he felt sweet pleasure in singing half-aloud the words he remembered one by one. It was homage to Mary. He smiled as if a cool breeze from his youth were blowing in his face. How happy he had been then! Of course, he could be happy again; he had not grown up; all he asked was the same joys, serene peace, a section of a chapel reserved for his knees, a lonely life brightened by beguiling childhood games. He began to sing louder and louder; he was singing in clear, flutelike tones when he saw the breach before him.

He looked surprised for a moment. Then he stopped smiling and murmured, "Albine must be waiting for me; the sun is already low."

But as he was climbing up to push aside the stones so he

could pass through, he was startled by a terrible snore. He had to go back down; he had almost stepped in the face of Brother Archangias, lying on the ground in a deep sleep. He had undoubtedly dozed off while guarding the entrance to Paradou, and he lay blocking the gate, his limbs extended in a shameful position. His right hand, thrown behind his head, had not released the dogwood stick, which he seemed to be brandishing like a flaming sword. And he was snoring in the middle of the brambles, his face in the sun, without any reaction from his tanned hide. A flock of fat flies was hovering over his open mouth.

Father Mouret watched him for a while. He was jealous of this sleep of a saint rolling in dust. He tried to chase the flies away; but they stubbornly returned and glued themselves to the friar's purple lips. He did not even feel them. Then the priest stepped over his large body. He entered Paradou.

XII BEHIND THE WALL, A FEW STEPS FROM THE BREACH, ALbine was sitting on a grassy carpet. She stood up when she saw Serge. "Here you are!" she cried, trembling from head to foot.

"Yes," he said tranquilly, "I came."

She threw her arms around his neck. But she did not kiss him. She had felt the chill of his canonical beads on her bare arm. She examined him, already worried, and said, "What's the matter, you didn't kiss my cheeks the way you used to. Don't you remember, when your lips sang? If you're sick I'll cure you again. Now that you're here we can start over with our happiness. No more sadness. You see, I'm smiling. We have to smile, Serge." And, when he remained serious, "Sure, I've had a lot of pain, too. I'm still very pale, aren't I? For a week I've been living on this grass, right here where you found me. I just wanted one thing, to see you come through that hole in the wall. Every time I heard a noise I got up and ran to meet you. And it wasn't you, it was leaves blowing in the wind. But I knew you would come. I would have waited for years."

Then she asked him, "Do you still love me?"

"Yes," he said, "I still love you."

They were facing one another, ill at ease, a huge silence between them. Serge was calm; he did not try to speak. Albine opened her mouth twice but closed it at once both times, astonished at the things she had been about to say. She could find only bitter words. She felt her eyes fill with tears. What could she be feeling not to be happy when her lover was back. "Listen," she said finally, "we can't stay here. That hole is freezing us. Let's go home. Give me your hand."

And they went into Paradou. Autumn was near; the trees were worried by yellow heads falling leaf by leaf. In the paths there was already a bed of dead green things, wet with moisture, which gave their steps the sound of muffled sighs. A haze floated over the back of the lawns, drowning the blue distance in mourning. And the entire garden was silent; it now released only melancholy breaths passing like a chill.

Serge was shivering in the walk lined with big trees they had taken. He said half-aloud, "How cold it is!"

"You are cold," Albine muttered sadly. "My hand doesn't make you warm anymore. Do you want me to wrap you up in my dress? Come on, we're going to relive all our feelings."

She led the way to the flower garden. The patch of roses still had a scent, the last blossoms gave off bitter perfume, and the limbs, grown out of all proportion, covered the ground like a stagnant pool. But Serge showed such resistance to the idea of entering these bushes that they stayed on the edge, seeking from afar the walks they had taken in the spring. She remembered every corner: she pointed to the grotto where the marble woman was sleeping, to the free-flowing hair of honeysuckle and clematis, to the fields of violets, to the fountain which spit out red carnations, to the huge staircase covered by a stream of wild wallflowers, to the ruined colonnade where the lilies had built a white pavilion. That was where they had both been born under the sun. And she recounted the smallest details of that first day, how they walked, how the air smelled in the shade. He seemed to be listening, but he asked a question which proved he had not understood. His trembling paleness never left him.

She led the way to the orchard, but the river was so swollen they could not even come near it. Serge no longer thought of taking Albine on his back to carry her to the other side in three leaps. But the apple and pear trees were still laden with fruit; the vine, its leaves farther apart now, was bent under the weight of bunches of amber grapes, each bearing its red spot of sunlight. How they had run in the ravenous shade of those venerable trees! They had been kids then. Albine still smiled at the shameless way she had displayed her legs when the branch broke. Did he at least recall the plums they had eaten? Serge answered by shaking his head. He already seemed tired. The orchard, with its greenish tunnels, its riot of mossy stems, collapsed and ruined scaffolding, bothered him, reminded him of a humid place inhabited by snakes and nettles.

She led the way to the meadows. There he had to go a few paces into the grass. It rose to his shoulders now; it seemed to have slender arms which were trying to bind up his limbs to roll him over and drown him deep in this endless green sea. And he begged Albine to go no farther. She did not stop, she kept walking forward; then, when she saw how he was suffering, she stood by his side, growing sadder and sadder, finally trembling as much as he. She continued to talk, however, and with a broad gesture she pointed to streams, rows of willows, patches of grass stretching to the horizon. All this had once been theirs. They had lived there for days at a time. Down there, among those three willows on the edge of that water, they had played lovers. Then they had wanted the grass to be taller than they were so they could get lost in its moving tide and be more alone, far from everything, like larks traveling to the end of a wheat field. So why did he shake today simply to feel the bottom of his feet disappear in the grass?

She led the way to the forest. The trees frightened Serge still more. Their black trunks were so serious that he did not recognize them. More than anywhere else, the past seemed dead to him in these stern trees where light descended freely. The first rains had erased their footprints from the sandy walks; the winds had carried away everything they had left in the bushes. But Albine, choked by sadness, protested with a look. She found the smallest traces of their walks in the sand; at every bush the old warmth which had rubbed off them as they passed rose to her face. And, begging with her eyes, she tried once more to evoke Serge's memories. Along this path they had walked in silence, very moved, without daring to say that they were in love. In this clearing they had forgotten everything until very late one evening, watching the stars rain drops of warmth. Over there, under the oak, they had exchanged their first kiss. The oak kept the smell of that kiss; the mosses themselves were still talking about it. It was a lie to say that the forest had become mute and empty. And Serge turned away to avoid meeting Albine's eyes, which made him tired.

She led the way to the big rocks. Perhaps there he would no longer quiver from that feebleness plunging her into despair. Only the big rocks were now warm from the red coal of the setting sun. They still had their tragic passion, their burning beds of pebbles where rolled lush, monstrously coupled plants. And, without speaking, without even turning her head, Albine led Serge up the steep incline. She wanted to lead him higher, beyond the springs, until they were both once more in the sunlight. They would find the cedar under which they had felt the first anguish of desire. They would lie on the ground, on the burning rocks, and wait to be won over by the earth's rut. But Serge's feet began very soon to stumble cruelly; he could walk no more. For the first time he fell to his knees. With a prodigious effort Albine pulled him up and carried him for a moment. And he fell again; he lay defeated in the middle of the path. Below him stretched the immensity of Paradou.

"You lied," cried Albine. "You don't love me anymore!"

And she began to weep as she stood by his side; she felt she did not have the strength to carry him higher. She was no longer angry; she wept for their dying love. He lay crushed on the ground.

"The garden is dead; I'm still cold," he muttered.

But she took his head and showed him Paradou. "Just look . . . Ah, it's your eyes that are dead, it's your ears, your limbs, your whole body. You passed through all our joys without seeing them, without hearing them, without feeling them. And all you did was stumble about, you came to fall here, you're tired and bored . . . You don't love me anymore."

He denied this gently and calmly. Then she became violently angry. "Shut up! Can the garden ever die? It will sleep this winter; it will wake up in May and give us back all the love we entrusted to it; our kisses will bloom again in the flower garden; our vows will break through the ground with the grass and the trees. If you could only see, if you could only hear, it feels with us, it loves more sweetly and more sadly in this autumn season when it goes to sleep in its fertility . . . You don't love me anymore, so you can't feel it now."

He raised his eyes to beg her not to be angry. His face was drawn, his childish fears made him pale. A shout caused him to tremble. He finally convinced her to agree to rest near him for a while, in the middle of the road. They would chat calmly and explain things. And, before Paradou, without even touching the tips of their fingers, they both spoke of their love.

"I love you, I love you," he said in his flat voice. "If I did not love you, I would not have come. I'm tired, and I don't know why. I should have thought I'd find here that good heat whose memory alone was a caress. And I'm cold, the garden is black, I don't see what I left in it. But it's not my fault. I'm trying hard to be like you, I want to make you happy."

"You don't love me anymore," Albine said once more.

"Yes, I love you. I suffered a lot the other day after I had to send you away . . . Oh, I was so insanely in love with you I would have crushed you in my arms if you had come back to me. Never have I wanted you so badly. For hours you stood alive before me, burning me with your lovely fingers. When I closed my eyes you were as bright as the sun, you took me in your flames . . . Then I walked over everything, I came to you."

He was dreamily silent for a time before continuing. "And now it's as if my arms were broken. If I wanted to press you to my chest I wouldn't know how to hold you. I'd drop you . . . Wait until this trembling goes away. Then give me your hands for me to kiss. Be kind; don't look at me with your flashing eyes. Help me get my heart back in the right place."

And his sadness was so real, his desire to start over in their tender life was so obvious, that Albine was touched. For a while she was gentle again. She asked him worriedly, "Where does it hurt? What's wrong with you?"

"I don't know. It seems to me that all my blood is flowing out through my veins. A little while ago, on the way here, I thought an icy cloak had been thrown over me. It stuck to my skin and turned my whole body to stone. I had already felt that cloak, but I can't remember now."

She interrupted him with a friendly laugh. "You're just a baby, you had a chill; that's all there was to it. Listen, at least I'm not scaring you, am I? In the winter we won't stay in this garden like two savages. We'll go where you want, to some big city. We'll love each other surrounded by people as calmly as when we're surrounded by trees. And I'll show you I'm good for something besides taking birds' nests out of trees and walking for hours without getting tired. When I was little I wore embroidered skirts with net stockings, all lace and frills. Somebody might have told you that?"

He was not listening. He cried out abruptly, "Oh, I remember!"

And when she questioned him he did not want to reply. He had just remembered the feeling of the seminary chapel on his shoulders. That was the icy cloak which turned his body to stone. Then he was irresistibly won over by his past as a priest. The vague memories which had awakened in him along the road from Artauds to Paradou grew more precise, imposed themselves with sovereign authority. While Albine kept talking about the happy life they would enjoy together, he listened to the bell ringing the elevation of the Host, watched monstrances outlining fiery crosses above kneeling crowds.

"All right," she said, "for you I'll wear my embroidered skirts again. I want you to be happy. We'll look for something to take your mind off your troubles. You might love me more when you see me beautiful, dressed up like a lady. My comb won't be stuck crossways; hairs won't fall all over my neck; I won't roll my sleeves up to my elbows; I'll fix my dress so my shoulders don't show. And I still know how to curtsy; I know how to walk so my chin moves just so. You'll have a pretty woman on your arm when you go down the streets."

"Did you ever go into churches when you were little?" he asked her softly, as if he were, in spite of himself, continuing aloud the daydream which had prevented his hearing. "I never could pass a church without going in. The moment the door closed behind me, I thought I was in paradise itself, angels' voices told me gentle stories, the saints' breath blew over my whole body. Yes, I would have liked to live there forever, lost in the depths of that bliss."

She stared at him, and a tiny flame lit the tenderness of her gaze. She went on, still submissive. "I'll be whatever you want. I used to play music, I was an educated young lady, I was taught every charm. I'll go back to school and take up music again. If you want to hear me play a tune you like, all you'll have to do is tell me. I'll spend months learning it so I can play it for you one evening in our locked room, after we've closed all the curtains. And you'll pay me with a kiss. Do you want to? One kiss on the lips will give my love back to you. You'll take me and crush me in your arms."

"Yes, yes," he muttered, still answering only his own thoughts, "my great joy was to light the candles, prepare the cruets, and carry the missal with my hands folded. Later I knew the slow approach of God and thought I would die of love. I have no other memories. I know nothing. When I raise my hand it's to give a blessing, when I open my lips it's to kiss the altar. If I look for my heart I can't find it: I have offered it to God and He has accepted it."

She became very pale, her eyes were fiery. She continued, her voice breaking, "And I never want my daughter to leave my side. If you think it's a good idea, you can send the boy to school. I'll keep the dear little blonde nestled in my petticoats. I'll teach her to read myself. Oh, I'll remember, I'll hire tutors if I've forgotten my letters. We'll live with all that little world under our feet. You'll be happy, won't you? Answer me, tell me that you'll be warm, that you'll smile, that you won't regret a thing."

"I often thought about the stone saints deep in their niches who had had incense burned in front of them for centuries," he said very softly. "After a time they must be soaked through with incense. And I'm like one of those saints. I have incense down to the smallest fold of my organs. This embalming gives me my serenity, the peaceful death of my flesh, the peace I taste by not living. Ah, may nothing disturb me as I remain motionless. I will always be cold and rigid with an eternal smile on my lips, impotent to come among men. That is my one desire."

She stood up, angry and threatening. She shook him and shouted, "What are you dreaming about? Aren't I your wife? Didn't you come to be my husband?"

He trembled and recoiled before her. "No! Leave me alone, I'm afraid," he stammered.

"And our life together, and our happiness, and our children?"

"No, no, I'm afraid." Then he said the final words, "I cannot! I cannot!"

For a time she was silent before the unhappy man quivering at her feet. A flame shot out of her face. She had opened her arms as if to take him and clasp him to her in an angry movement of desire. But she seemed to think better of it; she took only his hands and pulled him to his feet. "Come with me!" she said.

And she led the way to the giant tree, to the very place where she had given herself to him and he had possessed her. The same shade of bliss, the same trunk breathing like a chest, the same branches spreading far overhead like protective arms! The tree was still good, robust, powerful, fertile. As on their wedding day, the languor of an alcove, the glow of a summer's night fading on the bare shoulder of a woman in love, a barely audible exchange of lovers' moans abruptly becoming a great mute climax of passion, all this hovered in the clearing bathed in green brightness. And, far away, despite the first chill of autumn, Paradou too found once more its ardent whisper. It became their accomplice again. From the flower garden, from the orchard, from the big rocks, from the vast sky came laughter of sensual delight, borne on a wind which sowed dust of fertility as it blew. Never on the warmest spring evenings did the garden have the deep emotions it felt on the last beautiful days when the plants said good-bye and fell asleep. The odor of ripe seed blew across scattered leaves to bring them the intoxication of desire.

"Do you hear it? Do you hear it?" Albine whispered in Serge's ear when she had dropped him on the grass at the foot of the tree.

Serge was weeping.

"You see that Paradou is not dead. It's shouting for us to love. It still wants our marriage. Oh, remember! Take me. Let us belong to each other."

Serge was weeping.

She said nothing further. She took him herself. In a ferocious embrace, her lips glued themselves to this corpse to bring it back to life. And Serge still had only tears.

After a long silence, Albine spoke. She was standing now, contemptuous and resolute. "Go away," she said softly.

Serge stood with an effort and picked up his breviary, which had fallen in the grass. He went away.

"Go away," Albine repeated as she followed him, chasing him before her and raising her voice. And she pushed him from bush to bush; she guided him back to the breach under the serious trees. And there, when Serge hesitated, his head bowed, she shouted violently, "Go away! Go away!"

Then, without turning around, she slowly went back into Paradou. Night was falling. The garden was now only a great coffin of shadows.

XIII Brother archangias, awake now and standing in the breach, was hitting the stones with his stick and swearing frightfully. "May the devil break their backs! May he nail them together like dogs! May he grab their feet and drag their noses through their filth!"

He was astounded when he saw Albine chasing the priest

away. Then he hit the stones harder and was shaken by horrible laughter. "Good-bye, slut! Have a nice trip! Go back to fornicating with your wolves. Ah, you're not good enough for a holy man. You need stronger legs. You need oaks up you! Do you want my stick? Here, sleep with that! That's the lover to satisfy you." And in the gathering dusk he threw his stick as hard as he could behind Albine. Then he looked at Father Mouret and growled, "I knew you were in there. The stones had been moved. Listen, Father, your sin has made me your superior. God is using my mouth to tell you that hell has no torments fearful enough for priests who have jumped into flesh. If He deigns to forgive you, He will be too good, He will spoil His justice."

They moved slowly toward Artauds. The priest had not opened his mouth. No longer trembling, he gradually raised his head. When, far away against the violet sky, he saw the black bar of the Hermit and the red patch of tiles on the church roof, he smiled weakly. A vast serenity rose to his clear eyes.

The friar occasionally kicked a rock and turned to apostrophize his companion. "Is it over this time? When I was your age I was possessed: a demon ate my loins. And then he got bored and left. I don't have any loins now, I live in peace. Oh, I knew you would come. I've been keeping watch for three weeks. I looked in the garden through that hole in the wall. I wanted to cut down the trees. I threw rocks all the time, I was happy when I broke a limb. Tell me, is it really extraordinary, what you taste in there?"

Tortured by the delights glimpsed in Paradou, he had stopped Father Mouret in the middle of the road and was pinning him with eyes burning with terrible jealousy. He had remained on the threshold for weeks, sniffing distant, damnable joys. But when the priest remained silent, he began to walk again, mockingly growling dirty jokes. And, raising his voice, he said, "You see, when a priest does what you did, he hurts every other priest. Even I didn't feel chaste when I walked by your side. You poisoned our sex . . . Now you're reasonable again. You don't need to confess. I know what that blow is like. Heaven broke your back as it has other men's. So much the better!"

He was celebrating victory and clapping his hands. The priest, lost in dreams, was not listening; his smile had grown broader. And after the friar left him at the presbytery door, he walked to the front of the church and went in. It was all gray, as it had been on that terrible rainy evening when temptation had shaken him so roughly. But it remained poor and withdrawn, no streams of gold and no anguished sighs from the countryside. Its silence was solemn, it was filled with a breath of pity.

Kneeling before the large Christ of painted cardboard, shedding tears which were so many joys to his cheeks, the priest muttered, "Oh, my God, it is not true that You are merciless. I feel it, You have already forgiven me. I feel it in Your grace which has been descending to me for hours, drop by drop, slowly and surely bringing me salvation. Oh, my God! It was when I was abandoning You that You protected me most effectively. You hid in me in order better to deliver me from evil. You let my flesh go forward in order to hurl me against its impotence. And now, oh, my God, I see that You have branded me forever with Your seal, that awesome seal full of delights which sets a man outside of men and whose mark is so indelible that it reappears sooner or later even on guilty bodies. You broke me in sin and temptation. You laid waste to me with Your fire. You wanted me to be nothing but ruins so You could sit securely in me. I am an empty house where You can live. Blessed be Thy name forever, oh, my God."

He prostrated himself and babbled in the dust. The church was victorious. It remained standing above the priest's head with its altars, confessional, pulpit, holy pictures. The world no longer existed. Temptation had been extinguished like a fire now useless in the purification of this flesh. He was entering superhuman peace. He gave this supreme cry: "Outside of life, outside of creatures, outside of all things I am Yours, oh, my God, Yours alone, eternally!"

XIV In PARADOU AT THIS MOMENT, ALBINE WAS STILL PROWL-
ing about in the mute death agony of a wounded beast. She
was no longer crying. Her face was white; a large furrow ran
across her brow. Why was she being tortured like this? What
sin could she have committed to make the garden forget the
promises it had been making since she was a child? And she
examined herself as she walked on and on without seeing the
paths or the lengthening shadows flowing over them. But she
had always obeyed the trees. She could not remember breaking
a flower. She was still the girl loved by the greenery; she listened to it submissively; she gave herself to it, filled with faith
in the happiness for which it had destined her. When, on the
last day, Paradou had cried out for her to lie down under the
giant tree, she had lain down, she had opened her arms and
recited the lesson whispered to her by the grass. If she found
nothing to reproach herself with, then the garden was betray-
ing her, torturing her simply for the joy of seeing her suffer.

She stopped and looked around. The huge dark masses of
greenery still had their meditative silence; black walls were
being erected in the paths, making them shadowy dead ends.
In the distance, patches of grass were putting to sleep the winds
blowing through their blades. And she desperately spread her
hands and protested aloud: it could not end this way. But her
voice was choked off under the silent trees. Three times she
pleaded for Paradou to answer, and no explanation came from
the high limbs, no leaf took pity on her. When she began to
prowl again, she felt that she was walking into dead winter.
But now that she no longer interrogated the earth like a rebellious creature, she heard a soft voice running along the ground,
the voice of the plants saying good-bye, wishing one another a
happy death. To have drunk the sun for an entire season, to
have lived always in bloom, to evaporate in continuous perfume, and then to go away at the first sign of pain in the hope
of growing again somewhere, was this not enough life, was it

not a full existence which would be spoiled by a stubborn attempt to lengthen it? Ah, how comfortable death must be! To have endless night before you, to dream of the short day you lived, to fix its ephemeral joys for eternity!

She stopped again, but she protested no more in Paradou's great meditative silence. She thought she understood now. The garden was undoubtedly preparing her death as her supreme delight. It was toward death that it had guided her so tenderly. After love there was only death. And never had the garden loved her so much: it had been ungrateful of her to accuse it of abandoning her, for she was still its favorite daughter. The silent foliage, the paths barricaded by shadows, the lawns where the wind grew drowsy, were quiet only in order to invite her to the joy of lengthy silence. They wanted her with them in cold repose; they dreamed of taking her away, of sweeping her along in their dry leaves, her eyes frozen like the springs, her limbs stiff like the bare branches, her blood sleeping like the sap. She would live their life to the end, to their death. Perhaps they had already decided that next summer she would be a rosebush in the flower garden, a pale willow in the meadows, or a young birch in the forest. It was life's great law: she was going to die.

Then for the last time she walked across the garden, in search of death. What perfumed plant needed to hang the odor of its leaves on her hair? What flower was asking for the gift of her satin skin, for the pure whiteness of her arms, for the soft coloring of her breasts? To which sick shrub was she to offer her young blood? She would have liked to be useful to the grass growing along the walks, to kill herself there so green things would grow out of her, proud and lush, filled with birds in May and ardently caressed by the sun. But Paradou was mute for a long time; it had not yet decided to tell her what final kiss would bear her away. She had to go everywhere and make once more the pilgrimage of her walks. It was almost completely dark; it seemed that she was slowly entering the earth. She climbed to the big rocks to question them, to ask if it was on their beds of pebbles that she was to breathe her last.

She expectantly crossed the forest, slowed by a desire for some oak to collapse and bury her in the majesty of its fall. She walked along the meadow rivers, leaning over almost each time she took a step, looking for a couch prepared for her deep in the water, among the lilies. Nowhere did death call her, nowhere did it offer her its cool hands. Still, she was not mistaken. Paradou was truly going to teach her to die as it had taught her to love. She began beating the bushes again, hungrier than on the warm mornings when she was looking for love. And suddenly, as she came to the flower garden, she found death in the evening smells. She began running and laughing in sensual delight. She was to die with the flowers.

First she ran to the roses. There, in the last light of dusk, she thrust her hand into the thickets and picked all the languishing blooms. She picked them on the ground with no thought for the thorns; she picked them waist-high with both hands; she picked them above her by standing on her toes and bending the branches. She was driven by such a sense of urgency that she broke the branches, she who respected the smallest blade of grass. Soon her arms were filled with roses; she trembled under a load of roses. Then, after despoiling the bushes, she went to the summer house, taking even the fallen petals. And when she had let her cargo of roses slip to the floor of the blue-ceilinged bedroom, she went down the stairs to return to the flower garden.

She now picked violets. She made enormous bouquets and tied them one by one to her breast. She picked carnations, she even cut the buds; she tied giant bundles of white carnations, bowls of milk, and giant bundles of red carnations, bowls of blood. And she picked stocks, primroses, heliotropes, lilies; she grabbed handfuls of the last blooming stocks, pitilessly crumbling their quilled satin, laid waste to beds of primroses, barely open in the evening air, moved down the field of heliotropes and piled up her harvest of flowers, put sheaves of lilies under her arms like sheaves of wheat. When she was loaded again, she went back to the summer house to throw violets, carnations, stocks, primroses, heliotropes, and lilies beside the roses.

And, without pausing to catch her breath, she went down the stairs again.

This time she plundered the melancholy corner serving as the flower garden's cemetery. A burning autumn had put a second wave of spring flowers there. She was especially eager for tuberoses and hyacinths as she knelt in the grass and guarded her harvest with miserly care. The tuberoses seemed to be precious flowers which were to distill drop by drop extraordinary gold and riches. The hyacinths were covered with the pearls of their blossoming seeds, were necklaces whose every jewel would pour out joys which man had never dreamed of. And even though she was already hidden by armfuls of hyacinths and tuberoses, she went on to attack a field of poppies, and she still managed to cut down a field of marigolds. Above the tuberoses, above the hyacinths, grew marigolds and poppies. She ran to unload in the blue-ceilinged bedroom, careful not to let the wind steal a single pistil. She went down the stairs again.

What was she to pick now? She had harvested the entire garden. She stood on her toes and saw only a dead garden under gray shadow; it no longer had the soft eyes of its roses, the red laughter of its carnations, the perfumed hair of its heliotropes. But she could not go back empty-handed. And she swooped down on grass and leaves, dragged her breasts across the ground in an attempt to carry away the earth itself in one final passionate embrace. She harvested aromatic plants, filled her skirt with citronella, mint, verbena. She came upon a border of balsam and left not a single leaf. She even took two large fennels and slung them over her shoulder like two trees. If she could have gripped it between her teeth, she would have pulled away the garden's entire green carpet. Then, in the summer-house door, she turned to look at Paradou for the last time. It was black; night, which had fallen completely, had thrown a dark shroud over its face. And she went up the stairs, to go down them no more.

Everything was soon arranged in the large bedroom. She had lit the lamp and set it on the chest of drawers. She pulled piles of flowers to the middle of the floor, made huge clusters and put one in each corner. First she put lilies on the chest behind the lamp to make a lace curtain softening the light with white purity. Then she carried handfuls of carnations and stocks to the old sofa, whose painted upholstery was already covered with red bouquets which had been fading for a hundred years; and the upholstery vanished, the sofa stood against the wall as a mountain of stocks bristling with carnations. Then she lined the four armchairs before the alcove and filled the first with marigolds, the second with poppies, the third with primroses, the fourth with heliotropes: the chairs were drowned. Only the tips of their arms were visible; they looked like flowering hedges. Finally, she turned to the bed. She rolled a little table to its head and covered it with an enormous quantity of violets. And she completely buried the bed under hyacinths and tuberoses. The mattress overflowed on all sides, streams of flowers hung to the floor. The bed was nothing but a great blossom.

The roses remained. She scattered them at random, all over the room, not even looking to see where they fell; chest, sofa, armchairs, all caught some; they covered one corner of the bed. For a few minutes it rained roses in large clumps, a storm of flowers as heavy as the drops of a summer storm forming puddles in the floor's indentations. But she seemed to have just as many roses as when she had begun. She finally wove garlands and hung them on the walls. The plaster cupids doing their lewd things over the alcove had garlands of roses around their necks, arms, and loins; their bare bellies and rumps were dressed in roses. The blue ceiling, the oval panels framed in flesh-colored ribbons, the erotic paintings devoured by time, were covered by a mantle of roses, by drapes of roses. Everything was arranged in the large bedroom. Now she could die there.

She remained standing for a time and looked around her. She was thinking; she was looking to see if death was there. And she gathered the aromatic plants, citronella, mint, verbena, balsam, and fennel; she twisted them and folded them to make material to stop up every crack, every hole in the door and windows. Then she drew the primitively woven white calico curtains. And silently, without even sighing, she lay on the bed, on the blossom of hyacinths and tuberoses.

Now came her final sensual delights. Her eyes open wide, she smiled at the bedroom. How she had loved in this room! How happy she was to be dying there! Now nothing impure came to her from the plaster cupids; nothing disturbing came from the paintings of thrashing female legs. Only the flowers' suffocating perfume could now be found under the blue ceiling. And it seemed that this perfume was nothing but the smell of old love still warming the alcove, a smell increased, multiplied a hundredfold, become so strong that it was asphyxiating her. Perhaps it was the breath of that lady who had died there a century ago. And she was in her turn enraptured by this breath. Motionless, her hands folded on her heart, she still smiled as she listened to the perfumes whispering in her ringing head. They were playing a strange music of smells putting her to sleep slowly and very gently. First came a happy, childish prelude: her hands had twisted the aromatic greenery and gave off the bitterness of crushed grass, told her stories of her tomboy romps in Paradou's wilderness. Then a flute was heard, tiny musky notes dropping like seeds from the violets on the table at the head of the bed; and this flute, weaving its melody into the calm breath, accompanied by the lilies on the chest, sang the first charms of her love, the first vow, the first kiss in the forest. But it was growing more difficult to breathe; her passion arrived with a sudden outburst of acrid carnations, whose brassy voice dominated for an instant all the others. She thought she was going to die in the morbid phrasing of marigolds and poppies singing the torment of her desires. And suddenly everything became peaceful; she breathed more freely, slid deeper into gentleness, rocked by the descending scale of the stocks, which slowly died until an adoring hymn from the vanilla-breathed heliotropes told of the approach of her marriage. Primroses occasionally pierced this wedding music with a discreet trill. Then silence: the roses languorously made their entry. From the ceiling flowed the voices of a distant choir. It was a great ensemble; she shivered to hear it. The choir swelled, soon vibrating with prodigious harmonies bursting all around her. The marriage was prepared; the roses' fanfare announced the awesome moment. Swooning, dying, her hands pressed tighter and tighter to her heart, she was gasping, opening her mouth, searching for the kiss which was to smother her, when the hyacinths and tuberoses exhaled smoke and enveloped her in a final sigh, so deep it covered the choir of roses. Albine had died in the last gasp of the flowers.

◇◇◇◇◇◇◇◇◇◇◇◇◇◇◇◇◇◇◇◇◇◇◇◇◇◇◇◇◇◇◇◇◇◇

XV AROUND THREE O'CLOCK THE NEXT DAY, LA TEUSE AND Brother Archangias were chatting on the presbytery porch when they saw Dr. Pascal's carriage tearing through the village. His whip cracked loudly under the awning. "Where can he be going so fast?" the old servant said. "He's going to break his neck."

The carriage had reached the base of the hill on which the church was built. Suddenly the horse reared and stopped, and the doctor's head, all white and ruffled, came from under the awning. "Is Serge there?" he shouted furiously.

La Teuse, who had come to the edge of the hill, replied, "The Father is in his room. Do you have something to tell him? I could call him."

Uncle Pascal, his face frighteningly twisted, made a terrible movement with his right hand, the one holding the whip. He went on, leaning out so far he almost fell: "Oh, so he's reading his breviary. No, don't call him, I'd wring his neck and it wouldn't do a damned bit of good! I just wanted to tell him Albine is dead, do you hear me? Tell him for me she's dead!" And he disappeared, whipping his horse so hard that the beast ran off in a fury. But twenty yards down the road he stopped again, leaned his head out once more, and yelled, "Tell him for me too that she was pregnant! He'll be happy to hear it!"

The carriage again took up its insane course. With violent jolts it went up the rocky road leading to Paradou. La Teuse was left breathless. Brother Archangias was cackling in glee and staring at her with ferociously burning eyes. And she pushed him away; she almost pushed him down the porch steps.

"Go away," she stammered, angry in her turn and taking it out on him. "I'll end up hating you. Is it possible for a man to get pleasure from someone's death? I didn't love that girl one bit, but it's not funny when somebody dies so young. Go away, I said. Don't laugh like that anymore or I'll throw my scissors in your face!"

It had been around one o'clock that a peasant who had come to Plassans to sell his vegetables had told Dr. Pascal about Albine's death and added that Jeanbernat was asking for him. The doctor felt a little better after shouting what he had as he passed the church. He had come out of his way to have that satisfaction. He reproached himself with this death as if it were a crime he had had something to do with. He had cursed himself all along the road; he had to wipe his eyes continuously to see where he was going; he drove the carriage over piles of stones with the unspoken desire to turn it over and break a leg. When he entered the sunken road beside the endless park wall, he began to hope. Perhaps Albine was only in a coma. The peasant had told him some story about her asphyxiating herself with flowers. Ah, if he could only get there in time, if he could only save her! And he whipped his horse furiously, as if he were whipping himself.

It was a beautiful day. The summer house was bathed in sunlight as it was on lovely days in May. But the ivy covering the walls all the way to the roof was spotted with red, and the bees no longer buzzed around the wallflowers growing in the cracks. He quickly hitched his horse and pushed open the gate leading to the little garden. There was the same great silence in which Jeanbernat smoked his pipe. Only the old man was no longer on the bench by his greens. "Jeanbernat!" called the doctor.

There was no answer. Then, as he entered the vestibule, he saw something he had never seen before. At the back of the hall, at the bottom of the staircase, a door was open on Paradou; under the pale sun, the immense garden waved its yellow leaves and displayed its autumn melancholy. He went through the door and took a few steps on the damp grass.

"Ah, it's you, Doctor," said Jeanbernat's calm voice. The old man was digging a hole at the foot of a mulberry tree. He had straightened his tall body when he heard the doctor. Then he had gone back to work, removing enormous clumps of rich soil with each stroke of his shovel.

"What do you think you're doing?" asked Dr. Pascal.

Jeanbernat straightened again. He mopped his brow on his sleeve. "I'm digging a hole," he said simply. "She always loved the garden. She'll sleep well here."

The doctor was choked by emotion. He remained on the edge of the grave for a moment, unable to speak, watching Jeanbernat dig. "Where is she?" he said at last.

"Up there, in her room. I left her on the bed. I want you to listen to her heart before I put her in. I listened; I didn't hear anything at all."

The doctor went up the stairs. Except for an open window, the bedroom was undisturbed. The faded flowers, suffocated by their own perfume, now released only the stale odor of dead flesh. But asphyxiating heat lingered at the back of the alcove; it seemed to blow into the room and float away in thin curls of smoke. Albine, very white, her hands folded on her heart, was smiling as she slept on her mattress of hyacinths and tuberoses. And she was truly happy, she was truly dead. The doctor stood by the bed and watched her for a long time with that concentration of doctors who attempt resurrections. Then he decided he would not even disturb her folded hands; he kissed her forehead, where her maternity had already set a light shadow. Below, in the garden, Jeanbernat's spade was still making heavy, regular strokes.

After fifteen minutes, the old man came up. He had done his job. He found the doctor sitting by the bed, so lost in thought that he seemed not to feel the big tears flowing down his cheeks one by one. The two men only looked at each other. Then, after a time, Jeanbernat said slowly, "You see, I was right." He repeated his all-encompassing gesture. "There is nothing, nothing, nothing. All that's a bad joke." He remained standing and gathered the flowers which had fallen from the bed. One by one he threw them on Albine. "Flowers only live a day or two," he said, "and prickly nettles like me wear out the rocks they grow on . . . Now, good night, I'm going to call it quits. They blew out the last corner of my sun . . . It's a bad joke."

And he too sat down. He was not weeping; he had the stiff despair of a broken robot. Mechanically he stretched out his hand and took a book from the little table covered with violets. It was one of those books from the attic, a worn volume of Holbach's works which he had been reading as he kept watch over Albine's body. Since the doctor, overwhelmed, still said nothing, he began turning pages again. But an idea suddenly came to him. "If you helped me," he said to the doctor, "we could get her downstairs and bury all these flowers with her."

Uncle Pascal trembled. He explained that it was against the law to keep bodies like that.

"What do you mean, against the law!" shouted the old man. "Doesn't she belong to me? Do you think I'm going to let any-body take her and give her to the priests? Just let them try if they feel like getting shot at!"

He had stood up and was furiously shaking his book. The doctor took his hands and pressed them, begging him to calm down. He talked for a long time, saying everything that came into his head; he accused himself, made partial admissions, referred vaguely to those who had killed Albine. "Listen," he said finally, "she doesn't belong to you anymore. You have to give her to them."

But Jeanbernat refused. He was shaken, however, and in the end he said, "All right. Let them take her. I hope she breaks their arms! I'd like for her to come out of the ground and scare them all to death. Besides, there's something I have to take care of down there. I'll go tomorrow . . . Good-bye, Doctor, I'll use the hole myself."

And when the doctor had departed, he sat back down at the head of the bed and began to read his book seriously once more.

XVI THAT MORNING THERE WAS A GREAT TO-DO IN THE PRES-
bytery barnyard. The Artauds butcher had just slaughtered
Matthew, the pig, in the shed. Désirée, tremendously excited,
had held Matthew's feet while he was being stuck. She kissed
his back so he would not feel the knife and told him they
simply had to kill him now that he was so fat. No one was more
adept than she at cutting off a goose's head with one stroke or
at slitting a hen's throat with a pair of scissors. Her love of
animals had no difficulty accepting this massacre. It was necessary, she said; it made room for babies growing up. And she
was very gay.

"Miss Désirée," la Teuse grumbled constantly, "you're going
to hurt yourself. It doesn't make sense to get all excited just
because we're slaughtering a pig. You're as red as if you'd been
dancing all night."

But Désirée clapped her hands, spun around and kept busy.
La Teuse said she felt like her legs were turning to jelly. Since
one o'clock that morning she had been rolling her huge bulk
from kitchen to barnyard. She had to make the black pudding.
She was the one who had whipped the blood, two broad pots
all pink in the sun. And it seemed she would never finish, for
Miss Désirée kept calling her for no reason. It must be said that
when the butcher was sticking Matthew, Désirée had been
deeply moved as she entered the stable. Lisa, the cow, was in
labor there. Then, gripped by extraordinary joy, she had completely lost her senses. "One leaves, another comes," she yelled
as she jumped up and down and did pirouettes. "Just come
look, Teuse!"

It was eleven o'clock. At times snatches of song came from
the church. They could hear a confused murmur of grieving
voices and bits of prayer punctuated by loud Latin phrases.
"Come on!" Désirée said for the twentieth time.

"I have to go ring the bell," said the old servant. "I'll never
get through . . . What do you want this time, Miss?"

But she did not wait for an answer. She plunged into a group of hens ravenously drinking the blood in the pots; furious, she kicked them away. Then she covered the pots and said, "Okay, instead of bothering me, you'd better keep an eye on those things. If you let them do whatever they please, you won't get any pudding, understand?"

Désirée laughed. So what if the hens drank a little blood? It made them fat. Then she wanted to show la Teuse the cow, but the old servant refused. "I have to go ring the bell. The funeral's almost over. You hear them?"

At that moment, in the church, the voices swelled to hold a dying note. The women distinctly heard the sounds of steps. "No, come look," Désirée insisted as she pushed her to the stable. "Tell me what I should do."

The cow was lying on the straw. It turned its head and followed them with its big eyes. And Désirée maintained that she definitely needed something. Maybe they could do something to make her feel better. La Teuse shrugged her shoulders. Didn't animals know how to take care of themselves? People should just leave them alone and not bother them. And she was finally going to the sacristy when she passed the shed and cried out again, "Just look," she said, her fists clenched. "The little bitch!"

In the shed, Matthew had stretched out on his back, his paws in the air, waiting to be singed. The cut on his throat was fresh; drops of blood still beaded in it. And a small white hen was very delicately pecking the blood, drop by drop.

"Heavens! What a feast she's having!" was Désirée's only comment. She leaned over to punch the pig's swollen belly and added, "Well, fatso, you stole their food enough for them to deserve to eat your neck now."

La Teuse quickly removed her apron and used it to tie up Matthew's neck. Then she hurriedly disappeared into the church. The main door had just squeaked on its rusty hinges; a hymn rose in the open air and calm light. And the bell suddenly began to toll regular strokes. Désirée, who had remained kneeling by the pig, still punching its belly, smiled and raised her head to listen. Then, finding herself alone after furtively glancing around her, she slipped into the stable and closed the door. She was going to help the cow.

The small iron cemetery gate, which was supposed to be opened wide to admit the body, was hanging broken against the wall. In the empty field, the sun slept on the dry grass. The procession filed in, chanting the last verse of the *Miserere*. And silence fell.

"*Requiem aeternam dona ei,*" Father Mouret said seriously.

"*Et lux perpetua luceat ei,*" added Brother Archangias, in the deep voice of a cantor.

Vincent, in his surplice, was leading the way. He held the cross, a large brass cross which had lost half its silver, in both hands, very high. Next marched Father Mouret, pale in his black chasuble, his head erect, chanting without trembling, his eyes staring into the distance. His lighted candle barely spotted the bright sunlight with a warm drop. And, two paces behind him, almost touching his chasuble, came Albine's coffin, carried by four peasants on a kind of stretcher painted black. The coffin, draped in bunting too short for it, revealed at its foot new pine boards bearing the spangles of the bright steel heads of new nails. Flowers were strewn in the middle of the bunting, handfuls of white roses, hyacinths, and tuberoses, taken from the girl's deathbed.

"Be careful there!" shouted Brother Archangias to the peasants when they tilted the stretcher so he could pass without being caught on the gate. "You're going to drop the whole thing." And he held the coffin in his heavy hand. For lack of a second clerk, he was carrying the holy-water font as well as standing in for the cantor, the militiaman, who had been unable to attend. "You come in, too," he said as he turned around.

There was another procession, this one for Rosalie's baby, who had died in convulsions the day before. The father, mother, Mother Brichet, Catherine and two farm girls, la Rousse and Lisa, were all there. The last two were holding the baby's coffin, one at each end.

Suddenly all conversation ceased, and there was another silence. The bell was still tolling, slowly and deliberately, in heartrending tones. The procession crossed the entire cemetery on its way to the corner formed by the church and the barnyard wall. Flocks of grasshoppers flew into the air, lizards scurried to their holes. Oppressive heat beat on the rich soil. The tiny noise of grass crushed by this tramping procession began to sound like muffled sighs.

"Stop there," the friar said as he blocked the path so the two girls holding the baby could not pass. "Wait your turn. We don't need you underfoot."

And the girls put the baby on the ground. Rosalie, Fortuné, and Mother Brichet stopped in the middle of the cemetery while Catherine sneaked off behind Brother Archangias. Albine's grave had been dug to the left of Father Caffin's white tombstone, gleaming in the sun as if shot with rhinestones. The yawning hole, dug that morning, opened among big clumps of grass. Tall, half-uprooted plants leaned over to peer into it. At the bottom, a fallen flower spotted the black earth with its red petals. The soft soil sank under Father Mouret's feet; he had to back up in order not to fall into the grave.

"*Ego sum . . .*" he began in a full voice which dominated the lamenting bell.

And during the antiphon everyone instinctively cast furtive glances into the still-empty hole. Vincent, who had set the cross at the foot of the grave, across from the priest, loosened streams of dirt with his shoe and amused himself by watching them fall. This made Catherine laugh; she bent over behind him so she could watch, too. The peasants had laid the bier on the grass. They were stretching their arms while Brother Archangias prepared the sprinkler.

"Here Voriau," called Fortuné. The big black dog, who had gone to sniff the bier, retreated dourly.

"What's that dog doing here?" exclaimed Rosalie.

"He followed us, what do you think?" Lisa said, chuckling discreetly.

Everyone around the baby's coffin was whispering. The father and mother forgot it at times; then they fell silent when they noticed it there at their feet, between them.

"And didn't old Bambousse want to come?" Rosalie asked.

Mother Brichet raised her eyes to heaven. "He was talking like he was about to tear everything apart yesterday when the baby died. No, he's not a good man. I say it in front of you, Rosalie. Why, he almost choked me, yelling that he'd been robbed, that he would have given one of his wheat fields for the baby to die before the wedding!"

"There was no way to know," Fortuné said wickedly.

"So what if the old guy gets mad?" added Rosalie. "We're married for good now."

They smiled at each other over the tiny bier, their eyes shining. Lisa and la Rousse nudged each other. They all became quite serious again. Fortuné had picked up a dirt clod to chase away Voriau, who was now prowling among the old stones. "Ah, it looks like they're almost through," la Rousse whispered very softly.

At the grave, Father Mouret was completing the *De Profundis*. Then he slowly walked to the coffin and looked at it for an instant without blinking. He seemed larger; he was transfigured by the peace on his face. And he leaned over and picked up a handful of loose dirt which he let fall on the bier in such a way as to form a cross. He said in a voice so clear that not a syllable was lost, *"Revertitur in terram suam unde erat, et spiritus redit ad Deum qui dedit illum."*

A chill had run through the mourners. Lisa was thinking; she said in a disturbed voice, "Still, it's not much fun when you think it'll be your turn one day."

Brother Archangias had given the priest the sprinkler. He shook it over the body several times and said softly, *"Requiescat in pace."*

"Amen," Vincent and the friar responded together, in voices so high and so deep that Catherine had to bite her fist to keep from laughing.

"No, no, it's not much fun," continued Lisa. "There's not a soul at this funeral. If it weren't for us, the cemetery would be empty."

"They say she killed herself," Mother Brichet said.

"Yeah, I know," interjected la Rousse. "The friar didn't want her to be buried with Christians. But the Father said eternity was for everyone. I was there . . . Still, the Philosopher could have come."

But Rosalie quieted them by whispering, "Hey, look, there he is, the Philosopher."

And Jeanbernat was in fact entering the cemetery. He walked straight to the group around the grave. His step was as sprightly as ever; he was still so nimble that he made no noise. He stood behind Brother Archangias and seemed for an instant to be gazing intently at the back of his neck. Then, as Father Mouret was finishing the prayers, he calmly pulled a knife from his pocket, opened it, and chopped off the friar's ear.

No one had time to interfere. The friar screamed.

"The left one's for later," Jeanbernat said peacefully as he threw the ear to the ground. And he left. Everyone was so stunned that he was not even followed. Brother Archangias had fallen on the pile of fresh soil from the grave. He had tried to stop the bleeding with his handkerchief. One of the four pallbearers wanted to take him home. But he shook his head and remained there, ferocious, expectant, eager to see Albine lowered into the hole.

"At last; it's our turn now," Rosalie said with a sigh.

But Father Mouret was hesitating near the grave, watching the pallbearers tie ropes around the coffin so it could be lowered smoothly. The bell was still tolling, but la Teuse must have been growing tired, for the strokes were no longer regular; the bell seemed to be protesting the length of the ceremony. The sun was hotter; the shadow of the Hermit moved slowly across the grass dented by graves. When Father Mouret had to step back to get out of the way, his glance fell on the marble stone sacred to the memory of Father Caffin, of that priest who had loved and who was sleeping there, so tranquil under the wild flowers.

Then suddenly, as the coffin was being lowered on the ropes, whose knots tore groans from its wood, a frightening uproar arose in the barnyard behind the wall. The goat was bleating; ducks, geese, and turkeys were flapping their wings and clapping their beaks together; the hens were clucking as if they had all laid an egg at the same time; the tawny rooster, Alexander, gave his clarion call; even the rabbits could be heard as they leaped about and rattled the boards in their boxes. And above all this noisy life of the little nation of animals rang a huge laugh. There was a rustle of petticoats, Désirée appeared, her hair wild, her arms bare to the elbows, her face triumphantly red, her hands against the wall. She must have been standing on top of the dung heap. "Serge! Serge!" she called.

At this very moment, Albine's coffin reached the bottom of the hole. The ropes had just been pulled out. One of the peasants was throwing in the first spadeful of dirt.

"Serge! Serge!" she yelled, clapping her hands. "The cow had a calf."

AFTERWORD

◇◇

Emile Zola (1840–1902) is the most celebrated and accomplished representative of the ultra-realistic group of French writers known as naturalists. His major work is a monumental cycle of twenty novels entitled *The Rougon-Macquart: Natural and Social History of a Family under the Second Empire,* a series containing several masterpieces (*L'Assommoir, The Earth, Nana*), and one novel, *Germinal,* which stands among the great works of world literature. His style usually justifies his reputation of being realistic in the extreme. He attempted to incorporate into a fictional universe the "scientific" insights into the natural and human worlds rapidly accumulating in his day, and the description of physical objects, social conditions and historical circumstances is at least as important as the presentation of individual motives in explaining the development of his plots. His desire to duplicate objective reality within the novel is documented both in his critical pronouncements and in the multitudinous, painstaking notes he almost invariably accumulated before beginning his works.

Zola's descriptions fortunately never approach mathematical objectivity, however. There are vast differences between his style and that of France's current generation of realist authors, men like Robbe-Grillet and Claude Mauriac. Zola unquestionably devotes much energy to making his readers aware of the nature and importance of physical and historical reality, but he is as concerned with communicating the feeling that man's environment induces as with describing the environment itself. The reader is made to feel a presence while being shown an outline. Physical reality exists as part of the novel because of its human impact, and Zola's physical descriptions consequently often become mythic evocations of strange beings dominating human existence. It is this mythic vision which is responsible for the great critical attention accorded *The Rougon-Macquart* in recent years. The studiously consistent delineation of the objects and forces composing the world of Zola's characters transcends the material realm in which it is grounded to evoke a supernatural universe shaped by incomprehensible powers as independent of men's wishes as gods and fates. To take two of the most famous examples, in *Germinal* Zola communicates the terrors of a miner's life not only by giving minute descriptions of the conditions under which miners live and work but also by such poetic devices as transforming the mining company into a hidden god squatting in an invisible temple and demanding human sacrifices; in *The Earth* the effect of the new American wheat fields on nineteenth-century French farmers is described by a series of historically accurate quotations of the price of wheat on the world market, but the impact of these figures is immeasurably increased because Zola presents them as the outer signs of an unnameable Biblical plague destroying a land and sapping the will of all who live on it.

Zola's mythopoeic vision seldom dominates his concern with realistic detail, however. The universe in which we all live is often poetically transformed but almost never is it distorted beyond recognition. The unique, subjective vision of the world incarnated in *The Rougon-Macquart* is inseparable from its author's attempt to communicate his perception of an objective reality visible to all with eyes to see. The reader is never allowed to forget that he is reading about the world he knows, a world of time and space whose objects obey natural laws, a world where social and economic conditions are created by forces which, though vast and overpowering, can be determined and described in logical terms.

The most cursory reading of *The Sin of Father Mouret* (1875), the fifth work in the Rougon-Macquart cycle, reveals that the general description of Zola's realistic style in the preceding paragraphs does not in any sense apply to it. In this novel myth completely triumphs over imitation of reality. The author whose concern with the accurate reproduction of the physical universe is so scrupulous as to become occasionally oppressive is here blithely unconcerned with accuracy and logic: topography changes from chapter to chapter, distances telescope with dizzying speed, plants flower and bear fruit at impossible times and under impossible conditions, a girl runs two kilometers along a wall one day and says that she has never seen that wall a few weeks later. For all practical purposes time itself does not exist in this novel: a cow's gestation period is one tenth what it should be; Rosalie has a baby about three months after conception, Albine performs in the few minutes between dusk and darkness actions which should require many hours. The list of violations of the realist credo in *The Sin of Father Mouret* could be indefinitely extended, and we must ask what in this novel led Zola to an apparent rejection of his aesthetic beliefs.

In most of Zola's novels, myths arise from the fictional presentation of reality, and in *The Sin of Father Mouret* reality is manipulated by the exigencies of a myth. The novel is structured to retell the story of man's fall from grace, and this myth becomes the foundation of the entire work rather than one stylistic device among others. Poetic metaphor is no longer a method of description: it has become the primary—almost the exclusive—vehicle for the author's vision. Zola made his recasting of Genesis into a universally applicable moral tale, and he strove to make its universality obvious. The reader is viewing Man in Nature as well as individual men in a particular location at a certain time, so references to the novel's exact historical and geographic setting become much less important than in the other episodes of *The Rougon-Macquart*. *The Sin of Father Mouret* is Zola's most sustained evocation of the primal struggle between Life and Death, and his decision to begin the novel in the spring and end it in the fall to symbolize the victory of death obviously overrode concern with the proper length of a calf's prenatal development. Almost all of Zola's violations of the tenets of mimetic fiction can be similarly explained by reference to the myth he chose to tell. His universe cannot be understood in logical terms; it is a universe with a voice which shouts of man's agony, a universe such as might present itself to a monomaniac unable to perceive reality. Serge's hallucination of the countryside's attack on the church culminating in the Tree of Life's irruption into heaven is not qualitatively different from the hallucinatory setting of the novel as a whole. The reader, like Serge, comes to see all things as participants in the struggle between life and death for man's being.

There are obvious dangers inherent in the decision to give a novel a setting which can be manipulated at will so as to express a theme. The internal consistency of the fictional world must be created solely within the work itself, for in abandoning the imitation of reality the author has rejected a setting which his readers instinctively recognize and accept. It is frightfully easy to appear ridiculous and inconsequential by rebelling against such things as time and space, and Zola avoids this danger only by displaying the genius of a lyric poet. *The Sin of Father Mouret* creates a world sustained by language which commands acceptance. The hallucination is communicated because Zola's prose is so compelling that it seems to contain its own reality, is so powerful that it constrains the reader to respond to the vision it incarnates even if he does not fully accept the implications of that vision. The novel displays a stunning control of the French language, and it should be stated parenthetically that no translation can completely capture this compelling quality.

If Zola's great linguistic skills are applied to the purpose of giving acceptable fictional form to a myth, as we maintain, it is essential to examine that myth in detail. The superficial resemblances between *The Sin of Father Mouret* and the story of Adam and Eve are obvious. Serge and Albine's idyll in Paradou clearly echoes the story of Eden: Paradou equals Paradise; the couple's initiation into sex under the great tree is heavy with references to the Biblical description of Adam's Fall; the character representing the archangel who expels Serge from Eden is named Archangias and holds a stick resembling a flaming sword; the couple lives on fruits and among flowers growing as in Eden, without regard to the seasons; and the sense of timelessness and total isolation permeating the idyll duplicates the condition of man before he began to grow old and move toward death.

Father Mouret enters this Eden after an illness which has taken away his memory and made him, like Adam, a new man born at the age of twenty-five. He is baptised with a new name befitting his new being: invariably referred to as "Father Mouret" in Books I and III, he is always called "Serge" in Book II. The Eve to this Adam is Albine, who feels that she too is born again, that she emerges from Serge's rib when a deep sleep falls upon him. The park itself has the role of the serpent. Much serpentine imagery is applied to it, and it gives Albine constant assistance and advice as she initiates Serge into the awesome and joyous mysteries of procreation. The park, nature herself, prepares the marriage bed and helps the lovers find it, and the Tree of Life "whispers into Albine's ear what mothers tell brides on their wedding night."

Nature is thus the sinners' accomplice, and it is in this complicity that *The Sin of Father Mouret* diverges radically from its Christian model. God does not exist in Paradou, he does not walk in the garden in the cool of the day as he did in Eden. The only entity approaching divine power and creativity is Nature herself, and Nature wants Serge and Albine to know sex and be one with the rhythm of the world. When they yield to her wishes, they participate in the great cycle of coupling and birth moving the universe and know the ecstasy of being happy "in the certainty of a law obeyed." Adam and Eve disobey a commandment when their bodies unite, but Serge and Albine obey the only law they know, a law whose requirements have become ever clearer and more imperious.

In Zola's novel sexual union thus manifests submission rather than rebellion. But by an ironic twist it leads to the same anguish and shame which overcame the couple in Eden. Albine and Serge are immediately struck with dread, cover their bodies and run blindly through the garden in a desperate attempt to escape their fate. Their sin was only to love as they were told to love, they were neither proud nor disobedient, and yet they are cursed as surely as Adam and Eve. The dismembered Cupid standing in the poisonous exhalations of the flower plot serving as Paradou's cemetery is the perfect symbol of the deadly consequences of the idyllic love offered by the park, as Albine realizes when Paradou tells her to kill herself by breathing those same exhalations. The novel's plot justifies its title: sex is a sin carrying a horrible punishment.

But rejection of sex imposes punishment equally severe. Priestly asceticism violates the laws of nature imposed on all things, laws whose great power is evoked by the novel's most poetic lines, the descriptions of Paradou and the living country-side around Artauds. Virginity places men in opposition to these laws, opposition which can end only in the destruction of those who dare set themselves against the motive force of the universe; witness Father Mouret's critical illness in Book I and his stupor in Book III, Father Caffin's bathetic story, and Brother Archangias' repulsive depravity. On the other hand, the deaths of Albine and the woman who preceded her as mistress of Paradou, the subsequent misery of Serge and the eighteenth-century lord, clearly imply that obedience to these laws brings not salvation but simply another kind of despair. Man is damned to require the sexual act that dooms him to despair and death.

This is the desperately pessimistic meaning of the myth recounted in *The Sin of Father Mouret:* man is from birth condemned to abject misery because he can neither reject nature nor affirm it. The novel is not so much the story of man's fall from grace as of a quest for grace which can never succeed. The world calls man to join in the creation of life, but Zola's characters answer this call only to find the same death enveloping them before they responded to the rhythm of all creatures. The myth of Eden and *The Sin of Father Mouret* both describe the reason for the pain inherent in human existence, but Genesis describes man as responsible for his pain and Zola describes him as the helpless possessor of a being which can never fulfill itself, as a divided thing who cannot satisfy one part of his being without attacking other parts and destroying himself. Zola portrays in brilliant terms the age-old figure of man as a creature drawn both to heaven and earth, both to the Blessed Virgin Mary and Albine. The continual interplay between these two symbolic women is one of the novel's most effective expressions of the tension torturing Father Mouret. It is clear that Albine and Mary represent diametrically opposed goals and can never be joined, but they are often ironically identified with each other. The same imagery is used in reference to both; Désirée sees a strong physical resemblance between them, and the language describing Father Mouret's descent from mystical communion with Mary also describes Serge's descent from the bliss of physical union with Albine. Each woman leaves him incomplete, and it is impossible to possess both. The novel is symmetrically constructed around the idea of Serge's incompleteness. He is only part of a man in Book i, when he is a virgin unaware of life, and only part of a man in Book iii, after his sin has "deflowered" Mary and the blossoms on her altar have died. Father Mouret discovers life only to reject it and devote himself entirely to the lacerated, bleeding body of Christ crucified, to the great symbol of death which has become for him the entire meaning of the Church and his place in it.

It is important to emphasize that it is Father Mouret who gives this meaning to the Church and not the Church which kills Father Mouret. *The Sin of Father Mouret* is not a sophomoric, facile attack on Christianity's disastrous opposition to the satisfaction of man's natural desires, as it has occasionally been taken to be. While some of Zola's novels do imply that salvation is possible if man participates in natural processes, this theme is not to be found in the present novel. Serge's shame after intercourse is undoubtedly increased by the sound of the Angelus ringing in the church he has abandoned and betrayed but, if religion is solely responsible for the couple's fear, how explain the fact that Albine, the character completely unaware of the church's condemnation of sex, is the first to blush, the first to feel shame and attempt to hide. It is impossible to explain Albine's death by saying that she was oppressed by a religious sense of guilt, for she rejects the Church and defies its God. Zola's original notes called for her to commit suicide because she learned from books that she had committed the gravest of sins; that is, because she was made aware of the religious implications of her love. This plan was abandoned, however, and she dies because the park tells her to die, because nature teaches her that death is the consequence of love. This change is best explained by assuming that Zola wished to express the idea that the fault lies in the essence of the human condition, not in what man has made of that condition.

The Church would indeed be an unmitigated villain if its only effects were the pathological cruelty induced in Brother Archangias by his vows. But Father Mouret finds true peace and joy in the Church. His tragedy is that the happiness evoked in the lyrical chapters describing his elevation to the priesthood and his devotion to his sacerdotal duties is not sufficient. The Church gives Father Mouret all it has to offer, but his acceptance of its gifts, like his acceptance of Paradou's gifts, leads only to agony.

The novel's minor characters confirm the fact that man's pain is not caused by his religion. The residents of Artauds are liberated from the Church. The last word one would apply to these peasants is "repressed," and yet their hearts are cruel, their spirits dull and their lives bleak. Their sexual activity is a monotonous ritual producing not life but a baby who dies to be buried with Albine. Their misery is, like that of Serge and Albine, linked to mankind's primeval heritage. Father Mouret feels that the people of Artauds are a "handful of men beginning time over again." He looks at their huts and thinks he is "witnessing the slow birth of a race." The race is humanity, and its future is grim.

The Church does indeed represent death, as Father Mouret says in the powerful scene when he and Albine confront one another before the crude pictures of Christ's humiliation and crucifixion. But Albine is wrong when she says in the same scene that Paradou is life. She discovers her mistake when Serge comes to her in the park and she feels him become a "corpse" while Paradou itself becomes "a great coffin of shadows." Nature's message seemed to be to love and live, but it was in reality telling the couple to love and die. The contemplative life in an arid desert, the physical life in a green garden, obedience to the commandments of God, obedience to the commandments of nature, all lead to death. *The Sin of Father Mouret* is almost as darkly pessimistic as that other bitter work in the Rougon-Macquart cycle, ironically titled *La Joie de Vivre*.

But pessimism is not absolute. One character has conquered death, or rather has not herself been conquered by death: the priest's simple-minded sister, Désirée. Her name implies that she is the wished-for creature, that which every character needs to be. Dr. Pascal confirms the aptness of her name by saying that the world would be fit to live in if everyone were like her. She can experience sexual union, can participate in the great cycle of coupling and birth, without experiencing the shame and death which birth implies for everyone else. She is a kind of virginal nymphomaniac granted the satisfaction of a personal orgasm each time animals copulate, granted the joy of personal maternity each time an animal is born. Eternally pure, she is rent by none of the tensions caused by her brother's purity.

Désirée's conquest of death is implicit in almost every scene in which she appears and attains its ultimate expression in her joyous cry concluding the novel: "Serge! Serge! The cow had a calf!" Albine is dead, Rosalie's baby is dead, everyone in the cemetery is saddened by the thought that he too will one day lie under the earth, Brother Archangias is bleeding and his ear lies on the ground, but Désirée climbs on her cleansing manure heap, claps her hands and shouts of life. For her the cemetery is not a place of putrefaction but the source of lush plants which her animals devour with the maniacal fervor of creatures who know that they are eating the stuff of life.

Désirée is the earth, as Zola says in his notes for the novel, and both she and the countryside she incarnates are referred to as Cybele. Both are equated to the Great Mother of the Gods, of men and of all other living things, the goddess eternally reborn to be both the cause and the goal of life. The natural cycle absorbs and fulfills the land and its human representative, and Désirée is set apart from those whose reason is intact to be aligned with brute animals untroubled by contradictions between their natural and spiritual selves.

Désirée thus mitigates the pessimism of *The Sin of Father Mouret* but at the cost of her human reason, of that which distinguishes other characters from her animals. The priests of Cybele were self-emasculated eunuchs dressed in female clothes, and Désirée is the same kind of undefined creature, neither brute nor woman. Her joy is its own reward, she is unaware of her inadequacies, but her bliss is not open to her brother and Albine.

The main theme of the novel remains that man is so constituted that he cannot escape being rent by insoluble contradictions. The world Zola depicts is in essence out of harmony, and the tension created by its discord is conveyed in the story of Serge's dismemberment. Man can neither accept nor deny the vigor of physical life. Through poetic evocation of the glorious strength of nature and of the tranquil peace of spiritual devotion, through creating a character called equally by both, Zola communicates his mythic vision of a race torn apart.

The text used for this translation was the Pléiade edition of *Les Rougon-Macquart,* edited by Henri Mitterand. I should like to express my gratitude to M. Mitterand for the reliability of the text he established and for his extremely useful notes.